A

Basket Brigade
CHRISTMAS

A
Basket Brigade
CHRISTMAS

Three Women, Three Love Stories,
One Country Divided

Judith Miller, Nancy Moser
Stephanie Grace Whitson

BARBOUR BOOKS
An Imprint of Barbour Publishing, Inc.

Print ISBN 978-1-63058-450-4

eBook Editions:
Adobe Digital Edition (.epub) 978-1-63409-581-5
Kindle and MobiPocket Edition (.prc) 978-1-63409-582-2

All scripture quotations are taken from the King James Version of the Bible.

This book is a work of fiction. Names, characters, places, and incidents are either products of the author's imagination or used fictitiously. Any similarity to actual people, organizations, and/or events is purely coincidental.

Published by Barbour Books, an imprint of Barbour Publishing, Inc., P.O. Box 719, Uhrichsville, OH 44683, www.barbourbooks.com

Our mission is to publish and distribute inspirational products offering exceptional value and biblical encouragement to the masses.

 Member of the
Evangelical Christian
Publishers Association

Printed in Canada.

"When five o'clock came, there were twenty or thirty women on the platform waiting for the train. Baskets of hot buttered biscuits, cold meats, pies, cakes, and pickles, with gallons of milk and cream, were ready for the supper. . . . When the car drew up to the platform, the men in the soldiers' car crowded to the windows. . .and gave "three cheers for Decatur." Pale, emaciated, half starved, and disheveled, the men met us with apologies for their appearance, smoothed down their hair with their fingers, and tried to hide the dirty rags that covered their wounds. . . . It was a sight to make angels weep. This was only the beginning. . . the 'basket brigade' [was] called into service."

—Jane Martin Johns
Personal Recollections of Early Decatur, Abraham Lincoln,
Richard J. Oglesby, and the Civil War

A Stitch in Time

by

Stephanie Grace Whitson

"My dear boy, I have knit these socks expressly for you. How do you like them? How do you look, and where do you live when you are at home? I am of medium height, of slight build, with blue eyes, fair complexion, light hair, and a good deal of it. Write and tell me all about yourself and how you get on in the hospitals."

"P.S. If the recipient of these socks has a wife will he please exchange socks with some poor fellow not so fortunate."

—Note accompanying an aid society shipment to the US Sanitary Commission's Northwest Branch at Chicago

Chapter 1

Late September 1862
Decatur, Illinois

Unable to face what waited just beyond the black mourning wreath hanging on the Kincaids' front door, Lucy Maddox hesitated at the wrought-iron gate separating her property from the neighbors'. For the third time in as many hours, she pulled her gloved hand away from the gate and stepped back.

How could Jonah Kincaid possibly be dead? She could still hear his booming laughter, still see his curly blond hair glowing in the light of the auditorium lamps at the ball the ladies had given just before his volunteer regiment left Decatur. He'd been so proud, standing head and shoulders above everyone else, a favorite son of the city, promising to "whip the Rebels and be home before Christmas."

Tears threatened. Lucy swept her fingertips across her furrowed brow. *No.* She would not—could not call on the Kincaids just yet. Perhaps after a cup of strong tea. She startled when her housekeeper's voice sounded just over her shoulder.

Martha's voice was gentle. "Putting it off will only make it that much harder. Best get on with it."

Lucy turned to face her. "If I can't offer my condolences without crying, I'll be small comfort." She put a hand to the locket hanging on the thick gold chain about her neck—the locket bearing the images of Mother and Father, gone within six weeks of each other just three years ago. She still missed them every day, but saying farewell to the older generation was an expected part of life. The loss of someone as young and vibrant as Jonah—that was another thing entirely. Lucy shook her head. "I've no idea what to say."

"Truth be told, they probably won't remember what you say. But they'll be hurt if you don't go. And Lord knows, they're already hurting enough."

Lucy sighed. "I know you're right. Truly, I do, but—" Her voice broke. "It's *Jonah*." When tears spilled down her cheeks, she swiped them away. Why couldn't her feelings for Jonah fall in line with what she knew to be true? Jonah had never been more than a friend. Would *never* have been more than a friend, no matter what Lucy might daydream about. Why did she feel as if she'd lost more? *Because you, Lucy Maddox, are a fool, that's why. Obviously, you still harbored flickering hope.* Why couldn't she stamp out that flicker? Why?

Martha reached out and gave Lucy's arm an affectionate squeeze. "Young Mr. Kincaid was always fond of you. Everyone knows that."

Fond. Lucy knew it was true. Why should hearing Martha speak the truth hurt?

The beloved old woman put a calloused palm to Lucy's cheek. "Your mother would be so proud of you. Proud of the way you've taken up her role in the community, serving with the Ladies Aid, volunteering for every good cause. She was always a great comforter in times of distress. I've no doubt you will be, too."

Lucy thought back to the countless times there'd been a knock at the door and Mother had hastened to go to someone in need, armed with little more than her worn Bible and prodigious amounts of courage, compassion, and love for both her God and her fellow man. "I wish I'd paid closer attention to how she did it," Lucy murmured. She had no doubt that Mother would have known exactly what to say to the widowed Mrs. Kincaid, so cruelly bereft of Jonah, the eldest of her four sons.

"Mrs. Maddox always said that God gave the words just when she needed them, and not a minute before." Martha patted Lucy's arm. "Mrs. Kincaid knows you loved her son. She has no husband and no daughter to comfort her—only those three boys, Lord bless them. Be a daughter today. Sit beside her. Hold her hand. Weep with her. She will bless you for it."

One of Mother's oft-quoted Bible verses came to mind. "'In lowliness of mind let each esteem other better than themselves,'" Lucy murmured. "I suppose that's the key to it, isn't it. Think more about Jonah's mother and brothers and less about myself."

The deep wrinkles lining Martha's face crinkled as the old woman smiled. "That is it exactly." She made a little shooing motion with one hand. "Go along, now, and I'll have a good strong cup of tea waiting when you return. Perhaps even some of my Scotch cakes."

Lucy caught the old woman's hand and gave it a squeeze. "Thank you. As usual, I don't know what I'd do without you." Straightening her shoulders and lifting her chin, Lucy reached for the gate latch. This time, she did not turn back.

∽

Silas Tait tied the last black tassel in place over the Kincaids' entryway mirror. Gripping the top of the stepladder with one hand, he leaned back to inspect his work before looking down at the housekeeper. "Does that suit?"

The woman nodded. "That's just right, Mr. Tait. Thank you." She patted the remaining length of black cloth draped over her arm. "It was most thoughtful of you to deliver the mourning cloth personally."

Silas descended the ladder carefully as he spoke. "I imagine Jimmy was relieved to be assigned an errand, but once I'd read the note, it didn't seem right to let him bear the sad burden home all by himself."

"It's kind of you to remember that beneath his brave act as 'man of the house,' there's still a twelve-year-old boy who just lost a dear brother." The housekeeper's voice wavered. She cleared her throat and turned toward the parlor. "I'll just see to veiling Minerva with this last bit while you go on back to the kitchen. Cook insists that you take some refreshment before leaving."

Silas wasn't hungry, but he knew better than to argue with Cook. Still, he lingered beside the ladder after he stepped down, watching as the housekeeper draped black cloth over the marble bust of Minerva, Roman goddess of the arts. As manager of Maddox Mercantile, Silas was hardly part of the social scene in Decatur, but the arrival of the crate bearing the Italian sculpture at the train station and Minerva's subsequent placement next to the piano in the Kincaids' formal parlor had been the talk of the town for quite some time. With Jonah's death, Minerva would be veiled and the piano silent for weeks to come.

After gulping coffee and eating the sandwich Cook had prepared, Silas was taking his leave by way of the back door when he heard the housekeeper greet a caller. *Lucy.* He knew Lucy Maddox's voice almost as well as he knew his own. He'd been hired on by her father, the late Mr. Robert Maddox, as a tailor offering "the latest in menswear" to the dignitaries who frequented Maddox Mercantile.

A Stitch in Time

When Mr. Maddox passed away, Lucy surprised everyone by declaring that she had no intention of selling the mercantile. Instead, she retained ownership and asked Silas to take over the day-to-day management for her. He'd been thrilled to accept—and hopeful that Lucy's confidence in him might breathe life into his secret wish. It had not—yet—but Silas was a patient man.

Always happy to help was a personal motto, and nothing gave him more satisfaction than being called upon to live up to that mantra. Only days after the Rebels fired on Fort Sumter, when the ladies of Decatur convinced the owner of the *Magnet* to print small flags to be worn as badges, Silas donated yards of white muslin for the project. When the ladies decided to create a regimental flag for the local volunteers, he knew exactly where to procure silk thread and offered to make the journey to St. Louis himself. With the formation of the Decatur Soldiers' Aid Society, Silas spent hours driving Mrs. Kincaid and other members of the committee about town to collect shirts, sheets, pillowcases, quilts, and blankets for "the boys." He welcomed any opportunity to help, for in a day when every young man in Illinois wanted nothing more than to fight for God and country, the artificial lower leg and foot strapped in place below Silas's left knee meant that he would never be considered "fit for service."

He rarely thought of the unfortunate day years ago when a bad fall led to the serious injury that refused to heal. Amputation had saved his life, and over time, his wooden leg and foot became little more than an inconvenience. He thought of it now, though, as he stood at the back door of the Kincaids' house, listening to Lucy murmur comfort to Jonah's mother. Would Lucy ever see him as anything but the crippled tailor hired by her father? She had no idea how he cherished the occasional sweet smile that curled the corners of her mouth when Silas suggested something Maddox

Mercantile might undertake "for the cause." He would like nothing more than to stride confidently toward the front of the house right this moment and provide a shoulder for Lucy to cry on, for in the years since he'd worked for Miss Maddox, Silas had observed much. Jonah Kincaid's death would wound her deeply—more deeply than others might suspect. *And she would welcome neither your knowing that nor your displaying uninvited sympathy. You work for her. She appreciates you for that—and that is all. So do what is needed. Get back to work.*

With an inward sigh and a parting reminder to Cook to send word if there was anything more he could do to help the family, Silas stepped outside, turning the collar of his wool overcoat up to ward off a late-afternoon chill. At the end of the long drive, he glanced back at two carriages approaching from the opposite direction. Only God knew how long the stream of callers would flow this evening, but Jonah Kincaid was the first local boy to die of wounds received in battle, and that alone probably meant that Mrs. Kincaid and Jonah's three young brothers had a very long evening ahead of them.

As he turned toward Main Street, Silas thought of other Decatur boys who'd enlisted. Samuel McHenry and Doyle Lovett. Robert Pritchard and John Rutherford. As he walked, Silas prayed. *Lord, give our families grace to endure. Give our beloved president Your wisdom. Give comfort. To the Kincaids. To Lucy. And please, Lord, show me ways to serve.* Insofar as the United States Army was concerned, Silas Tait was "unfit for service." The term stung. He was determined to prove it wrong.

Chapter 2

As the evening wore on and the stream of callers continued, Lucy realized Martha was right. Words weren't all that important. The very fact that people came—and that Lucy remained—was what mattered. Mrs. Kincaid said as much.

"You are such a comfort to me, dear."

Shadows were lengthening, and Lucy was sitting next to Mrs. Kincaid in the parlor when the housekeeper opened the front door and admitted, along with more well-meaning callers, the familiar sound of the whistle announcing the arrival of the northbound train.

Mrs. Kincaid started and looked at Lucy. "I didn't realize the time. Aren't you needed at the depot?"

"They'll understand," Lucy said.

Mrs. Kincaid's hazel eyes sparkled with fresh tears. "The best way to honor our dear Jonah is to care for the living. And so I must insist, dear girl, that you fulfill your duty to the Basket Brigade." She took Lucy's hand and rose from the settee they'd shared. "Come along, now." Like a mother, she led the way to the foyer, took Lucy's shawl and bonnet down from the hall tree, and pointed her to the door.

Lucy paused at the base of the porch steps, suddenly aware of just how weary she felt. Adjusting her shawl so that it hugged her neck, she hurried to Main Street, passing Maddox Mercantile just as the Widow Tompkins was locking up.

"You poor dear," the widow said. "Mr. Tait said you were the first caller to arrive at the house earlier today. Have you been with the Kincaids all this time?"

"I have, but—Silas was there? I didn't see him."

When young Master Kincaid brought the note regarding the need for crape, Mr. Tait wasn't about to let the poor boy complete such a sad errand alone. He was at the house for at least a couple of hours, helping the housekeeper with the draping. He was just leaving by way of the back door when he heard you speaking to Mrs. Kincaid. 'She'll be all right,' he told me when he returned. 'Miss Maddox is with her.' "

Lucy looked past the gray-haired woman toward the store. "Is Silas still working, then?"

"Oh, no. He's gone back to the Kincaids. Making a 'proper call,' he said." Mrs. Tompkins smiled. "I think it was just an excuse to check on those three boys, the poor dears. Would you believe that Mr. Tait knows the favorite candy of every boy in that family? He took a few pieces of each with him. Wasn't that the nicest thing?"

Lucy agreed that it was. "We heard the train whistle, and Jonah's mother insisted that I keep my promise to the Basket Brigade. She said it's more important now than ever."

"God bless her," the widow said. "What's Mrs. McHenry assigned you?"

"I'll find out when we get there," Lucy said. "It's very good of you to help, by the way. I can't imagine how tired you must be after a day on your feet at the store."

"Oh, it's not so terrible," the widow said. "I'm thankful for your willingness to allow me the job."

"You've Mr. Tait to thank for that," Lucy said. "He made an excellent case for hiring you, and you've proven him right." In truth, it had taken some convincing to get Lucy to agree to it, for they lived in a world where the only legitimate employment for a woman like the Widow Tompkins—who had no father or brother to provide for her—was teaching or sewing. Mrs. Tompkins had talent for neither, and she lived in a tiny two-room cottage that barely rated as a house. Taking in boarders was not possible.

"Mr. Tait would never go against your wishes, Miss Maddox, and so I thank you for saving me the indignity of becoming an object of pity—or contempt."

Uncomfortable with the woman's praise, Lucy was relieved that they had arrived at the depot. Several pairs of ladies with baskets brimming with food for the soldiers on board the train were already hurrying across the platform toward the hospital cars. Lucy followed Mrs. Tompkins inside, grateful for the warmth and the welcoming aroma of fresh coffee, unexpectedly overwhelmed with a sense of pride in what the ladies of Decatur had accomplished in recent months.

Every day when the hospital train reached Centralia one hundred miles to the south, the agent of the Illinois Central there telegraphed the agent in Decatur to relay how many wounded men were on the train. Armed with that information, the ladies prepared to serve them during a half-hour layover in Decatur. Over the months, Lucy and the ladies of the Basket Brigade had doled out fried chicken, pickled peaches, pound cake, apples, biscuits, sandwiches, doughnuts, and more. For a city of only six thousand souls, with at least a third of the population gone to war, it had been a monumental undertaking. The first train full of hungry, hurting men cheered the ladies, and after that no one would have dared consider suspending the project. They would serve the boys until the very last patient had been transported from overcrowded hospitals farther south to better equipped facilities in Chicago.

Hurrying to the table laden with filled baskets, Lucy and Mrs. Tompkins each grabbed one. Together, they made their way to the most distant car, where a soldier waited to help them up the steep stairs. As soon as Lucy stepped through the door, another soldier with a lilting Irish accent called out, "What did I tell you, boys? They may not have wings as we can see them, but sure as Decatur brings us angels, may the saints be praised." When Lucy handed him a bit of pound cake, he held it up for all to see. "Angels with cake!"

There was laughter and good humor as the two women made their way down the aisle—so much laughter and good humor that Lucy's heart broke a dozen times, humbled by the men's gratitude and once again amazed that they could put on such a brave face. Bandaged or missing limbs and faces either too pale or blazing with fever evidenced their suffering. Some eyes glittered with unspilled tears and yet, almost to a man, the soldiers had nothing but good words for the ladies.

Lucy had emptied her basket and was waiting for Mrs. Tompkins when the young man nearest her said quietly, "Please tell whoever made the pound cake that she gave a boy from New York a taste of home." His voice wavered as he choked out the words, "Tell her that Private Joe Donlin blesses her for it."

"I'll make sure she hears of it," Lucy said, wondering which of the two dozen pound cakes he'd tasted. Of course, it didn't matter. She'd tell all the bakers about Private Donlin.

"Beware of that one," a soldier across the way called out. "Next thing you know, he'll be writing love letters, just to get more pound cake."

"Or a pair of socks," someone hollered.

"If it's socks you want, you'd better write a poem."

"A poem? I'd write an entire ode if it'd earn me a blanket without holes."

"An ode to holes? Why'd you write an ode to holes?"

Private Donlin looked up at Lucy with a grin. "Don't mind Lyle. He doesn't hear very well these days. Artillery gunner. Too many shells exploded with too little cotton in his ears."

Good-natured banter continued until a blast of the train whistle signaled departure. Mrs. Tompkins joined Lucy, and with a wave and a "God bless you," the two of them descended to the platform. Empty baskets in hand, they waved to the men until the train was out of sight.

"That was quite the group," Lucy said as she and Mrs. Tompkins hurried toward the depot.

"Indeed," Mrs. Tompkins said. "I hope Lyle regains his hearing."

Lucy agreed. "All that nonsense about writing love letters just to get a pair of socks." She looked over at Mrs. Tompkins. "Surely they'll get fresh socks and new blankets when they reach the hospital—won't they?"

"One can only hope."

Inside the depot, the ladies were preparing to leave, gathering up the empty baskets to be taken home, refilled, and brought back on the morrow. Lucy stood by the door and called them to order. "I've a message to pass on to the pound cake bakers." She told them about Private Donlin of New York.

"One of the boys on my car said he hadn't had yeast bread for weeks. He showed me a piece of hard tack." The speaker shuddered. "I can't believe we expect them to fight when that's what they're eating."

"I know," another woman said. "If only there were a way, we'd want them all to have steak or roast beef every night."

"And pound cake," someone called out.

Lucy was about to mention socks and blankets when Jimmy Kincaid trotted into the depot. He hurried to Lucy's side. "Ma asked me to see if you'd stop back in once the Brigade work is finished." He leaned close and lowered his voice. "She's in a tizzy about the Ladies Aid meetings."

The Ladies Aid. Of course. As chairwoman of the group, Mrs. Kincaid hosted weekly meetings in her home. A woman in mourning could not host social events. Lucy nodded at Jimmy. "All right. Let's go."

"I've got to stop at the mercantile, too," he said. "We're out of sugar. Seems like at least a thousand people have called. And they stay and stay. We ran out of biscuits a while ago." Jimmy looked over at Lucy. "Your Mrs. Jefferson rescued that. Came to the back door with a plate of her Scotch cakes, and when Cook started to cry 'cause she was so relieved, Mrs. Jefferson said she'd rustle up more. Seems like she's delivered more every hour since. And folks just keep coming. And now we're out of sugar and Cook's in a panic about it." Jimmy grunted his disapproval. "As if it's the worst thing in the world not to have sugar for people to put in their coffee. *Hunh.* The worst thing in the world already happened."

Lucy patted him on the back. "Cook just wants things to go smoothly. It's her way of helping out. So let's get her that sugar." Together, Lucy, Mrs. Tompkins, and Jimmy departed the depot. They stopped at the mercantile just long enough for Mrs. Tompkins to wrap two cones of sugar. Bidding a good evening to the woman, Lucy led Jimmy out into the night. The moon rose as they rounded the corner of Main and Poplar.

Jimmy gestured toward the line of carriages in the distance, some with coach lights burning, others dark and silent. "See what

I mean? People just keep coming. Your Mr. Jefferson put lanterns out on the porch so nobody would break their necks in the dark."

Indeed, the Kincaids' expansive front porch was crowded with people who'd gathered in the light of several lanterns positioned at intervals along the wide railing. Light spilled out of every first-floor window of the house. Just as they reached the front porch steps, Lucy glanced toward home and saw Martha coming through the Maddoxes side gate, then hurrying across the yard toward the back door.

"More cakes, I suppose," Jimmy said.

Lucy frowned. It was one thing for people to call and express their condolences, but there was something unseemly about their lingering. Didn't they know how weary Mrs. Kincaid had to be? Shouldn't Jonah's brothers have some time alone with their mother?

Lucy sent Jimmy to the back door with the sugar. The moment she entered the front, Mrs. Kincaid latched on to her like a drowning woman reaching for the rope that would pull her to safety. "Thank goodness you've come." She glanced toward the back of the house. "The sugar?"

"Jimmy's taking it around back."

The poor woman's shoulders sagged with relief. "Thank God." She looked back at Lucy. "I knew Jonah was popular, but I had no idea—" Her eyes filled with tears.

"You need to rest," Lucy said.

"Yes. I do. And I will, as soon as I know you'll see to the Ladies Aid."

"Of course," Lucy said quickly. "Don't give it another thought."

"You know all the members, but you'll need the roster to make certain everyone is kept informed. There's a copy in the entryway table drawer."

"Perfect," Lucy said. "Now, please. Go upstairs and lie down.

And—where are the boys?"

"In the back, I suppose. Or upstairs. I think maybe Cook sent Boyd and William to bed." She frowned. "But I don't quite recall."

"They're in bed," Jimmy said as he stepped up and put his arm about his mother. "And Lucy's right. You should rest." When his mother looked toward the parlor, Jimmy said quickly, "I'll keep watch."

Ah, yes. The watch. Lucy glanced toward the parlor. Someone must always be with the casket until the funeral.

"I asked Silas about it earlier," Jimmy said. "He's already in the parlor, and he said that he'll stay with us."

"God bless him," Mrs. Kincaid said. Without another word, she grasped the stair railing and proceeded up the stairs.

Lucy watched her go, thinking that the poor woman seemed to age with every step.

Chapter 3

At Jimmy's request, Lucy stood beside him to receive callers. Finally, the crowd began to wane. Cook came to get the boy, insisting that he eat something before he joined those keeping watch in the parlor. As the last carriage pulled away, Lucy made her way back to the kitchen, deeply touched when Jimmy jumped to his feet to give her what he called a "thank-you hug." The unusual show of emotion left her speechless. Feeling awkward, she patted the boy on the shoulder, nodded at Cook, and made her way through the house and past the parlor where Silas Tait, the Kincaids' pastor, and a handful of others would remain through the night. Lucy bid them a silent farewell with a raised hand.

Henry Jefferson was on the front porch, dousing the lanterns. "I can carry a couple of those," Lucy said, and grabbed two. Henry carried two more with one hand, raising a third before them to illuminate the way home. A fine mist had blown in early in the evening. Now, as Lucy and Henry made their way past Mrs. Kincaid's dormant rose garden, the grass crunched softly as their footsteps broke through a thin sheen of frosted mist.

Martha was waiting for them in the kitchen. She'd just taken another tray of cakes out of the oven, and while Henry and Lucy removed their wraps, Martha poured cups of tea. When Lucy thanked her for the evening of baking and the regular deliveries to the Kincaids', Martha only shrugged. "That's what neighbors do."

The three sat around the kitchen table for a few moments until Henry gave a soft grunt and said, "Time for these old bones to say good night."

"Thank you for taking the lanterns over," Lucy said. "They probably saved a few necks."

"Necks that should have had sense not to linger so long," Henry grumbled. He shook his head. "That poor family."

Wishing Martha and Henry a good night, Lucy ascended the back stairs to the second floor. She undressed quickly, but instead of going to bed, she waited for the sound of the back door closing and the faint click of the lock. Certain that Martha and Henry were gone, she pulled on her wrapper and tiptoed into the wide upstairs hall and, from there, down the front stairs toward the foyer. Instead of going all the way down, though, she perched on the fifth step from the top, staring down at the patch of moonlight shining on the polished floor. Thinking. She'd promised Mrs. Kincaid that she would "take care" of the situation with the Ladies Aid. They would need a new place to meet. Almost as if to protest the logical solution to that dilemma, the house creaked. Lucy looked about her. Nodded. *Yes, I know. Father would not approve. He'd never have allowed it.*

Robert Maddox had insisted on calling the house a "cottage," but with its broad veranda and two-story central gable, the ten-room Gothic Revival mansion made the use of that word ridiculous. Even though she'd been only a child when the house was built, Lucy remembered the stir it had caused. But the curious were to suffer their curiosity unsatisfied, for Father declared the new home a sanctuary, not a showcase. Only close friends would ever be invited in. Only the kind of people who would appreciate nice things but never gossip about them.

As the only child of middle-aged parents, Lucy eventually learned that one could be alone without being lonely. She grew up in solitude, spending hours at a time entertaining herself, her imagination transforming this nook or that cranny into a castle tower or a pirate ship as the need arose. Father's expansive library offered unending delights in the form of cherished books.

After her parents died, Lucy faithfully continued her mother's legacy of doing good—elsewhere. The house remained as it had always been, private and protected from the curious. Tonight, though, the intersection of two obvious needs was challenging the way things had always been. First was Mrs. Kincaid's need for someone to step into her place of leadership for the Ladies Aid. The organization had done a superb job of helping the war effort in recent months. They'd shipped barrels of bandages west to Rolla, Missouri, and south to Cairo and Paducah. After the Battle of Fort Donelson this past February, they'd collected dozens of shirts, sheets, and pillowcases and sent them to St. Louis. They'd also supported the Basket Brigade. Lucy had done her part at every turn, but as she sat alone on the stairs, listening to the house creak, she pondered a new possibility. The men on the daily train needed so much more than food. If Lucy provided a place to work, what more might the ladies accomplish? *With help from Maddox Mercantile.* She had unique access to an abundant supply of calico and yarn, needles—and more.

Descending to the foyer, she tiptoed into the formal parlor and opened the drapes. When moonlight spilled into the room, Lucy turned her attention to the formal portrait of Mother as a young woman. When, Lucy wondered, had Mother begun to "think more highly of others than herself"? Had she always had a servant's heart? She'd been quite a beauty. A fresh pang of regret coursed through Lucy as she looked up at the portrait. *If only I looked like Mother. Jonah might have—* She forced an end to that foolishness. *If wishes were horses, beggars would ride—and you would be a very young widow.* The realization sent chills up her spine.

Taking a deep breath, Lucy crossed the foyer and went into the dining room, where Father's portrait hung above the sideboard. Opening first the heavy drapes at one window and then the interior shutters, she made her way down the row of upholstered dining chairs toward the far end of the room and the massive sideboard. She stood for a long while, staring up at the uniformed young man mounted on a dark bay horse. *You were a soldier once. We can do so much more for the men, Father. Please understand.*

Her confidence wavered. What would Mrs. Collins think of Lucy's plan? Ever since moving to Decatur not long ago, the banker's wife had fought to become one of the leaders of Decatur society. She would expect to be consulted first about—well, about everything to do with the Ladies Aid. Lucy wasn't even an officer of the organization. Mrs. Kincaid had asked only that Lucy contact the ladies to make arrangements for the next meeting. Now that Lucy thought about it, the other ladies might resent it if she seemed to be going off on a tangent. Lucy Maddox had never been at the forefront of anything. That was not her way. She stayed in the background, lending her assistance—and Maddox money—to worthwhile projects, but never assuming a leadership role.

Taking a deep breath, Lucy mounted the stairs to the second floor, newly aware of the rooms to her left. Mother and Father's rooms, still exactly as they had been three years ago. Martha dusted faithfully. Every spring, she aired the bedding and beat the carpets. The windows were opened until spring breezes banished the staleness of the winter. And then the rooms were closed up again.

A Stitch in Time

"I'd write an entire ode if it'd earn me a blanket without holes." Lucy thought about the soldier who'd said that—and then about the blankets on the unused beds in that wing of the house. The dozen or so blankets stored in a chest beneath the window in Mother's sitting room. It had never occurred to Lucy to donate things from those rooms. But. . .why not? Why hadn't she ever challenged the notion that the Maddox mansion was a sanctuary that must not be invaded?

For the first time in Lucy's life, the empty house felt cavernous instead of comforting. She frowned. Should she be ashamed of her wealth? *No. You should use it. You must use it. The time has come.* Lucy looked down the stairs toward the first floor. Yes, indeed. The time had come for things to change.

⚭

The aroma of coffee brewing woke Lucy at first light. Dressing quickly, she crossed the hall into Mother's sitting room and opened the trunk sitting beneath the east-facing window. She stared down at the woven blanket lying atop the contents. Draping it over one arm, she descended the back stairs to the kitchen. Martha was standing at the stove. When she heard Lucy's footsteps, she turned around.

"What's this?" She nodded at the blanket Lucy draped over the back of a kitchen chair.

"A blanket from atop the pile of things in that chest in Mother's sitting room."

"What's it doing in my kitchen?"

Lucy waited until she was seated at the table and Martha had served coffee before answering. "Something happened on the train yesterday." She told Martha about Private Donlin and the mention of socks and blankets.

Martha nodded. "Are you taking that to the train, then?"

Lucy sighed. "I don't know. I just thought—there's so much in this house that could be put to good use. I think the Ladies Aid has quite a stack of things stored over at the Presbyterian Church, just waiting to be packed up and sent off somewhere. And those boys coming through Decatur without decent blankets. There's always been such a rush to feed them, I doubt anyone's taken the time to realize—I don't even know why I noticed, but I did."

"And. . . ? I suspect there's more to this than blankets."

Lucy took a deep breath. "Mrs. Kincaid asked for my help with the Ladies Aid, now that she can't host the meetings." She glanced toward the front of the house. "She didn't really ask me to take over, but. . .I was thinking. . ." She glanced at Martha. Shrugged. "Two needs crossed paths. . .here. In this house."

Martha chuckled. "That explains the open drapes in the parlor and the dining room."

Lucy nodded. Looking down at the light reflecting off the surface of her coffee, she circled the rim of the cup with her finger. Martha returned to the stove, humming while she rolled out biscuit dough. Lucy finished her first cup of coffee and poured a second. Finally, she said, "The parlors. The formal dining room. Father's library. All of those rooms just sitting here. Not doing anyone any good."

Martha said nothing.

"But Father was always adamant that we not open the house to just anyone."

Martha worked the pump at the sink and rinsed her hands. As she dried them, she said quietly, "Mr. Maddox was a very private man. But he left the house—and the mercantile—to you."

Lucy took Martha's gentle reminder for encouragement. "If we opened the pocket doors between the two parlors, more than a dozen women would have ample space for knitting and stitching."

She swallowed. Might as well tell it all. "And if we moved the chairs away from the dining table, we'd have a grand surface for spreading out fabric."

"A cutting table," Martha said. "Of imported rosewood."

"It's—probably not a good idea."

Martha's tone was slightly mocking as she said, "What were you thinking, dearie? Using all this space for the good of our boys? Creating a place where the ladies of Decatur could work together to relieve misery?"

Lucy allowed a little smile. "So you *don't* think it's a terrible idea?"

"I'd call it inspired. I'll put a pot of soup on every morning. We'll offer soup and fresh rolls to anyone who cares to come and stay over the noon hour. And endless tea and cakes to the rest." Martha nodded. "Your mother would be so proud, Lucy. So very proud."

"And Father?"

Martha didn't answer for a moment. Finally, she said, "He would understand—eventually."

Chapter 4

A few days after Jonah Kincaid's funeral, Silas began his day at the mercantile as usual—by opening the weekly *Decatur Magnet* newspaper to check the store's quarter-page advertisement for accuracy. As he scanned the page, his attention was drawn to an announcement that appeared just above the mercantile ad. He read it more than once.

LADIES
who wish to participate in a special project
intended to expand the ministry of our beloved Basket Brigade
are invited to attend an organizational meeting on
Tuesday, October 7, at ten o'clock in the morning
at the home of Miss Lucy Maddox,
6 Poplar Street.
A light luncheon will be served.

Mrs. Tompkins stepped in the back door. One glance at Silas and she asked, "Something of particular interest in the *Magnet*, Mr. Tait? A unique announcement, perhaps?"

"You are aware of Miss Maddox's plan?"

"Not until I read the paper. Then I remembered. Miss Maddox was singularly moved by something that happened on the train the last time she and I shared duty in one of the hospital cars." Mrs. Tompkins hung her bonnet on the hook beside the storeroom door and donned her blue-and-white work apron. "Whatever she has planned, though, I imagine she'll get plenty of interest. It's not every day the hoi polloi are invited to a mansion for tea."

"Not *any* day, when it comes to the Maddox place," Silas said, folding the paper as he spoke. "Do you have any idea what she means by 'expanding the ministry' of the Basket Brigade?"

"No, sir." Feather duster in hand, Mrs. Tompkins proceeded to the front display window then glanced back at Silas. "But in about two minutes you'll be able to ask the lady herself. Miss Maddox is headed this way."

Silas shoved the folded newspaper onto a shelf just beneath the counter. He smoothed his thinning hair and straightened his cravat. Tugging at each of his sleeves so that precisely the right amount of cuff was showing, he strode to the door and pulled it open just as Lucy reached for the handle. "Good morning, Miss Maddox. It's a pleasure to see you."

Miss Maddox's cheeks flushed a lovely shade of pink. "I've done something—well—impetuous. At first I thought it was the perfect solution to Mrs. Kincaid's quandary about the Ladies Aid. And then, once I'd decided I might open the house for meetings—the idea grew." She glanced over at Mrs. Tompkins. "You were there—on the train—those poor men."

Mrs. Tompkins nodded. "Yes. And I could tell that you were unusually moved by what you saw that evening."

"I was." She gave a nervous little laugh, put one gloved palm to her waist, and took a deep breath. "And I only have a week to finish preparations before that meeting at my home."

She looked over at Silas. "If it's to be a success, I'll need the mercantile's support, as well."

"As always, Miss Maddox, I am at your service." *You sound like a butler, you idiot.* Ah, well. Stuffy as it was, the response garnered another pretty smile. That was something. "It would help, however, to know exactly what it is you're talking about. The announcement mentions expanding the ministry of the Basket Brigade."

"Exactly." Quickly, Lucy told Silas about the men who'd teased one another over poems for socks and odes for blankets. "And it occurred to me after I returned home that evening, that while the collections and drives have had wonderful results—as far as we know—that there are men coming through Decatur every evening with needs we might meet—with a little planning and a lot of hard work." Her warm brown eyes lit up as she laid out her plan to transform her mansion into a production center for the benefit of the wounded soldiers on the daily train.

"You mean to turn your home into a factory?"

"Yes," Lucy said, and followed it quickly with, "and I know that Father would have trouble with the idea." She lifted her chin. "I've thought about that. Carefully. I don't mean to be disrespectful to his memory, but he entrusted everything to me. If I want to use it for good, shouldn't that be my decision?"

Silas looked over at Mrs. Tompkins, who immediately busied herself with dusting. With all the dignity he could muster, he said firmly, "No one with any sense at all would dare question your devotion to your parents. I do not think it possible for someone as kind as you to dishonor their memory." He clenched his hands behind his back as he continued. "As to your plans to serve the men, it seems to me a superb way to honor the memory of one of the greatest civic servants this region has ever been privileged to know—the late Mrs. Maddox. In my opinion, your plans merely expand upon your own gracious habit of following in your mother's beloved footsteps." He could feel the heat crawling up the back of his neck as he spoke. Had he said too much? Had he betrayed himself? Lucy must not see him blush. In desperation, he looked toward Mrs. Tompkins, dismayed by the older woman's expression. *She knows.*

Retreating to a safer spot behind the counter, Silas quickly changed the subject. "You said that you would require the mercantile's support. May I ask you to elaborate on the specifics?"

Lucy had just opened her mouth to answer when the door burst open to admit Mrs. Collins. The feather adorning the woman's stylish bonnet bobbed as she scanned the interior. She nodded at Mrs. Tompkins, ignored Lucy, and addressed Silas. "I've just come from the Maddoxes', where Martha informed me that I'd find Lucy here. If you'd please give us just a moment"—she acknowledged Lucy's presence with a well-fixed glare—"Miss Maddox and I have important business to discuss. *Ladies Aid* business."

Silas looked toward Lucy for guidance. He saw the joy she'd just displayed fade. In its place came uncertainty, shown by the way she clenched her gloved hands and glanced down at the floor. He was reminded of a child about to endure a scolding. How he would have loved to step to her side and put an encouraging arm about her. Squelching the thought, he stayed put behind the counter.

Mrs. Tompkins, bless her, spoke up. "You were speaking of the mercantile's role in the new project, Miss Maddox? I'm certain Mrs. Collins would be pleased to offer her support for such a worthy cause—her being someone the entire city looks up to." She glanced at Mrs. Collins. "If you don't mind my saying so, ma'am."

It was clear the domineering Mrs. Collins did not mind. In fact, she fairly preened beneath the implied praise. "Mr. Collins and I are most interested in doing our civic duty." She peered down her long nose at Lucy. "I was, however, taken aback when I saw the announcement in this morning's newspaper. When I called late the day of the visitation, Mrs. Kincaid mentioned that she had asked for your help contacting the women of the committee. I had no idea she'd asked you to take over." She sighed. "I don't blame her, of course. Anyone in her position can be forgiven the oversight. The poor dear. But surely *you* know, Miss Maddox, that there are bylaws in place. The president cannot simply hand over the running of the Ladies Aid to whomever she wishes."

"Of course not," Lucy said quickly. "I have no intention of doing so."

"Really?" Doubt sounded in Mrs. Collins's voice. "This morning's newspaper would seem to indicate otherwise."

"My announcement didn't mention the Ladies Aid," Lucy said.

"Not specifically." Mrs. Collins sniffed. "But it's obvious you're making rather impressive plans."

"I hope so," Lucy said. "In the end, that will be up to the ladies who attend the meeting."

"Yes, well." Mrs. Collins tapped the floor with the tip of her parasol. "I'm here to offer my assistance in advance. If you'll be so kind as to tell me what you have in mind, I'll know how best to lend my support."

Silas shot a sympathetic glance Lucy's way and then pretended to study the ledger open before him on the counter. Poor Lucy. Her first attempt at leadership had put her in the crosshairs of one of the most intimidating women Silas had ever met.

Lucy, however, seemed to be recovering from an initial bout of self-doubt. "In truth, I've come to the mercantile to consult with Mr. Tait regarding the matter. It's much too early in the planning for me to ask anything of others. But I do appreciate your kind offer of assistance."

There was an uncomfortable silence before Mrs. Collins said, "Well then. Perhaps I shall call later today. After you and Mr. Tait have spoken."

"As you can imagine," Lucy said, "my enthusiasm for the cause has outstripped my experience. I'm afraid I'm a bit overwhelmed at the moment. I'm not certain I'll be able to receive callers today."

Mrs. Collins peered at Lucy with all the intensity of a gambler sizing up his opposition. "I see. Well, accept this bit of advice at least, and have your people prepare for a large crowd." She gave a deep sigh. "There will always be those who attend these things simply to take note of the drapes and the wall coverings in our fine homes, and I have had occasion to hear yours wondered about more than once. Be advised that many in attendance will be there merely to gawk. They will depart without committing to the cause—but only after consuming more than their fair share of refreshments."

A low clearing of Lucy's throat—Silas thought it sounded suspiciously like a stifled laugh—preceded Lucy's response. "I shall be certain to have Mrs. Jefferson prepare accordingly, Mrs. Collins." She crossed to the door and opened it, inviting the woman to leave even as she smiled sweetly and said, "I hope it isn't imposing on your time to ask that you personally reassure Mrs. Kincaid that you have the Ladies Aid matter well in hand. She may not be accepting callers, but you could perhaps stop by with a note?"

Mrs. Collins frowned. "I'm not certain that I do have things 'in hand.' "

Lucy sighed. "I'm not plotting a takeover, Mrs. Collins. The Ladies Aid membership will hopefully want to attend my gathering. I did intend to speak with you about conducting a meeting in concert with my event, simply as a matter of convenience to them. However, if you object, then please be prepared to announce the next meeting date and location at my gathering. I hope I can count on you to attend?"

"Of course."

"Good. I'll look forward to seeing you then. Now, if you will excuse me, I do have some private business to conduct with Mr. Tait and Mrs. Tompkins." The moment the sputtering Mrs. Collins bustled out the door, Lucy flipped the OPEN sign in the window to read CLOSED. She looked from Mrs. Tompkins to Silas. "Did you ever?"

"Only several times a week," Silas replied. "Mrs. Collins is a woman of very pronounced opinions and tastes, and she is a frequent customer."

"And a good one," Mrs. Tompkins added, "as long as she gets exactly what she wants."

"I see that with greater clarity now," Lucy said. And then she grinned. "I never quite understood how you could let her purchase all those yards of bright blue plaid last fall. I mean—the scale of it on such a. . .large frame."

Mrs. Tompkins chuckled. "I did everything I could to steer her away from that plaid and toward an understated vertical stripe, but Mrs. Collins is not easily steered."

Lucy sighed. "I suppose I've just bought myself a world of trouble by refusing her offer to help with the meeting."

"You mean her offer to take over?"

"Yes, but—she's probably right about ladies attending merely to see the house." Lucy frowned. "I really don't want gawkers. I need *workers*."

Silas spoke up. "How can we help?"

Lucy described the plan that had resulted from what Silas could only think of as an epiphany. It would have taken something that dramatic to effect such a change. The Maddox mansion opened to the public? Transformed into a wartime production center? When Lucy mentioned that Martha Jefferson had offered to serve luncheon every day to whoever was there working, Silas interrupted with applause. "Bravo, Miss Maddox. It's a superb idea. Inspired."

"You really think so?"

"With not one scintilla of doubt." The confident approbation earned him the kind of smile he had grown to cherish. "Mrs. Collins was right about one thing, though. Expect a very large crowd at that first meeting."

Lucy nodded. "It's a shame public curiosity can't benefit the cause."

"Perhaps it can," Mrs. Tompkins said. "You could charge admission."

"I couldn't!" Lucy sounded horrified.

"Hear me out," Mrs. Tompkins insisted. "It's going to take a lot of fabric and yarn to accomplish what you want to do."

Lucy looked over at Silas. "That's why I wanted to talk to you. Would you agree to donating older stock to the cause?"

"It is your mercantile, Miss Maddox. You can 'donate' the entire dry goods department if you so wish."

"I don't," Lucy said. "I just want to get off to a good start, but the point isn't to draw attention to the Maddoxes. We need others to invest in the effort."

"And so," Mrs. Tompkins began again, "you ask them to invest from the beginning. Admission to the first meeting is gained by donating a bag of scraps or a twist of yarn."

"I wish I'd thought to suggest that in the announcement. It's too late now."

"We can put up a notice in the store window," Silas said. "Decatur has a very active grapevine. And you needn't require it.

Merely suggest it." He reached up to pull down a few bolts of the older stock and then swept his hand over the surface of the top bolt of fabric. "A few women working together cutting these up into, say, four-inch squares while another few stitch them together could piece cot-sized quilt tops rather quickly, don't you think?"

Mrs. Tompkins nodded. She glanced over at Lucy. "You'd want to tie comforters, though, instead of quilting—assuming speed is important."

"It is," Lucy said. "We don't know that the trains will continue much past December."

"Depending on how many ladies offer their assistance, it might be possible to tie several comforters in a day. Of course, someone would still need to bind them."

"It's a shame you don't know a good tailor," Silas said.

"Why a tailor?" Lucy asked.

"Because a good tailor with a sewing machine could apply binding in a fraction of the time required to stitch it by hand."

Lucy nodded. "How many sewing machines do you suppose there are in Decatur?"

"I've ordered two for customers," Silas said, "but only one is still here in the city. Mrs. Jenkins ordered a machine last winter after visiting the aid society in Salem and seeing firsthand what could be accomplished with one."

"Jenkins," Lucy murmured. "Didn't they move this past summer?"

"They did. The other machine belongs to Mrs. Collins. She ordered hers about a week after Mrs. Jenkins's was delivered. With more attachments and a nicer cabinet."

Mrs. Collins. Again. "I don't dare ask Mrs. Collins to loan hers," Lucy said.

"I doubt it's been used once," Mrs. Tompkins said. "It was more the principle of the thing."

"What principle?"

Silas interrupted, hoping that his explanation showed due respect for poor Mrs. Collins, never satisfied and rarely happy. "She is somewhat. . .competitive. . .when it comes to things like fashion and the latest innovation. She wishes to be at the forefront of everything. I believe she sees it as part of her role as a community leader."

Mrs. Tompkins chuckled. "That's a very kind way to put it, Mr. Tait." She smiled at Lucy. "It's too bad the ladies of Decatur can't be enticed to compete over something like comforter tying or sock production."

"Perhaps they could," Silas said. "Especially if public recognition for their accomplishment were part of it."

Lucy was doubtful. "Wouldn't they object to something like that? I mean. . .being singled out in a public way?"

"Object?" Mrs. Tompkins laughed. "They'd love the attention. In fact, recognition would likely entice scores of the women in our fair city to participate."

"We could publish the winner's name in the *Magnet*," Lucy said.

Silas was half joking when he proposed a "Golden Needle Award" for "the most pairs of socks produced by one fair lady's knitting needles."

"That's a superb idea," Lucy enthused. She looked over at Silas. "Would you be willing to have socks submitted here at the mercantile? Someone would need to keep an official count."

"We could string up a clothesline across the front window," Mrs. Tompkins said. "Hang each pair on display. To keep the interest going."

"And a count. A board in the window announcing the total number of pairs thus far. No names attached, to keep the mystery of who will win alive."

"What's a reasonable end date?" Lucy asked. She glanced over at Mrs. Tompkins. "Do you think Miss Evans would allow the winner to be announced at her Christmas musicale?"

"We can but ask," Mrs. Tompkins said, "but first I'd like to return to something Mr. Tait said." She glanced at Silas. "I know you were joking about the 'Golden Needle Award,' but what if the award itself were more than just an announcement and mention in the newspaper? What if it were something that would make the recognition more lasting. Perhaps something wearable?"

"That's brilliant," Lucy said. "A ladies' version of a medal. Lasting recognition for exceptional service. To be worn with pride."

"A brooch, perhaps?" Mrs. Tompkins offered.

"Large enough to be noticed but tasteful." Lucy crossed the store to the jewelry display. She pointed to an oval brooch. "Something on the order of that. Except—do you think we could have something made specifically for the contest?"

"I could consult with the jeweler who made that one," Silas offered. "I was actually planning a trip to St. Louis soon to make the rounds at a few of our suppliers."

"Thank you," Lucy said, and again Silas was graced with a sweet smile. "You are so good to offer." She laughed and clasped her hands together. "It's all coming together perfectly."

She laughed. The sound was more beautiful than any music Silas Tait had ever heard.

Chapter 5

The day before Lucy's meeting to establish a sewing arm of the Basket Brigade, she was wielding a feather duster in the library when she heard the muffled sound of hoofbeats coming toward the house. She peered out the window. *Please. Not Mrs. Collins.* She'd been expecting the woman to call ever since reading a note Jimmy Kincaid had delivered for his mother.

> *Dear Lucy,*
>
> *I hope you don't mind my addressing you as a friend, for I feel that you have become one in recent days. I write to forewarn you. Mrs. Collins called to express her displeasure with what she sees as my encouraging you to take over (her term, not mine) the Ladies Aid. Please do not allow her to intimidate. Proceed with your good work. Gertie has a good heart. She will eventually see that a shared meeting and a few weeks of shared effort to support the Basket Brigade is the best thing. You have my utmost confidence and my best wishes.*
>
> *The demands of full mourning should not keep friends from sharing important news. Please call some afternoon to share your progress.*

I only wish I could support them in a more visible way.

Lucy had read the note to Martha before laying it aside. "Can you believe the temerity? Mrs. Collins made a social call to a woman in mourning. That's very nearly scandalous." Thinking back on it now gave Lucy fresh resolve to be quite firm when she faced Mrs. Collins on the morrow. She glanced over at Martha. "Perhaps I should simply step out on the veranda and tell her in so many words that I don't *care* who runs the Ladies Aid. Before she so much as alights from the carriage."

"If you want to try it, I'll stand by you," Martha said, "but I doubt the lady will believe you. She seems bent on assuming the worst."

Laying her feather duster aside, Lucy hurried to the front of the house to greet whoever it was. *Please. Not Mrs. Collins.* The Maddox home sat in the middle of two acres bordered with a low stone wall. Guests approached by way of a winding drive that led from an iron gate suspended between two pillars, each one topped with elegant lanterns. Deliveries were made via a much less impressive double gate at the back of the property. It wasn't until Lucy had stepped through the front door that she realized what she'd really heard. Someone was coming in the back way. Hurrying around the side of the house, she recognized the mercantile delivery wagon.

Martha had followed her and was the first to speak. "Why, that's Mr. Tait sitting beside the driver. I wasn't expecting a delivery. Were you?"

"No." Lucy's tone was teasing as she called out to Mr. Tait, "Do you really think we need an entire wagonload of refreshments for tomorrow?"

Mr. Tait lowered himself from the wagon seat, taking just a fraction of a moment to steady himself before turning around and tipping his hat. "Miss Maddox. Mrs. Jefferson. I've taken the liberty of delivering a few supplies in advance of the meeting." He nodded at Lucy. "You asked if I would check for old stock. We have perhaps two dozen ends of bolts—a half yard here, a quarter yard there—and a good supply of remnants, for which there is often very little call." He took a couple of steps and pointed at the oak cabinet in the wagon box. "I also thought you might make use of my sewing machine for the next few weeks. There hasn't really been much demand for tailoring of late. It could be put to much better use here. If you're willing to have it."

Stunned by the generosity, for Mr. Tait's machine belonged to him, not to the mercantile, Lucy said nothing for a moment. Mr. Tait misunderstood.

"I hope you'll forgive me if I've overstepped. I didn't mean—"

Lucy interrupted him. "No. Of course you haven't overstepped. It's. . .wonderful. It's just. . .I don't know if any of the ladies will know how to run it."

"It's a brilliant invention," Silas said, "and quite simple to operate. It would be my honor to give you a demonstration, and I'd be happy to instruct anyone willing to learn. I thought its presence might make a silent statement as to the sincerity of the mercantile's commitment to your endeavor."

When he touched the brim of his hat and said something about interrupting her at a very busy time, Lucy's hand went to the kerchief wrapped about her head. *Oh dear.* How embarrassing to be caught in such a state. "Well, obviously, I didn't expect to be receiving." She glanced back toward the house. "Martha and I have been giving the main floor a last polish, and when I heard someone coming up the drive—I thought it might be Mrs. Collins."

"Mrs. Collins? Is she helping with the preparations?"

"I suppose that would be her way of seeing it." Lucy chuckled. "But no, Mrs. Collins has not called today. Thank goodness." She motioned toward the contents of the wagon. "It's very kind of you to have done all of this. And I think you're right. The presence of a sewing machine will make a very good impression." She led the way inside. "You can see what we've done and look around a bit while I make myself more presentable. I'm sure you'll know better than I where we should set up your machine. The fabric goes on the dining room table. If you've a mind to do so, you might suggest a way to display it to its best advantage. In fact, we might create a vignette—calico, a sewing basket—all the tools needed to facilitate the project. Can we do that?"

"Of course," Silas said. "I'll have Mrs. Tompkins gather up an assortment of materials and return whenever you wish. It will be ready to greet those in attendance tomorrow."

Lucy nodded. "Good. I rather like the idea of everyone who comes through the door seeing that Maddox Mercantile has made a substantial commitment to get things started."

∞

Trusted employee or not, Silas Tait had never stepped through the door to the Maddox home. Even with Miss Maddox leading the way inside, Silas could not quite shake the feeling of trespass. He hesitated just inside the back door, trying his best not to stare. Miss Maddox directed Mrs. Jefferson to "show Mr. Tait what we've done to ready the house for tomorrow," and then she retreated via a steep flight of stairs just off the kitchen.

"This way," Mrs. Jefferson said, waving him through a door that led into a wide front hall with polished floors boasting an intricate inlaid border. Silas was reminded of the way Mrs. Collins had scoffed at people she labeled *gawkers*. How, he wondered, could one be expected not to gawk at exquisite silk wall coverings and crystal chandeliers? It was a glorious house—the finest he'd ever seen. Mrs. Jefferson showed him about with a combination of pride and deference. It was clear that she loved the house—and also clear that she respected him as the able manager of one of Mr. Maddox's businesses. As the two of them returned to the front hall, she apologized for not taking the hat he had removed but still held in his hands.

"I don't know what I was thinking, making you hold on to your hat like some delivery boy. Please forgive me, Mr. Tait."

"You needn't apologize," Silas said with a smile. "I rather appreciate having something to hold on to." He stared about him with open amazement. "I don't know what I expected, but it was never anything this grand."

Lucy's voice sounded from the top of the stairs. "But surely you've seen the house before."

"No, ma'am. There would have been no occasion for a mere tailor to be invited here."

"But—Father thought so highly of you." She frowned and then shrugged. "Ah, well. I am sorry." She descended the stairs. "What do you think? Are we prepared for tomorrow?" She crossed the hall to the formal parlor, pausing in the wide doorway. "We've opened the pocket doors to make the space as accommodating as possible, but even counting the piano stool and the footstools, we can only provide seating for about thirty. There are more chairs in the ballroom, but I didn't have the heart to ask Henry to haul them down from the third floor."

Silas scanned the two rooms. He didn't dare mention anything so intimate as *hoops*, but the fact of the matter was that once even a couple of dozen ladies wearing stylish hoop skirts arrived, the spacious rooms would be crowded. "I think it's reasonable to expect that those in attendance will wear their best for the occasion. Taking that into consideration. . ." He hesitated.

"My thought exactly," Lucy said. "It's not really a matter of chairs, is it? It's more a matter of our hoop skirts."

Feeling awkward, Silas motioned toward the dining room. "Are you certain you want a display on that exquisite table? I will of course take great care, but—"

Mrs. Jefferson spoke up. "Henry's working on a false top, backing a smooth piece of pine with felt. The pine will be the actual work surface."

"That's very wise," Silas said.

"Where should we put the machine?" Lucy asked.

"By a window to provide the best light possible. Beyond that, it doesn't really matter." He looked about them. "I assume you'd prefer not to move the settee in the parlor?"

"I don't mind it, but is the machine noisy?" Lucy asked. "I should know the answer to that, but I can't recall hearing it in operation, and you know the ladies will want to be able to chatter while they work. On the other hand, it shouldn't be tucked away where they won't be aware of the work that's getting done."

"If you are willing to have the settee moved away from the parlor window, we can set up the machine and I'll give you a demonstration," Silas said. "Once you've seen it operate, you'll have a better idea as to how to arrange things."

"Whether it stays there or not, though, I very much like the idea of it being on display in the parlor for tomorrow's meeting. It will do more than just show the mercantile's commitment to the project. It will make a statement—that the point is work, not socializing. Although I will also say that as I've thought about this, I've rather liked the notion of these rooms echoing with voices and laughter instead of midnight creaks." She walked to where a beautifully upholstered settee stood before one of the parlor windows. "We can just slide this over to the other window."

"I'll get Harker." Silas hurried to fetch the driver. Together the men moved the settee and returned to the wagon for the machine. Silas had hoped that Henry Jefferson would be available to help haul the machine in. A wooden leg and carrying heavy equipment didn't mix well. But Silas had no intention of looking like a weakling in Lucy's presence. Fortunately, he had just positioned himself at the back of the wagon when Henry Jefferson came trotting around the back of the house. He'd been working on the cover for the dining table out in his workshop.

"Mr. Maddox would have my head for letting the manager of one of his businesses do the work of a common laborer. No sir, he wouldn't never want that and neither does Henry Jefferson. Stand aside and let me help."

Thank goodness for Henry Jefferson.

⚭

"You said it was simple," Lucy said, watching as Silas opened the cabinet and lifted the machine itself into view.

"It is." He pointed to the platform shaped like the soles of two shoes. "The operator places his or her feet there to pedal. That turns this wheel." He touched the large wheel mounted on the right side of the cabinet, which was attached to the pedal with an iron bar. "This belt"—he indicated a leather belt that connected the large wheel to a smaller one—"transfers the power between wheels and from there to the finer mechanical parts that move the needle up and down. Meanwhile," he said, removing a small plate near the needle, "the shuttle and bobbin work together to feed the thread in a way that produces a lock stitch."

"That may seem simple to you," Lucy said, "but to me it's a bit of wizardry."

Martha agreed about the "wizardry" involved, although she didn't see it as a plus. "Wizardry from a monstrosity," she said.

Silas smiled. "I suppose it is a bit of a monstrosity on display here in the formal parlor. In most homes, it would be hidden in the servant's quarters—perhaps even given its own room."

Martha snorted. "Over my lifeless body. I'll have none of it. God gave me two good hands, and I can keep up with the mending just fine. Don't have any use for a newfangled concoction of wheels and shuttles that could send a needle right through me at a moment's notice. I'll be back in the kitchen if you need me—doing what the good Lord intended a housekeeper to do."

After Martha had retreated, Lucy apologized for her outburst.

"There's no need to apologize," Silas said. "A great many people are suspicious of machinery. Truly, though, there's no wizardry involved. You could be running it efficiently in no time."

Lucy sounded doubtful as she peered at the machine. "So says the man who's a professional tailor."

"Want to try it?"

"No." She folded her arms. "I don't want to chance being blamed for breaking it before we've even had a chance to use it."

"The only thing you could break would be a needle."

"Exactly. Broken before we sew a stitch for the cause."

Silas reached into his pocket and produced a small wooden vial. "A good tailor always has a spare."

Lucy reconsidered. "You're sure you don't mind?"

"I'd be delighted." Silas grinned. "And Mrs. Collins will be incensed to think she's not the only woman in Decatur who can operate a sewing machine."

Lucy gave a low laugh. "If she does operate it."

Amusement shone in Silas's dark eyes.

Mrs. Collins aside, Lucy was surprised at just how much the idea of mastering a machine appealed to her. She nodded. "All right. Tell me what to do." Silas carried the piano stool over. Lucy sat down, and in a matter of minutes, Silas had shown her how to fill the bobbin and thread the shuttle. Regulating the tension was a challenge.

"Just remember that a very slight movement of the screw makes a considerable change in the tension," Silas said as he handed Lucy a tiny screwdriver.

She tried to hand it back. "You should do it."

"No, you've a talent for machines. I can see it. You'll be fine."

She *was* fine, but there was a great deal more to learn. Threading the needle required guiding thread through half a dozen precise places on the machine head.

"If you miss a single one," Silas said, "you won't get a good result. There can be no shortcuts."

Martha had returned from the kitchen and was standing in the doorway, her arms folded, her expression still wary. Yet, when Silas mentioned no shortcuts, Martha spoke up. "That's just like with baking. Sloppy measurements or a missed ingredient and you've got yourself a failure."

"Just so," Silas said, nodding as he handed Lucy two squares of cloth. "Right sides together," he said. "Just as you do when you're hand stitching a seam."

With trembling hands, Lucy lifted the presser foot on the machine and slid the fabric into place.

"Remember not to pull on the work," Silas said. "That's a good way to break a needle. All you need to do is guide the fabric. Let the machine do the work for you. That is, after all, the point. Now, you begin by placing your hand on the flywheel and moving it—gently. Once the motion is begun, keep it going by pedaling. The more evenly you can pedal, the more even will be your stitches."

Lucy put her hand to the flywheel. Her heart thumped from nerves—and then thumped again when, as she barely moved the flywheel, Silas put his hand over hers.

"Not that way," he said. "This way." He corrected the movement.

For a fraction of a moment there was. . .something. Lucy didn't quite know what, but it made her catch her breath.

Silas snatched his hand away. "I beg your pardon, Miss Maddox." He took a step back.

Tentatively, Lucy moved the flywheel and then, placing both hands on the fabric, guided it beneath the presser foot while she pedaled. The result was a long line of stitches in a fraction of the time it would have taken her with needle and thread. Lifting the presser foot, she pulled the fabric away, snipped the threads, and held the result up with a triumphant smile. "God bless you, Silas. The ladies will bless you, as well." She hesitated. "Is it asking too much for you to come to the first workday—just in case I have trouble with the machine?" She glanced over at Martha, who was still standing in the doorway. "You may think it a monstrosity, but I think it's nothing short of a miracle."

"And you're to be the miracle worker, I suppose?" Martha asked.

"No," Lucy replied. "Silas is the miracle worker for suggesting it and for teaching me how to use it." She looked up at him. "What do you say, Mr. Tait? Will you agree to 'hover' here at the house in case the monster breathes fire?"

Silas bowed. "It would be my pleasure, Miss Maddox."

Chapter 6

On Tuesday morning Silas arrived at the Maddox mansion fully one hour before the ten o'clock meeting. Even so, as he drove the light rig carrying everything Mrs. Tompkins had gathered for the sewing display atop Lucy's dining room table, he was startled to see several carriages waiting at the front gate.

Henry Jefferson had donned ancient livery for the occasion and was standing before those gates like a sentry. Which was a good idea, since the first carriage in line was Mrs. Collins's flashy rig. Silas saluted Henry Jefferson as he drove by, bound for the back entrance. He was hitching the buggy when Mrs. Jefferson flung open the back door and called out, "Thank goodness you're here."

"Is something wrong?"

"Not yet, but if Miss Maddox doesn't settle down, she's going to have an apoplectic fit before her guests arrive." She descended the porch steps, and Silas handed over a couple of baskets of props and then took up a larger box for himself. Mrs. Jefferson continued, "She rose before dawn and has been second-guessing everything from how the chairs are arranged to what we're serving and on to every other detail. And she's convinced herself that what she's planned to say is entirely insufficient."

The two of them had barely entered the kitchen when Lucy swept in with such force that her hooped skirt swung about her like a bell. "Thank goodness you're here!" she cried out.

Silas set the box of sewing paraphernalia on the table. He'd never seen Lucy so lovely. She'd coiled her dark hair about her head in a new way that made her look regal.

She put her hand to the fringe of black lace accenting the square neckline of her day dress. "Is it too much?" She looked down, nervously trying to smooth out the black-and-white striped ivory skirt. "I didn't want to appear to be casual about the project, but now. . ." She patted the wide lace extending from beneath her bell-shaped sleeves and glanced at Mrs. Jefferson. "It is too much, isn't it? They'll think I'm flaunting my—"

The housekeeper interrupted her. "I haven't changed my mind since the last time you asked me ten minutes ago. It's perfect. They'll expect you to look like the lady of this house, and that dress says that you are."

Miss Maddox turned to Silas. "What do you think, Mr. Tait?"

He looked up. "Of. . . ?"

"The dress," Miss Maddox said. "Is it too ostentatious?" She touched one of the scarlet silk rosettes at her waist.

Silas looked over at Mrs. Jefferson, dismayed by the housekeeper's knowing smile. "Well, Mr. Tait. What do you think? Since the opinion I've given at least half a dozen times since dawn doesn't seem to have convinced her that she looks lovely, perhaps you can."

Silas cleared his throat. Swallowed. "I am hardly a proper judge of ladies' fashion, Miss Maddox. However, since you've requested an opinion. . ." He could feel the warmth climbing up the back of his neck again. He could not meet Lucy's gaze, and so he grabbed the two baskets Mrs. Jefferson had helped him bring in and motioned toward the front of the house. "You are a vision. The dress is perfect. Everything is perfect. Now, if I may, I should be preparing the display you wanted in the dining room."

Lucy stood at the base of the stairs in the front hall, her hands folded in a way she hoped belied the pounding of her heart. She was trembling with fear. Not just nerves but true fear, for Mrs. Collins was standing on the other side of the front door. Of course she would be the first to arrive.

Lucy looked across to the dining room, where a perfectly composed Silas Tait stood beside the perfectly composed display of sewing goods and cloth he'd arranged atop the dining room table. He'd protested what he called "such a prominent station" and suggested that he should wait in the kitchen until she called the meeting to order, at which time he would quietly slip in and stand beside the sewing machine at the back of the room. But Lucy had insisted.

"I need every friendly face I can muster," she'd said. "And if I try to flee, you're ordered to stop me." She'd laughed nervously as if making a joke, but at the moment every fiber of her being wanted to do just that. She actually glanced behind her toward the upstairs hall.

"You'll be fine," Silas said. His quiet voice steadied her.

"He's right," Martha said. "Just think about the suffering you'll relieve through this work."

Lucy nodded. Yes. That was the secret, wasn't it? Serving the wounded was the thing—not what others thought of her or the house or—anything. If only the ladies would agree to help. "All right," she said. "Let us begin."

Martha nodded. And opened the door.

"How kind of you to come," Lucy said, smiling as Mrs. Collins stepped through the doorway.

The older woman did not even try to hide her curiosity. Instead, she ignored Martha's offer to take her wrap and swept across the foyer to drop a calling card on the silver tray atop the hall table. She looked up. She looked down. She looked into the dining room and nodded. "Mr. Tait."

"Mrs. Collins." Silas bowed. "May I have the honor of seeing you into the parlor while Miss Maddox greets her guests?" He glanced at Lucy. "She has requested that you be seated at the front to facilitate your addressing the Ladies Aid—when the time comes."

Mrs. Collins looked at Lucy with open suspicion. "She has, has she?"

"This way, if you please." Silas escorted her across the hall to the parlor entrance.

Mrs. Collins peered into the parlor. "Is that—a *sewing machine?*"

"It is," Silas said. "Not nearly as new as yours, I'm afraid, but—"

Mrs. Collins followed him into the parlor. And so it began.

Lucy was gratified by the enthusiasm that greeted her presentation. She quickly described the inspiration for opening her home—the intersection of the loss of "one of their own," her encounter on the train, and Mrs. Kincaid's request for help with a meeting place for the Ladies Aid. She hurried to do what she could to smooth Mrs. Collins's ruffled feathers.

"I wish to make it clear that the work I am proposing to relieve the suffering of the wounded men who pass through Decatur is in no way intended to be in competition with the Ladies Aid. While I have offered my home for future meetings, I have done so only as a personal favor to my dear neighbor, Mrs. Philip Kincaid. The fact that I am playing the part of hostess today should in no way be perceived as a desire to be involved in leadership."

She glanced at Mrs. Collins, who did not appear in the least convinced.

"Those who know me surely know that I have always been content to remain in the background while others far more able than I take up leadership roles. I have no desire to change that.

"After a brief time of refreshment, I will be yielding the floor to Mrs. Bernard Collins so that she can conduct a proper Ladies Aid meeting." She forced a nervous smile and nodded at the irascible old woman sitting just a few feet away. "I do ask that if you are interested in joining my little project, you leave your card in the basket that Mr. Tait has provided in the dining room alongside his fine display. The display shows some of the materials Maddox Mercantile has donated to inspire us."

Lucy went on to detail what she had in mind. She limited the proposed project to tied patchwork comforters and socks. The announcement of the Golden Needle Award was met with enthusiastic applause. Lucy smiled. "I wish to thank Mr. Tait for his support of the project and ask that he come forward and describe how the mercantile will be participating with us."

Silas looked surprised when Lucy motioned for him to come forward. As he stepped up beside her, she said quietly, "Just describe your plans for the display window, please. So the ladies know that everyone who participates will be acknowledged."

Silas described the planned display and the public signage that would keep citizens apprised of the rising number of donations. "Each time a pair of socks is donated, the knitter will be asked to sign a small ledger monitored by Mrs. Tompkins at the mercantile. The entire city will be able to watch as the laundry line spanning the main window is filled with pair upon pair of socks. The sign in the window will announce the total number, and it will be changed each day as the contest proceeds."

Portia Dameron spoke up. "When's it over? How long do we have to win?"

Silas stepped back, effectively yielding the floor to Lucy.

"December 1st," Lucy said. "That way, the soldiers will benefit before the coldest months of winter set in."

From the back of the room, a plaintive voice called out, "That's less than two months away."

Mrs. Collins looked behind her with a scowl. "I personally could produce a dozen pairs of socks in half the time."

Portia retorted, "Yes, but will you?"

Mrs. Collins jumped to her feet and wheeled about. Before she could say anything, Lucy said, "I see that Martha is ready for us. Refreshments are being served in the dining room. Please don't forget to leave your card if you think you might be joining us here tomorrow for our first production day. We'll be cutting scraps into squares, stitching cot-sized comforter tops, and knitting socks. As I said earlier, Martha has graciously agreed to keep a pot of soup at the ready for those who work through the noon hour. Tea and cake will be set out throughout the day. I look forward to the opportunity to work alongside each of you. Are there any questions?"

Several hands went up.

Lucy thought that she handled the questions well—until Mrs. John Pritchard, whose son, Robert, was with the 35th Illinois, suggested they distribute the socks and blankets the Ladies Aid had already gathered as part of a project begun earlier in the year. "They've just been sitting over at the Presbyterian Church, waiting until we receive a specific request. I don't see any reason to ship them off to parts unknown when, as Miss Maddox has so clearly explained—and as many of us have had occasion to witness— there's a more immediate way to alleviate suffering. I move that we bring the Ladies Aid blankets and socks here to Miss Maddox's for distribution to the men on the train."

Mrs. Collins didn't give Lucy a chance to respond before jumping to her feet and saying in clipped tones, "As Miss Maddox has clearly stated, the Ladies Aid meeting will proceed *after* we have had time to take advantage of her kind hospitality."

"I don't see why we have to wait," Mrs. Pritchard argued. "Who could possibly object to the idea?"

"It isn't a matter of objecting to the *idea*," Mrs. Collins said.

Portia Dameron chimed in. "Then what is it a matter of?"

"Bylaws exist for a reason," Mrs. Collins said. "Ideas are presented as 'new business' and voted upon by the membership." She looked out across the women in the room. "Not everyone here is a member in good standing. That means not everyone can have a voice when it comes to the Ladies Aid materials."

"Perhaps not," someone else said, "but nearly everyone here is a mother or a sister or an aunt or a wife of a soldier, and we'd all agree that if there's a chance to relieve suffering, we should do it. We'd want it done for our boys."

"Exactly." Mrs. Pritchard nodded.

"That's not the point," Mrs. Collins insisted.

"Gertie."

Lucy started and looked behind her in the direction of the voice. She took a step back and bumped into Silas as a woman garbed in black stepped into the room, which became instantly quiet. Full mourning meant that Mrs. Kincaid's face was obscured by a black, knee-length veil.

"I beg your forgiveness for interrupting," she said, "as sincerely as I ask that you forgive this breach of etiquette on my part. I should not be making calls. In truth, I am not. But I have a personal interest in what Miss Maddox has proposed, and I wish to thank her for stepping forward and doing something that has required great courage on her part. I intended to listen from the kitchen and to return home without anyone knowing I came. I thought it would bring comfort to hear my friends take up the cause. I would like to think that all of this is at least in part because of the ultimate sacrifice recently paid by one of our own." Her voice wavered.

The veil did not hide the tremendous resolve required for Mrs. Kincaid to continue without breaking down. Lucy crossed to where she was standing. When a gloved hand was extended from beneath the veil, Lucy took it. "Thank you, my dear," the older woman said quietly. She cleared her throat.

"Gertie," she repeated. "You and I have had our differences, but in this instance, I hope that we can agree to conduct ourselves in the spirit of Proverbs 3:27: 'Withhold not good from them to whom it is due, when it is in the power of thine hand to do it.' It seems to me that for those of us living in this place at this sad time in our nation's history, it is well within our power to relieve suffering close to home. Let's not be concerned with bylaws just now, Gertie. Let the Basket Brigade ladies distribute our stores to the needy on those trains. Please. In Jonah's memory and in our dear Lord's name. Let's not squabble over who gets the credit. Let's just do good." ·

Lucy saw that she was not the only woman in the room struggling to hold back tears. Robert Pritchard's mother wasn't the only one with a loved one who'd enlisted. Doyle Lovett's sister was here. And John Rutherford's fiancée.

The stubborn set of Mrs. Collins's jaw relaxed. She nodded and said in a hoarse whisper. "Of course, Dorothy. As you wish."

Mrs. Kincaid released Lucy's hand. "Thank you," she said and retreated from the room.

Stunned silence reigned for a moment, and then someone in the back said softly, "Can you really knit a dozen pairs of socks by December 1st, Mrs. Collins?"

Mrs. Collins turned about to face the ladies in the room. She was smiling as she said, "Do you mean to challenge me in regards to the contest, Mrs. Miller?"

Mrs. Miller, a ramrod-straight octogenarian, rose from the settee she'd been sharing with her seventy-five-year-old baby sister. "I believe I do."

Mrs. Collins nodded. "I believe I'll accept that challenge." She glanced over at Lucy. "Now, what was that about refreshments, dear?"

Chapter 7

Silas and Mrs. Tompkins had stepped onto the sidewalk to view the latest addition to the Golden Needle display when he saw Lucy cross the street about a block away. As soon as she was within earshot, he called out, "Wait until you see Mrs. Tompkins's latest idea." He stood back, watching for Lucy's reaction as she took in the veiled display case in the front window and the sign encouraging citizens to "Watch for the Unveiling of the Golden Needle Award."

Lucy's face beamed with pleasure. "You've both gone far beyond duty to support this effort. I promise you that your faithfulness will be rewarded in due time."

"The work is its own reward," Silas said, and ushered the two ladies inside.

Mrs. Tompkins agreed with Silas. "We'll all cherish the smiles and thanks we receive from the men on the train until the end of our days."

"Is there any word on the award itself?" Lucy asked.

"I expect it to arrive any day now," Silas said. At Lucy's behest, he'd traveled to St. Louis and ordered a special design from Mr. Meyer Friede, one of the city's top jewelers. "You'll be pleased."

"I expect I will," Lucy said. The gold hollowware and blue

enamel brooch was to feature seed pearls surrounding a center oval crystal. Beneath the crystal, which would normally have showcased hair art, crossed miniature golden knitting needles would be mounted over a blue background. The back was to be engraved with the presentation date and the winner's initials.

What Lucy did not know was that when Silas told Mr. Friede the reason behind the design, the jeweler suggested a change. "What if, instead of seed pearls, I made that border red, white, and blue. More patriotic, isn't it?"

"I like the idea," Silas said, "but my employer didn't authorize a more expensive version of her design. I'll have to check with her and telegraph a reply."

"It wouldn't be any more expensive if I donated the gemstones."

"You'd do that?"

"I would. They won't be first quality, mind you, but I'd wager the ladies will be a lot more excited about a border that sparkles."

Silas hesitated. "Perhaps, but Miss Maddox isn't—" He broke off. Lucy would be horrified with anything gaudy. Then again, it wouldn't do to offend the man making the suggestion.

"You needn't worry, Mr. Tait." Mr. Friede indicated the showcase nearby. "As with all of my wares, everything will be done in good taste. Small chips—but still beautiful. Garnet, diamond, and topaz. Understated but elegant."

"If you're certain. I will admit, however, that your generosity is a bit overwhelming."

"I am certain. In fact," the jeweler said, "I'll personally deliver it so that I can see the fair lady's reaction."

"She'll be very pleased," Silas said. All the way home he contemplated the "fair lady's reaction" to the surprise. It would be a moment to cherish. A memory that he would treasure far more than sparkling gems.

A Stitch in Time

As fall painted the leaves of the trees in town and the air turned cool and crisp, Silas's anticipation of seeing Lucy's delight when the jeweler delivered the brooch grew. More than once he very nearly ruined the surprise by telling her. Finally, he told Mrs. Tompkins—in confidence. "She's going to be so pleased."

"Indeed," Mrs. Tompkins said with an odd smile.

Silas tilted his head. "What?"

"Oh. . .nothing. It just seems that you've been unusually happy since Miss Maddox took on her new project—in spite of the fact that the project requires so much of your time. It's not every shopkeeper who'd risk being gone from his business for so many hours every day. Not to mention the evenings you spend catching up the ledgers and keeping track of shipments."

"Lucy asked—I mean, Miss Maddox requested that I 'hover' a bit until she feels more at ease operating the machine. I'm sorry if my doing so has put an undue burden on you." He frowned. "And of course it has. I apologize, Mrs. Tompkins."

The widow waved a hand in denial. "No, no, no, Mr. Tait. I intended my words as nothing more than good-natured teasing. It does my old heart good to see you two working so well together. It's I who should be apologizing if I seemed to be complaining. I am not. Your support of the Basket Brigade is wonderful."

Silas shrugged. "I want to do my part." He bent his knee and lifted his false leg. "Some would say that since I can't fight, I should do *more* than my part."

"Well, you are. All the squares you've cut after the store closes each evening. I know you'll deny spending your own funds, but really, Mr. Tait, I'm not quite so absentminded as to have lost track of entire bolts of cloth that you seem to find a reason to declare as 'old stock we need to be rid of.' And please allow an old woman her dreams. There's no better way to court a lady than to show yourself willing to support what's important to her. Miss Maddox has fairly blossomed in recent days, and I suspect it has as much to do with the gentleman who calls each day as it does with her pet project."

"That's absurd," Silas protested. "What's more, such a thing would be—unsuitable. Please don't mention it again."

Mrs. Tompkins frowned. "What an odd use of a word. Why would you say it's 'unsuitable'?"

"You need ask?" Again, Silas indicated his false leg. He allowed a sad laugh. "I learned long ago that ladies see me as 'unsuitable' when it comes to—that kind of relationship."

"And now who's being absurd?" Mrs. Tompkins said firmly.

"Only the woman in the room who refuses to acknowledge the evidence presented in this store every single day. Silas Tait is the skilled tailor. The capable storekeeper. The dependable errand boy. I will never be more, and I have accepted that."

"Balderdash. I've seen the way you look at Miss Maddox. And I see the way she's blossoming before our very eyes as she works with the Basket Brigade—and you. Your feelings for her are certainly nothing to be ashamed of. She's a kind, unselfish, intelligent woman."

"You don't have to defend Miss Maddox's virtues to me. I am well aware of every single one of them." *And they've caused me no small amount of anguish.*

"And you, Mr. Tait, are equally kind, unselfish, and intelligent."

"Thank you. Now it is your turn to be kind and find something to do besides tempting me to hope."

Mrs. Tompkins sighed. "As you wish. I shall keep my own counsel in the matter. And take it up with the Lord."

Silas said no more. He and the Lord had shared many discussions over the years regarding Miss Lucy Maddox. For a very long while, Silas had insisted on believing the Lord's answer was *"Have patience. Not yet."* The fact that Lucy kept the mercantile and asked him to stay on after Mr. Maddox's death helped the flame of hope continue to flicker. Until, at some point in the last year, he'd faced the truth. She was ten years his junior. She was far above him in social standing. She thought of him only as a reliable fixture in her life. The real answer to his longing was *No. Not in this lifetime. Not ever.* Facing that truth had been the most difficult thing he'd ever done.

Mrs. Tompkins's teasing aside, Silas gained a deep sense of satisfaction from supporting Lucy's "Golden Needle endeavor," for the phrase had been adopted by everyone involved. They welcomed Silas's assistance with open arms, and their kindness not only soothed his sense of guilt at not being able to fight but also applied balm to the deep loneliness he'd felt ever since moving to Decatur.

Lucy was pedaling away on the treadle sewing machine when, one week late in October, Silas strode into the parlor and leaned down to say quietly, "I have news. May I speak with you privately?"

Lucy rose, took her cape down from the hall tree, and led the way onto the front veranda. She had barely closed the door behind them when she asked, "Is it the award? Is it ready?"

He sighed with exasperation. "Is it even possible to surprise you, Miss Maddox?"

"Probably not." Lucy grinned. "I know you too well. I could see happy news in your eyes. I immediately thought of the award."

"Mr. Friede sent a telegram. He will bring it day after tomorrow on the morning train from St. Louis. How do you wish to proceed? Shall I bring him here to the house, where you can share the award with the ladies here at the time, or do you wish to make the unveiling more of a ceremony?"

"Which do you prefer?"

"If you unveiled it in the display case in the windows. . ."

". . .there'd be a crowd."

"And more attention brought to the effort."

"As well as more anticipation for the contest participants." Lucy laughed. "I like the way you think, Mr. Tait. We could meet Mr. Friede at the depot, perhaps have tea in the hotel café, and then have a ceremonial unveiling at the store thereafter. Say, at eleven o'clock. It will give people something to talk about."

Mr. Tait agreed. "Word of mouth is the best promotion a project could receive."

"I should like to ask Mrs. Tompkins to join us at the depot," Lucy said. "If you'll agree to closing the store until the unveiling. The display case was her idea and a very good one."

"Closing the store will emphasize the importance of the moment," Silas said. "Shall Mrs. Tompkins and I call for you at nine in the morning, then?"

"There's no need for you to go to so much trouble," Lucy said. "Henry and I will call for you both at the mercantile."

⌒⌒

Silas barely slept on Thursday night for the pure excitement of seeing Lucy when she caught her first glimpse of the Golden Needle Award. He had, however, been a bit taken aback by her refusal to let him do the calling.

"I hear the disappointment in your voice, Mr. Tait," Mrs. Tompkins said when Silas explained the plan to her. "She wasn't refusing you personally. The mercantile is on the way to the depot for her. You would have had to rent a carriage. She has a fine one that hardly gets used. It's more efficient this way. Don't take it as anything more than that. She isn't sending an unspoken message that you must never call on her."

"I believe I've already made it clear that I would never expect such a thing," Silas said.

"You have certainly made a valiant effort in that regard. But the heart will do what it will do. Someday, I hope you'll have the courage to take down those iron gates you've locked around yours and at least let her know how you feel. You might be surprised by her reaction. 'Nothing ventured, nothing gained,' as the saying goes."

Thankfully there was no time for more nonsense, for Lucy's carriage had come into view. Silas led the way outside, locking the mercantile door behind them. In moments, they were at the depot and he was helping the ladies down from the carriage. Together, the trio made their way inside to garner a table in the café while they waited.

"You wouldn't believe the chatter going on over at the house today," Lucy said. "There are nearly a dozen ladies working together, and the unveiling of the Golden Needle Award is the main topic. There is going to be a virtual parade from my house to the mercantile midmorning." She chuckled. "Mrs. Collins was distinctly put out with me that I wouldn't so much as hint at the design. She must always have some little tidbit of news that no one else has. But I resisted. She will be just as surprised as everyone else."

Silas suppressed a smile. He and Mrs. Tompkins exchanged knowing glances.

Lucy cocked an eyebrow and looked from Silas to the widow and back again. "Is there something I should know?"

"Absolutely nothing," Silas said.

"At least not about the award," the widow said.

At last, the train huffed its way into the station. Brakes squealed and steam hissed. Mr. Friede was the first one off the train. "Welcome to Decatur," Silas said. "Miss Maddox and Mrs. Tompkins await us in the café." As the two entered the depot, Silas explained the plan to make the unveiling a public event. "But Lucy—Miss Maddox—did not want to wait, of course."

Lucy and Mrs. Tompkins rose as the two of them entered the café. As soon as Silas had introduced everyone, Mr. Friede reached into his pocket and withdrew a beautiful dark blue box. "I hope you are pleased, Miss Maddox. I made a slight change to the design—with Mr. Tait's approval, of course."

Lucy opened the box with trembling hands. Staring down at the sparkling gemstones surrounding the center crystal, she gasped with delight. "It's—stunning. But—" She looked over at Silas. "We said seed pearls."

Mr. Friede nodded. "I thought, given the purpose, you might prefer the red, white, and blue."

"It's more beautiful than anything I imagined," Lucy said.

Mr. Friede's eyes misted over a bit. "My nephew was on one of the first trains. He wrote me about your Basket Brigade. As I worked on this design, I realized how much I was enjoying the idea of supporting your good work. With your permission, I would like to donate this Golden Needle Award to the cause."

⊙

By the time Lucy and Silas, Mrs. Tompkins and Mr. Friede had climbed aboard the carriage for the drive back to the mercantile, a sizable crowd had already gathered in anticipation of the unveiling.

"Look! Just look!" Lucy enthused. She leaned forward to tell Henry to drive around to the back entrance. "Oh, this is just wonderful. Thank you, Mr. Friede, for such a beautiful award. Thank you, Mr. Tait, for making it more than I ever dreamed! And thank you, Mrs. Tompkins, for that inspired decision to put a veiled display case in the window!" She wanted to hug someone.

But she did not.

At last, it was time. Mr. Tait lifted the display case from the window and set it atop the counter. He and Mr. Friede stood shoulder to shoulder to block the view of the eager crowd outside while Lucy put the brooch in place. After Mrs. Tompkins redraped the case with the black veil, Mr. Tait returned it to the window, front and center.

"Someone should perhaps say a few words," Mr. Tait said. "It's quite a crowd. We might at least thank them for their support."

"You do it," Lucy said. "You're the store manager. Besides that, without your and Mrs. Tompkins's enthusiasm, this wouldn't be happening at all."

Mr. Tait—never one to call attention to himself, Lucy realized—asked Mr. Friede to join him. As the door opened, a titter of expectation sounded from the gathered ladies—and, Lucy noted, more than one gentleman. Mr. Tait began by introducing "one of the finest jewelers in the Midwest." He lauded Mr. Friede's generosity and then looked toward Mrs. Tompkins as he said, "And now, without further ado, the Golden Needle Award."

The instant Mrs. Tompkins removed the veil, Mrs. Collins, who had been sure to arrive early enough to be standing right in front of the display case, leaned close. It seemed that every other woman in the crowd held her breath, waiting for the irascible woman to suggest what they should think. When Mrs. Collins finally spoke, Lucy sighed with relief.

"It's magnificent," she said, and then looked over at Mr. Tait. "What did I tell you? Speak with Meyer Friede. He does fine work." She glanced about her. "Mr. Collins had a piece designed for me just last year."

As ladies spilled into the mercantile, Lucy pulled Mr. Tait to the side. "I didn't know you'd consulted with Mrs. Collins about the award."

Silas shrugged. "Neither did I. Although now that I think about it, I might have mentioned Mr. Friede in a conversation right before I left for St. Louis. I don't recall that she said anything about his skill one way or the other. How fortuitous for us all that she approves the design."

"I know you were at least partly joking when you first mentioned a Golden Needle Award, but it was an inspired idea. Truly inspired, Silas. Thank you." *Silas.* Somehow the familiarity felt right. After all, hadn't they become more than employer-employee in recent weeks? Still, she shouldn't presume. "I hope you don't mind my calling you by your Christian name," she said. "I don't mean any disrespect."

"I would never think you did. You needn't have asked permission." He hesitated. "I would not, however, want you to invite disapproval on the part of Mrs. Collins. She's already caused you quite enough difficulty questioning your decisions in matters that were not her concern."

Lucy pondered the warning. Finally, she said, "Perhaps we shouldn't worry quite so much about Mrs. Collins. In fact, if we're going to give her something to disapprove, let's do it right. Please call me Lucy."

Chapter 8

Once the Golden Needle Award was on display at the mercantile, the number of ladies joining in the work at Lucy's house increased daily. Mrs. Collins began to come every day. Lucy suspected that her motivation was a desire to keep an eye on her competition. Whatever the reason, Lucy was thrilled to see how well the community had responded overall. It made her wish that she'd opened her home on behalf of the cause long ago.

When someone suggested that the ladies tuck anonymous notes of encouragement in with their gifts to the wounded, Lucy cleared off her father's desk in the library to facilitate that part of the project. On days when there were more notes than blankets or socks, the ladies simply handed notes out along with the food. No soldier ever refused. Every soldier was pleased.

Lucy began to join the ladies writing notes at every opportunity, especially when Silas was using the machine to attach binding to comforters. Unexpected friendship blossomed at Father's desk, as Portia Dameron, who was, like Lucy, still single, threatened to sign her letters and to invite soldiers to Decatur to meet an "old maid" who wasn't yet "totally resigned to spinsterhood."

"You wouldn't!" Lucy said, horrified.

"Of course not," Portia replied. But then she gave a wicked grin and leaned forward to whisper, "but wouldn't it give Mrs. Collins a shock."

Lucy frowned. "Mrs. Collins? How so?"

"You don't think I'd sign *my* name?" Portia chuckled.

Lucy clamped her hand over her mouth to keep from laughing aloud. Her composure regained, she tapped the notepaper before Portia. "Back to work, Miss Dameron. This is serious business."

"As you wish, Miss Maddox."

Lucy dipped her fountain pen in the inkwell and began to write.

I do not know your name, but our kind Creator does. You have been prayed for today by the author of this missive.

When she completed her first comforter top, she changed the wording a bit.

You have been prayed for by the maker of this patchwork. May our Redeemer give you peace.

Thank-you notes began to arrive and, along with the notes, a few letters. Some of the latter made the ladies blush, for they contained outlandish praise and, on occasion, a promise to come to Decatur one day. It was all nonsense, of course, but everyone agreed that it would be an unforgettable day if that actually happened.

There was one letter in particular that tugged at Lucy's heartstrings. A Private Oscar Greene wrote that the Basket Brigade missive was the first mail he'd received since joining up. He had no family, he said, and if some kind soul would care to write again, he would be grateful. He apologized for his "abominable penmanship," which he blamed on his injuries. His grammar was impeccable, his spelling excellent. Lucy thought that Oscar Greene must be an educated man. Perhaps even a gentleman.

She wrote again, although she did not sign her name. Initials would have to suffice. After all, a lady had to be careful.

Write and tell me all about yourself and how you get on in the hospitals. Where do you live when you are at home?

She wrote of the weather and the work of the Basket Brigade. She spoke of opening her "huge, drafty house" to the work and how grateful she was for the help of many. She wished he could hear the pleasant murmurings of a dozen or more voices working together each day in the parlor, intent on bringing comfort to others. Her faithful housekeeper and the gardener had been a great support. She wrote a humorous account of Henry Jefferson dressed in old livery and standing guard at the gate on the morning of the first meeting. She hoped it would make the private smile.

She took Mr. Greene's mention of the president as an interest in politics and told the well-known local story of how the future president's first political speech had been delivered from atop a tree stump in front of a Decatur hotel. She boasted on behalf of a local tailor employed by her father who had had the honor of fitting Mr. Lincoln for a suit of clothing.

I hope you do not think it silly for me to write of such things as speeches and suits.

Private Greene did not think her silly. Her letters, he said, were the only light in his dismal days. He had nearly come to fisticuffs with another soldier over the cherished patchwork that would forever be a treasured reminder that there was, indeed, kindness in the world.

The private's words made Lucy blush. She moved her correspondence with him to her bedroom, writing by lamplight late into the night, counting the hours until a reply came, and wondering. . .*is this what it is like to fall in love?* She caught her breath when Oscar first mentioned a visit. What a gift it had been that the mail could be carried between them so quickly, he said. How thankful he was for the frequent train service between Decatur and Chicago. He would soon be leaving the hospital. Decatur was not so far from Chicago.

> *It would be my great joy to one day meet you. However, I consider it the height of impropriety to force oneself on others without an invitation. You have my promise that if we were to meet—which would be the granting of a secret wish—it would be only after you have granted your permission.*

Lucy studied herself in the mirror. She was still just plain Lucy Maddox. Nothing would ever change that. And yet. . .perhaps Oscar was different. He wrote with such grace. Such intelligence. How he would adore Father's library. Lucy pictured him there with her, the two of them reading in the golden glow of the lamps. Fond hopes kept Lucy awake for the better part of a night.

She signed the next letter. *Lucy A. Maddox.*

∽

November brought frigid air and cold winds. Silas barely noticed. He rose with newfound joy as he anticipated what he might do that day to help the ladies of the Golden Needle. To help *Lucy.* She might never love him, but she had befriended him, and Silas told himself that that was enough. He relished their time together, no matter what it entailed. He cut fabric, applied binding to comforters with his machine, and ran errands. All of it took on a new glow, because he was doing it for his friend. For *Lucy*.

All in all, November of 1862 provided some of the happiest days of Silas Tait's life. Until, that is, a square-jawed, flinty-eyed man in uniform stepped into the mercantile to inquire after "Miss Lucy A. Maddox."

"Mr. Slade over at the depot sent me here," the man said, grimacing as he reached into the sling supporting his left hand. He produced several envelopes tied together with a bit of string. "I didn't realize I was asking after someone quite so prominent in the community. I hope it doesn't cause her any trouble." When Silas did not offer to take the letters, the soldier laid them on the counter. He tapped the addressee's name. "That's me."

Silas looked down. His heart sank. After years of working with Lucy, he'd recognize her handwriting anywhere.

"I'm Oscar Greene," the soldier said. "I told her I'd come as soon as I was given leave."

Silas's heart sank. *Oh, Lucy.* He was suddenly aware of Mrs. Tompkins standing in the doorway to the storeroom, looking his way.

"If you could just point the way to the house," the soldier said. "Unless—I hope it isn't too far." He put his hand to the sling. "I'm healing up just fine, but cold air seems to make things worse."

Silas glanced over at Mrs. Tompkins. He was not about to send some stranger to Lucy's front door. He did not like it one bit that the man had flashed private correspondence from a lady in such a cavalier manner. Letters he claimed to treasure. Didn't the man have any sense of propriety at all?

"As it happens," Silas said, "I have a small delivery to make to Miss Maddox's residence. I can show you the way. If you'll just give me a few moments."

Mrs. Tompkins spoke up. "I've got those things collected right back here in the storeroom. If you'll just lend me a hand?"

Silas excused himself and went into the storeroom. Mrs. Tompkins pulled the door closed and whispered, "You are quite right to offer to drive the man over. I can mind the store for the rest of the day. You help the ladies of the Golden Needle—and keep an eye on the stranger." She put an arthritic hand on his shoulder and gave it a light pat. "Don't despair, Mr. Tait. Miss Maddox is a sensible young woman. I'm sure it's all very innocent."

⌒⌒

Mrs. Tompkins might think the man's appearance in Decatur innocent, but Silas did not. His suspicions had already been aroused by the man's casual attitude in plopping those letters on the counter. Where was the man's sense of propriety? And what did his reference to her being "prominent in the community" mean, anyway? Did he know that about Lucy, or was he trying to find out?

As they pulled away from the mercantile in the light delivery wagon, Greene looked back with an admiring glance. "Maddox Mercantile is an impressive place."

"We take pride in serving the community as best we can," Silas said.

"The largest mercantile in Decatur?"

Silas said yes.

"It seems a growing concern—the town, I mean." Greene gave a casual laugh. "I only mention it because on my way here from the depot I think I noticed four banks. Bankers can be trusted not to invest in a losing concern, can't they?"

"I wouldn't know. I am a tailor by trade and a merchant, thanks to Miss Maddox's good graces. I know nothing of banking."

"But you have to deal with them, don't you? For the business, I mean. Someone's money has to back all that inventory."

"I make it my business not to know that part of Miss Maddox's business," Silas said firmly. "It is not my place."

"It's not my place, either," Greene said quickly. "I was merely trying to make conversation." They rounded the corner of Main and moved past the Kincaid house. Greene gave a low whistle as he stared at the well-groomed lawns and formal gardens. Colorful foliage still clung to many of the old trees. When they came to the corner of Lucy's property, Greene pointed at the low stone wall. "Don't tell me. Bank president or judge. Am I right?"

Silas reined the mare pulling the wagon into the front drive.

"No," Greene protested, then looked over at Silas. "She lives *here?*" As they approached the mansion, he spoke again. "How lonely she must be, rattling around in a place like that all by herself."

Silas frowned. "Miss Maddox hardly 'rattles around.' Dozens of women depend upon her leadership. Hundreds of brave men have benefited from her kindness. She is a tireless servant and one of the more important citizens of Decatur."

Greene looked over at him with an odd expression. "You obviously think very highly of her."

"I do. I am honored to be in her employ."

Greene gave a low grunt. He spoke sotto voce—just loud enough for Silas to hear the comment. "You sure that's all it is?" Then he said in a normal tone, "I am indebted to you for showing me the way."

As he pulled the wagon up at Lucy's front door, Silas cleared his throat. "I shall also be happy to drive you back to the depot for the five-thirty train." He supposed that sounded rude, but he didn't care.

Greene looked at him with a knowing smile. "Thank you kindly. If you're still here when I take my leave, I'll be happy to accept a ride. There's no hurry, though. I've a few days before I have to report back, so I decided to take advantage of the opportunity to meet my faithful correspondent. I'm staying at the depot hotel."

∞

When the knock on the front door echoed down the hall and into the kitchen where Lucy was indulging in a second Scotch cake, she didn't pay it any mind. Stitchers had been coming at all hours of the day and evening for some time now, and Lucy had finally realized that they felt more welcome if she didn't treat each arrival and departure like a formal event. Someone would answer the door. This time, though, Martha came for Lucy.

"It's Mr. Tait—with another gentleman asking to see you."

Lucy paused midbite and looked at Portia Dameron, who was sitting across from her at the kitchen table. Portia arched one eyebrow. "Do tell?"

"Someone who wants to see me?" Lucy asked.

With a glance behind her, Martha stepped into the kitchen and lowered her voice. "He came in on the train. Stopped at the mercantile asking about you. Mr. Tait said something about letters? Says the stranger's name is Greene. Private Oscar Greene."

Lucy dropped the piece of Scotch bread. It broke in half when it landed on her plate. Portia leaned forward and hissed, "You *signed* one? Why didn't you *say* anything?" She scolded softly, "And I thought we were friends."

For a moment, Lucy could not think. Finally, she spoke to Martha. "Give me a moment and then. . .show them into the library." She was not about to have a half-dozen women witness what could be the most important meeting of her life. Or the most embarrassing, depending on Oscar's reaction when he saw her. She would always be too thin, she would never be pretty, and she would never forget Jonah Kincaid's determined ignorance regarding how she really felt. He'd made a point of telling her how much she appreciated their *friendship*. She told herself not to expect

A Stitch in Time

anything different from Private Greene, and to prove to herself that she meant it, she refused the impulse to hurry upstairs and try to do something—anything—to improve her appearance. She was plain Lucy Maddox—for better or worse, and it would probably be worse. Best to get it over with.

Chapter 9

Was it her imagination, or was the house suddenly quiet? As Lucy waited in the library for Martha to escort Oscar—Private Greene—in, she felt like she imagined a parent would feel with curious children lurking just outside the door, barely breathing as they tried to hear what was going on in the room where the grown-ups were speaking in low tones about something of the utmost importance.

She heard each step in the hall. She forced herself to relax her clenched hands and to fold one over the other in an attempt to at least appear relaxed. Still, it was necessary to lean against Father's desk for extra support because she was trembling so. She knew she was blushing but hoped it would simply put a nice rosy tint to her sallow complexion. She smoothed her hair, straightened her collar, and started when Martha knocked lightly on the library door. She inwardly winced at the hoarse tone when she said, as calmly as possible, "Come in."

"Mr. Tait with a Private Oscar Greene to see you, miss," Martha said as she motioned the men into the library and closed the door firmly behind them. Behind them all, for Martha remained, presumably to guard the door.

"Miss Maddox."

Private Oscar Greene was not handsome. The word didn't do him justice. He was beautiful. Sun-washed curls tumbled to his shoulders. A perfectly trimmed mustache bordered full lips. Lucy had never been one to admire goatees, but Oscar's only served to accent the strength of his jawline. And those eyes. The warmth in those gray eyes sent goosebumps chasing up the back of her neck, for nothing in his expression hinted at disappointment when he looked at Lucy.

"Private Greene." Lucy held out her hand with all the dignity she could muster.

He took it, and for a moment she thought he might actually kiss it. But he did not, and with Martha and Silas watching his every move, Lucy was glad he didn't.

"The ladies will be expecting tea," Martha said, looking past Oscar to Lucy. "Shall I serve you and your guest here in the library?"

Smiling warmly, Oscar said, "It is very kind of you to offer."

Martha arched one eyebrow. "If you'll excuse me, sir, I was speaking with Miss Maddox." She directed her attention back to Lucy.

Lucy cleared her throat. "Yes, well. Other men who've benefited from our service have mentioned stopping in Decatur. We never dared to hope it would happen. I should think they would all like to meet Private Greene."

"I can think of nothing I would enjoy more," Oscar said.

Martha opened the door—rather abruptly. "I'll be preparing tea, then, while Miss Maddox introduces you."

When Martha departed, Silas followed her. Lucy was once again aware of the unnatural silence in the rest of the house. Oscar gestured toward the dining room and said in a low voice, "After you, dear one."

A Stitch in Time

Dear one. Just when she thought she could introduce him to the ladies without revealing any untoward emotion, two words transported this visit to an entirely new plane. And yet, as he stepped into the dining room with her, Oscar was the perfect gentleman in every way.

He met Portia Dameron and Ina Porter first. The two of them had been working in the dining room when he arrived. Now they stood, scissors in hand, a length of indigo calico spread out before them as Oscar said, "I hope you don't mind my impromptu visit. When I realized I only had to get off the train for a chance to meet you all, I simply could not resist." He beamed down at Lucy. "You are so good to welcome me."

"You'll stay for tea?" Portia looked pointedly at Lucy. "He *is* staying for tea. You must insist, Lucy."

"There is no need to insist," Oscar said with a gallant little bow. "As long as I am welcome, I can think of nowhere I would rather be than in such wonderful company." He touched his sling. "You have no idea what a balm it is to someone like me to be in the presence of such gentility." A shadow flitted across his handsome face. "You simply have no idea."

Ina put her scissors down. "Please, Private Greene, come meet the others." She led the way into the parlor, with an unhappy Lucy following. *He is here because of me. To see me. I should be the one introducing him.*

"Ladies, we've a visitor. Private Greene came all the way from Chicago to thank us for our work on the hospital trains." Ina looked up at him. "What was it you received?"

"Much-needed warmth," the private said, beaming at the half-dozen women gathered in the parlor. "Patchwork that I shall treasure until the end of my days and a missive that spread nearly as much warmth as did the comforter."

Ina introduced the knitters, and Oscar bowed deeply as each of the ladies in the parlor was named. Martha announced that tea was ready, and in the next few moments Oscar proved himself to be gallant, charming, thoughtful, and gracious. He was wonderful. His eyes glistened with unspilled tears when Portia asked about family and he said that he was not "so blessed."

When Mrs. Pritchard inquired as to his regiment, it was discovered that Oscar and her Robert had probably met, although sadly, Oscar was unable to remember some of the details. He seemed embarrassed by the fact.

When Lucy saw him put his good hand to his wounded arm, she realized that he was gallantly trying to mask pain. She interrupted the talk of regiments and battles and insisted that he sit down in the parlor and allow her to serve him. He did so with a sigh of relief. Lucy hurried off to the kitchen, overwhelmed with joy. Oscar had come to meet her. He had stayed. He was seated in her parlor. And he was happy to be there.

She rejoiced.

∞

Even though it caused him pain to see it, Silas could not simply slink away so that he didn't have to watch Lucy's lovely face aglow with happiness in the presence of Private Oscar Greene. After all, only an immature cad would sulk in the kitchen while the women he'd worked alongside for weeks now chatted with a visitor. Silas could not shake the suspicion that Private Greene bore watching. Why would a casual visitor take note of the number of banks in a town? And why that comment about the cost of the inventory at the mercantile? If he was wrong to feel that way, time would reveal his error. But Silas did not think he was wrong.

Apparently, Mrs. Jefferson had her own suspicions, for after she'd laid out tea in the dining room, she retreated to the kitchen and asked Silas several very pointed questions—in a tone of voice intended not to be overheard. "You said the private asked for Miss Maddox by name?"

Silas nodded.

"I don't understand how he knew it. I was there when the subject of writing notes was first introduced, and everyone agreed. They would sign on behalf of the Basket Brigade of Decatur, Illinois. No individual names."

It wasn't Silas's place to tell Mrs. Jefferson that he'd seen the letters. Lucy had not only signed her name, she'd been carrying on a personal correspondence with a man she'd never met. But he would not behave like a schoolboy tattling on a friend. "Perhaps you could ask Lucy about that later this evening. After everyone has departed for home."

Mrs. Jefferson nodded. "Don't think I won't. Lucy is not my own child, but I care for her as if she were. No mother would be pleased to have a stranger appear at her door in this manner. There are rules, and Private Greene should have abided by them. At the very least, he should have asked permission to come."

"I am under the impression that he did."

Mrs. Jefferson frowned. "If what you say is true, the situation is more serious than I thought."

Silas didn't know what to say to that. He felt guilty, hiding out here in the kitchen, assuming the worst about the situation. Assuming that Lucy needed protecting. And yet, he could not ignore the odd things Greene had asked about. The look on his face when he realized that Lucy lived in a mansion far grander than the one he'd admired next door. The assumption that Lucy was lonely.

Mrs. Jefferson looked past Silas toward the dining room. "I should be seeing if anyone cares for more tea. Tell me this, though. Did I hear correctly? Did he say something about the depot hotel?"

"Yes. He told me he'd gotten a room there when I offered to wait and take him back in time for the five-thirty train."

Mrs. Jefferson nodded. "If only he'd taken the hint." She paused for a moment then said, "Might be I'll have Henry see what he can find out—without letting the miss know, of course." When laughter rang out from the front parlor, she sighed. "I do hope that we are wrong in our suspicions, Mr. Tait. Either way, it seems we have an interesting few days ahead of us."

As time for the day's hospital train to arrive approached, Silas offered to take Lucy to the depot and Oscar to the hotel. Oscar declined in favor of lingering with Lucy. The time was short, he said, and he wished to savor every moment. But then he looked down at her with those beautiful gray eyes and said quietly, "I do not wish to be the reason you abandon your post with the Basket Brigade. Perhaps I should go."

"There are plenty of ladies to help," Lucy said. "They won't miss me just this once." She bade Silas a fond good evening and then asked Martha to please set an extra place at the supper table for Private Greene. She felt as if she were in a dream, for not only did Oscar hang on her every word, he also expressed an interest in Father's library.

"I'd have given anything to have access to so many books as a child."

"This room has always been a sanctuary to me," Lucy said.

"The house must have been a favorite of all your friends. It's so grand." He looked above them. "I can only imagine all the delightful haunts. And the grounds. The picnics you must have hosted! The games at sunset. Now be honest," he said, and the candlelight danced in his beautiful eyes. "Did you climb every tree on the place? I hope you don't mind that I see you that way—as an adventurous soul."

She wished she had done every single thing he mentioned. But she hadn't. Her childhood had consisted of reading and playing quietly in her room. Spending time with her mother and helping Martha in the garden. Hearing Oscar speak of other things made it seem that she had had a joyless childhood, indeed. He would think her so common. So boring. And so she tried to deflect the conversation back to him.

"I hate to disappoint you, but I was a very typical little girl." She leaned forward and rested her chin in her palm. "But I suspect you had all kinds of adventures. Tell me about them. What were you like as a boy?"

He grimaced. "I am sorry, my dear, but I have no sweet stories to tell. I wish I did. I could certainly make one up, but I won't have you look back on this evening and have it tainted by a lie— even a harmless one created to avoid a sad tale of profound loss." He took a long, slow breath.

"I am sorry," Lucy said quickly. "I didn't mean to cause you unhappiness."

"Please don't think ill of me if I don't wish to revisit a painful past." He took a sip of water and settled back in his chair. "Let us live in the delightful present. Tell me the story of your Basket Brigade. How did you come to the moment of opening your home?"

Lucy told him the story. She shared how fearful she'd been that first day, how upset Mrs. Collins had been.

"Mrs. Collins," Oscar murmured. "The matron who sits in the green chair?"

"You remembered."

"Impossible to forget a woman of such. . .strength of character, shall I say?" His eyes twinkled with humor.

"I suppose you could put it that way."

"I would *always* put it that way." Oscar laughed. "I do not think

Mrs. Collins a woman to be trifled with. You have won her over, though."

"I think not."

"Don't be so self-deprecating, sweet Lucy. I could tell they all admire you greatly. You should take pride in what you've done."

And so went the evening. It seemed that in a matter of moments the clock in the hall was striking nine o'clock. Lucy started as if waking from a dream. "Goodness!" She twisted about to look toward the kitchen. "Poor Martha. She must feel that the evening will never end." She rose. "Shall I ask Henry to drive you to the station?"

"I wouldn't dream of asking such a thing," Oscar said. "Let Henry have his wife and Martha have her rest. I shall enjoy the walk." He took his cloak off the hall tree. Tried but failed to drape it across the wounded arm.

"Here, let me help you," Lucy said. When he bent down so that she could accomplish the matter, something in his gray eyes made her draw a quick breath.

He caught her hand. "Until tomorrow," he whispered, and kissed her palm.

"Are you saying good night, then?" Martha's voice sounded from the doorway to the kitchen. Lucy pulled away. "I am sorry, miss," she said as she strode up the hall to where Lucy stood with Oscar. "I sat down at the kitchen table to have a cup of tea, and I'm afraid I nodded off."

"I apologize for staying so late," Oscar said.

Martha opened the door. "It's a brisk night, Private Greene. I wouldn't waste any time getting to the hotel if I were you. We wouldn't want you to take ill, now, would we?"

Lucy longed to linger at the window, watching Oscar make his way up the drive to the street. Instead, she helped Martha clear the supper dishes and take them to the kitchen.

"Mind if I leave them until morning?" Martha asked.

"Not at all. I am sorry we lingered so long. I simply lost track of time."

Martha said nothing.

Lucy took a deep breath. "He is a. . .handsome man, is he not?"

"He is. And I know it's not my place to say it, but I'm saying it anyway. The only beauty that really matters is the beauty a body can't see."

"I suppose that means you're suspicious of Oscar just because he's handsome. After all, no one that beautiful could possibly be interested in plain Lucy Maddox."

"I didn't say that. I was merely reminding you to make certain about what's beneath that handsome face before you give your heart."

"I'm not a child."

"And I didn't say you were, miss." Martha sighed. "I have prayed a long time for a man with a beautiful *soul* to see the beauty that lies inside of you. If Private Greene is the answer to those prayers, then I'll thank the good Lord with all my heart. But I won't lie to you. I don't like the idea that he just turned up in Decatur. What do you know about him, really? And why in the name of heaven above did you sign your name to something that got sent off to a complete stranger?"

"I don't know," Lucy said. "But I'm glad I did. Why can't you be happy for me?"

"Perhaps in time, I will be." Martha sighed and put her palm to her back. "At this hour, I just don't know."

Henry came lumbering in the back door. "Are you ready, then? It's about time." He hadn't seen Lucy. When he did, he apologized. "Sorry, miss. I didn't see you there."

"It's I who should be apologizing," Lucy said. "I'm sorry for keeping you so long, Martha. Henry." She wished them good night and retreated up the back stairs.

But when they were gone, she descended again. She sat in the dining chair Oscar had occupied. She put her hands where his had been. And she dreamed.

∽

Lucy had always thought Silas Tait a unique man in his willingness to be part of an endeavor that required him to be in the company of women for hours at a time. She supposed it was at least in part due to his being a tailor. No one questioned his participation in the sewing project. He was the brother-son-cousin-friend that everyone appreciated for his dependability and his general good nature. She had never known another man like Silas.

She still didn't. Oscar was different from Silas in myriad ways. None of the ladies treated Oscar like a brother-son-cousin-friend. Part of that was his striking appearance. One simply did not forget that Oscar Greene was in the room. He drew the eye of every woman in his presence. Even Mrs. Collins was not immune.

Oscar knew nothing of sewing or knitting or any other feminine pursuits, and yet, for the few days he remained in Decatur, he made himself useful in countless ways. He created pleasing arrangements of calico squares destined to be patchwork comforters. He marveled at Lucy's skill with the sewing machine. He tried to assist Ina and Mrs. Rutherford in the tying of a comforter—but when he freed his arm from the sling to facilitate the process, pain quickly cut the effort short. Sinking into a chair with a regretful sigh, he came up with the idea of reading to the workers.

The ladies accepted his offer with a resounding yes, for Private Greene had a voice that resonated with warmth. Accompanying Lucy into the library, Oscar said that she must make the selection.

"Some of these volumes are surely quite valuable. I don't want to be responsible for anything like that. If I broke a binding or tore a page, I'd never forgive myself."

"That's very thoughtful of you." Lucy pointed across the room. "As long as we stay away from the ones over there—behind the glass."

Oscar peered through the glass. "I don't see any titles that are likely to appeal."

"Indeed not," Lucy said. "They're all political essays. Father was a particular admirer of James Madison. And Jefferson, of course. I think there are one or two volumes printed by Benjamin Franklin himself." She'd been perusing titles as she talked, and when she came to an old favorite, she pulled it off the shelf, then reached for a second book. Holding one in each hand, she said, "Chateaubriand or Dickens?"

"I haven't had the pleasure of indulging in novels," Oscar said. "I defer to your wisdom."

Lucy laughed. "Well then, since Monsieur Chateaubriand is decidedly *not* a novelist, we shall proceed with the ever-popular Monsieur Dickens. *En anglais.*"

Oscar seemed confused. "I'm afraid I don't understand."

"Didn't you tell me you studied French at university before the war?"

"Yes, but—I'm sorry. My memory has never fully recovered since my unfortunate encounter with an artillery shell."

"Forgive me," Lucy said. "I shouldn't have teased."

"There is nothing to forgive," Oscar said quickly. "I do remember a little, *chérie.*"

Lucy stepped closer. "You mustn't make me blush today. The ladies will talk."

"I don't think you need worry today," Oscar said. "Mrs. Collins hasn't arrived yet. She's the one who seems to watch us so closely.

She and Mr. Tait."

"I do hope Mrs. Collins isn't ill. She is absolutely determined to win the Golden Needle Award."

"The award in the window at your mercantile."

"You saw it?"

"I did. On my way here this morning. And I was most impressed. No one would ever suspect that it isn't real gold and gemstones."

"Well, of course it's real," Lucy said with a low laugh. "Cheap metal and glass wouldn't inspire competition. Silas carried the idea to a jeweler in St. Louis, and when he learned of the cause it would support, he donated it. Wasn't that kind?"

"Very," Oscar said. "May I say that you amaze me, Lucy Maddox?"

"Why? I've done nothing different from what dozens of women all over the state do—hundreds all over the country, for that matter."

"I disagree," Oscar said. "Others donate what they can. You've put your heart and soul into service, and you fairly glow with honest joy. It really is quite attractive." He reached for the book in her hand. "To the parlor. Lest the ladies gossip."

Lucy led the way into the parlor, thinking all the while that at the moment, she didn't care two whits about gossip. Let them gossip. It was a small price to pay for another moment alone with Private Oscar Greene.

Chapter 10

On the Friday when Private Oscar Greene was due to depart Decatur—please, God, let it be—Silas oversaw the unloading of an unusually large shipment of goods at the mercantile. He was concentrating on a rather complex bit of mathematics when Greene stepped into the store.

"I was wondering," he said, looking about at the merchandise, "if you might assist me in a rather delicate matter. You've. . .um. . . you've known Lucy for a long time, yes?"

Silas gave a wary nod.

"I was hoping you might be able to advise me in a purchase. The thing is, though, I am in the embarrassing position of being short on cash. I've sent word home and asked that a transfer be initiated to Mr. Collins's bank. But I'm afraid I'm going to have to leave Decatur before the cash arrives, and I'm loathe to leave without giving Lucy a token of my admiration. You understand, surely?"

"What is it, exactly, that you are asking, Private Greene?"

"Your advice. And help selecting a gift. A book, perhaps? But I want it to be something special." Greene lingered at the jewelry counter.

"I believe the convention is to limit oneself to flowers or candy,"

Silas said. Mrs. Tompkins was just coming in, and he called to her. "Am I right in that, Mrs. Tompkins? Appropriate gifts from a gentleman to a lady?"

"Married, courting, or"—Mrs. Tompkins stopped midsentence when she saw who was in the store—"merely an acquaintance?"

Greene made a show of considering his answer. "Something more than a mere acquaintance. From someone hoping for much more." He gave a nervous little laugh. "You'll keep that to yourself, now, won't you, old man?"

"I should think Mr. Tait's advice was the best," Mrs. Tompkins said. "Flowers or candy. A book is always appropriate, but Miss Maddox has the finest library in the region."

"Candy, then," Greene said. "But not something ordinary." Again, he appealed to Silas. "And you'll assist me in that. . .other matter? I'll give Mr. Collins instructions to handle things for me."

Silas opened the store ledger. At the top of a fresh page he wrote *Private Oscar Greene.*

Greene nodded. "Thank you." He spent the next half hour selecting an absurd amount of the most expensive imported chocolate in the store. He asked Mrs. Tompkins to see the "various wrapping papers" available and pretended great disappointment when she said that what they had was that roll of brown paper right there on the counter. "Well. If that's the best you can do," he said. "And you'll deliver it on the same day of my departure?"

"That isn't today?" Silas asked.

"I sincerely hope not," Greene said. "I'm awaiting word from the regiment. I've made the case for a delay." He grimaced as he made a show of trying to raise his arm. "It just isn't healing as it ought."

"What a shame," Silas said. "Perhaps you'd want to have our Dr. Kirkland take a look at it. His office is just there." Silas pointed across the street. "See the sign? He's probably there right now. He's an excellent physician."

"You're very kind to suggest it," Greene said. "Perhaps I will consult the good doctor." He looked up at the clock on the wall. "At the moment, though, I must check back at the telegraph office and then make my way to Lucy's. I promised I'd be there by ten o'clock this morning, whether I had good news or not. She and the ladies have some idea that the work goes better when I'm reading to them. Will you be coming to help today?"

"You'll have to carry on without me," Silas said. He pointed to the crates and boxes lining the far wall. "What you see there is only about half the shipment. I expect it will take Mrs. Tompkins and me most of the day to check it all in."

The moment Greene had exited the mercantile, Mrs. Tompkins exploded. "The nerve of the man! Who does he think he is? And what on earth is he thinking, trying to delay his return to his regiment? 'Not healing' indeed. How dare he saunter in here like some dandy, expecting to be waited on. Insinuating and prodding. And asking you to extend credit? I declare!" She sputtered for the next few minutes before finally calming down enough to notice that Silas hadn't said anything.

"If he's made a favorable impression on you, I apologize."

"Quite the contrary," Silas said. "I was hoping the illustrious Private Greene would be on the evening train the day he arrived. It was obvious he had designs on Lucy." He bit his lower lip to keep from saying more and turned his attention to opening one of the crates.

Yarn. Lucy would be pleased. If she noticed. She hadn't been to the mercantile since Private Greene's arrival.

" 'Designs on Miss Maddox,' you say?" Mrs. Tompkins frowned. "Surely she hasn't fallen for him."

"Should we put this yarn in the contest window?" Silas held up a twist of red. "Red, white, and blue, perhaps?"

Mrs. Tompkins reached over and took the twist of yarn. Setting it aside, she took one of Silas's hands between hers and held it fast. "Silas Tait. Are you really going to stand by and let that—interloper—steal your girl?"

Silas pulled free. "She is not 'my girl.' "

"And why is that?"

"You and I have had this discussion before," Silas said, "and I distinctly remember asking you not to raise the subject again."

"And I have respected your wishes. But only because I thought that, given time, you'd come to your senses and speak your mind."

"To you?"

"Heavens above, no. Not to me. I'm not important. To Lucy. Fight for her. Don't let that—don't let him win her over."

The door opened and a gaggle of young women came tittering in. One asked about the new shipment, wondering if there was a fresh supply of winter gloves.

"Come back this afternoon," Mrs. Tompkins said. "We'll have checked in the new merchandise by then and you can try on gloves to your heart's content."

The girls started to leave, then retreated to the far side of the store, exclaiming over a selection of cameos in a display case before moving on to hair combs and lace collars.

Thankful for the distraction, Silas busied himself with the new stock.

❧

Lucy had tried not to count days. She had done her best to cherish moments. Still, time had flown. It was Friday, and absent a miracle, Oscar would be leaving on the five-thirty train. She could barely control her tears. She thought back to that awful day in October when they'd received news of battles in Corinth, Mississippi, and Perryville, Kentucky. Between those two battles, the toll on Illinois had included more than 200 killed, more than 1,000 wounded, and 260 captured or missing. She had cried with the ladies over the news. And yet, apart from Jonah Kincaid, she hadn't known anyone who died. Now, facing Oscar's departure and his return to his regiment, a knot of fear clutched at her midsection. Every once in a while she had to remind herself to take a deep breath. She relaxed momentarily, but then, moments later, the fear returned.

Whatever would she do if something happened to Oscar? Would she even know? Unless he chose to tuck a note in a pocket that requested she be notified, Oscar Greene could simply disappear. She would never know what had happened to him. For the rest of her life, she would wonder. How would she ever bear that? It would break her heart. She looked down at the watch pinned to her blouse. It was after ten o'clock. He had promised to be here by ten o'clock.

She must be calm. And brave. She must not make a scene, for then surely Oscar would know—and he must not know just how dear he had become to her. Not yet. A lady must be certain of a man's feelings before exposing her own. She had done so prematurely with Jonah Kincaid. She would not make that mistake again.

She pedaled away at the machine, telling herself to be calm. Suddenly, there was an odd click. She'd broken a needle. She sat back, exasperated. Where was Silas, anyway? He was supposed to do the binding. Didn't he know that he was needed?

Oscar stepped in the front door. The broken needle was forgotten when Lucy looked at his smiling face. He motioned for her to come to him. She went, her heart pounding. He led her to the library. One look at the two of them and the ladies who'd been gathered about Father's desk rose and left the room. They were alone.

"May I close the door?" he asked.

Lucy nodded.

"Let us sit together for a moment."

She sat.

He pulled a telegram out of his coat pocket and, with a flourish, read. "'Change in orders. Stop. Report to Jefferson Barracks, St. Louis, Tuesday, December 2, 1700 hours. Stop. Acknowledge receipt.'" He folded the piece of paper and put it back in his coat pocket. Then he leaned forward and held out his good hand, palm up.

Lucy took it.

"Sweet Lucy Maddox, would it be presumptuous of me to remain in Decatur for a few extra days? I know we've just met. I've told myself I'm a fool to hope. But—if only you'll tell me I have a chance." He looked away. "Perhaps I presume too much," he murmured. "If you send me away, I will understand."

Lucy felt herself blush. She leaned forward and kissed his cheek. "I could never send you away."

Church was supposed to be a place of comfort. At least Silas had always found it to be so. He loved congregational singing. He wondered at the wealth hidden in the scriptures. He appreciated the idea that people greeted him with honest warmth. More often than not, he received more than one invitation to join a family for dinner. He had always loved the Sabbath, and when Lucy showed up at the early service on Oscar Greene's arm, Silas determined that he would not let the vision ruin his day. He was there to worship. To sing to God. To join others in the contemplation of the eternal. To be fed God's Word. And he tried with all that was in him to do those things, in spite of the fact that Oscar Greene gave every indication of being there for the sole purpose of being seen in the company of Miss Lucy Maddox. Greene did not sing. He sat, looking straight ahead, expressionless during the homily. Silas suspected the man was bored. How was it possible to be bored in God's house on Sabbath?

Silas was not the only parishioner who was shocked. He knew this because at the close of the service, as he was helping Mrs. Tompkins gather up hymnals to return to the shelf at the back of the sanctuary, he overheard someone say, "What on earth could someone as handsome as that private see in Lucy Maddox?"

The reply, spoken in a low voice that Silas did not recognize, made him long to interrupt in Lucy's defense. But he could not, for whoever it was had merely put words to his own unspoken fear.

"Her money, of course."

∞

Lucy woke before dawn on December 1st, and her first thought was that today they would learn who had won the Golden Needle Award. Her second thought was of Oscar. When the two thoughts intersected, Lucy had a wonderful idea. She shared it with Martha over breakfast.

"I've been remiss in making plans in regards to the award, but everything fell into place for me the moment I woke this morning."

"That's good to know," Martha said, "because I've heard more than one of the ladies comment on the lack of 'fanfare.' It isn't like you to let something go until the last minute."

"I know. But I'll make up for it." Lucy smiled with confidence. "First, I'm going to ask Oscar to present the award to the winner. He's the perfect person to do it. He's personally benefited from what we're doing, and the ladies all love him. I can't think of a better person."

"You can't?" Martha stared at her as if she'd lost her mind.

Lucy went on. "We'll have the name announced in the *Magnet*—I think if I rush the news over to the office this afternoon, it'll be just in time to make tomorrow's edition. Then Oscar and I will personally call on the winner and give her the news. I'll make sure the newspaper includes an invitation to a social hour at the auditorium for the official presentation and ask Miss Evans's choral group to sing. Voilà. A respectable celebration." She sat back with a satisfied smile—until she realized that Martha still had that same look of disapproval on her face.

"I know I should have planned further ahead, but you don't have to lift a finger. I'll order all the refreshments from McHenry's bakery."

"Have I ever complained about the cooking?"

"No, but perhaps you should have," Lucy said. "Oscar noticed that you've seemed tired the last couple of days, and once he mentioned it, I felt guilty that I hadn't noticed. You do seem short-tempered. I hope you haven't driven yourself to the point of illness. In fact," Lucy said quickly, "let me send Jimmy Kincaid to McHenry's today and see if they might be able to give you a respite from all the cooking for the ladies. We could ask for volunteers to supply the soup, as well. You've earned a rest, Martha."

"If ever I want a rest, I'll let you know," Martha said crisply. "And I'll not be ordered to take one when I don't need it, thank you very much. If you must know, I'm not tired. But I am sick to death of Private Oscar Greene." She nodded. "There. I've said it. The man waltzed in here and took over a place that was rightly another's."

"What are you talking about?"

"Not. *What*. Who. And Silas Tait is the *who*. Mr. Tait came up with the idea for the award in the first place. He traveled to St. Louis to find just the right jeweler to make it. He has done nothing but support you in every way possible since the day your father died. But he's been cast aside for the likes of a pretty face with a golden voice who you've known for exactly one week. And don't tell me about the letters, because anyone can write a fancy letter. I'd wager Mr. Tait could write a pretty letter if he took a notion to. Come to think of it, the man has been writing you love letters almost since the day your father hired him. It's a pity you haven't had the eyes to read them."

"Don't be absurd," Lucy said. "Oscar hasn't taken anyone's place. And Silas is still my friend. He has no interest—he doesn't think of me in that way. I'd have known."

"How?" Martha said. "You've been too busy writing letters to strangers to pay anyone else any mind at all."

Martha had never spoken to her in such a manner. Lucy sat staring down at the eggs on her plate, speechless. She hadn't thought that Silas might be hurt if Oscar presented the award. *No. You haven't thought about Silas at all since the day he brought Oscar to your front door.* Of course she'd thought about Silas, hadn't she? She'd missed him. *The only time you've missed Silas since Oscar came into town was the day you broke that needle and needed him to help you replace it.* She didn't like thinking that about herself. Not one bit. Falling in love shouldn't make you forget your friends. Should it?

"If you were. . .doubtful. . .about Oscar, why didn't you say something?"

"I've said plenty," Martha said. "To the good Lord and to Henry. All three of us have been waiting for the intelligent, sensible girl we love to open her eyes."

"But—don't you want me to be happy?"

"Oh, sweet girl, *yes*. Of course we do. And if Private Greene is meant to make you happy, then we won't object. But, Lucy. You don't *know* him. He's swept you off your feet, and no one can blame you for that. But who is he? Where is he from? Who are his people?"

"His family is gone," Lucy said. "His past is—painful. He

doesn't like to talk about it."

She didn't want to admit it, but hearing herself say the words gave her pause. It did seem that he would have shared *something*. Especially when he was so interested in her stories. How the house was planned. Where the furniture came from. Father's library. He'd wondered aloud at the success of the mercantile. He didn't think a single store could ever be so successful as to provide so well for a family. It hadn't, Lucy explained. Pride surged through her as she told Oscar about Father's wise investments. The farm over in Sangamon County. The other two stores, one in Salem and one in Springfield. Oscar listened with enthusiasm. He loved hearing stories of success, he said. How good of God to bless a good man with abundance.

Thinking back on it now put a new kind of knot in Lucy's stomach. She had unwittingly revealed a great deal of private information. A gentleman would have stopped her. Wouldn't he?

"Something just doesn't feel quite honest about the man," Martha continued. "For instance, I don't know about the military, but Henry does, and he's never heard of a soldier being given a longer leave because of an injury without a doctor's say. Did you actually see that telegram?"

"He read it to me."

"But he could have just been holding any piece of paper."

Lucy did not want to think about that. Not now, when she had to dress and meet Oscar at the mercantile. Martha was right about one thing, though. Silas should present the award, and Lucy said so. "He has most certainly earned the right."

"Indeed he has," Martha agreed. "But he would never seek it for himself. He's a living example of 'not seeking his own,' as the Good Book recommends."

Martha was right about that, too. Father had insisted that Lucy memorize the passage Martha was referencing. More of it came to mind now: *"Charity suffereth long, and is kind; charity envieth not; charity vaunteth not itself, is not puffed up, doth not behave itself unseemly, seeketh not her own, is not easily provoked, thinketh no evil; rejoiceth not in iniquity, but rejoiceth in the truth; beareth all things, believeth all things, hopeth all things, endureth all things."*

The words described Silas, and that word *charity*, Lucy knew, could be substituted with the word *love*. *Agape* love, Father had told her—the kind of love that sacrificed self to do what was best for another. As she thought back over the weeks since she'd first had the idea to open her home on behalf of the cause, Lucy thought of the untold hours Silas had given to the project. To *her* project. It must have cost him dearly to be away from the store so often. Lucy hadn't considered how many late nights he must have put in at the store after spending most of a day working here with the stitchers. After all, books still had to be kept, ledgers balanced, orders placed, and stock unpacked. Silas would never have allowed Mrs. Tompkins to shoulder the burden alone. He was too kind. Nor would he ever complain about the extra hours. He was too selfless. Too humble.

Why had she never thought of it until now?

Chapter 11

Oscar was already at the mercantile when Lucy arrived. He'd promised to meet her there so they would hear the news of the Golden Needle Award winner together, and when she stepped into the store, his smile reassured her. Everything would be all right. Martha was right, though. It took time to know another person as well as she knew Silas.

Silas stood behind the counter with Mrs. Tompkins beside him. She was holding the ledger she'd used to keep track of the contest entries.

"Don't keep me in suspense," Lucy said. "Just tell me. Is it Mrs. Collins?"

Silas shook his head. "I'm afraid not."

Lucy gulped. "Are you sure?"

Mrs. Tompkins spoke up. "I added the numbers twice and then asked Mr. Tait to check my work."

Lucy sighed. "At the very least, she'll demand a recount."

"If it will save you any difficulty at all," Silas said, "we can certainly do one."

The door swung open and in rushed Mrs. Collins. "I've three more pair," she said, and plopped them on the counter. She looked from Lucy to Silas and then over at Oscar. "I told my husband you'd be here," she said. "I'm glad to see I was correct. He wanted me to ask that you stop in the bank at your earliest convenience. Something about an account you wanted to establish?"

Oscar nodded. "Thank you. I'll be sure to do that."

"I'd be happy to show you the way."

"I know the way," Oscar said, and looked over at Lucy with a sweet smile. "But I was hoping that Miss Maddox and I might have time for a cup of tea at the café as part of our morning together."

Lucy tried to hide her surprise. They hadn't made any such plans. It was nice of him to surprise her, but surely he knew that her morning was more than full already. They must congratulate the winner, submit the announcement to the newspaper, and stop in McHenry's bakery to consult with Mr. McHenry in regards to the celebration. And Oscar wanted to take tea? Just the two of them? A glimmer of hope made her wonder if he was possibly going to declare himself, but it was merely a glimmer and it flickered out when it became obvious that Mrs. Collins was not to be denied.

"I would say that *now* is your earliest convenience, Private Greene. Mr. Collins does not like to be kept waiting."

"I'll walk with you," Lucy said. "I can stop at the bakery and make the order for our celebration while you meet with your banker." *His* banker. How fortuitous that he had selected Father's bank to be his own. Again, hope flickered. If a man established a banking relationship, that meant that he intended residency, didn't it?

"If there is one thing I know about ladies," Oscar said with an odd laugh, "it's that they despise business meetings. I hate to leave you alone to make all those calls, dear Lucy, but—"

"Actually," Mrs. Collins interrupted, "I have a private matter to discuss with Miss Maddox. We can all walk down together."

She nodded at Lucy. "You and I can speak while the gentlemen have their little meeting. How does that suit?" She smiled brightly at Oscar. "I'm sure it's nothing to be too concerned about, Private Greene. My husband knows that you've become a favorite of the Basket Brigade."

Oscar offered his arm to Lucy. "I do apologize, Mrs. Collins. If it weren't for the infernal Rebels, I'd be able to offer you my other arm."

Mrs. Collins brushed past him. "Now, now, Private Greene. There's no need for gallantry today. Come along."

∞

Something was wrong. That was quite clear. Whatever Mr. Collins's business with Oscar might be, Lucy couldn't imagine that it was so urgent as to merit being nearly dragged out of the mercantile. As Mrs. Collins led the way to the bank, Lucy could not quite shake the feeling that she and Oscar were naughty children being herded into the schoolmaster's office for a scolding. And whatever Mrs. Collins had to say to her could certainly be said in the presence of Silas and Mrs. Tompkins. It was likely some petty complaint about the way the contest had been run. She'd probably gotten wind of the fact that she wasn't the winner.

Lucy glanced up at Oscar as they hurried along. His expression told her that he was upset, too. A shadow flitted across his face when, as they entered the bank, they nearly collided with Mr. Slade of the depot hotel. Something passed between Oscar and Mr. Slade. Something unpleasant. Lucy told herself that it was only the natural animosity between a man who'd been wounded in the war and a civilian who was doing everything in his power to avoid service. Mr. Slade's mother had insisted that giving one son to the cause was enough, and apparently, Mr. Slade agreed. Lucy supposed that a brave man like Oscar would dislike someone like that. That must be what it was.

The moment the three of them entered the bank, Mr. Collins's assistant rose from a desk and hurried over to greet them. "Right this way." He led them toward Mr. Collins's office. Apparently, whatever Mrs. Collins needed to discuss with Lucy could wait.

"We'll just see what my husband has to say first, dear," Mrs. Collins said, and motioned for Lucy and Oscar to go ahead of her.

Oscar stopped abruptly just inside the bank president's office door. He almost took a step back, but Mrs. Collins and Mr. Collins's assistant were standing right behind them, effectively blocking the door. Why were soldiers in the office? What was happening?

A lanky private looked to his superior and nodded. "That's him. That's 'Gamblin' Greene.'" He smirked as he said to Oscar, "Guess they'll be calling you 'Deserter Greene' from now on."

"I don't know what you're talking about," Oscar protested.

When a third soldier stepped forward with a pair of handcuffs, Lucy released Oscar's arm and took a step away from him.

"You've got the wrong man." He appealed to Lucy. "It's not— they're lying. I've never—"

"Come on, Greene," the man with the handcuffs said. "I lost half a month's pay to you not two weeks before you went missing."

"This is all a misunderstanding," Oscar insisted. He looked over at Lucy. "On my honor, my dear. I did not desert. I was given leave."

"One week," the officer snapped. "Long enough to return to your regiment. But you failed to report for duty." He glanced at Lucy and then back at Oscar. "It would appear you decided to seek out the charms of Decatur instead. And now," he said, "Private Oscar Greene, it is my duty to place you under arrest."

Oscar paled. For a moment, Lucy thought he might try to flee. But then, his shoulders slumped and he submitted to the handcuffs.

"But, Oscar," Lucy croaked. "You said—" She broke off. Handcuffed, he would not even look at her.

Mrs. Collins reached over to support Lucy's arm. "I imagine you'd like to sit down, dear."

Lucy resisted. "I'd like an explanation. Oscar?"

Still, he would not meet her gaze as he muttered, "I'm sorry. You're a nice girl. I—I honestly did grow fond of you."

Fond. That word again. Turning her back to him, she allowed Mrs. Collins to lead her to a chair. The soldiers left with Oscar in tow. Her head swam. *I've been a fool. Again. First there was Jonah, and now—this.* How would she ever show her face in public again? She'd be a laughingstock.

Mrs. Collins sat next to her, patting her arm. "There, there, now, my dear. It will be all right. Everything's going to be all right."

Mr. Collins dismissed his assistant. Once the office door was closed, he said quietly, "You have Mrs. Collins to thank for this rescue, by the way." Lucy looked up just in time to see the banker beaming at his wife with affection. "She was very concerned when Private Greene appeared at your door. In the end, however, Greene's own hubris gave him away. He talked his way into a hotel room and an account at your store, but—"

"Wait." Lucy held up a hand, frowning. "Who gave him an account at the mercantile?"

"Mr. Tait didn't want to say anything to anyone," Mr. Collins explained. "But once I told him I was already looking into the man, he said that Greene had come in and asked to have credit extended so that he might purchase a gift for you—just until he could receive a transfer from another bank." Mr. Collins grimaced. "The problem was with the other bank. There wasn't one. No money ever arrived, and when I checked with the one he named, they'd never heard of an Oscar Greene." He sat back and folded his hands across his expansive midsection. "Next came a concern about the hotel bill. Mr. Slade came to me about that after overhearing one of the men on the hospital train call out to Oscar from the car. 'Gambling Greene,' he called him."

Gambling Greene. The same moniker the soldier had used moments ago.

"As it turns out," Mr. Collins continued, "Private Greene was to have returned to his regiment two weeks ago."

Anger flared. "Was everything a lie?" Lucy asked. "Did he even come about my name honestly—or did he steal a letter from some poor wounded soldier?" The idea made Lucy shudder with revulsion.

"His wound was real. It just wasn't nearly as severe as he made it out to be. He was perfectly fit for duty when he got off the train here in Decatur."

Lucy hung her head. "I've been such a fool."

Mrs. Collins reached over and squeezed her hand. "No more than the rest of us, my dear. He took us all in. With the exception of the people who work for you. Mr. Tait had his suspicions early on. He's a very good judge of character, it would seem."

"But—he didn't say anything. Why wouldn't he have tried to warn me?"

Mrs. Collins didn't answer right away. "Perhaps you'd better ask him about that."

Lucy sighed. Silas was too kind, for one thing. He wouldn't have wanted to hurt her feelings. The dear man. Always thinking of others first. And Martha. She owed Martha an apology. "Martha tried to warn me this morning. I didn't want to hear it." Lucy looked over at Mrs. Collins. "Is unmasking Private Greene the real reason you wanted me to come with you to the bank?"

Mrs. Collins nodded. "It was the only way we could think of

to protect you. Of course there will be gossip, since Private Greene disappeared so quickly. Someone will have seen him being taken away. But you can be assured, my dear, that neither my husband nor I will say a word. We never discuss bank business with anyone other than the client affected. It has always been thus and it shall ever be thus."

Lucy took a deep breath. "How will I ever thank you?"

Mrs. Collins smiled. "Just try not to poke me when you pin that gorgeous brooch on me."

The morning after Oscar Greene was hauled onto the train to be taken away to wherever deserters went, Lucy was still in her room when the doorbell rang. She hadn't even gone down to breakfast yet. She had no appetite. She could not bear the thought of facing the stitchers. No one save Martha knew she'd cared for Jonah. That had been a private disappointment, but it made the fiasco with Private Greene even more painful. And everyone knew about him. She might never show her face in public again.

The doorbell again. Where was Martha? And who was calling this early? She thought for a moment that Mrs. Collins might be here to flaunt her success. There had, indeed, been a recount, and while Lucy had no idea yet who had won the Golden Needle Award, if it was Mrs. Collins, she would surely want to arrive first today in order to receive everyone's accolades. Somehow, Lucy didn't mind.

There was more to Mrs. Gertie Collins than Lucy had ever seen. Beneath that annoying habit of drawing attention to herself, beneath the strong will to rule the women of the city, there beat a kind heart. It might not be too horrible to see Mrs. Collins this morning. Perhaps she would have some words of wisdom for Lucy. Heaven knew, Lucy could use the wisdom of the older women in her life.

Crossing to her parents' wing, Lucy went to the front window in Father's room and peered through the shutters. *No carriage.* Not Mrs. Collins, after all. The insistent knocking continued, and Martha continued to ignore it.

Lucy hurried down the back stairs. Martha was just taking a pan of her Scotch cakes from the oven. "Don't you hear that? There's someone at the door."

"It's for you," Martha said as she set the pan on the counter.

"I'm not receiving today. I need time. Surely you can understand that."

"I do. But you don't have time, miss. There is no less work to be accomplished today than there was yesterday, and no less need for your leadership. There is no better way to assuage a disappointment than to carry on." As if to illustrate the point, Martha began to transfer warm cakes to a serving platter. "A caller wishes to see you, and you are definitely receiving." She looked pointedly at Lucy as she said, "The Maddoxes do not hide, Miss Lucy. They hold their heads high and they do their duty." She returned her attention to her work.

"I cannot bear the thought of being the object of laughter."

Martha's tone was almost stern. "Then refuse to be one. Laugh at yourself in whatever way you deem best and move on."

The door again.

Martha set the spatula on the counter and leaned against it. Her voice was gentle when she next spoke. "There's not a woman alive who hasn't had her heart broken at least once. Not a person alive who hasn't believed in someone who disappointed them. It's called life, Lucy, and you should live it." She pointed toward the front of the house. "There is nothing I wouldn't do for you, but you must do this yourself. I pray that you will."

The old woman was growing more mysterious by the minute.

And whoever was at the door wasn't leaving. Taking a deep breath, Lucy hurried up the hall and opened the door. *Silas Tait*. With a massive bouquet of lilies.

Lucy stepped back.

Silas stepped in. "I hope I'm not intruding."

"Well, it *is* only about seven o'clock in the morning." She closed the door.

"But you were up?"

"I was. Although I had no intention of coming out of my room for the next year or so." Lucy looked behind her. "Martha wouldn't answer the door."

"I. . .um. . .I was afraid. . .I mean. . .the work you're doing. It's very important. You shouldn't feel any need to retreat from your friends. They all. . .*we* all—" He broke off.

Lucy pointed at the flowers. "Are those for me?"

He thrust them at her.

"You probably didn't know this," she said softly, "but I adore lilies."

"As a matter of fact, I did know that."

She tilted her head. "What else do you know about me?"

"Dickens is your favorite author. You love the color red, but you don't wear it often. You take sugar in your coffee but never in tea. And"—he gulped—"you have no idea how lovely you look when you smile."

She glanced down at the lilies and then back at him. "You know quite a lot. I'm confused, though. Why tell me now?"

"The Widow Tompkins."

"What?"

He swept a hand across his furrowed brow. "I worked late last night. Mrs. Tompkins insisted we put a new display in the window that's been dedicated to the Golden Needle Award all these weeks.

I think it was a ruse—an excuse to tell me in a dozen different ways that if I didn't speak up now, I didn't deserve you. And I realized she's right. Not that I think I do—deserve you, that is. But that doesn't mean I shouldn't express my—complete—devotion."

He was blushing. Lucy thought it charming. Silas knew things that only a man who cared would notice. *Dickens. Red. Sugar. Black tea.* Why didn't she know such things about him? Why hadn't she ever really *seen* him? "Do you know what I know about *you*?"

He shook his head.

"Not enough." She touched the petal of a lily. "I feel rather ashamed that after all the years I've known you, I don't know *your* favorite author."

"Dickens," Silas said quickly.

"Or your favorite color."

"I don't have one."

"Or how you take your coffee or tea."

"Black. Both."

Lucy nodded. "I shall remember. Just as I'll remember what a good friend you've been to me, even when I was playing the fool."

Silas protested. "You mustn't speak ill of the lady I most admire in this world."

The warm sincerity in his voice almost made her cry. She'd nearly thrown her life away because a handsome fop smiled at her, and Silas Tait, one of the best men she'd ever known, still admired her. Fearing that she'd lose courage if she didn't speak immediately, she blurted out an invitation. "Would you consider escorting me to the award ceremony?"

"Nothing would make me happier."

"And I'll ask Martha to prepare a light supper for us beforehand."

"That would be lovely."

"And—did you mean what you said just now about—admiring

me? Because I—I've come to realize that I—admire—you, too."

He stared at her for so long that Lucy began to think maybe she'd overstepped. Her heart pounded. A creak sounded from down the hall. She imagined Martha standing just on the other side of the door to the kitchen, listening.

"Of course I admire you," Silas finally said. "And if you will allow it, I shall spend the rest of my life proving just how much."

He didn't need to prove it, Lucy realized. He'd already done so, in countless ways she'd somehow failed to see. She couldn't trust her voice to say that just yet, and so she reached for his hand. "You'll stay for breakfast, won't you, dear?"

About the Author

Stephanie Grace Whitson, bestselling author and two-time Christy finalist, pursues a full-time writing and speaking career from her home studio in southeast Nebraska. Her husband and blended family, her church, quilting, and Kitty—her motorcycle—all rank high on her list of "favorite things."

A Pinch of Love

by

Judith Miller

"A well filled basket was the necessary card of admission to the soldiers' car."

— Jane Martin Johns, *Personal Recollections of Decatur, Abraham Lincoln, Richard J. Oglesby, and the Civil War*

Chapter 1

October 1862
Decatur, Illinois

Sarah McHenry placed a cool, damp rag on her mother's forehead. She hoped Mama would finally sleep. "You'll feel better soon, Mama. Just rest—"

At the sound of pounding below, her mother's eyes flew open. "What's that racket?"

Sarah sighed. Just when Mama was finally drifting off. "It's probably just someone at the door, Mama. Papa will get it."

But when the pounding continued, Sarah left her mother's bedside and raced down the stairs into the bakery kitchen. Her father stood behind one of the long wooden tables, humming an unmelodic tune while sifting flour into a velvety white mountain. Calm. Unconcerned.

She let out an exasperated breath and swiped an unruly auburn curl from her forehead. "Papa!" She turned toward the bakery door.

"Can you not hear the pounding? Someone is at the door."

He merely nodded and continued to hum.

"Why didn't you answer?"

Flour floated from the sifter like a flurry of snow. "Because we are closed. When it is time to open the bakery, I'll unlock the door."

"There are other reasons someone might be at the door, Papa, and Mama was almost asleep." Sarah's high-topped shoes tapped out a determined beat as she crossed the room and yanked open the door.

Johnny Folson lowered his fisted hand and greeted her with a gap-toothed grin. "Sorry for making such a ruckus, but I didn't think anyone was gonna answer unless I kept pounding. I could see your pa through the window, but he wouldn't look my way." His forehead wrinkled, and a glimmer of confusion shone in his eyes.

"I'm sorry you had to wait, but Papa doesn't like to be disturbed when he's baking—especially when we're not officially open for the day." After directing a quick look of disapproval toward her father, she turned back to the young messenger. "Tell me what brings you out so early this morning." A cold breeze rushed through the open door, and Sarah waved Johnny inside.

The boy doffed his cap as he stepped into the kitchen and peered longingly at the warm buns her father had recently removed from the large brick oven. "Matthew Slade from down at the depot sent me. He got a telegraph from the Centralia depot a short time ago and said to tell your ma that there's gonna be sixty-five injured soldiers on the five thirty train, so the ladies in her Basket Brigade will need to get lots more food ready for them."

"S–s–sixty-five?" The number caught in Sarah's throat. Instinctively, she looked toward the upstairs bedroom. Though she longed to remain calm, her thoughts cascaded like a swollen stream plunging over towering falls. Being prepared to feed an additional twenty-five or thirty men was daunting, especially given her mother's illness.

The boy bobbed his head. "That's what came in over the telegraph." He shoved his cap atop his unruly hair. "I best go and tell him I delivered the message and then get back to the livery and help Grandpa."

Before he could turn the doorknob, Sarah grasped Johnny's coat sleeve. "Not yet—I need to speak to my mother. The ladies of the Basket Brigade may not be able to feed sixty-five soldiers. Mother may want Matthew to send a message to the Centralia depot." She held tight to the boy's sleeve as he edged a step closer to the door. "This is important, Johnny. You mustn't leave." She leaned in and lowered her voice. "I'll give you a warm bun if you wait right here."

He arched his thin eyebrows and held up two fingers. When Sarah nodded her agreement, he smiled and scooted onto a stool near the front window, his attention fixed upon the yeasty buns resting on a cooling rack.

Before Sarah could exit the room, her father tapped one of the huge pans of rising dough. "I could use a bit of help if your ma is sleeping."

"I'm going to check on her now." Matters other than rising dough gnawed at Sarah as she ran back upstairs.

Her mother shifted and turned toward her when Sarah burst into the room. "You must quit running up the steps, Sarah. One of these days you're going to trip over your skirt and fall." Her mother's reprimand fell away when she looked into Sarah's worried eyes. "Has something happened? You're as white as this bedsheet." Her mother reached to feel her forehead. "I hope you're not taking ill, too."

"I'm not ill, but something terrible has happened." She went on to convey Johnny's message and then dropped to the chair beside her mother's bed. "Should I tell Johnny to have Matthew Slade send a message to Centralia saying we can't feed that many soldiers?"

"No, of course not. But you must take charge for me. The other ladies will help. You and Johnny divide the list of ladies in the Basket Brigade and tell them they need to supplement their contributions so that we have food enough for all the soldiers. The list is tacked to the far worktable in the kitchen. You can also post a message on the board at Logan's General Store and ask Mr. Logan if he can help with some additional supplies. After that, go to Maddox Mercantile and ask Silas Tait if he'll do the same. When you return, I'll go over what needs to be done before the train arrives."

"But Papa said he needs help in the bakery, and you know I don't—"

"There isn't time to argue, Sarah. Hurry downstairs and do as I've asked. Your father will understand. He knows the wounded soldiers must come first."

Shoulders slumped, Sarah plodded from the room. Organizing the Basket Brigade was her mother's passion. It was the way she'd chosen to support the men fighting for the Union. While Sarah admired the women who trundled off to the train depot each evening to board the trains with baskets of food and cheery smiles on their faces, she'd been unwilling to participate. She longed to help in the war effort and had prayed that God would reveal to her where she *could* serve, but so far, her prayers had gone unanswered.

She'd searched for some other way to show her loyalty, but one thing was certain: she didn't want to be a member of the Basket Brigade. Seeing those young men with battered bodies and broken spirits would be too great a reminder of her twin brother, Samuel, and what might happen to him. Though their father had tried to convince Samuel he should wait to enlist, her brother wouldn't be dissuaded. When the call went out for men to enlist in the 41st Illinois Volunteer Infantry Regiment, Samuel was among the first to sign up. More than a year ago, he'd left Decatur with the other volunteers.

Since then, Sarah had done her best to cope with Samuel's decision, but when the ladies of Decatur met and formulated their plans to deliver food baskets to the injured soldiers on the hospital trains passing through town, she knew she couldn't participate. She'd told the ladies, and she'd been clear with her mother. Now, to be required to take charge in her mother's stead? Her stomach churned at the thought.

When she once again entered the kitchen, Johnny eyed the cooling buns and licked his lips. After removing two of the buns and placing them on the table in front of the boy, she turned to her father. "Mama says I'm needed to help deliver a message to the ladies of the Basket Brigade."

"Whatever she says, but hurry back so you can help. Soon it will be time to open."

She nodded and stepped to the other side of the room. After examining several of Mama's lists, she turned to Johnny. "We need to go to the homes and tell the ladies what's happening so they can prepare more food. We'll divide them between us."

Johnny frowned. "Grandpa said to come right back. Besides, some of them ladies live outside of town, and I didn't ride a horse over here."

Sarah's eyes widened when her father clanged several metal trays atop a cooling rack then signaled her to give Johnny the list. "Feeding our boys is more important than anything else, Johnny. You take my horse and get busy delivering that message to the ladies. If your grandpa scolds you, you tell him Mr. McHenry made you go and that he should come and talk to me."

Before handing over the list, Sarah carefully marked which houses he should visit. "I'll call on all the ladies who live here in town. You go to the Fieldings' house first. That way, you can stop by the livery and tell your grandfather I've asked for your help. Go to the depot and tell Matthew, too."

He nodded and wrapped his remaining bun in the piece of paper she handed him. "I'll bring your horse back quick as I can, Mr. McHenry."

Sarah donned her wool cloak and pulled the hood tight around her head before stepping outside. The clouds appeared heavy with moisture and the sky gray and threatening—as though waiting to make this day even more problematic. She hesitated before opening the door and turned to her father. "Should I ask Dr. Kirkland to stop and check on Mama?"

He nodded. "Tell him she has a fever and a bad cough and we think it might be winter fever."

Sarah's mind reeled at the thought. If her mother had winter fever, she'd be abed for much more than a day or two. Would she expect Sarah to take charge of the Basket Brigade until she returned to health? Sarah gave a slight shake of her head as she opened the front door and stepped outside. This was going to be a dreadful day. Like the freezing air that whipped at her cape, contemplating the tasks that lay ahead chilled her to the bone.

Chapter 2

Corporal Jacob Curtis leaned against a wooden post outside the Cairo depot and inhaled a lungful of crisp, cold air. He could have gone inside the sprawling brick building, but he wasn't seeking warmth. Instead, he wanted time alone to once again reflect on what had happened to all of his grand plans. When he'd enlisted, he'd had one objective: to be assigned to the front lines where he would fight for the Union. But that hadn't happened. Instead, he'd been ordered to escort wounded soldiers from Cairo, Illinois, to Chicago where they'd receive additional medical treatment. The train headed north through Centralia and Decatur, eventually taking a more easterly route into Chicago.

Many considered the hospital trains a duty without danger while others thought the trains could come under attack. Thus far, that hadn't occurred, and Jacob didn't fool himself with such notions. His duty aboard the trains wasn't dangerous. There was no chance he'd see any action while escorting injured soldiers.

With the train's three bright red lanterns swinging by night and a shiny red engine, smokestack, and tender car to identify it by day, neither side had ever fired upon any train transporting invalids. This train was a sheltered environment where he'd never have need of a weapon.

A recent letter from his father had said as much. Though his words had been carefully chosen, his father's derision had been obvious. Most of the letter had been a comparison of Jacob's military duties with those of his older brother, Malcolm, who had fought at Antietam. Whenever his father mentioned Malcolm, his pride bled from the pages—just as Malcolm's blood had flowed from his veins when he'd been shot with a minié ball. No doubt Jacob's blood would also need to flow before his father considered him a real soldier.

The train hooted three short blasts to announce their departure, pulling him back to the present. After stepping onto the train, he lowered his collar, tucked a pair of thick gloves into his pockets, and entered his assigned car.

Frost lay thick on the ground outside the train, and a young soldier in the first hammock was using a corner of his blanket to clear vapor from the train window. He glanced up as Jacob approached. "Mighty cold out there, ain't it?"

Jacob nodded. "Looks like it could snow any minute now, but I hope I'm wrong. Don't need any bad weather slowing us down." He touched the soldier's arm. "You need anything?"

"Naw, I'm doing fine. Ain't had this much rest since afore I joined up."

The boy's comments turned into a fit of coughing, and Jacob held a tin cup filled with water to his lips. "Take a few sips and see if it helps."

Once the young fellow's cough abated, Jacob continued down

the aisle of the train, stopping to inquire about the needs of each soldier. On his return, a man who looked to be much older signaled to Jacob. "I hear there's a real treat in store for us when we get to Decatur." He grimaced with pain but didn't let the discomfort stop him. " 'Fore we was put on the train, one of the fellows told me that the ladies of Decatur are true angels of mercy. He said they board the train and deliver a hot meal to each of the soldiers. Is that true?"

"You heard right. The ladies started coming on board the trains back in March. At first they served only warm homemade bread and coffee, but with each train that passed through the Decatur station, they added more food. I'm not for sure how they manage it all, but it means a lot. Besides the food and other provisions, they spread a lot of good cheer to everyone on board." He glanced outside at the freezing rain that now pelted the window.

The soldier followed Jacob's gaze. "They come even if the weather ain't good?"

Jacob chuckled. "Don't you worry. Good weather or bad, they'll be waiting for us. Most of them have husbands, sons, or sweethearts that are off fighting, so they won't let the weather stand in their way."

A soldier across the aisle called to him, and Jacob stepped to the litter. He smiled at the soldier, who rested on the second row of hanging beds that had been arranged three tiers high. "What can I help you with, Private?"

"Could you bring me some water when you have a minute?"

Jacob rested his hand on the litter. "Of course."

He picked his way down the aisle of the car, careful to maintain his balance as the train moved along sections of rough track. The soldiers' makeshift beds had been securely attached to stanchions and suspended by stout tugs of India rubber so that they gently swayed with the motion of the train. Though Jacob used caution as he traversed the car, the careful arrangement of the litters protected the injured men from the train's jarring movement. After passing by several invalid chairs, he stopped at the end of a wide couch, where a few men with less threatening wounds sat visiting with one another.

He poured water from a canteen and returned to the soldier's bed. The fellow drank his fill and then handed the cup to Jacob. "You think one of them Decatur ladies could write a letter for me?" His voice cracked as he looked at Jacob with mournful eyes. "I don't think I'm going to make it home, and I need someone to write a letter to my Susie."

Jacob's hold on the cup tightened. The boy couldn't be more than eighteen. "Is Susie your sweetheart?"

With a slight nod, he momentarily closed his eyes. "We got married the day before I left home. I need her to know about this." He looked at his right arm, which had been amputated above the elbow, and his bandage-wrapped chest and stomach. "Too bad I'm not left-handed." He attempted a feeble smile.

"I'm sure one of the ladies will write a letter for you, but I think you're going to make it back home." Jacob prayed he was right. The soldier was too young to die, and his wife too young to be a widow. He glanced around the car. The same could be said for most all the soldiers riding this train.

"You got a gal back home?"

The question jarred Jacob from his thoughts. "A girl? No. I don't have a girl back home, but I'm going to be praying you make it back to your Susie."

After the soldier murmured his thanks, Jacob returned to his chair at the far end of the car and contemplated what had happened between him and Laura Monroe, the girl who was no longer waiting for him. The girl who'd written to tell him she'd found someone else only two months after he'd departed. She'd written four pages in an effort to make him understand, but what she wrote could have been said in only a few words. She'd found someone else. That was all he needed to know. Why she thought he'd want a list of her new beau's many fine qualities still baffled him. Didn't she realize that breaking their engagement would be a knife to his heart and hearing about her new love would only deepen the wound?

By now, she was already married to someone else, and Jacob didn't want to know anything more. He didn't care why she'd decided to marry another man or even what his name was. Jacob leaned forward and rested his elbows on his knees. Over and over, he'd asked God to heal the gaping hole in his heart and give him the ability to forgive. He wasn't sure he'd completely forgiven Laura, but he didn't think about her much anymore. Besides, it was better to have learned that she didn't really love him before they'd married. Would he ever be able to trust another woman? He doubted that would happen. One broken heart in a lifetime was enough for anyone.

Chapter 3

Sarah was only a short distance from the Decatur depot when the dark, swollen clouds that had loomed overhead throughout the day burst open and pelted her buggy with freezing rain. She didn't know whether to be thankful or distraught. If the train couldn't make it, she wouldn't have to face any of the wounded soldiers or worry over completing arrangements in the depot to serve them. On the other hand, the women who had worked from early this morning to increase their contributions into food enough to feed sixty-five soldiers would be sorely disappointed. Much food would go to waste, and waste was not a matter to be taken lightly during wartime.

The wooden sidewalk outside the depot had turned slick, and the plummeting temperature and freezing rain chilled her to the bone as she carried the covered trays of rolls into the building. A fire crackled in the large, wood-burning stove, and she stepped toward the welcome warmth, still holding the trays.

"Let me take those, Sarah. I'm always here to help the ladies. Especially you." Matthew Slade approached from the doorway leading from the depot restaurant kitchen into the main terminal.

She forced a smile as he lifted the trays from her arms and placed them on one of the long dining tables. Matthew was yet another reason she'd avoided helping with the Basket Brigade. For the past two years, he'd attempted to court her. For the past two years, she'd steadfastly refused. While Matthew was attractive, appearance wasn't on the top of her list of requirements for a husband. Integrity, a strong faith in God, and a kind heart were the traits she valued and desired in a future mate, not a man like Matthew who couldn't be trusted.

While still in school, she'd attempted to overlook his unpredictable conduct, thinking he would change as an adult. He could turn on the charm, but if you caught a look at him when he thought he was safe from sight, there was a brooding there. Even an element of danger. And she knew he could be dangerous.

He'd attempted to take advantage of her dear friend Elsie after a New Year's Eve party several years ago. Convinced that her beau would never understand why she'd agreed to let Matthew take her home after the party, Elsie had tearfully begged Sarah to forever keep her secret. At first, she'd encouraged Elsie to tell her parents what had happened, but when the girl wouldn't relent, Sarah had agreed.

Though she had hoped Matthew's character would transform with age, the only thing she'd seen improve was his ability to fool those around him. One minute he could be charming and the next minute become self-serving and hostile. Even though Sarah had rejected the idea of a romantic relationship with him long ago, he continued to pursue her, avowing that she would one day change her mind. Sarah remained certain she would not. Ever.

A Pinch of Love

Last year, when his older brother joined the army, Matthew had done his mother's bidding and remained behind to operate the depot hotel and help her in the café. Mrs. Slade had insisted one son was enough for any mother to sacrifice. Those who didn't agree with Mrs. Slade's way of thinking had taken to labeling Matthew a mama's boy or coward, and he'd become more and more unpleasant over the past year. He was like a pot on a fire—capable of boiling over at any moment.

Matthew leaned close and reached for the trays. "I'd do anything for the prettiest gal in town. Johnny told me you were going to be helping the ladies of the Basket Brigade today. I wasn't sure he knew what he was talking about, but I'm glad he was right."

When his hand remained atop her own, she pulled away. "I don't have time to visit with you, Matthew. There are still several trays of bread and rolls in the buggy. I need to retrieve them before they're ruined."

"Don't you worry one more minute. I'll go get the trays. I don't want you out in that freezing rain. A person could catch a terrible cold in this weather."

She shuddered when he winked at her. How she longed to tell him she'd get the trays herself. Yet refusing his help would create an argument—and she didn't have time to match wits with him.

Clara Wingard bustled into the room carrying a large kettle of stew. "Did you count how many kettles of stew we have coming, Sarah? If we don't have at least twelve, we'll have to be careful we don't overfill the bowls. Nothing worse than running out before the last soldier gets his share."

Sarah ran her finger down the list. "There are thirteen kettles promised, so we should be fine if everyone arrives as expected. With this weather, I'm worried some of the ladies may not want to get out."

"Pshaw!" Clara waved her arm in a dismissive motion. "Don't you worry 'bout the ladies of the Basket Brigade. The weather's never stopped them before and it won't stop them today. You mark my word—they'll be here, and they'll be on time, too."

Sarah glanced toward the ticket counter, where the huge clock was clicking off the minutes. "Mother's list says everyone should be here to divide the food and fill the baskets by quarter to five. Is that going to give us enough time?"

"Your mother's been in charge of the Basket Brigade since we first started eight months ago, and quarter to five has always worked before." Clara pointed to a table along the far wall. "Grab the end of that table and let's move it over by the other one. We need to leave enough space so there's a walkway between the tables where the ladies can work."

In spite of the cool draft that pervaded the room once she'd moved away from the stove, perspiration dampened Sarah's hands. "I never thought to ask Mother how we're to serve everything."

If her trembling voice revealed fear and a lack of confidence, Mrs. Wingard didn't let on. Instead, she stepped toward another table. "No need to fret. We use tin cups to serve coffee, and they work fine for serving soup and stew, too. Once the boys have finished eating, we pass through a final time and pick up the dirty cups and utensils." As Sarah and Clara set the last table in place, the depot door opened and several ladies trundled inside, their arms laden with their dinner offerings. Clara nodded toward the group. "See? I told you they'd be here on time."

Nellie Hanson was in the lead as the group marched forward to place their food on the table and rid themselves of their dampened wraps. Once they'd hung their cloaks on hooks near the stove, the women gathered in a huddled group and stared at Sarah. Finally, Nellie cleared her throat. "We're waiting to hear our assignments."

She pointed toward the tables. "Tell us where you want us."

Sarah momentarily met the inquisitive stares of the women before glancing at the clock. This wasn't a time to be indecisive or fearful. If they didn't begin their work, they wouldn't be prepared when the train arrived.

Inhaling a deep breath, she summoned her courage and appointed several women to work each of the tables. "Divide the stew into ten kettles so they won't be too cumbersome to handle. We'll send two kettles to each of the five cars. Several of you need to take care of the bread tables." She forced a slight smile before picking up a stack of the baskets and carrying them to the tables. "These can be used for the bread items. Please line them with the cloth napkins and have another lady follow behind you with butter, jam, apple butter, and any other preserves." After a quick survey of the tables, she noted numerous bundles of dried fruit. "Miss Wilhoite, would you and your sister, Emma, please take charge of the dried fruit? You can divide it into individual servings—perhaps wrap it in brown paper and twist the top or tie it with string."

"We've been doing this for eight months, Sarah. Just assign who is to handle each of the food items." Before Sarah could respond, Emma pursed her lips in a tight knot and pointed to the fruit. "I don't think there's enough fruit for sixty-five packets." She perched her hands on her hips and raised up on her toes. "Who else was supposed to bring dried fruit?"

Janine Brown waved. "I brought the rest of the fruit, Emma. I put the crate over by the stove when I hung my coat then forgot to set it on the table."

Emma lowered her arms, but her eyes shone with disapproval. "You know we always place our food on the tables. There isn't time to scurry around the depot looking for baskets and crates, Janine."

"Now, now, sister." Maggie patted Emma's arm. "You don't

need to make such a fuss. I keep telling you that faultfinding is not a spiritual gift."

"Well, if people would do as they're supposed to, I wouldn't be required to point out their errors." Emma lifted her nose high in the air when several of the ladies chuckled, whispered comments, and nudged one another.

Sarah circled around one of the tables and positioned herself in the center of the room. "Ladies! Let's keep to our work so we'll be ready when the train arrives." Every woman was needed, and Sarah didn't want Emma stomping out of the depot with hurt feelings.

Emma cleared her throat and pointed toward the small depot kitchen. "The coffee's not going to be ready if you don't get out to the kitchen and set the pots to boiling. That's your mother's job, so that makes it your task today."

Sarah noted Emma's smug smile as she hurried toward the door leading into the depot restaurant. Right now, there wasn't time to dwell on Emma and her negative attitude. Besides, she had needed the reminder about the coffee. Sarah rushed past the scarred wooden tables covered with frayed checkered cloths and a multitude of mismatched chairs awaiting the next trainload of passengers.

In the kitchen, the aroma of brewed coffee wafted through the warm room. Three pots sat atop the large wood cookstove, and several kettles of water had been hung in the large brick fireplace. Surely Mrs. Slade hadn't made all this coffee for the hotel guests and the few passengers who would eat in the depot restaurant. From the information Sarah had gleaned from her mother, the only passengers who ate in the restaurant were soldiers who worked as aides on the trains and the few soldiers able to disembark the train. There was another train due a few hours after the five-thirty departed, but it was far too early to prepare coffee for those passengers.

Without warning, Matthew approached from behind her. "I

thought you'd forgotten about the coffee, so I went ahead and put it on for you." His lips curved in a lopsided grin. "Mother said if I had free time, I should be helping clean the hotel, but I didn't want you to be without coffee when the train arrived."

Sarah cringed. Why did it have to be Matthew who'd come to her aid? "That was kind, but your mother is right. You shouldn't neglect your own duties."

Matthew jerked his head toward the stove. "I expected a sweet thank-you. Instead, you're taking my mother's side." He cast a doleful look at her. "I thought you'd be pleased when you saw that I'd prepared the coffee. Without me, it wouldn't have been ready by the time the train arrived."

Guilt momentarily pierced her, but she knew Matthew far too well. By helping her, he hoped to win her favor. While she appreciated his assistance, she wasn't going to be manipulated.

"Thank you, Matthew, but in the future, you need not trouble yourself. I will handle it." She was careful to offer only a fleeting smile. "Since you've already taken care of the coffee, I'll return to the depot and help the ladies with the baskets. Some of the ladies from Lucy's sewing circle will soon be arriving. I need to make certain they don't have any questions for me before the train arrives."

Sarah doubted Lucy's group would need any instruction from her. They'd been delivering their comforters, knitted socks, and other handmade items for many months now. As a special way of ministering to the wounded soldiers, the ladies in town had even taken to writing letters to the boys—notes they hoped would add a bit of cheer and thank them for serving the Union. Several of the soldiers had now begun a regular correspondence with some of the ladies who had taken them under their wings and considered them surrogate sons.

Matthew nodded toward one of the tables in the café. "I thought you might at least sit and have a cup of coffee with me since I went to all this trouble."

She clasped a hand to her bodice and gave a slight shake of her head. "Whatever would the other ladies think if I sat here drinking a leisurely cup of coffee while they're hard at work? That simply wouldn't be fair—or proper. We're all here because we want to support our boys, and when that train pulls into the station, I know they're going to be thankful for that hot coffee you've made."

His frown made it clear that her response hadn't pleased him.

Chapter 4

At the sound of the clanging bell and hooting train whistle, Sarah's stomach tightened in a knot. If she was going to step in for her mother, she'd need more than good intentions. She'd need help from the Lord.

With a quick wave, she motioned to the workers. "Ladies! Could we gather in a circle for a word of prayer before the train arrives?" The women hurried toward her and joined hands. After glancing around the circle, Sarah met Emma's aloof stare. "Would you lead us, Emma?"

The older woman arched her brows then gave a nod. "Lord, You know we have our work cut out for us getting all these boys served some food afore the train leaves the station. Help us reflect Your love, and give us the speed, kindness, and courage we need to complete our mission this evening. Amen." The simple prayer whooshed from her lips in one long breath. She drew close to Sarah and lowered her voice. "That courage part was for you. When you walk onto the platform, take a deep breath and paste a brave smile on your lips. Don't cry. They don't need to see tears; they need smiles of encouragement and laughter. That's the best medicine. Except for my stew, of course." Emma grinned before she turned to resume filling a large basket with the tin cups she'd be using to serve.

Moments later, the train chugged into the station. Gripping the handles of her basket with enough force to turn her fingers white, Sarah crossed the station platform.

When she neared the train, a young corporal with broad shoulders and a wavy shock of chestnut brown hair blocked the steps. Though his full lips curved in a slight smile, he didn't move to permit Sarah entry. Instead, he remained steadfast and watched as the other women flooded through the station doors and onto the platform. When he'd completed his inspection of the crowd, he looked down at Sarah. Disappointment shone in his hazel eyes. "Mrs. McHenry is assigned to my car. Isn't she going to be here today?"

"I'm Sarah McHenry, her daughter. My mother's health prevented her from being present today, but I'll do my best to stand in for her."

He reached for Sarah's hand and assisted her up the steep metal steps. "Let me welcome you aboard, Miss McHenry. I'm Corporal Jacob Curtis, assigned as the aide to assist the wounded riding in this car. I'm also here to provide any help you may need while you're on board."

"I'm pleased to meet you, Corporal Curtis." Her hands trembled as she shifted the basket. "I must admit I'm quite nervous. This is the first time I've come to help with the Basket Brigade."

His eyes twinkled. "Then I'm pleased I'm the one assigned to accompany you. You can set your mind at ease about serving these men. Since leaving the station in Cairo, they've been talking about you ladies and the fine food they'll receive here in Decatur."

"Are you the one who told them about the food, Corporal Curtis?"

He chuckled and traced his fingers through his thick crop of hair. "I plead guilty, but I have to admit it pleases me to give them something to look forward to. I enjoy bringing a smile to their faces, even if it's only for a short time."

Sarah steeled herself as Corporal Curtis pushed open the door and led her into the car. She forced her lips into a smile she hoped would appear warm and compassionate rather than cold and detached. Her breath caught as she spied a soldier with a missing arm in the first swinging cot on her right. *Please help me, Lord. Let my service to these men represent a glimpse of Your love for them.*

The young man's sober countenance immediately brightened when Sarah reached into her basket and withdrew a buttered roll wrapped in brown paper. "There will be stew, so you may want to wait and eat that when the ladies come through with the kettles."

"Thank you, ma'am." He pulled back the paper, lifted the soft roll to his nose, and inhaled a deep breath. "This smells like home."

Sarah fought off the tears that threatened. "I'm so glad." The young soldier's comment was a stark reminder of Samuel. She could imagine him saying those very same words if someone handed him a fresh roll or slice of bread.

From the time the two of them had been old enough to help in the bakery, they had enjoyed working side by side. By the time they finished school, their father's arthritic hands had worsened and he had relied upon their help—especially Samuel, who had the same talent as her father for kneading the dough and keeping the fires in their brick ovens at just the right temperature. Once Samuel enlisted, her father insisted his hands were fine, and he'd returned to kneading and wouldn't accept help. She wasn't certain if he considered the pain to be his contribution to the war effort or if the pain blotted out thoughts of Samuel off fighting, but she no longer argued with her father.

They'd had only two letters from Samuel since he'd left Decatur, but they'd known his letters would be few and far between. Samuel wasn't fond of letter writing. Besides, the mail to and from the front lines moved like molasses on a winter day.

Her father continued to insist she help her mother with the pastries and serve the customers who came to their shop each day. Sarah's sweet disposition appealed to everyone who daily visited their bakery. She wanted that same personality to shine through today.

Sarah's confidence increased as she made her way down the aisle. After glimpsing the men's good humor and pleasure, her initial wariness vanished. Her smile deepened when she noticed several of them slicking down their hair. They could do nothing to make their tattered clothing more presentable, but she was touched by their efforts to appear tidy and neat.

As she turned to a soldier on the other side of the car, he greeted her with a huge smile—a smile so reminiscent of Samuel that her heart skipped a beat. She reached into the basket then handed him a buttered roll. "You have a wonderful smile, soldier."

He beamed and a dimple formed along his right cheek. "Your beauty could put a smile on any fellow's face, ma'am."

"I don't know about that, but I thank you for your kind compliment. What's your name?"

"Joseph Oleen. Private Joseph Oleen."

"An honor to meet you, Private Oleen." She patted his shoulder before continuing onward, touched by the soldier's sweet words.

Her confidence emboldened, Sarah continued to exchange warm greetings and a cheery smile with each of the remaining soldiers. As she neared the end of the aisle, Jacob nodded toward the ailing men. "These soldiers haven't seen a young lady in a while, so it might be best if you weren't quite so friendly with them."

Sarah's bright smile wavered. "I was merely attempting to extend a bit of hospitality along with their meal. While I appreciate your warning, I don't think any of the men mistook my behavior as anything other than kindness. Not one of them said anything untoward."

"That's good to hear. I know the efforts of all the ladies are greatly appreciated." He excused himself to tend to a soldier as Sarah emptied her basket.

When she passed by Jacob a short time later, she hesitated. "I'm going into the depot to gather cups so we can begin serving coffee and dessert."

Several of the women joined Sarah in the station, all of them carrying empty baskets and tales of the fine young men they'd met while on board the train, when Emma bustled into the depot. One glance at the chatting ladies and her eyes flashed a warning that caused the room to still. "You're in charge, Sarah. These ladies need to be filling baskets and getting back on the train. Why are you all standing here visiting like there's no need to hurry?" Without waiting for an answer, she scooped up an armful of tin cups and dropped them into her basket. "Flora, bring a pot of coffee and follow me."

Flora rushed off to the kitchen to fetch a pot of coffee, with several other ladies following on her heels. Sarah filled her basket with tin cups while she waited for the ladies to return with additional pots of coffee. She was completing the task when Jacob stepped inside and strode toward her.

He held a coin in his hand. "The young fellow with the big smile wanted to pay you for his dinner."

Sarah shook her head. "Absolutely not. His smile was thanks enough." She took the coin from Jacob's hand. "I'll return it to him when we go through with coffee and dessert."

"Since you seem to be doing fine, I'll stay here in the depot and get me something to eat before we leave."

Embarrassment washed over Sarah. She hadn't even offered the aide so much as a cup of coffee or piece of bread. "I'm sorry, Corporal Curtis. I should have offered you something to eat before now. We have more than enough." She reached inside her basket to remove a tin cup, but he shook his head.

"No need for an apology. I enjoy a little time off the train when we make our stops. I'm sure your food is better than what they serve in the depot restaurant, but I'd rather you save it for the wounded men. I think they'll be happy to receive seconds if there's any extra."

Sarah briefly considered disagreeing with him, but he turned and walked into the restaurant before she could form an argument. It was understandable he needed a time of respite after hours of aiding the wounded soldiers. The men required a great deal of assistance, and there would be many long hours before the train reached Chicago.

The ladies made several passes down the aisle of each train car, distributing food and coffee. Once the men had eaten their fill, the ladies collected the used cups and utensils. As Sarah gathered the items, she silently thanked God for the change He'd wrought in her heart. The thankfulness and appreciation of the men had wiped away her fear and apprehension. While she harbored a modicum of regret that she'd refused to serve in the past, she would eagerly do her part in the future. As Sarah entered the depot, Lucy Maddox and the ladies of her sewing guild crossed the platform and stepped onto the train to offer each of the soldiers a word of cheer, along with a handmade comforter and socks to help them ward off the cold.

Inside the depot, Jacob greeted Sarah before nodding toward Lucy and her group. "The fellas are sure going to appreciate those items. Any blankets they have are in tatters, and many of them shiver even when it isn't cold." His eyes shone with compassion. "You probably noticed that when you were on the train. I'm not sure if it's due to their injuries or because of all they've seen and experienced on the battlefield."

His sympathetic tone touched her, and she instinctively looked over her shoulder toward the train. If Samuel should be injured, she hoped there would be a man with the compassion of Jacob Curtis to help him. "You're very kind, Corporal Curtis. The men on that train may have been unlucky on the battlefield, but they're fortunate to have you with them on this journey." His cheeks reddened, and he glanced toward the wooden floor. "I'm sorry. It wasn't my intention to embarrass you, but your work is so important. You must have been very pleased to receive this assignment."

"I'd like to say you're right, but escorting the wounded isn't what I hoped for. What I really wanted was to fight on the front lines."

They walked to one of the tables, where Sarah poured coffee into a tin cup and handed it to him. "My brother was filled with the same passion when he enlisted, but you must know that you're a great help to these men. And your encouragement and kindness were exactly what *I* needed to get me through my initial fears. I can't thank you enough for being so understanding and helpful." She chuckled. "Now, I have trouble remembering why I was so afraid or why I had to be forced into joining the Basket Brigade."

He grinned. "Maybe it was because we were destined to meet on this particular day." The train whistled a long, piercing blast. "I need to get on board, Miss Sarah." He handed her the empty coffee cup. When his fingers lingered on her hand for a moment longer than necessary, unexpected warmth flooded her cheeks. "I won't be coming back to Decatur for a few days, but I hope I'll see you again."

Her heart fluttered. "I hope so, too, Corporal Curtis."

Chapter 5

Using the frayed sleeve of his uniform jacket, Jacob wiped the haze of condensation from the train window and leaned forward to capture a final glimpse of Sarah. His heart hammered an extra beat when she stepped onto the depot platform and waved one final time. He wanted to believe that last friendly gesture had been meant for him and not the entire trainload of wounded soldiers.

For the first time since enlisting in the army, he could truly be thankful for this assignment. How he'd railed against God when he learned that he would be acting as an escort for injured soldiers. He'd launched into a fierce argument with his sergeant—which hadn't helped his situation. In truth, his behavior had created even greater consequences: the duty had been extended for an indefinite term. He didn't know whether the order would eventually be rescinded or whether he'd spend his entire enlistment shuttling soldiers back and forth to the hospital in Chicago.

More than a year ago, Jacob's commanding officer had declared him a fortunate young man. The officer's words remained etched in Jacob's memory: *"Once you step onto that hospital train and see all the wounded soldiers, you'll be grateful for this assignment."* But his commanding officer had been wrong. He'd never given thanks for this assignment.

Not until today. Not until he'd met Miss Sarah McHenry.

Before today, it was guilt rather than gratefulness that gnawed at him. When injured soldiers stared at him with vacant eyes, he worried what they thought of him. They all wore the same uniform, but did they think him a coward whose family had pulled strings to keep him out of harm's way? He hoped they understood he'd had no say in his orders. A time or two, he'd been tempted to ask their opinion but decided his worries were small compared to the problems they faced.

Wedged between one of the cots and the edge of a wooden seat, Jacob let his thoughts run free and return to Sarah and their time together. His lips curved as he recalled the twinkle in her eyes as she'd become more confident. He rested his head against the seat and closed his eyes. The clack of the train soon lulled him into a peaceful cocoon.

Suddenly he jerked to attention when a soldier mentioned Sarah's name. Hoping to hear over the din of the train and chattering men, he leaned forward.

A young amputee a few cots down rested his head in his palm. "She's one beautiful gal. I think maybe she liked me. I asked her if she had a beau."

A loud hoot came from across the aisle. "What did she say to that?"

"She shook her head no and gave me a real sweet smile. When I told her my name, she said her name was Sarah and she'd be praying for me."

Another soldier chortled. "Well, that don't mean she's hankerin' after you, Chester—just means she's gonna say a prayer you get better. Besides, I'm thinking she's a might more interested in me. She stopped and asked me about my family and if I was going to be coming back to Decatur. That probably means she wants to marry me, don't ya think?"

As the men continued to discuss Sarah's beauty and charm, their laughter and jibes assaulted Jacob's ears. Had they been discussing anyone other than Sarah, he might have ignored the comments. Instead, he felt his muscles knot and his lips tighten. Hadn't he advised Sarah the men might mistake her sociable demeanor for more than just a friendly exchange? Could he have misunderstood her intentions? Had her interest in him been no more than the same kindness she'd extended to the other men? Instead of worrying about the wounded soldiers, perhaps he should have guarded his own heart.

∞

Sarah lowered her arm and silently chided herself for her impulsive behavior. Had the other ladies been watching from inside the station as she'd stood on tiptoe and waved to the departing train— to Corporal Curtis? Bowing her head against the snow, she pulled her gray quilted cape close and strode across the platform.

Once inside, loud applause and cheers greeted her. The silk-lined hood dropped from her auburn curls and rested lightly on her shoulders. Embarrassment seized her. "What's all this fuss about?"

Nadine Greer stepped forward and patted Sarah's shoulder. "We're proud of you, my dear. You did a stellar job today, and we are hopeful you'll agree to remain a member of the Brigade." She leaned a bit closer. "In fact, while your mother is convalescing, we'd like you to continue to take charge. We all agree you're the best choice." The older woman glanced about the group. "Don't we, ladies?"

The assembled women nodded and murmured their agreement. From the doorway of the depot restaurant, Matthew's deep bass blended with the women's voices. He leaned against the doorjamb, his eyes fixed on her. "I'd say Sarah's the best choice for just about anything."

She frowned when he winked at her. She feared that Matthew would use her daily visits as an opportunity to try to woo her. She'd need to keep him at arm's length, but she wouldn't let his conduct determine her decision. After all, the wounded soldiers had been willing to sacrifice their lives. Surely she could avoid Matthew's advances and convince him there was no possibility they'd share a future together.

Keeping her eyes upon Mrs. Greer, Sarah gave a resolute nod. "I would be honored to lead the Brigade for as long as you need me."

Nadine led another round of applause then squared her shoulders and motioned the ladies to silence. "Please remain available to assist Sarah as needed. We have no way of knowing how many men to expect until word is received from Centralia. Do your best to be prepared, and Sarah will do the same."

After the ladies donned their wraps, they gathered their kettles, baskets, and serving utensils. Before they departed, Nadine once again waved them to silence. "And don't forget that Lucy can use additional help making lap quilts. If you can't donate your time, perhaps you have some fabric or thread the other ladies can use."

After seeing the condition of the tattered clothing and blankets worn by the injured men, Sarah was certain Lucy would need more than a few scraps of fabric and a spool of thread to furnish their needs. However, Sarah was confident the ladies would scour their sewing baskets and do even more than they'd been asked.

Nadine walked alongside Sarah. "Do tell your mother we're all very proud of the work you accomplished today. I know she must have been praying from her sickbed, and she needs to know her prayers were answered. She will be most proud of you, Sarah."

When the two women parted, Sarah lifted her face toward the sky and stuck out her tongue to catch a few snowflakes. A flurry of white coated her eyelashes, and she swiped away the dampness with her gloved fingers. What a wonderful evening this had been. Not only had the Lord helped her overcome her fears, He'd also revealed that this truly was where she was needed—where she could serve. Her fears had been dispelled, and she looked forward to meeting the future trains that would arrive in Decatur—and to seeing Corporal Jacob Curtis again.

Chapter 6

Sarah hurried toward the train station, eager to begin preparations for the train's arrival. Though her mother was gaining strength, the doctor had declared it unwise for her to resume any duties with the Basket Brigade. While she was able to be up and about for short periods of time, her progress remained tenuous. One day she would appear much stronger, but the next she'd be abed the entire day.

Uncertain if her mother was napping, Sarah peeked around the bedroom door. Her mother smiled and waved her forward. "Leaving so soon? It seems you leave a little earlier each day."

"I'm going early so I can have the tables arranged before the ladies arrive with their food."

Her mother nodded. "How wise of you. I can see how that would hasten preparations once the ladies arrive. I'm thankful you've adjusted so well. I don't want to be one who says I told you so, but. . ."

Sarah chuckled. "You're allowed, Mama. I only wish I hadn't

waited until you became ill before doing your bidding. Now I look forward to hearing the train whistle each day."

The late-afternoon sunlight flickered through the bedroom curtains and cast a lopsided design on the wooden floor. "Do you have someone to help you move those tables? They're much too heavy for you to move about on your own."

"Johnny Folson comes over when he can. After school, he mucks stalls at the livery and then, if his grandfather gives him permission, he comes to the depot to help move the tables." If necessary, Sarah could move them by herself, but she'd enlisted Johnny's help as a ploy to discourage Matthew's unwanted attention. A fact she didn't share with her mother.

Before leaning down to brush a kiss on her mother's cheek, Sarah tucked a letter into her skirt pocket. "Pray that all goes well on the train today."

"I always do." Her mother nodded toward her pocket. "Another letter for Jacob?"

A smile tugged at Sarah's lips. "He was right about the letters. It's proved to be a good way to learn more about each other."

Her mother's gaze wavered. "Be careful to protect your heart, Sarah. You never know when he may receive a change of orders. I don't want to dishearten you, but I think you need to be prepared for such an event."

"You need not worry, Mother. I understand the possibility." She glanced toward the door. "I really must be going." She squeezed her mother's hand and hurried from the room. She didn't want to think about Jacob receiving another assignment. She'd had to say goodbye to Samuel. Surely that was enough.

She patted the pocket of her skirt, and the stiff envelope crinkled beneath her hand. She hoped Jacob would enjoy her letter. He had such a way with words that reading his letters filled her with joy.

After she'd observed his writing skills, Sarah promised herself she wouldn't compare their missives—but it was difficult. His letters read like poetry while hers resembled rambling prose.

They did their best to visit as much as possible each time the train passed through Decatur. However, Sarah's primary duty was to help the ailing soldiers, not develop a kinship with Jacob, so they'd agreed upon the idea of writing letters as a method to become better acquainted.

Jacob had given Sarah a letter on their third meeting and suggested exchanging letters. They'd continued the practice ever since. Sometimes Sarah told him about her daily activities, but at other times she included details of her childhood and family.

Though exchanging letters several times a week wasn't a perfect solution, they permitted a deeper familiarity—much more than their brief visits at the depot would have provided. Yet rather than beautiful words, Sarah sometimes longed for Jacob to give her more details of his life before joining the military. While he was willing to answer questions about his family and friends, when she'd once made a lighthearted remark about the sweetheart he'd left behind, he'd become brooding and withdrawn. She'd attempted to push aside his startling reaction to her playful question, but his behavior still baffled her. His abrupt negative response to her question had made it clear that he didn't wish to discuss the matter further. There had been little time to dwell on his response—the soldiers on board the train had far more pressing needs.

The icy wind whipped at Sarah's cape as she entered the train depot. Matthew stood in the doorway leading to the café. The moment he spied her, he leaned forward and swooped his arm in a giant wave as if greeting a member of royalty. She arched her brows and glanced around the depot, surprised to see the tables had already been arranged.

He grinned as he approached. "I hope you appreciate my efforts. When Johnny didn't arrive, I set up the tables—all for you."

Sarah sighed. Nothing she said or did discouraged Matthew's attempts to impress her. "I would rather believe your help was for the ailing soldiers who will be arriving."

His longing gaze remained riveted on her. "Believe what you like, but it's you that I care about, not a train filled with soldiers."

His words erased the kindness of his deed, and she gave a slight shake of her head. "Thank you for setting up the tables, but there's no need for you to do so in the future. I wouldn't want to take you away from your duties in the hotel." She removed her cape and hung it on a peg near the stove. When she turned around, the letter escaped her pocket and fluttered to the floor. Before she could retrieve it, Matthew snatched it up by one corner.

"Nothing's too much trouble for you, Sarah." He stepped closer and turned the envelope over. His jaw twitched as his gaze settled on Jacob's name. "You know Jacob Curtis ain't gonna be around forever, but I'm gonna be here. We can build a future together." When she attempted to step away, he blocked her path. "You need to think about the future instead of that soldier boy who's gonna leave ya and go home to his sweetheart."

With mention of a past love, Sarah's anger mounted. Matthew had no right to interfere in her life. She didn't want or need his opinions. She waved for him to step aside. "You need not worry about Jacob or his plans for the future. They don't concern you. Leave me alone, Matthew!"

Had there not been so much work to complete, she wouldn't have gathered the courage to speak in such a bold manner.

"We'll see if ya feel the same way once he's gone." He thrust the letter at her before stomping off toward the hotel lobby.

Sarah inhaled a deep breath, thankful for his retreat. If only

Samuel had been around, she would have requested he speak to Matthew. She gave fleeting thought to asking Jacob, but that would likely make matters worse. Yet she was also proud of herself for standing up to him.

Sarah pushed thoughts of Matthew aside as the other ladies arrived and they busied themselves with the final preparations. With each passing day, her confidence increased, and she now looked forward to time with the wounded soldiers. While the train hissed to a stop outside the depot, she filled the last of the large kettles with warm beef and vegetable soup.

Moments later, Jacob was at her side, his smile as warm as the fire that crackled in the depot stove. "You look particularly lovely today." He glanced around the room. "What can I do to help?"

"If you'd like to carry one of the soup kettles, I'll carry the basket of cups and utensils." Sarah took a quick survey of the room and, once assured all the ladies were prepared to begin, she followed Jacob to his train car. Sarah made her way down the aisle handing out the cups and spoons while Jacob followed behind and filled them with the thick soup. She stopped occasionally to explain that they would be delivering sandwiches and either fruit or dessert once the soup was served. On the few occasions when she lingered to visit with the soldiers, Jacob encouraged her to move along.

They were nearing the rear of the car when Jacob drew close. "I've told you before that you should be careful around the men. They'll think you're flirting with them, and that could lead to trouble. I don't want you to say or do anything that causes one of them to disrespect you."

She was getting weary of his admonitions. "How could asking about their families or inquiring if they have a special need be considered flirtatious? I have received nothing but respect. You're being overly protective where there's no need."

Jacob frowned but said nothing more until he'd finished serving the soup. "I'll get the sandwiches if you want to begin collecting the empty cups at the other end of the car."

Sarah nodded, but as she made her way through the aisle, the cup of soup given to a badly burned soldier remained untouched. She smiled and nodded toward the soup. "Not hungry?"

His gaze settled on his bandaged hands. "I'm hungry, but the spoon didn't cooperate." He dropped against his pillow and groaned.

Sarah glanced across the aisle, where another soldier was beckoning to her. When she approached, he leaned closer. "When we got on the train, the doc said he didn't think that young fella would make it to Chicago. He was burned real bad—and not jest his hands. I think his name is Thomas Reed or Reedy—not for sure about his last name."

After whispering her thanks, Sarah moved back across the aisle. The young soldier's eyes had closed. She hesitated, uncertain if she should awaken him, but he'd said he was hungry. Keeping her voice to a whisper, she said his name.

His eyes fluttered open. "You look like an angel. Is that how you knew my name? Have I died and gone to heaven?"

"No, Thomas. You're still on the train, and I'm not an angel. My name is Sarah, and I'm going to help you with your soup so you don't become any weaker on the rest of your journey. Will it hurt if we prop you up just a little?"

"I'm willing to try." He attempted to scooch into a sitting position but groaned in pain.

Sarah stayed him with a touch of her hand. "Here. Let me put these folded blankets behind you."

He grimaced but nodded his approval as she positioned him and then dipped a spoon into the cup of soup. He opened his mouth and gave a slight nod after he'd swallowed. "That's good."

Pleased by his willingness to let her feed him, Sarah continued until the cup was empty. "There will be some sandwiches coming soon. Do you think you'd like one?"

He dropped back against his pillow and shook his head. "Don't think my stomach can hold any more right now. Besides, I'm tuckered out from eating the soup." When he closed his eyes, Sarah removed the napkin she'd placed beneath his chin. "You're as kind as my very own mother. She fed me soup when I was sick, and then she'd give me a kiss and tell me I'd soon feel better."

Tears welled in Sarah's eyes. The thought that the young soldier wasn't expected to live much longer tugged at her heart and she lightly touched his cheek. "Take care, Thomas. I understand they have wonderful doctors in Chicago." Her voice cracked, and she turned away but stopped short when she saw Jacob in the middle of the aisle, glaring at her.

Chapter 7

Jacob turned away from Sarah and strode down the aisle, thankful he'd emptied the basket of sandwiches. Even if the basket had been full, he couldn't have stayed on the train any longer. Seeing Sarah touch the cheek of a complete stranger had sparked a fiery anger that burned deep in his belly.

When Clara Wingard stopped him inside the depot and reached for the empty basket, he struggled to maintain his composure. Clara took a small backward step. "I'll refill that basket for you, Corporal. That way, you can take it to one of the other cars. I don't think all of the soldiers have received sandwiches and dessert."

Jacob shook his head. "One of the ladies should deliver to the other cars. I need to stay here right now."

Though her eyebrows shot high on her forehead, she didn't argue. He strode to the far side of the depot and waited until he caught sight of Sarah stepping down from the train. Not wanting to be overheard, he pulled open the door and met her on the platform. Taking her elbow, he guided her to an area sheltered from the cold wind.

"Why don't we go inside? It's too cold to stand out here and talk." Still holding the hamper of dirty tin cups and utensils, Sarah shifted the basket and tugged the hood of her cape tight around her neck.

When she began to move toward the door, Jacob gently grasped her arm. "I don't want others to overhear this conversation. I wouldn't want to embarrass you."

"Embarrass me? What could you have to say that would embarrass me?" She arched her brows as though her behavior only minutes ago had been completely proper.

Did she believe he would overlook her actions? Was she so naive she thought he would applaud her outlandish performance? He gritted his teeth in an attempt to maintain an even temper. They'd exchanged enough letters that he thought he knew Sarah, and thought she was a young woman who could be trusted. Now, he feared he'd made the same mistake for a second time. Was Sarah no different from Laura? Had he chosen another woman who couldn't remain true to one man?

"I saw you stroking that soldier's cheek. What do you think the other men on the train thought when they saw that spectacle? You looked like a loose woman. They'll be talking all the way to Chicago about the young woman willing to share affection along with a cup of soup."

Sarah glowered at him. "Will they? I thought they might think they'd seen an act of compassion toward a fellow soldier. I would hope someone would do the same if that were my brother." She hesitated a moment. "Or you." Before he could stop her, she stalked off and hurried inside the depot.

He moved from the shelter and let the cold wind whip around

him, cooling the heat of his anger. Was she right? Was he acting like a peevish schoolboy? He bowed his head against the wind, letting his thoughts settle.

What did it matter if the soldiers made comments about her actions? Sarah had fully explained her reasons. If the men made any rude remarks, he could easily defend her honor, for he knew he'd be thankful for the same kind treatment had he been suffering. He mustn't let Laura's behavior destroy his trust in Sarah.

Jacob startled when the train whistled three short blasts to announce the impending departure. He sprinted toward the depot doors, knowing he couldn't leave Decatur with this disagreement still standing between them. He glanced around the room, but Sarah was nowhere in sight. He rushed to Mrs. Wingard's side. "Where's Sarah? I need to speak to her before I leave, and the train's going to depart any minute."

The older woman nodded toward the door. "She left to speak with Johnny Folson's grandfather. The boy didn't appear this afternoon, and Sarah wanted to see if he's sick or if his grandfather simply wouldn't let him help today."

Jacob sighed. There wasn't time to write her a note. He'd have to rely upon Mrs. Wingard. "Tell her I was wrong and I'm sorry." He grasped the older woman's hand. "Will you do that for me?"

"Of course I will. Anything else?"

He shook his head then hesitated. "Yes. Tell her I'll give her a proper apology next time I come through Decatur."

The older woman smiled and patted his hand. "I'll give her your message. Now, hurry or you'll have to run to catch the train."

Mrs. Wingard had been right. Had he remained in the station a few more seconds, he would have missed the train. Still gasping for breath when he entered the car, Jacob dropped onto one of the seats. Over the chugging of the train, he heard someone mention

Sarah's name. Wanting to know what was being said, he stood and moved down the aisle a short distance.

One of the soldiers said, "I think that young lady should get a medal for kindness."

Another agreed and added, "She'd get my vote, for sure. Too bad he died so quick. Would have been nice if he could have had a little more time to recall the kindness shown to him."

Stunned by the response, Jacob continued down the aisle. A blanket had been drawn across the burned soldier's face. Jacob looked at the man across the aisle. "When?"

"Right after she left the train. He breathed one of them long ragged breaths. This time it rattled deep in his chest and that was it." The soldier nodded toward the dead man. "Another soldier checked him, said he was dead, and covered him up. Sure am glad that lady was so nice to him. If you see her again, be sure and tell her, would ya?"

Jacob swallowed hard and gave a slight nod. "I'll do that." He should have said more, but the words stuck in his throat. When he returned to his seat, Jacob bowed his head and asked God to help him overcome his jealous nature and direct his future—a future he hoped would include Sarah.

On the way back to the depot, Sarah considered how she'd reacted to Jacob's reprimand. Granted, he had no right to speak to her in a condemning fashion, yet part of what he'd said was true. She'd let her emotions rule her actions—something her own mother had advised against. Yet she didn't feel a great deal of regret. The boy had been so thankful for her meager offering of kindness. She prayed he'd get well, yet it was clear his prognosis was dismal.

Her thoughts skittered between the badly burned soldier, Jacob, and Johnny's grandpa, Herman Folson, who'd kept Johnny at the livery stable today. When she'd approached Mr. Folson, he'd been annoyed and had dodged her questions with a curt remark that he had work to complete and that he needed Johnny's help. He'd added that the boy was gone far too much helping everyone else when he was needed there. She'd attempted to gain more insight, but the old man had shooed her away as though she were a pesky fly.

When she stepped inside the depot, the train had been gone for more than fifteen minutes and only a handful of the women remained. Most of them hurried home once they finished serving the soldiers each day, and Sarah understood their need to depart. They had families waiting on their evening meal. Once inside the depot, Clara Wingard waved Sarah forward. "I have a message for you from the good-looking soldier." When Sarah didn't respond, Clara continued. "The one who seeks you out each time he passes through. The corporal. Jacob Curtis."

Sarah gave a slight nod and waited.

With her gaze fastened upon Sarah, Clara repeated Jacob's message then added, "Oh, and he said the next time he's in Decatur he'll give you a proper apology." She winked and tapped her fingers against the bodice of her dress. "I think you've won his heart. He seems like a nice young fellow."

Heat raced up Sarah's neck. "Thank you for delivering the message, Clara." Sarah gestured toward the empty tables as she twisted around. "Let's move these tables, and then we can go. I'm sure you have work at home that needs your attention."

"Not much. Without a husband or children around, I don't have to worry about serving supper on time like some of the other ladies." She grinned. "We're kind of alike in that regard, Sarah, but I'm thinking maybe that's going to change for you. There's no denying that corporal has set his sights on winning your heart."

Sarah's cheeks flamed. While she hoped Jacob truly desired to win her heart, his jealous outburst had dampened her increasing affection for him. Although his words had struck a chord of truth, she'd been less than pleased with his bitter avowals. Still, he'd attempted to apologize. Only time would reveal if he'd been sincere.

Two days later, an apologetic Jacob arrived on the train returning from Chicago to Cairo. Though she'd expected to see him later in the week, Sarah was surprised when he walked into the bakery. He'd never stopped to see her on his return trips from Chicago. Because the train didn't stop long enough for him to come and visit her home, he'd normally make a dash to the livery and leave a letter with Johnny Folson. As soon as Johnny's grandpa would give him permission to leave, he'd deliver the missive to Sarah.

Jacob grinned as he approached the interior of the bakery. "I'm pleased you're here. Are you surprised to see me?"

"How did you manage? Has the train already departed for Centralia? Will you get in trouble?"

He shook his head. "I won't get in trouble. I had a little extra money, so I caught the early train out of Chicago. There's another train passing through going to Cairo in about an hour. I'll get on board when it stops."

She was pleased to see him but was sorry their argument was the reason he'd spent his extra money on a train ticket. When she heard her father's footsteps, she turned.

"Papa, this is Corporal Jacob Curtis, the soldier who has been helping me when I board the train with the Basket Brigade."

Her father beamed and hurried forward with his hand outstretched. "I am pleased to meet you, Corporal. Our son, Samuel, is serving at the front with the Union troops. We hear very little from him, but when he has free time, it is more important he rest than write letters—at least that is what I tell my wife. I'm sure Sarah has already told you about Samuel."

Jacob nodded. "She has, and I know you must be very proud of him. I had hoped to serve at the front, but instead I'm assigned to the hospital trains."

"All soldiers must serve where they are sent, Corporal. In wartime, every position is important." Her father pointed to the case of bakery items. "Tell Sarah what you'd like. It is my small gift to you for helping her and the injured soldiers. I must return to my wife upstairs, but I am pleased to have met you."

"Thank you, Mr. McHenry. It is a pleasure." After her father left the room, the two of them sat at one of the tables near the front window and Jacob reached into his pocket. "I brought this for you." He'd tied a piece of twine around his letter and attached a sprig of holly with red berries. "I wanted to tell you in person how sorry I am for the way I spoke to you. I needed to know if you would forgive me."

She brushed his fingers as she accepted the envelope. "Of course I forgive you. Clara told me you had apologized. You didn't need to make a special trip." She hesitated and smiled. "But I'm pleased you did."

"So am I." He clasped her hand. "Very glad."

Chapter 8

Sarah glanced at the bakery clock before rushing toward the door. She grabbed her woolen cloak from the peg as her father returned downstairs. "Where are you rushing off to? It's not time for the train to arrive."

"I need to stop at the mercantile before I go to the depot. We're in need of some additional napkins, and Silas Tait said he had some old ones the store would donate. I want to pick them up before the store closes."

"If you have time, you should stop at the doctor's office. He said he would bring some cough medicine for your mother, but I haven't seen him."

"I will, Papa." With a quick wave, she exited the bakery. A sigh of relief escaped her lips when she spotted the glow of a lamp in Dr. Kirkland's office window.

The bell over the door jangled, and the doctor looked up as she stepped inside. "Sarah! I'm sorry you had to come out in the cold. I didn't get the medicine over to your mother. I was needed at a farm out in the country and just returned."

"No need to apologize, Dr. Kirkland. I was on my way to the mercantile, so stopping here isn't an inconvenience."

The doctor pushed back from his desk and strode toward the adjacent room. "It won't take me long to prepare the mixture."

As Sarah turned toward the window, she caught sight of Johnny Folson across the street. She yanked open the door and waved at him. "Johnny, can you come over here? I need to speak to you."

The jangling bell and her loud comment brought Dr. Kirkland rushing back to the front office. "Is something wrong, Sarah?"

Heat rushed to her cheeks. She didn't usually exhibit such a lack of decorum. "No, I want to speak with Johnny Folson."

The moment Dr. Kirkland returned to the adjacent office, she again motioned to Johnny. He'd stopped in the middle of the street, no doubt hoping to escape her questions. Moving ever so slowly, he finally drew near.

She kept her tone soft. "Where have you been? You promised to help at the depot."

He danced from foot to foot and attempted to answer in sputters and spurts before finally meeting her gaze. "Guess I should just tell you the truth. Matthew told me to stay away. He said I wasn't needed so often."

Sarah frowned. "Why didn't you check with me to make sure that was what I wanted?"

The boy hiked one shoulder. "Matthew said if I knew what was good for me, I wouldn't tell you. He acted like it was a surprise and that you'd be pleased." The boy pointed his thumb over his shoulder. "I gotta get going."

Her stomach roiled at the thought of Matthew going behind her back to keep Johnny away. How dare he do such a thing! Then again, she shouldn't be surprised by Matthew's cunning behavior. He'd seen through her efforts to elude him and had done his best to outwit her. Perhaps a confrontation was now in order. They'd been playing this game of cat and mouse far too long.

While she completed her errands, Sarah silently rehearsed what she would say to Matthew. He needed a good upbraiding, and she needed to be prepared to meet the challenge. It wasn't until she was tying her horse outside the depot that she recalled Matthew's warning to Johnny Folson. She couldn't confront Matthew unless she betrayed Johnny's confidence. Would he hurt the boy? She wilted like a flower in need of a drink.

Sarah braced herself as she entered the depot. "Hello, Sarah. I was beginning to think you weren't going to appear." Matthew stepped to her side as she crossed the threshold. He glanced at the clock. "You're a little late, aren't you?"

Sarah shrugged and continued across the depot. When Matthew attempted to help her remove her cape, she turned. "I don't need your assistance. I can remove my own cape, and I can set up the room by myself. Surely you must have work in the hotel that requires your attention. If not, I'm sure your mother would appreciate extra help in the café."

His eyes opened wide, as though her remark came as a surprise. "I know you are able to set up the room on your own, but I *want* to help you." He stepped closer. "I like being near you. I care for you, Sarah. If you'd just give me a chance, I'll show you I can offer you more than Corporal Curtis ever can."

She blew out a long breath. After what she'd learned from Johnny, she wasn't going to engage in a conversation about Jacob or any other soldier. "I have work to do, Matthew." The sound of his footsteps followed her as she crossed the room.

When she came to an abrupt halt, he stopped at her side. "A group is going ice-skating tomorrow, and I thought you might want to join us. I could come by the bakery and we could ride out to the pond in my sleigh. More gals than fellas, but it should still be fun."

Of course there would be more girls. Most of the able-bodied men were off fighting in the war. "Since there are so few men, I'm sure one of those girls you mentioned will be pleased to have you as an escort."

He rested his hip against the doorjamb. "Do you plan to sit at home and pine for Corporal Curtis until the war ends? Even if he doesn't get orders to the front, once this war is over, do you really think you'll see him again?" He didn't give her a chance to respond before he continued. "Soldiers don't get much of a chance to talk to womenfolk anymore, so they'll say just about anything to gain a woman's attention for a few minutes. You need to remember that I'm the one who's here right now. And I'm the one who's gonna be here when the war ends. I don't think you can count on Jacob Curtis."

Rather than displaying his usual anger, Matthew remained calm, his demeanor more confident than when he'd previously spoken to her about these matters. Instead of creating the softening effect he'd likely hoped for, his attitude only served to deepen her anger.

She wheeled around to face him. How she longed to confront him and tell him she knew he'd gone behind her back and told Johnny to stay away. She balled her hands into tight fists and dug her fingernails into her palms.

"I'm still waiting for an answer about the ice-skating party."

Her anger mounted, and she glared at him. "Stop it, Matthew! I don't want to go anywhere with you, so quit asking me. In fact, I prefer if you didn't talk to me at all!"

For a moment, it appeared he would heed her request to remain silent, but he soon regained his composure. "You need to think about the future, Sarah. There won't be many men coming home from the war—at least not men who will be the same as when they left. Either they'll be missing an arm or leg, or their minds will be messed up from all the bloodshed that's surrounded them. Is that what you want for yourself? To be tied to half a man who won't be able to take care of you? I've talked to Jacob. He wants to go to the front. He told me so himself. If you think he's set his mind on courting you and traveling back and forth on that hospital train, you're sadly mistaken. Me and Jacob have had us a couple of sensible talks about the future."

His last comment stung. Jacob had told her of his desire to go to the front and fight—but he'd added that his aspirations had changed upon meeting her. Was he still making attempts to have his orders changed and not telling her? She couldn't be certain, but she wouldn't give Matthew the satisfaction of knowing his remarks had caused her worry. She'd have a talk with Jacob when he arrived.

Though she'd privately vowed to ignore Matthew's attempts to talk to her, Sarah felt a need to dispel his observations. "Jacob told me that he'd enlisted because he wanted to fight and he'd been unhappy to be assigned to the hospital trains." She wanted to ask when he'd talked to Jacob about a reassignment but decided any questions would give Matthew too much satisfaction.

Matthew arched his brows. "And what about your brother?"

She jutted her chin. "What does Samuel have to do with any of this?"

"I thought you two were going to take over the bakery and go into business together." He tapped himself on the chest. "Me? I understand that idea because I live here and know you and Samuel, but do you think Jacob is gonna marry you and move to Decatur?

What's he supposed to do while you and Samuel run the bakery? You gonna teach him how to make cakes and expect him to be happy? I got me a job right here at the depot hotel, and I'd be happy to have my wife working with her brother at the bakery."

Sarah's eyes widened. It seemed as if Matthew had been giving a lot of thought to her future. Truth be told, she'd not even considered what might happen if she and Jacob eventually decided to wed. Their letters had provided an opportunity to learn about each other, but letters weren't the same as personal visits, in which matters of importance could be discussed. And there hadn't been much time together. With a letter, one could take time to think of a proper response, but inquiries made in person required a direct answer. And though she'd asked Jacob numerous questions, Sarah hadn't asked if he would ever consider living in Decatur. Such an inquiry would be far too bold.

"What Jacob and I decide about the future is none of your business!"

Though she'd responded with conviction, Matthew's question created a modicum of doubt. Had Jacob and Matthew discussed the future? Perhaps she'd been wrong to discourage him when he'd mentioned using his pay to purchase train tickets as he had when he'd delivered his apology letter. They would have had additional time together, yet she didn't believe the expense warranted the short visits they would have gained.

"I'm glad you're taking a little time to reconsider my offer."

Matthew's remark was enough to pull Sarah from her thoughts of Jacob. "I was *not* reconsidering your offer." She straightened her shoulders and marched toward the far side of the room. "Please leave me alone. I need to get set up for the train's arrival."

"You go right ahead with your duties. I wouldn't want you to be unprepared when it's time to serve those soldier boys. But when the war is over and all the soldiers have gone home, don't forget I made a proposal." He shrugged. "Who knows? I might let you take me up on my offer if I haven't married someone else by then."

As if anyone would have him.

Sarah set to work with thoughts of Jacob and the future weighing heavy on her mind.

Chapter 9

By the time the train arrived, Sarah had been able to think of nothing but her conversation with Matthew. He'd spoken with such authority that she worried there might be a speck of truth in his words. Had Jacob indicated that he wouldn't want to live in Decatur? Bold as it might be, there was only one way to find out.

Sarah gathered her courage as the train came to a halt outside the station. While the other ladies exited the station, she checked her basket one last time and watched for Jacob. Working together, they'd developed a routine that permitted them to serve the soldiers in Jacob's car as well as lend additional help to some of the other ladies. Panic knotted inside her stomach. Where was he? All the other ladies had boarded the train, yet he still hadn't disembarked.

Grasping the basket in one hand and holding her cloak tight against the freezing wind, she hurried toward the train. No doubt he'd been detained helping one of the soldiers. She clambered up the steps and was surprised when the door leading into the car swung open.

A smiling young private greeted her. "You must be Sarah McHenry. I'm Private Nelson."

Sarah's mind whirred as she attempted to peek over the shoulder of the young private. "I'm pleased to meet you, Private. Where is Corporal Curtis?"

"He's back in Centralia. He had to meet with the commander about his assignment, but he sent a letter for you and said he'd be on the train coming through tomorrow." The soldier reached inside his uniform jacket, withdrew an envelope, and handed it to her.

Sarah's gaze settled on the slightly crumpled envelope, but she couldn't bring herself to take it from Private Nelson's hand. She suspected there was nothing in that letter she wanted to read. Jacob still wanted to be reassigned to the front lines. He'd said he was pleased with his duty on the hospital trains now that he'd met her, but according to Matthew, that was a lie. He was meeting with his commander about another assignment. Clearly he wanted to march into battle more than he wanted to be with her.

"Corporal Curtis said you'd tell me what I should do to help you, Miss McHenry."

Sarah pushed aside the disturbing thought that Jacob hadn't been honest with her. She took the letter from Private Nelson and tucked it into her pocket. "Yes, of course." She forced a smile. "We need to hurry. We're already behind schedule." She handed him her hamper and gave him instructions.

She began her own duties down the aisle, though her mind and heart weren't in it. As if in a cloud, she welcomed each of the men, handing them the items from her basket and thanking them for serving the Union. Some looked at her with dazed eyes, while others offered a crooked smile or word of thanks, each one of them reminding her what might lie ahead for Jacob should he be sent to the front.

For the remainder of their time together, Private Nelson followed her directions with exacting precision. When the whistle signaled their departure, Sarah thanked him for his help and wished him Godspeed on the rest of their journey.

As she turned to leave the train, the private touched her arm. "Wait! Corporal Curtis said you would have a letter for him. He said I should take it just in case something happens and he doesn't arrive on tomorrow's train."

Sarah shook her head. "No. I'll keep it with me and give it to him the next time he comes through."

The private lifted his hand to his forehead and gave her an informal salute. "Whatever you say, ma'am. Tell all the ladies thank you for their kindness—it means a lot to all of us."

"We're pleased to serve you." Although she meant the sentiment, her words sounded flat. Sarah stepped down from the train and crossed the platform. She glanced over her shoulder as the train slowly gained momentum and departed the station. Only then did she permit herself to fully feel the weight of what the future might hold. How silly of her to think that a simple exchange of letters and their time at the train depot would be enough to discourage Jacob from his desire to be a "real soldier."

The women had already cleared the tables when Sarah entered the depot, and some had already departed. She slogged through the remainder of her tasks with thoughts of Jacob flashing through her mind. After she swept the floor, she gathered the dirty napkins into a hamper to launder and then retrieved her woolen cape.

"I hear tell Jacob had a meeting with his commander today." Sarah twisted around to see Matthew standing in the doorway to the dining room, one hand resting on his hip. She swallowed hard, annoyed that he'd obviously managed to elicit the information from Private Nelson. "Seems I was right about him. He's more interested in being a soldier than a husband." His face creased in a satisfied grin.

The words bit Sarah's ears like an early frost pinching blossoms from fruit trees. He'd said aloud the words that she'd been thinking only a short time ago, and she groaned inwardly. She didn't want to spar any further with Matthew. "You are entitled to your opinion. Good night, Matthew."

She walked to the depot doors, her shoulders as rigid as a broomstick while her fingers clung to the envelope in her pocket. Though she had her doubts, she prayed Jacob's letter would contain the lifeline she needed. She pushed open the door and rushed outside before Matthew had any further opportunity to hurt her with his cutting remarks. The skies unfurled in a gloomy winter darkness that matched her mood. She plodded toward home, the cold wind chilling the bones beneath her flesh. When she entered the bakery a short time later, neither her father's warm smile nor the familiar yeasty smells were enough to lessen her concerns.

"Good news. Your mother is feeling much better. The doctor says if she continues to improve, she can return downstairs one time each day."

While Sarah was pleased to hear the news, she could offer no more than a feeble smile. "I'm glad for the good report, Papa."

His smile wavered. "I expected to see more than half a smile. You should go up and tell your mother you are pleased to have the good news."

Although she'd wanted to read Jacob's letter the minute she stepped inside the door, she hurried upstairs and kissed her mother's cheek. "I hear there is cause for celebration. Papa tells me the doctor says you are making fine improvement."

Her mother smiled and clung to Sarah's hand. "I hope that I can soon return and help with the Basket Brigade." She squeezed her fingers. "Unless I'm no longer needed."

"You know better, Mama. The ladies will be full of good cheer when they learn of your progress. They pray for you and daily inquire about your health. All of them look forward to your return."

Her mother's eyes clouded with concern. "You don't seem yourself. Did something happen? Is there bad news you're withholding from me?"

"Of course not. I'm tired, that's all. I brought home some leftover soup. I'll warm it and bring it up to you."

Her mother nodded. "There's no hurry."

Apprehension followed Sarah with a gnawing tenacity as she stepped down the hallway and into her bedroom. Finally alone, she dropped into the worn, chintz-covered chair and withdrew the letter. Fear took hold as she unfolded the page and began to read.

When she finished reading the letter, Sarah slumped back and let the pages flutter to the floor. Either the letter had been written before he learned of the meeting with his commander or he intentionally hadn't included details. The only mention of the meeting was a hastily added postscript saying he hoped to have some important news for her the next time they met. She folded her hands in her lap and stared at her entwined fingers.

Her mind flitted from thought to thought so quickly that she couldn't even form a prayer, but she took refuge in the knowledge that God knew her heart.

Chapter 10

Jacob hadn't been on the train the next day, so on Friday Sarah steeled herself for the possibility she might never see him again. She hoped if he didn't appear today, at least there would be a letter telling her what had happened in the meeting with his commander. She strode into the depot prepared for Matthew's barbs but was relieved when she spied Clara Wingard already at work.

"Am I late or are you early, Clara?"

The older woman swung around and waved a napkin in the air. "I'm early. It was either come here and help you set up or listen to some of the ladies at the general store argue about whether the president should have replaced General McClellan with General Burnside. Personally, I don't think any of them know enough about fighting a war to offer an opinion, but to hear some of them go on, you'd think they'd been planning battles all their lives." Clara hesitated a moment. "Maybe if you count some of the battles they've had with their husbands. . ." She unfolded an apron and tied it around her waist. "With many of their men gone, I'm sure they sorely regret those now."

Sarah strode toward one of the tables and nodded to Clara to grab the other end. "There's a lesson to be learned from this, Sarah."

Sarah's brows knit in confusion. "I don't have a husband, and my brother and I quit squabbling when we were children. Why do you think this applies to me?"

"You don't need a husband to learn that it isn't wise to argue with those you love. Even more, you should never part on bad terms." Clara's eyes clouded. "One time I had a close friend, a girl I loved like a sister. We had a fight over a fella when we were nineteen years old, and I told her I never wanted to see her again. Two days later she was struck by a runaway wagon and died. I've lived with regret over that argument and what I said to my friend ever since." She shook her head as if trying to shake off the gloom that colored her story and the sadness that still shone in her eyes. "So you see? You don't need a husband to understand the importance of what I'm saying."

"I understand it's important, but how do things get settled if you don't let the other person know how you feel?"

Clara grinned. "You speak the truth in kindness, and keep on talking until you're sure there's no hard feelings left between you."

That sounded well and good in theory, but Sarah wasn't certain it would work. Right now, she didn't have time to dwell on the matter. The ladies of the Basket Brigade were bustling into the station, and she needed to keep her mind on the task at hand.

By the time the train arrived at the station, all was in good order, and Sarah did her best to keep her hopes in check. If Jacob wasn't on the train, she promised herself she would remain in good spirits. The wounded men on the train deserved her very best.

Still, when the train came to a halt, her gaze focused on Jacob's car, hoping, praying. . .

Then he bounded down the steps and across the platform. With the basket swinging from her arm, she hurried out the door to greet him.

He met her with a broad smile and grasped her hands between his. "I'm so happy to see you. I've been praying we'll have some extra time so we can talk."

Her heart lurched. Did he want the additional time so he could tell her he had received a new assignment and was going into battle? If so, she wasn't certain she wanted time for a lengthy talk. Together, they strode toward the train, and as he took her hand to help her up the steps, he leaned a bit closer. "I've missed you very much. Did you receive my letter?"

She nodded. "Private Nelson delivered it to me. He was a very helpful young man."

When he lifted his foot to climb up behind her, she gestured toward the station. "You've forgotten that we'll need the coffeepot, and you can bring the kettle at the end of the table."

He grinned. "Away for only two days and I've already forgotten the routine."

She watched as he loped toward the station. Her stomach tumbled like a bucket of rocks, and she felt worry crease her brow. How many more days would he be away? She pushed the thought from her mind. She barely had time to pass out the cups and utensils before Jacob reappeared. While he poured coffee, Sarah passed out ham sandwiches on thick slices of bakery bread, along with Clara's doughnuts that had been dusted with sugar and cinnamon. The boys cheered when they caught sight of the sweets. She wished Clara had been there to hear them.

One of the soldiers pointed to the basket. "If there's any extras, I'd be happy to help you out."

With a smile, Sarah handed him another doughnut. "I must

remember to tell Clara how much you liked her doughnuts."

Her basket was almost empty when Jacob stepped behind her. "I'm finished with the coffee. I'll pick up any empty cups as I pass back through the car. Come as quickly as you can so we can talk."

"I'll do my best."

Sarah took a moment to stare after him as he exited the car. Since his arrival, he'd been in good spirits. If he came bearing bad news, he was hiding it well. Then again, Jacob might consider his news pleasing while she would consider it disagreeable.

On the one hand, she wanted to hear what he would say, yet she also feared he would tell her he'd been reassigned. As she prepared to exit the train, Clara opened the door leading to the next car and waved Sarah forward. "I need some help in here. Two of the fellows with arm injuries have spilled their soup, and it needs to be cleaned up. Can you help?"

Sarah glanced toward the depot. Jacob would be waiting for her. Yet she couldn't refuse Clara's request. As she stepped into the adjacent train car, Sarah withdrew several of the dirty napkins and prepared to help sop up the mixture of broth and vegetables that had trickled down the aisle and beneath the swinging hammocks.

The task took far longer than she'd anticipated, and when they'd finally finished, Sarah rushed from the train and back to the depot. Jacob met her the moment she stepped inside. He took the basket from her arm and nodded toward a small alcove on the other side of the room.

"I'm sorry to keep you waiting. There was an accident in another car, and I needed to help Clara."

They'd just stepped into the alcove when the train hooted the warning whistle. Jacob frowned. "We don't have much time, but I wanted to tell you that the meeting with my commander went very well."

Sarah clenched her hands. "So he's agreed to send you to the front?"

"The front?" Jacob shook his head. "I didn't ask to be transferred into battle. I met with him to see if I could be permanently assigned to travel with the hospital trains."

Relief washed over her. "And?" Her heart pounded a new beat as she awaited his response.

"And he agreed." His lips curved into a generous smile, and his eyes twinkled in the glimmer of the candlelight that brightened the depot.

Without thinking, she reached forward and grasped his hand. "When Private Nelson told me you were meeting with your commander, I was sure it was because you wanted to request a change in your assignment. I'm so relieved—and happy."

He glanced down at her hand, and she immediately dropped her hold. "You're not the only one surprised by my news."

She arched her brows. "Who else have you told?"

He nodded toward the other side of the depot. "Matthew was in the café when I came inside the depot. He saw me and asked about my new orders—said Private Nelson had told him about my meeting with the commander. He seemed disappointed by the news and left me with the impression there was something more than friendship between the two of you."

Sarah bristled at the idea of Matthew filling Jacob's head with such a notion. Would he never cease with his interfering ways? Though she didn't want to use their few minutes together talking about Matthew, she didn't want Jacob to leave Decatur thinking she'd ever thought of Matthew as more than a casual friend.

When three short blasts suddenly sounded from the train, she knew she'd have to talk fast. "Matthew has wanted to court me for some time now, but I've told him in no uncertain terms I have no interest in him as a suitor."

Jacob looked toward the train. "I have to go."

He'd given her a slight nod, but he hadn't said he believed her. She hurried along beside him. "You believe me, don't you?"

"Yes, I believe you." He cupped her cheek in his hand. "We'll talk about our future when I return."

All the way home, Sarah hummed a happy melody. Jacob's parting words had planted a seed of happiness, a commodity in short supply. They didn't know each other well enough to make a lifelong commitment yet, but knowing he considered her a part of his future was enough to quicken her senses.

Just as she'd done when she'd been a little girl, Sarah spread her arms wide, turned in a wide circle, and took pleasure in the wet snowflakes that dampened her face.

Jacob walked down the narrow aisle of the train, his thoughts hopscotching between what Matthew had revealed and Sarah's parting words—her almost desperate plea that he believe her. When he'd said good-bye and stepped onto the train, he'd harbored no doubt she'd been truthful.

Now, with miles of train track separating them, his thoughts returned to Laura—the woman he'd expected to marry. The woman who had gone behind his back and married another. When he'd first heard rumors Laura was seeing another man, he'd quizzed her at length. For several weeks, she'd told him the gossip was unfounded. She, too, had begged him to believe her.

Back then, he'd set aside warnings from his parents and friends and had chosen to trust Laura. Two weeks later, she'd rewarded his faith in her with a broken engagement, a broken heart, and a broken hope for the future.

He wanted to believe Sarah but now wondered if her pleading words had been complete truth or merely words shaded by dishonesty. Was she, like Laura, hoping for someone better to come along while keeping him on a string? He wanted to believe that wasn't true. He wanted to believe Sarah was a woman with high principles. A woman who wouldn't toy with his feelings.

Chapter 11

The following afternoon, with her father's help, Sarah loaded their buggy with loaves of bread and fresh rolls.

"I think that's the last of it. Thank you for your help." She slid one last basket onto the seat before perching on tiptoe to kiss his cheek.

Her father leaned into the rear of the buggy and rearranged two of the bread trays. "Drive slowly or you'll have bread flying every which way. And make sure you return with all of the trays. I'll need them before morning."

"I know, Papa. Don't I return them each evening?"

He chuckled and nodded his head. "Yes, but a reminder never hurts. There's always a first time for everything. Besides, you would not be happy if you had to make a return trip to the train depot to retrieve them. Am I right?"

"Yes, Papa, you're right."

Her father assisted her into the buggy. She held the reins loosely in her hand, but before she flicked the leather straps, she met her father's gaze. "I think you should have the doctor call on Mama again. She was making progress, but last evening when I returned home and again today, it seemed she wasn't doing well."

"I'm afraid you're right. I think she pushed herself too much once the doctor said she was doing better. I'll go over and fetch him once I close the bakery."

Sarah hesitated. "I have time to go by his office before I go to the depot. Why don't I see if he's there? If not, I'll leave a note on his desk and ask him to call on her when he returns."

"That would be good." Her father gave a quick wave before hurrying back inside to the warmth of the bakery. Though summers in the shop were brutal, the heat provided by their ovens during the winter months was welcomed by both the family and their customers.

Sarah lightly flicked the reins, and when the horse didn't respond with much enthusiasm, she slapped the leather straps with a bit more gusto. "Get along, Blaze. I don't have time for you to move at that slow gait." The horse hearkened to her command and changed from a walk to a trot. When they arrived at the doctor's office a short time later, she tied the horse and hurried inside. She called out to the doctor, but the fading echo of the bell over the front door was the only response.

She had hoped to visit with Dr. Kirkland, but there was no telling when he might return. Instead, she used the pen and paper left on the desk for such purposes. Fortunately, no other notes requesting his ministrations littered the desk, so Mama should be his first visit when he returned to the office. Sarah uttered a silent prayer that he wasn't delivering a baby. When those blessed events took place, the doctor could sometimes be away for several hours or even the entire day.

Her inability to visit with the doctor would give her a little extra time at the depot. For once, she hoped none of the other women would arrive early. She wanted to have a talk with Matthew. He'd created discord with his comments to Jacob, and she was going to be clear: Matthew must refrain from such behavior in the future.

After traveling the short distance to the depot, Sarah stepped down from the buggy and tied Blaze to one of the iron posts situated outside the depot before removing two of the bread trays. Learning to balance two of the trays at one time had saved her countless minutes in the cold weather.

In spite of her pleas that he leave her alone, Matthew appeared at the door wearing his heavy coat. "Let me take those for you."

Sarah shook her head. "I'm fine. I've told you I don't need your help."

"Whether you need it or not, it's a gentleman's place to offer assistance to a lady in need."

Sarah didn't return his smile. "Is it a gentleman's place to hinder and hurt a lady, as well?"

"What's that supposed to mean?"

"It means you've both hindered and hurt me by telling Corporal Curtis untruths."

He reeled back as though she'd slapped him. "Are you saying I lied?"

She narrowed her eyes and gripped the trays harder. "Yes, that's exactly what I'm saying. What's more, I expect you to set matters aright when he comes through on the train this evening. You need to tell him that I have been consistent in my refusal to be courted by you and have been clear that I have no interest in you as a suitor. You know the truth, but you chose to mislead Jacob." She pushed past him and strode inside with Matthew close on her heels.

"I stretched the truth, but I did it for your own good. I'm a much better choice than Jacob Curtis. You barely know him."

Her eyes blazed with conviction. "You're right. I don't know him well, but in these past weeks we've learned a great deal about each other. Besides, how well I know him isn't any of your business!"

They both looked up as Clara Wingard and Nellie Hanson bustled into the depot with a rush of cold air following them. Nellie's gaze immediately settled on Matthew. "Since you're just standing around, could you go out to my buggy and get my other baskets? They're filled with jars of pickled peaches, and my rheumatism is acting up in this cold weather. Go on now."

Matthew's features creased in annoyance when he turned toward the door. He'd made certain neither Clara nor Nellie had seen his scowl, but Sarah hadn't missed it.

He grunted and pulled his cap low on his head. "I'll be going over to the hotel as soon as I bring your baskets inside, so don't plan any other work for me."

The depot door banged, and Clara rubbed her arms against the cold air as she stared after Matthew. "The way he slammed that door, I'm thinking he's mad as a wet hen."

Nellie chuckled. "That's 'cause he doesn't want to spend his time helping us old ladies. He's wanting to impress Sarah." She nudged Sarah's arm. "We all know how jealous he is because of Jacob."

Clara nodded. "She's right on that account. I've seen it with my own eyes. Matthew's not one who can hide his feelings."

Sarah's features creased into a frown. "If Matthew's said anything to make you believe there's something between us, it bears no truth."

Nellie winked. "Don't worry. We know what's what."

Matthew returned with the baskets of pickled peaches slung

over his arms and a pound cake in each hand. He placed the items on the table with a thud and stalked out of the depot.

Sarah watched as he snaked his way around the dining tables in the café and continued through the door leading to the hotel lobby. She'd no doubt angered him, but he'd overstepped his bounds. She'd had quite enough of Matthew Slade.

Chapter 12

As the train belched and hissed into the station, Sarah's anticipation reached new heights. Her stomach fluttered, and her heart pounded so hard she was certain anyone who came near would hear the thrumming beat. Her eagerness to hear what Jacob had to say about their future had monopolized her thoughts after she'd gone to bed last night. While she knew it was best to keep a level head in unknown circumstances, she wasn't certain how one attained such a feat.

This evening, she was determined to make time for him. Though he hadn't been wounded, Jacob was a soldier serving the Union and worthy of her uninterrupted attention. That's what she'd told herself, though she doubted the other ladies in the Basket Brigade would agree. Still, she wouldn't be deterred. The moment he stepped down from the train she exited the depot and motioned for him to join her.

His eyebrows dipped low and his features creased in confusion as he approached her side. "Are you not serving the men in my car tonight?"

"I'll go and finish once we've talked, but I asked two of the other ladies to attend to your car and they agreed."

A generous smile curved his lips. "You've made me very happy by taking special measures so that we can have time together."

"When you departed, you said you wanted to talk about our future. I'd like to discuss our future as well."

He lightly grasped her elbow and led her to the small alcove where they would have a bit of privacy. As she looked deep into Jacob's eyes, an unexpected yearning ignited deep inside. He cupped her cheek and whispered her name. In the flickering lamplight, his eyes shone with undeniable longing, and she tipped her cheek deeper into his hand, reveling in his touch.

"Although we've known each other only a short time, I asked to be reassigned because I wanted to be with you more often. In our short visits together, I've come to care for you a great deal. I think you already know that. I admit that Matthew's comments gave me some momentary concern, and I let my jealousy get the best of me. I'm sorry for my behavior. I handled the matter poorly, but I'm thankful we parted on good terms yesterday." His voice reedy, he inhaled a deep breath as if to gain the strength needed to continue. "Since then, I've had a chance to pray about the future, and I truly believe you are the woman I am destined to wed."

Sincerity laced his words, and Sarah's heart leaped with joy. He'd spoken the words she had hoped to hear—had prayed she would hear. She reached for his hand and clasped it within her own. "You've made me so happy, Jacob. I prayed your thoughts were the same as my own."

"Then you'll permit me to court you?" He lightly squeezed her fingers. "At least as much courting as I can manage, what with my travels back and forth."

"I can't think of anything that would give me greater joy. And you can be sure that I understand your time is not your own. The Union must come first for all of us, but I do feel much more fortunate than the ladies who love a man who has been sent to the front."

His eyes radiated love as he leaned down and placed a tender kiss on her lips. Then he smiled down at her. "I hope my kiss didn't offend you. I should have asked your permission."

She touched her fingers to the stubble that darkened his jawline. How wonderful to have these moments alone, for with their responsibilities, who could say when they would have another opportunity? When she voiced her thoughts, Jacob tapped his breast pocket.

"I have already received permission to return to Decatur by private train rather than on one of the hospital trains. That way, I can return as soon as the wounded soldiers are settled in at the hospital in Chicago. I figure that will give us at least two or three hours each trip, and there will be some days when there will be delays, so I may even have an extra day or two. And I don't want to hear any objections due to train fare. I've been saving my money, and I can think of no better way to spend it."

Sarah momentarily considered telling him that it might be best to save the money for their household needs should they decide to marry in the future, but she immediately pushed aside the thought. Even though they'd been discussing the future, voicing such a presumptuous statement would be unseemly. Talk of household furnishings should wait until there was a proposal and wedding plans. Besides, Jacob was right. They needed more time together, so purchasing train tickets made perfect sense.

"May I have one more kiss before we get back to our duties?"

Her stomach fluttered in anticipation as she tipped her head to look into his eyes. Her pulse thudded as she lifted her hands to his chest. She gave a slight nod, and he slowly lowered his head. His mouth took hers, his lips gentle and then more urgent as he deepened the kiss. She turned weak at his touch, and when he suddenly pulled away, her knees buckled and she leaned into him to gain her balance.

A shiver raced through her as he traced his finger along her lips. "I think we'd better get back to our duties before someone comes looking for us."

He was right. To have someone find them would cause no end of embarrassment—not to mention the gossip. Her name would be the main course at every dinner table in Decatur and a humiliation to her family. She took his arm as they stepped from the alcove, but already she missed the warmth of his embrace.

∞

Gray clouds draped the morning sky and were a close match for her father's gloom as he shuffled around the bakery. He'd been in a sour mood all morning. The doctor had arrived to examine her mother before Sarah had returned home last evening. While she understood her father's despair, the doctor's report hadn't been devastating. Perhaps something else was causing his glum behavior. Her stomach knotted. Was something wrong with Samuel? Had they received word but not told her?

Her father's shoulders slumped over the worktable as he kneaded a mound of dough, a job that could tire the arms of the strongest, especially when her mother wasn't here to take over for a short time so his arms could regain their strength.

Instead of sifting the flour for the next batch of loaves, Sarah stepped to his side and nudged his shoulder. "Let's exchange jobs for a while, Papa. I'll knead the dough and you mix up the next batch of bread."

She reached in front of him and plunged her hands into the dough, not permitting him an opportunity to object. He gave a slight nod. "I could use a rest. I miss your mama's help."

"I know you do, and I'll try to do more to help you."

His jaw twitched. "You can't do your job and mine, too."

"You're doing your job and Mama's, so if we divide the work, it will be easier. I'll do as much as I can when I'm not helping customers or making the deliveries."

Samuel was the one who had devised the plan to deliver bread. No matter the weather and no matter how weary he might have been, her brother had made certain that the orders were made in a timely fashion each day. When he'd joined the army, the deliveries had fallen to Sarah. While she didn't mind on days when the weather cooperated, she'd grown to abhor making the rounds when sleet pelted the buggy or the snow became so deep that she had to use the old sleigh. Her father had threatened to cease the deliveries when Samuel departed, but their customers had raised a hue and cry that made the cessation impossible. With many of the men away from home, having their bread delivered was one less chore for the ladies, and a time-saving pleasure they'd come to depend upon. They'd rallied against the idea with such vigor that neither her father nor Sarah had been left with a choice. The deliveries would continue, and Sarah would make them.

The frown that tightened her father's features slowly eased, and he nodded. "We will give it a try and see how it works—for both of us. You have your mother's duties at the train depot each day, too."

Though his mood had lightened, he still appeared lost in thought. "Are you worried about Mama—or Samuel?"

He glanced her way. "Both."

Sarah dug her fingers into the dough. "Have you had any news of Samuel? Something you haven't told me?" Her scalp prickled when her father didn't immediately answer. She withdrew her hands from the mound of sticky dough as panic seized her. "You have, haven't you?"

"We received a letter that had been sent by one of his friends. He'd given it to the fellow and asked him to send it to us if he was injured in battle. The letter held no particulars about his wounds or what had happened. Only a note in Samuel's handwriting, explaining that if we received the letter, we would know that he'd been injured." His voice cracked. "Or killed."

Sarah swiped her hands down the front of her apron as if the gesture could sweep away the unwanted news. A lump formed in her throat, but she pressed her father for further information. She wanted to know where the battle had occurred, if the letter had any sort of marking to indicate the place from which it had been mailed or any snippet that could offer a clue as to Samuel's whereabouts and the extent of his injuries, and when had it been received.

Her father waved her toward the worktable and the mound of resting dough. "You need to work the dough or the bread will not rise as it should. There isn't time to be idle." Instead of his usual commanding tone, his voice was thin and somber.

"Yes, Papa, but can I read the letter when I've finished?" She was hurt that she hadn't been told immediately upon her return home last evening or when she'd entered the kitchen this morning. If she hadn't quizzed her father, she wondered if he would have waited even longer to give her the news.

He nodded. "You can read it. I picked it up at the general store yesterday, but you'll discover the letter says nothing more than what I've told you."

Sarah had been in the general store to make bread deliveries to Mr. Logan yesterday morning, and he'd not mentioned any mail for their family. Then again, ever since Milo Wilson had left his job at the store to join the army, the mail didn't get sorted with any regularity. There was no telling how long it might have been sitting in one of the mailbags dropped at the depot. There was no denying Mr. Logan put the needs of his store first and his position as postmaster second, and many wondered if the town would be better served if the position was given to Silas Tait over at Maddox Mercantile. Of course, Silas wasn't the type who would agree to the position without first making certain that Mr. Logan had no objection.

When her father finally placed the first loaves in the oven and set the other bread to rise, he relieved her of her kneading duties and handed her the letter.

Her heart caught at the familiar sight of her brother's hand-writing. To think of him injured and lying in a hospital tent in the freezing cold caused her hands to tremble. What would she do without Samuel? Until Samuel went off to war, they'd always been together. Inseparable twins, they had been more than brother and sister—they were best friends and confidants.

Sarah pored over the letter, seeking any word or phrase that might give her some clue, but her father had been right. She gleaned nothing further from the missive. Disappointed, she scooted off the stool and shuffled across the room. Her father gestured toward a shelf where he stored supplies, and she tucked the letter alongside a large crock.

"Does Mama know?"

"Yes. I asked the doctor if I should tell her. He said it wouldn't affect her condition and thought I shouldn't withhold the truth, but I'm not so sure I did right. She barely slept, and I heard her crying last night. I think it would have been better if I hadn't said anything." After a glance toward the stairway, he turned back toward Sarah. "Maybe you should go up and spend some time— cheer her a bit. The bread won't be ready to deliver for quite a while."

She nodded and turned toward the stairs. Her father's request was reasonable, yet how could Sarah cheer her mother when she needed cheering herself? She silently chastised herself as she climbed the steps. Her mother needed to be comforted, and her needs should come first if she was going to recover. Sarah straightened her shoulders and silently prayed that the Lord would heal her mother and that He would give Sarah the peace she needed to encourage her.

The carpet runner in the hallway muffled Sarah's footsteps as she approached her parents' bedroom. She stopped near the door and peeked into the room. Her mother's hair lay fanned across her pillow, and her eyes were closed. But then, her mother's eyes fluttered open, and she motioned Sarah forward. "I'm not asleep. I was praying. Come sit with me. Your father has told you the sad news. I can see it in your face."

Sarah sat near her mother's side. "I don't think he would have told me if I hadn't asked why he was so gloomy."

Her mother's lips tipped into a sad smile. "You know your father. He thinks he should keep all the bad news to himself and bear the burden on his shoulders alone. If Dr. Kirkland hadn't told him I was strong enough, I think he would have withheld it from me. If he had done so, I would have been furious when I finally discovered he'd heard something and hadn't told me." Her forehead creased in a frown. "We must increase our prayers for Samuel and all of our boys who are fighting for us. The Almighty is our only answer in all of this."

Her mother burst into a fit of coughing, and Sarah reached behind her pillow to lift her into a more upright position. "You should remain calm, Mama. When you become emotional, your cough worsens. We have all been praying for the safe return of our boys. Every evening after we've prepared to serve the wounded, the ladies of the Basket Brigade gather together and we pray until the train arrives. And you know that I have been praying for Samuel's safekeeping since the day he departed."

"I know." Her mother's response was barely audible before she began to cough anew.

Sarah shook her head. "Don't try to talk right now."

When the raspy coughs finally subsided, Sarah held a cup of water to her mother's lips. After her mother took several swallows, Sarah lowered her to the pillow. "Maybe I should come back later."

Her mother grasped her hand. "No. I want you to stay with me a bit. I'll be fine. Tell me about the ladies of the Brigade and how things have been going."

For the next half hour, Sarah set aside her own sadness and regaled her mother with the success she'd experienced working with the ladies. "They have been so helpful and willing to do whatever I ask of them. The challenge of meeting the trains and serving the men has changed me so much, Mama."

"I'm very proud of you, Sarah. I do wish I could be at the depot serving our wounded soldiers, but I rest easier knowing you're there. I know that meeting that first train and seeing the soldiers was very difficult for you, but your success is truly admirable."

"I'm only sorry it took me so long to trust that the Lord would be with me when I'm serving the wounded soldiers."

"And He is with you in every other circumstance, as well. At times, we all tend to forget that whether good or bad—the Lord is with us always." Her mother squeezed her hand, and her features brightened. "Now, tell me whatever happened to that soldier you thought was so nice? The one who was so kind to you during your first days on the train."

Sarah was surprised her father hadn't mentioned Jacob's visit to the bakery, but perhaps he'd thought it would cause her mother undue worry. Sarah had refrained from mentioning Jacob, as well. Not because she worried that news of a beau would concern her mother, but because she'd wanted to know Jacob better before talking about him. In truth, Jacob's jealous nature and lack of trust had been troubling. However, yesterday's apology had erased any problems between them, so Sarah was now eager to share news of Jacob.

An unexpected warmth spread across her cheeks as she recalled Jacob's kisses, and she wondered whether her mother had noticed a change in the way she spoke or acted. Did her eyes twinkle when she mentioned his name, or did the flicker of a smile play upon her lips and reveal the bloom of first love?

"The nice soldier is Corporal Jacob Curtis, and we have become quite fond of each other. I've never been in love with a man before, but I believe I am in love with Jacob."

There was a glint of apprehension in her mother's eyes. "In love? You haven't known him for very long, my dear. Don't you think it's a bit soon to speak of love?"

Sarah sighed and placed her palm across her heart. "I know we haven't been able to spend a lot of time together, but my heart tells me this is love."

"I understand, but sometimes the heart can deceive us. What we think is love could be merely infatuation and doesn't last for long. I think before you speak of love, you need to know this young man much, much better. Your papa courted me for two years, and I had known him for several years before that. Even with all that passage of time, there was much we didn't learn about each other until after we married. What of his past? Has he spoken of his life before he joined the army?"

Her mother's brow furrowed with worry. Perhaps Sarah shouldn't have confided so much. "We have exchanged letters each time Jacob comes through on the train. I have told him about growing up in Decatur and my life with you and Papa and Samuel. His letters have been filled with much of the same. I understand that letters are not the same as time with one another, but it has helped us become better acquainted. Jacob is a good man, and I believe he would be an even better husband. But you need not worry—he hasn't asked me to marry him."

She had hoped her lighthearted tone would ease her mother's concern, but tight lines continued to border her mother's lips. Sarah's effort had fallen short. Reaching for her mother's hands, she clasped them within her own. "Let's pray, Mama—for Samuel and his comrades, for our country, for your healing, and for the peace that only the Lord can provide."

Chapter 13

As the days passed, Sarah stopped at the general store each morning, hoping there would be word from Samuel. Each morning she'd been disappointed, and today was no different. She didn't want to believe her brother's injuries were so extensive that he couldn't take pen to paper, and she wouldn't let her thoughts go far enough to even consider the possibility that he might be dead. She would not let that word become a part of her vocabulary.

When she arrived at the depot, her cape was heavy with the wet snow that had begun to fall earlier in the morning. The weather had been much warmer over the past few days so the flakes melted as they drifted to the ground. The pristine white had turned the roadways into a murky sea of slush. Sarah had remained as far from the roadway as possible to avoid the passing carriages and wagons that showered all in their path with a slurry of snow and mud, but one racing carriage had spattered the side of her cape and her wool skirt.

Once inside the depot, she strode across the room and stood near the fire hoping the muck would quickly dry. Any attempt to brush off the damp mixture would further stain her garments. She'd had little time to dry off before Matthew ventured into the room.

His gaze settled on her sullied clothing. "Appears you may have been walking too close to the road. I went out a little while ago. It's a mess out there."

She didn't want to converse with Matthew and hoped her silence would cause his return to the hotel desk. When he strode off, she exhaled a sigh, pleased her silence had garnered success. The heat from the fire had created the desired effect, and Sarah turned to the side to dry the remainder of her cloak.

As the warmth enveloped her, Sarah's thoughts returned to Samuel. Was he in a hospital tent without a fire or blankets to warm him while she enjoyed the warmth of the bakery ovens and the wood-burning stoves that heated the depot?

She startled when Matthew touched her shoulder. "I brought you a clothes brush."

His gesture was kind, but she didn't wish to encourage him. She refrained from looking at him and offered only a quick thank-you.

"I'd be glad to brush it for you after you begin setting up for the train." His broad smile revealed an uneven front tooth, the result of a fight over an apple when Matthew had been only nine or ten.

Apparently, even her quick thank-you was too much encouragement. "That's kind of you, but I can take care of it myself. Thank you for the use of the brush. I'll see that it's returned before I depart." Her dismissive tone was intended to end their conversation, but Matthew remained at her side.

"Any further word about Samuel?"

Word of her brother's letter had quickly spread through the

town. Her father had told every person who came into the bakery and then asked for their prayers for his son. Sarah shook her head. "Nothing more."

"I'm sorry. Other than his recent letter, how long had it been since you'd heard from Samuel?"

"We had a short note after the siege at Corinth telling us that he'd made it through without injury, but nothing else until his recent letter."

Matthew's brows knit. "If I remember right, the battle at Corinth was last spring. I'm surprised Samuel doesn't write more often."

Would he never leave? "He may be writing more often, but who can say if or when we'll ever get his mail? The only information we have to rely upon is what we read in the newspapers and even that information is outdated by the time it's printed."

"You're right about the newspapers, and most of the time you can believe only about half of what you read." He shook his head. "I know it must be hard. The not knowing." The sympathetic words had barely escaped his lips when he gestured across the depot to a large message board, where community notices were often posted. "I was wondering if you planned to attend the Christmas musicale. Miss Evans brought me an announcement to put up in the hotel and another for the depot."

The quick change of topic caused Sarah to suspect that his concerns for her family might be less than genuine. She stared at him, overwhelmed by his lack of sensitivity, once again certain that her silence would bring him to his senses.

Instead, he continued to blather on. "I hear tell Miss Evans has the group practicing most every day, so it should be a good program. I think you should attend. The music would lift your spirits, and I think we owe it to the singers to support their efforts." He stopped only long enough to inhale another breath. "So, do you think you'll be going?"

Sarah hiked a shoulder and glanced toward the tables that still required her attention. "Much will depend upon my mother's health. I'm not making many plans right now. I'm. . .busy."

His features tightened. "Seems you're able to make time for Corporal Curtis when he's around."

She longed to escape this conversation but had nowhere to go. "I make time for him because we work on the train together."

He shook his head. "Do you think I believe that's the only reason you're around him every time he arrives at the station? I'm not a fool, Sarah. You may believe you're quite sensible, but I'm not so sure."

Matthew turned and stomped off. Clearly, she'd angered him.

Jacob leaned close, whispering in Sarah's ear. "I wish I could draw you into my arms and comfort you right here. And then I'd kiss you in front of all these ladies."

In spite of the cold, Sarah's cheeks warmed at his words. "I don't think that would be wise, but it pleases me to know you'd like to kiss me. And that you care about my pain."

"How are your parents—how are they faring?"

His kindness touched her heart. "They're about the same. The only thing that will bring joy is word that Samuel is alive and well, but who can say how long that may take? In the meantime, let's see to the soldiers. I'm sure they're eager for something warm to eat."

Jacob had only a few minutes to tell Sarah he would return on the train coming back from Chicago the following evening before offering a hasty good-bye. They would have had more time together if Sarah hadn't taken so long with one of the soldiers near the rear of the car. He'd done his best to hurry her along, but she'd taken extra time with the fellow, who had been far too forward—at least that's how Jacob had viewed the situation. Still, he'd said nothing to Sarah. His jealous nature had already caused problems in the past, and he didn't want Sarah to accuse him again of thinking her untrustworthy. Especially since she was worried about Samuel.

The train rumbled through the darkness that had descended over the bucolic countryside between Decatur and Chicago. The fleeting glimmer of candlelight in distant farmhouse windows was the only evidence of life outside the train. The darkness provided the soldiers ample time to sleep or be alone with their private thoughts.

Jacob's eyes were heavy with sleep when one of the wounded called to him. A low groan escaped his lips. He had hoped for at least a couple of hours of sleep. As he pushed to his feet, he silently chastised himself for his selfish thoughts. His body remained unscathed by battle wounds, and his mind didn't reel with haunting visions of dying and maimed comrades or the frightening sounds of canon fire.

Careful to maintain his footing, Jacob picked his way down the narrow aisle toward the soldier. Snores of the sleeping men were occasionally interrupted by the shouts of a soldier frightened by a nightmare, but except for the soldier who had called to him, all remained quiet this evening.

When he arrived at the young man's cot, Jacob leaned close. "How can I help? Do you need a drink of water?"

"No. I wanted to ask if you come through Decatur often?"

"Yes. I travel with most all of the trains that carry wounded soldiers from Cairo to Chicago. Once I arrive in Chicago, I return with the hospital train. Why do you ask?"

The soldier reached into his breast pocket. "There was a young lady—real pretty—who brought one of the baskets through. She was serving us soup, and then she brought some biscuits and rolls for us, too. You know which one I mean?"

Jacob smiled and nodded. "That was Miss McHenry. She helps me in my car most every time we stop in Decatur."

"Is her first name Sarah?"

Jacob's voice caught in his throat. What was this about? How did this soldier know Sarah's given name? Had she been overly friendly and told him her name? Did this fellow now harbor some romantic notion about a possible future with her? Surely she wouldn't have encouraged such a thing. He and Sarah had healed their earlier misunderstandings, and he didn't want to believe she would do anything to jeopardize their blossoming relationship. No—he was letting his imagination take flight and plant foolish thoughts in his mind. The last thing he needed to do was rush to judgment.

"Well, is it?"

The soldier's question pulled Jacob from his wandering thoughts. He nodded. "Yes. Her name is Sarah. How did you know? Did she tell you?"

The soldier shook his head and slowly uncurled his fingers. A silver, heart-shaped locket lay in his palm. "This here locket has the name 'Sarah' etched on the outside. I was thinking it must belong to her." He tapped his finger to the clasp. "Looks like this here fastener broke and it ended up on my cot."

Jacob reached forward and lifted the locket from the young man's palm. He rubbed his thumb over the etched impression that formed Sarah's name in a delicate script. Jacob tucked it into his pocket. "I'll make certain it's returned to Miss McHenry." He hesitated a moment. "In the unlikely event it doesn't belong to her, please know that I'll search for the rightful owner."

The soldier thanked him, and Jacob returned to his seat, his hand tucked deep in his pocket. As he lowered himself onto his seat, he withdrew the locket and turned it over in his hand. He'd never seen the locket around Sarah's neck, but perhaps she placed it beneath her clothing. He'd heard tell that many ladies wore lockets given to them by their loved ones beneath their dresses so that it would be closer to their heart. The thought sent fear racing through him. His pulse quickened as he tightened his fingers around the silver heart. He longed to push down on the tiny clasp along the outer edge of the heart, the metal closure that would open the heart and reveal the inner contents of the locket. However, opening the piece of jewelry in the darkness of the train made little sense. He'd wait until they arrived at their next stop and he'd go inside the Wenona Depot, where he'd be able to gain a good look.

His fingers remained wrapped around the locket until he stepped off the train in Wenona. He bowed his head low against the blowing snow that assaulted him as he hurried toward the doors of the depot. Suddenly, his foot slipped on the snow-dampened wooden platform and sent him sailing. With the locket still tight in his fist, he yanked his hand from his pocket to break his fall. He hit hard on his hip and wrenched his ankle, but he soon managed to push to his feet and hobbled inside.

A lone man stood behind the ticket counter inside the depot. "You all right? Looked like you took quite a fall out there. I told the supervisor they need to post some signs about the platform being slick, but he didn't listen."

"A few lanterns would help, too. I don't think I could have read any signs even if they'd been posted." Jacob transferred the locket to his left hand and briefly massaged his hip. No doubt there would be a huge bruise by the time the train arrived in Chicago—and he'd be required to endure the soreness that would surely follow such a spill. When pain shot through his ankle, he leaned forward to loosen the laces of his boot to allow for any swelling.

The old man behind the counter pointed at Jacob's boot. "Be sure you tie that up before you go back out to the train. Don't want to step on one of those laces and end up on your backside again. You want some coffee? I got some boiling over there on the stove. You can help yourself." When Jacob shook his head, the man stepped from behind the counter. "Well, I guess I could get it for ya, what with you not walking so good."

Jacob didn't really want the coffee, but he accepted the cup and thanked the man. Though he didn't encourage him, the ticket master sat down on the bench beside Jacob and chattered about the weather, news of the war, and the number of trains that would be coming through in the next few hours. He was relieved when an older couple entered the depot and walked to the ticket counter.

The depot manager sighed and pushed to his feet. "Sorry to leave ya alone, but I need to see to these folks."

"That's quite all right. I know you have a job to do." Jacob downed a swallow of the coffee and immediately sputtered at the bitter taste of the hot liquid. After placing the cup on the bench, he removed the locket from his jacket. Their stop in the small town would be only long enough to take on wood and water, and he was sure the whistle would soon alert him to their impending departure.

He snapped open the clasp and the locket fell open. His breath caught as he read the inscription: *To the Sweetest Girl.* On the opposing side of the locket was the picture of a handsome young man in uniform.

How could Sarah do this to him? No doubt the young soldier had given her the locket before he marched off to join his regiment—to remember him—to hold him close to her heart. Well, she may have held his locket close to her heart, but she hadn't remembered him or held him close. And it now seemed that, like Laura, she hadn't been true either to him or Jacob.

Chapter 14

For the remainder of the journey to Chicago, Jacob was besieged by a combination of confusion and sorrow. The pain from his fall at the depot only served to make matters worse. His ankle continued to swell, and his hip throbbed with an ache that matched the gnawing pain in his heart.

His hand remained deep in his pocket, with the locket chain threaded through his fingers. Though his duty required him to assist each of the men off the train and into the makeshift ambulances that would deliver them to the hospital, his own injuries now prohibited him from performing his duties. When an attendant from the hospital finally entered their car, Jacob explained his mishap.

"I'm not going to be any help getting the men off the train. Corporal Franklin is in charge of the injured soldiers in the adjoining car. Once they've unloaded, I think he'd be willing to help you with my men."

The hospital attendant stooped down to inspect Jacob's ankle. "You'd best stay right here until we get you a crutch. That ankle might be broken, so it will be better if you don't put any weight on your foot. I'll see if I can find one for you, and then I'll speak to Corporal Franklin."

Jacob thanked the soldier and scooted down to rest his head against the hard wooden seat. He felt useless sitting there while the soldiers remained in their cots, each one eager to be off the train and transported to a hospital bed. Yet he had no choice, for even before the hospital attendant had examined his ankle, Jacob suspected it was more than a slight sprain. Fortunately, the men understood his plight and didn't complain—at least not much.

When the last of the men had been moved from the train, the attendant returned with a pair of crutches for Jacob. With the attendant holding one of his arms, Jacob gingerly stood on his good foot and situated the crutches beneath each of his arms. The attendant moved back and Jacob took a swinging step. Careful to keep his right knee bent and the injured foot in the air, Jacob and the attendant made their way to the steps where another man awaited them.

"We'll lift you down. We don't want you trying to use those crutches on the steps." The attendant didn't wait for Jacob to agree. Instead, the two men took his crutches and hoisted him down from the train.

Being lifted from the train into a makeshift ambulance left Jacob feeling dependent in a way he'd never before experienced. He hoped he wouldn't ever again face such a need. No doubt the injured soldiers suffered the same feelings each time they required help. Jacob hadn't considered how the need for assistance could gnaw at his manhood. Little wonder some of the soldiers became angry and abrupt whenever he attempted to lend aid.

The fact that Jacob's injuries had occurred on a slick depot platform rather than during a skirmish only caused him further anguish. The doctors were needed to treat wounded soldiers, men who had been injured in battle—not a clumsy corporal assigned as an escort. If his father, who already considered Jacob's military assignment an embarrassment, ever got wind of this event, Jacob would never hear the end of it. When Jacob closed his eyes, he could still hear the pride in his father's voice as he spoke of his brother, Malcolm, fighting at Antietam. Indeed, a fall on a slippery platform would provide his father with enough ridicule to last a lifetime.

The wagon ride to the hospital had been bumpy, and with each lurch of the wagon, pain stabbed his hip like a hot poker. Though the wagon had been covered with a makeshift canvas and the men were wrapped in the quilts and blankets the good ladies of Decatur had provided, their teeth chattered and they huddled close together. The freezing winds that crossed Lake Michigan assailed them with a piercing iciness that cut to the bone, but Jacob didn't complain. Shivering, he held fast to the locket and prayed his heart wouldn't turn as cold as his freezing fingers.

Once the wounded soldiers had been assisted into the hospital, the medical staff took charge with tactical precision and assigned each of the injured soldiers to a specific hospital ward. Jacob, however, was taken to an examination room, where the doctor pronounced his ankle badly sprained. Though Jacob objected, the doctor insisted the ankle would be more seriously injured if he returned to duty before the swelling diminished and the ankle had time to strengthen. Had the doctor been a civilian rather than an officer in the army, Jacob might have disobeyed. He silently cringed when he was transported to a ward filled with amputees who'd lost limbs while fighting for the Union. They'd likely have a good laugh at him when they discovered his injury had been received while trying to navigate a slippery depot platform.

He threaded the locket's chain through his fingers and settled his head against a lifeless pillow. When Jacob had departed the train, Corporal Franklin had offered to notify friends or family of Jacob's whereabouts. For a fleeting moment, he'd considered sending word to Sarah but then changed his mind. Perhaps she could use the additional time to write letters to the fellow whose picture she carried in her locket.

∞

Sarah stood inside the depot as the train returning from Chicago huffed into the station the following day. She remained with her nose pressed near the glass until the train eventually departed. Maybe she'd misunderstood, but she was sure that Jacob had said he'd return on this train. Slowly, she made her way out of the depot and returned home. There had been no word of a mishap with the train. If an accident had occurred, a message would have been received at the depot. And if Jacob had been detained somehow, she was certain he would have sent word.

Her breath caught. Maybe Jacob sent word and Matthew hadn't told her. Sarah turned on her heel and hurried back to the station. Once inside, she passed through the café and entered the hotel.

Matthew leaned across the counter as she approached. "This is a surprise. Have you come to join me in a cup of coffee?"

Sarah shook her head. "No. I wondered if a telegraph had come about the hospital trains. The ones that return from Chicago to Cairo to pick up more of the wounded soldiers."

He pushed up from the counter and squared his shoulders. "This is about Corporal Curtis. Am I right?"

She gave a slight nod. "I thought perhaps he sent word he'd been detained in Chicago. He was supposed to have come through on the train returning to Cairo today."

Matthew hiked a shoulder. "How many times have I told you that you can't depend upon the promises of a soldier during wartime, Sarah? You think Corporal Curtis is different, but I'm telling you that he isn't. Maybe he was offered an opportunity to leave his assignment on the hospital trains and he jumped at the chance."

"You're wrong. Jacob has no intention of requesting a change of assignment."

Matthew arched his brows. "You go ahead and believe whatever you want. I know how men think. Jacob may tell you he's happy to stay away from the fighting, but I know better."

Sarah studied him a moment, regretting the entire conversation. Matthew wouldn't tell her the truth even if he had received word from Jacob. "You may think you know better about other men, but I know Jacob, and I'm certain he's told me the truth."

"Why do you think some soldier you barely know is more trustworthy than me?"

Recollections of Matthew's many half truths and deceptions flooded her mind. She wanted to tell him she knew how he'd tried to take advantage of Elsie and how he'd told Johnny Folson to stay away from the depot, but she'd given them both her word. She'd have to remain silent, but hearing Matthew continue to argue against Jacob only strengthened her resolve.

"Is it because I'm not wearing a uniform? Is that why you want nothing to do with me? You think I don't know half the town calls me a coward behind my back? Why wouldn't I believe you think the same way?"

She was weary of him and just wanted to be home. "You know this has nothing to do with wearing a uniform or joining the army. If I had my way, not one man in this town would be off fighting in the war, so don't accuse me of refusing your suit because you aren't wearing a uniform."

By the way he just stood there, she knew there was no need to continue their conversation. She wasn't going to change her mind, and neither was he.

"If Jacob should send a message, can I rely upon you to deliver it to me?"

"That's my job." His jaw was tight as he met her eyes.

She turned to leave but stopped short. "No one has mentioned finding a locket, have they? I thought I'd worn it when I came to the depot yesterday, but now I can't seem to locate it anywhere. I've looked at home and I've asked most of the ladies of the Basket Brigade, but no one has seen it. I thought perhaps someone might have found it while sweeping up."

"The locket Samuel gave you?"

Sarah bobbed her head. "Yes, have you seen it?"

"There's been nothing turned in to me, and I'm sure my mother would have known it was yours and given it to you if she'd found it. If it should turn up, I'll let you know."

Sarah mumbled her thanks and trudged toward home. The loss of her locket had been foremost in her mind until she'd been confronted with Jacob's unexplained absence at the depot. She bowed her head low against the frigid wind as feelings of hammering defeat assailed her. Where was her locket—where was Samuel—and where was Jacob?

The bell over the bakery jingled, and her father glanced up when she stepped inside. "Hurry and close the door, Sarah. It's cold out there."

Tears stung her eyes. She'd barely cleared the threshold before he'd chastised her. "I'm sorry, Papa. I know it's cold. I walked home from the depot." She pulled her scarf from around her neck and strode toward the stairs.

"I'm sorry, Sarah. I was more worried about keeping the bakery warm than about my daughter's welfare. Forgive me. You should go upstairs and fix yourself some tea and warm up. Maybe sit with your mother for a while. I know she misses you."

"I'll do that, Papa."

Once she'd brewed the tea, Sarah carried the tray to her parents' bedroom.

"What a lovely surprise. How did you know I was longing for a cup of tea and some time to visit with you?" Her mother scooted higher in her bed while Sarah placed the tray on a nearby table.

"Let me arrange your bedding so that you're more comfortable." Sarah plumped the pillows and then stepped to the table and poured tea into the two cups. "I'm sorry I haven't spent more time with you, but it seems there's always something. . . ."

"No need to apologize. I know you're kept busy with your duties in the bakery and with the Basket Brigade. I don't want to be an additional burden."

"You're not a burden, Mama. I love spending time with you, but there aren't enough hours in the day."

"Is that why you appear so sad? You've forced a smile onto your lips, but I see sorrow in your eyes. Is there something beyond the letter from Samuel that's caused you unhappiness?"

She nodded her head and quietly revealed her concern that Jacob hadn't been on the train from Chicago. "To make matters worse, I've lost the locket Samuel gave me before he left Decatur. I've looked everywhere and haven't been able to find it. Nothing seems to be happening as it should. You're ill and the doctor can't seem to help; Samuel's whereabouts and well-being are a mystery; Jacob has gone missing; and my locket has vanished."

Her mother brushed a strand of hair from Sarah's forehead.

"Tell me—have you prayed and asked for God's help?"

"No, I haven't." A pang of guilt stabbed her. Why hadn't she thought to pray? "I seem to always think I must solve problems on my own, and forget to pray, until I realize I have no solution."

"Don't be so hard on yourself, Sarah. All of us have times when we are so consumed by our problems that we rush to solve them ourselves instead of stopping and seeking God's guidance. God understands, but He does want us to come to Him with our needs. Now that you've done everything you can think of to resolve your problems, maybe the two of us should pray together. Would you like that?"

Sarah reached forward and lightly grasped her mother's hand. "There's nothing that would help me more. Thank you, Mama."

Together, they bowed their heads. When they'd said their final amen, Jacob and Samuel still hadn't appeared and her locket hadn't been found, but a sense of peace had settled in Sarah's heart. Finally, she had released her worries into God's loving hands.

Chapter 15

Jacob didn't particularly want to attend the church service that a local pastor conducted each Sunday at the hospital, but he did want to escape the confines of the medical ward. Since his arrival, he'd been quizzed by almost every patient—at least those who were conscious enough to be aware of his existence. Though none of them had laughed at his mishap and a few had even expressed their thankfulness for the help they'd received from military attendants on the hospital trains, feelings of inadequacy and the picture in Sarah's locket continued to plague him. The church service would provide a brief diversion.

"All them that's coming to hear the preacher, raise your hand if you need help getting down the hall." A young medical attendant stood in the doorway leading into their ward.

"If I ain't got a hand anymore, can I raise my foot?" A patient who looked to be about thirty years old guffawed and raised his leg high in the air after he'd shouted the question.

The attendant laughed with him. "You can raise anything you want as long as it ain't a ruckus. Glad to know you're in such good humor today, Corporal Williams."

"I aim to please. Now, find someone to help me out of this bed so I can go to the church meeting."

Jacob longed to help the man, but the doctor had adamantly refused to let him bear weight on his ankle. Although he was now permitted the occasional use of crutches, the amount of help he could offer the other patients was limited.

Once inside the meeting room, Jacob took a seat near the front and glanced around. Though it was good the hospital allowed space for church services, the room was a close match to the one he'd just left. Granted, no beds lined the walls, but he was certain the chipped plaster and thin, faded window coverings were a far cry from the stained-glass windows and ornately carved wooden pews that likely adorned the large Chicago churches. Though he'd never attended a church with such finery, he wondered if the city had a group of women like those in Decatur—women dedicated to doing their best to help the wounded soldiers. If so, a bit of refurbishing to make the room more appealing and providing the men with Bibles would likely be appreciated. Maybe he'd mention his idea to the doctor when he next visited. Surely the doctor would know if the women of Chicago had formed a Ladies Auxiliary to aid in the war effort.

Jacob pushed aside thoughts of the gloomy surroundings as a young private stepped forward.

The young man motioned to his left and then his right. "I'm in charge of the music, and as you can see, there's no piano or other instruments to accompany us. You need to sing out, and I'll do my best to lead you. We're going to sing Christmas carols, so most of you will know the words. Let's start with 'Silent Night.' "

A Pinch of Love

The men joined in, their voices blending—at least for the most part. Corporal Williams sang with gusto, although he was off-key for most of the song. He didn't seem to notice the arched eyebrows and shudders of those around him. Corporal Williams was a man filled with joy in spite of his injuries, and the realization caused Jacob a twinge of guilt. How could a man be so joyful even though he'd lost his right hand as well as his left arm up to his shoulder?

They'd barely finished the last notes of "Silent Night" when Corporal Williams called out, "How about 'Away in a Manger'? That's my little boy's favorite."

A son? How would Corporal Williams ever teach the boy to fish or hunt? Even more, how would he earn a living to support his wife and that little boy? Jacob wondered whether the man had even considered life beyond the walls of the hospital. If so, it was difficult to imagine how he maintained such a positive outlook.

When they had finished singing, the pastor stood and greeted them before thanking God for the opportunity to meet and worship. After the prayer, he opened his Bible to the second chapter of Luke and read the familiar verses about the birth of Jesus.

When he finished reading, he closed the Bible and glanced around the room. "I know that each of you is suffering, and this Christmas is going to be very different from any other Christmas you've ever celebrated. So I thought that instead of me preaching a sermon, maybe some of you would like to share a little with each other. Christmas away from home and family is challenging. It's even more difficult when you've suffered injuries that will forever change your life."

A deafening silence fell over the room. Jacob had been sure Corporal Williams would speak up, but the boisterous man quietly stared at the floor. Moments later, the shuffle of feet could be heard near the back of the room, and a dark-haired soldier stepped forward.

"I believe I have something I'd like to share with all of you."

Jacob's breath caught as he stared at the man. He reached into his pocket, removed the locket, and snapped the clasp. He stared at the young man pictured in the locket and then looked at the soldier standing at the front of the room. The likeness was undeniable. His stomach clenched, and he tightened his hold on the silver locket. So this was Sarah's beau. He was as handsome in person as in the picture. Jacob moved to the edge of his seat, not wanting to miss a word.

The young soldier glanced around the room and smiled. "Most of you don't know me. I've been here for a while, but when I arrived at the hospital, I wasn't conscious. The last thing I remember was being in the middle of canon fire and the lieutenant shouting orders for us to charge the lines. I'm not sure what happened to me. The doctor says I was probably struck on the head and knocked out. He was beginning to wonder if I'd ever wake up. Now that I realize how long I've been lying in a bed resting, I'm amazed, too. In fact, I count it a real miracle that I was carried off the battlefield and brought to this hospital, where the doctors have declared me fit as a fiddle."

The muscles in Jacob's stomach tightened. *Fit as a fiddle—and likely going back to Decatur to Sarah.* He should be pleased for the young man, but the thought of losing Sarah to someone else had taken hold and now consumed him.

The young man cleared his throat. "Since regaining consciousness, one thing has become very clear to me: we don't know how long we have on this earth, and while we're here, we need to use our time wisely. Instead of holding grudges, finding fault, and harboring jealousy, we need to truly love one another as the Bible commands. With God's help, I know I can do better from here on out. I know some of you are facing terrible hardship with your injuries, and it's easier for me to say these things now that I've returned to good health. Turning free of grudges and jealousy won't heal our bodies, but it will heal our hearts and our souls."

The words pierced Jacob's heart. Maybe he wouldn't enjoy a future with Sarah, but wasn't it more important that he do what this young man suggested so that he could move forward and accept God's plan for his future? He bowed his head and silently prayed that God would grant him the capacity to release any feelings of jealousy and give thanks that Sarah's beau hadn't been killed. When he lifted his head, the knot in his stomach was gone. While several other men were speaking, the hurt, confusion, and jealousy he'd experienced over the past days was now replaced by a sense of acceptance and peace.

At the end of the meeting, the song leader stepped to the front. "Let's end our time together with one final Christmas carol. Let's join together in 'O Come, All Ye Faithful.'"

Jacob lifted his voice along with the other men, and as he sang the words, he prayed that he would remain joyful and triumphant no matter what the future might hold. As the song ended and the men filed from the room, Jacob waited and, leaning heavily on his crutches, moved alongside Sarah's beau.

He reached into his pocket and clasped his finger around the locket. "I have something I'd like to give you."

A flicker of doubt shone in the young man's eyes. "You don't look familiar. Should I know you?"

Jacob shook his head. "No. We've never met."

"You had me doubting myself for a minute. I was worried that my memory hadn't returned as well as I'd thought."

"I think this belongs to someone you love." Jacob opened his hand to reveal the locket resting in his palm.

The young soldier's eyes opened wide and then glistened with tears. "Sarah." His voice was no more than a whisper and cracked with emotion. "How did you get this? I gave it to her the day before I left Decatur."

Jacob gestured to a wooden bench in the hallway. "Why don't we sit down? I'm not very good with these crutches." Once they were seated, Jacob shoved his hand into his pocket, already missing the touch of the heart-shaped locket. "The locket was found on the hospital train that passes through Decatur. One of the wounded soldiers found it. He gave it to me so I could return it to her. I saw the picture inside the locket and could barely believe my eyes when you stepped forward to speak this morning."

The young man wiped away his tears while Jacob continued to explain his assignment on the hospital trains and describe the injury that had caused him to become a patient at the hospital.

"I can't believe Sarah is working with the wounded. I've received only a letter or two from her since leaving Decatur. The mail doesn't keep up when you're on the march as often as we were. In her last letter, she wrote about the women helping on the trains, but I was sure she said she couldn't bear the thought of seeing the wounded men so she wasn't going to help."

"She had a change of heart and is in charge of organizing the distributions each evening. Most of the ladies think she's an excellent leader. She did have a bit of trouble being accepted by a couple of the ladies, but they've come around and accepted her as a leader."

The young soldier chuckled. "I'm guessing one of those ladies would be Emma Wilhoite. She's not a woman who's quick to take orders from anyone, especially by someone Sarah's age. The Wilhoite sisters are very active in church and community events. Maggie is rather quiet and unassuming, but Emma prefers to take charge whenever possible."

A faraway look shone in the soldier's eyes, and Jacob guessed that he was attempting to picture the scene with Miss Wilhoite. Then again, perhaps he was simply remembering Sarah's beauty and sweet spirit. The thought pained Jacob. Though his decision to rely upon God was firm, his wound remained deep. He'd had to suffer through this same agony with Laura and had determined that he'd never allow another woman to steal his heart. He marveled at how easily he'd broken that personal vow when he met Sarah. Yet if he didn't forgive, he'd remain bitter and never move forward—his life would be worthless.

"Don't you agree?" The soldier lightly nudged Jacob's arm.

Jacob's brow creased. He'd been lost in thought and hadn't even heard the young man's question. "Agree?"

"That the ladies of Decatur are quite fine to come up with their Basket Brigade?"

Jacob gave a firm nod. "Absolutely. You can't imagine the excitement on the train once the men learn there will be home-cooked food as well as personal items to help keep them warm. When the train comes to a stop in Decatur, you see a spark of hope return to their eyes."

"You are a fortunate man to have had the privilege of serving them."

Jacob nodded as he recalled the anger he'd harbored when he'd first been assigned to the trains. How much had changed in such a short time. "You're right. It is an honor to serve them, though I must admit that wasn't my initial reaction to the assignment, and my request to be permanently assigned to the trains wasn't completely noble."

"How's that?" The soldier leaned forward and rested his arms across his knees.

Jacob revealed how he'd initially railed against the assignment with his commander. "I wanted to go to the front and fight. I knew

I would never receive my father's praise unless I was off in the middle of a skirmish."

The young soldier arched his brows. "Sad to hear that a father would wish his son assigned to a position of danger. I'm glad to hear you had the courage to go against his wishes and request the permanent assignment. What was it that caused you to make that decision?"

Jacob inwardly winced. "As I said—it wasn't completely honorable. I met a young woman, and I didn't want to miss out on seeing her when I was traveling back and forth between Cairo and Chicago."

"So you met a nice young lady on one of the stops along the way. I can see how that would influence your decision, but I think you were placed in your position because you truly have the heart of a caring person who is willing to serve others. Have you considered the fact that the nice young lady might be a special gift from God? Perhaps the Lord saw a change in your heart and sent the girl into your life because you have willingly been serving others."

Jacob shook his head. "No. I didn't willingly serve until after I met the young lady. It turns out she wasn't such a special gift—at least not for me." He pointed toward the locket the soldier still grasped in his hand. "Seems we both love the same woman."

The soldier's jaw dropped, and his eyes shone with surprise. "Sarah? You're in love with my sister?"

"S–s–sister?" Jacob gestured back and forth between the soldier and the locket. "Sarah McHenry is your sister and not your sweetheart?"

A boisterous laugh escaped Samuel's lips. "She's my twin sister and I love her dearly, but what caused you to think. . ." His gaze drifted to the locket. "Oh, I understand. You read the inscription and thought it was from her beau. I can see how that happened, but Sarah really is the sweetest girl I've ever known, so that's why I chose to have it engraved in the locket. One day I may meet and fall in love with a woman I find as sweet as Sarah, but that hasn't happened yet."

"So you're Samuel." Jacob looked away as a rush of heat infused his cheeks. His heart pounded inside his chest with such force that he thought it might explode. After the despair of believing Sarah had betrayed him, he could barely comprehend the depth of what Samuel had just now told him. His mind reeled as he attempted to grasp the truth. If he revealed that he'd ever doubted Sarah, Samuel would likely think him unworthy of her affection.

The thought caused Jacob to scoot to the edge of the bench. "Unfortunately, I sometimes tend to jump to conclusions, especially when it comes to young ladies."

While Samuel quietly listened, Jacob detailed the overwhelming sense of loss and betrayal he'd experienced when Laura had broken their engagement and soon married another man.

"I can understand how such an experience would cause a man to view the actions of other women with a lack of trust, but that's unfair, don't you think? You can't expect Sarah to step in and take the punishment for the misdeeds of another woman. When you falsely accuse her and believe she's lied to you before you've even talked to her, that's what you're doing—you're shifting your anger and loss from that other woman onto Sarah."

"I know you're right. After you spoke in the service this morning, I prayed and asked God to help me overcome my ill feelings so that I could move forward with my life without bitterness and doubts. Your words made me realize how wrong I'd been."

"I believe it is God's providence that we met today, don't you?" He patted Jacob on the shoulder.

Jacob choked back the emotion that flooded over him. If it

hadn't been for that accident at the train station, he would have already returned to Decatur and likely would have falsely accused Sarah. Would he have even given her a chance to explain? If he'd given her an opportunity, would he have believed her without affirmation from someone else? The thought that a severely sprained ankle had given him the opportunity to save his future with Sarah was a gift beyond measure.

Jacob met Samuel's gaze. "Yes, I do believe God intervened and saved me from making a complete fool of myself and ruining my future with Sarah. Who would ever think a person could be thankful for taking a spill on a train platform."

Samuel chuckled. "Just proves that God can use even painful circumstances to change our lives."

The two men stood, and Jacob positioned the crutches beneath his arms. "Has the doctor said when you'll be released from the hospital? I know your parents and Sarah have been worried about you. Have you written to them?"

Samuel shook his head. "I was unconscious until day before yesterday, and the doctor said he's sending me home, so I figured I'd get there before the mail. Unless something changes, I'm leaving on the hospital train that passes through Decatur tomorrow. I'll have two weeks at home before I report back to duty. I'm looking forward to surprising them."

"You know your mother's been ill? Sarah said she wrote and told you."

Samuel's eyes widened. "If she wrote, I never got the letter. What's wrong? Nothing serious, is it?"

"I'm not sure. Sarah tells me there's some improvement for a short time and then she worsens again. I'm sure that seeing you will have a good effect on her."

Samuel appeared lost in thought, but shouts from one of the

rooms brought him back to the present. "How about you, Jacob? The doc ever going to let you get off those crutches and return to duty?"

"He says a few more days and he'll let me get out of here. Wish I could return on the train with you, but I think one surprise at a time is enough."

Samuel frowned. "I'm not sure I understand. Why would Sarah be surprised to see you?"

"I never sent word back to Sarah after I was injured. In the past, whenever I had a change of orders, I made sure I sent a message with one of the other soldiers, but this time I didn't."

"Because you were confused and hurt about the locket?"

Jacob bowed his head. "I didn't know what to say to her. Maybe I could write a letter and you could take it when you go back."

Samuel shook his head. "I think some things are better said in person. I'll tell Sarah that you're in the hospital and, once you're released, you'll explain things to her."

Jacob hesitated. "That's fine, but I'm not sure exactly what I'm going to tell her. If I reveal my doubts, she may not want to have anything more to do with me."

Samuel sighed. "I won't tell her what we've discussed—that's up to you to decide. But good relationships aren't built on lies or deceit. They're built on trust, and love and truth. Why don't you pray about what you should do when you return to Decatur?"

Jacob agreed he needed to do his part to build a strong foundation. But if he told Sarah of his misconception that she cared for another, would she reject him? The risk seemed far too great.

Chapter 16

Since Jacob's absence, Sarah had met all the trains that returned from Chicago. Matthew had been reticent to give her the schedule, but he'd finally relented. He now appeared pleased he'd done so. Each time the trains arrived, he took pleasure in pointing out Jacob's absence. This afternoon had been no different.

When Jacob didn't appear, Matthew came alongside Sarah. "I see Jacob is still nowhere to be found."

"It's unkind to take pleasure in my unhappiness."

He shrugged and several strands of dark hair dropped across his forehead. "I'm sorry you're sad, but I'm not surprised by what has happened. I knew you couldn't trust him."

"That's your opinion, Matthew, but I know I'll hear from Jacob, and I don't believe he requested a change of orders."

Sarah turned to leave, but as she looked out the window and across the platform, she caught sight of a man in uniform. "Samuel!" She ran toward the doors, and as he entered, she flung herself into his arms.

Her brother hugged her in a tight embrace. "I'm glad I saw you coming and had a good footing. Otherwise, we would have both landed on the floor. You are as wonderful as I remember."

"We've been so worried. Your friend sent the letter you'd written, and we've all been fervently praying." She stepped away and let her gaze linger on him. "You don't appear to be injured. Tell me what happened."

"Let's go home and I'll tell you everything. I want to see Mama and Papa as soon as possible."

Matthew stepped forward and clapped Samuel on the shoulder. "Good to have you home, Samuel. We've all been worried about you. Care for a cup of coffee?"

"Thanks, Matthew, but I'll have coffee with you tomorrow or the following day. Right now, I want to see my parents." Samuel placed his arm around Sarah's shoulder. "Let's go and see if Mama and Papa are pleased to have another mouth to feed for a couple of weeks."

∞

After their joyful but exhausted parents had gone to bed, Samuel and Sarah remained in the small parlor enjoying the warmth of the crackling fire.

Samuel stretched his hands toward the heat. "I'd forgotten how nice it was always to have a fire burning in the hearth. When the enemy was close, we weren't allowed to light fires, and the cold became unbearable at times. It's good to be home."

She reached forward and patted his shoulder. "We're so thankful to have you here and to know that you are safe. Your presence is the best Christmas present we could have. God has truly answered our prayers."

"There's something else I wanted to talk to you about now that Mama and Papa have gone to bed."

Sarah arched her brows. She could think of nothing he would share with her that he wouldn't tell their parents. "What is it?"

"I met a young corporal who is a patient at the hospital in Chicago. We met at a chapel service there." Samuel reached into his pocket and withdrew the locket. "He gave me this."

Sarah stared at the necklace, unable to believe her eyes. "My locket! I've looked everywhere for it."

"It appears the clasp is broken. One of the men on the hospital train found it and gave it to Corporal Curtis. I believe you know him quite well."

"Jacob? You met Jacob?" She reached for his hand, unable to contain the urgency swelling in her chest. "Tell me. Where is he? Did he receive orders sending him to the front?" One after another, the questions spilled from her lips until her brother finally waved her to silence.

"I'll answer what questions I'm able to, and Jacob can answer the rest when he arrives in Decatur."

"He's coming here? So he wasn't sent to the front?"

Her brother chuckled. "How can I answer if you continue asking more questions?"

"All right. I promise I'll be quiet. Just tell me what you know."

When he'd completed the brief tale of their meeting in the Chicago hospital, Sarah smiled. "I'm so glad that he found the locket and recognized you. It's astounding that the two of you met. He's wonderful, isn't he?"

Samuel smiled. "He seems like a fine man who is growing in his faith, and I believe he loves you very much."

Warmth spread through her when he spoke those words. She had believed Jacob loved her, but when he'd disappeared without a word, she'd begun to doubt his intentions. Her brother's confirmation of Jacob's love gave her comfort. Yet why hadn't he sent word?

"Whenever Jacob wasn't going to be on his regular route, he would always send a note with one of the other soldiers so that I wouldn't worry. This time, he didn't send word. I've been so worried about what happened to him, and I don't understand why he didn't send a message. I'm sure there must have been opportunity for him to do so during the past few days."

She stared at her brother, hoping he would give her some explanation. While she could understand Samuel's inability to communicate with his family, Jacob had only an ankle injury. He could still write a note.

"I think you should talk to Jacob about that. If all goes as expected, he should be on the train the day after tomorrow. I think he can better explain his reasons."

Sarah had hoped for more, but she wouldn't pursue the matter. Her brother didn't like to be pushed.

"How are plans for the Christmas musicale? Does Miss Evans have everyone hard at work practicing their parts?"

The sudden change in topic affirmed the fact that the subject of Jacob was now closed.

∽

When Jacob arrived at the station two days later, Sarah was eagerly awaiting him. His crutches had been replaced by a cane. He'd attempted to convince the doctor he didn't need either but had lost the battle. His heart swelled as Sarah rushed toward him, and in spite of the many passengers on the platform, he wrapped her in a warm embrace.

"I'm so happy to see you. I didn't expect you to be here."

She lifted her face and looked into his eyes. "I've met every train coming from Chicago since the day after you left Decatur. I knew you'd be on one of them. I just wish it hadn't taken so long or that I would have known that you were in the hospital so I wouldn't have worried."

A pang of guilt stabbed him and he nodded. "I know I should have sent word. I'll explain everything."

Sarah clung to his arm as they crossed the platform and entered the station. "I have the buggy waiting out front. I didn't want you to have to walk far."

Her thoughtfulness touched him. He didn't deserve her kindness. He didn't deserve her trust. He didn't deserve her. Since his talk with Samuel, Jacob had spent a great deal of time in thought and prayer. While he knew he was soon going to tell her about his past betrayal and his recent confusion and pain, he had hoped to wait for just a little longer. He had planned to enjoy a short reprieve and delight in her presence before telling her why she hadn't heard from him. But she was eager for answers to countless questions, and she shouldn't have to wait any longer.

He leaned heavily on the cane as they crossed the station and walked outside to the awaiting buggy. A light snow had begun to fall, and Sarah tipped her head back, looked toward the sky, and stuck out her tongue. "I love to try and catch snowflakes on my tongue. When Samuel and I were children, we would sit on the steps outside the bakery doing this. Eventually the customers became familiar with our antics and didn't think we were sticking our tongues out at them."

Jacob chuckled and then stopped and stuck out his tongue. He waited until he felt the dampness of a snowflake before he closed his mouth. "I'm not sure I'd have had the patience to do this when I was a child. I was more interested in making snowballs and tossing them at my friends."

"I must admit we had our share of snowball fights, too." She pointed to his leg. "Since your ankle isn't completely healed, are you expected to return to Cairo before Christmas?"

"No. The doctor released me from the hospital, but he signed orders that I couldn't return to duty until after the first of the year. Even then, I have to be examined by one of the military doctors in Cairo before they'll let me return to my duties on the hospital trains."

"So you'll be here with us for Christmas? How perfect it will be to have both you and Samuel at the table for Christmas dinner."

"I'm not so sure you'll want me at the dinner table once you hear what I have to tell you." His voice caught when he saw the fear that shone in her eyes. "We need to go somewhere quiet where we can be alone."

"Well, home won't work because I know my parents and Samuel are eager to visit with you." She hesitated a moment. "We could stop at the church. Choir practice doesn't begin for another hour."

Jacob nodded. The church would be the perfect place for him to reveal Laura's betrayal as well as the recent fears and jealousy he'd harbored since receiving her locket. He'd already confessed and received God's forgiveness. Whether Sarah would be as understanding remained to be seen. He'd done his best to prepare himself, but if Sarah walked away, he'd need every ounce of faith he could muster to carry on.

The church door creaked when Jacob pulled on the handle, but once they slipped into a rear pew, the building was eerily quiet. Sarah folded her hands in her lap and turned toward him. Detecting her fear and apprehension, he resolved to keep her waiting no longer.

As the story unfolded, he maintained a close watch on her. She pulled back when he revealed what he'd thought upon seeing the soldier's picture inside the locket and disclosed that his bewilderment and jealousy had taken hold. "I didn't send word because I didn't know what to say or think when I saw the picture inside your locket."

Jacob went on to detail all that Samuel had said in the chapel meeting at the hospital and how the message had impacted him.

"Even when I still thought Samuel was your beau, I asked God to forgive me, and I promised to accept whatever plans He had for my future. I know I don't deserve your understanding, but I'm begging you to give me another chance."

For several moments, Sarah remained quiet and seemed to consider all he'd told her. "Knowing what happened to you with Laura helps me understand so much of what's happened between us. I wish you would have told me before now. It also explains your confusion and lack of trust when you saw Samuel's picture in the locket. Still, I thought that you knew me better and believed me when I told you I didn't have a beau."

He bowed his head. "I know I've wronged you, and I apologize. If you can't forgive me, I understand."

Sarah reached forward and lifted his chin. "I forgive you, Jacob. I want to build a future with you, and I believe that what began as only a pinch of love will continue to grow if we are careful to leaven our union with truth and love. Please promise me there will be no more secrets."

"You have my word." He leaned forward and lightly kissed her lips. "I love you, Sarah. You're the best Christmas gift any man could ever hope for."

On Christmas Eve, Sarah, Jacob, and Samuel hurried off to the station to help prepare for the arrival of the hospital train. Sarah and the other ladies of the Basket Brigade had taken unusual care to prepare their best treats for the soldiers they would serve on this evening.

Along with sandwiches and kettles of soup and stew the ladies filled their baskets with jars of jams and jellies, a variety of cookies, and the oranges that had been specially ordered by Silas Tait. Bright red and green bows adorned the basket handles, and a few of the ladies even tied small bells to their hampers. Lucy Maddox and her group of ladies arrived with knitted socks, scarves, blankets, and quilts. Many of the items had been wrapped in brown paper and tied with colorful pieces of leftover yarn. They'd almost completed their preparations when Zona Evans and members of her singing group arrived and gathered on the platform where they would entertain the soldiers with Christmas carols while the Basket Brigade boarded the train with their food and gifts.

Excitement pulsed through the depot when the train chugged into the station and squealed to a stop. Though the doctor would not have approved, Jacob insisted upon helping Sarah deliver food to his regular car. He didn't know any of the wounded soldiers, but feelings of gratitude assailed him as he walked through the car handing out food and delivering cheer where he could. Gratitude that he'd been assigned to this position; gratitude that he'd met Sarah; and gratitude that God had forgiven him and directed his steps toward a future with Sarah.

After completing their deliveries, they stepped back to the platform and listened as the carolers continued to sing for the men. When the train whistled to signal the departure, looks of wistfulness shone in the eyes of soldiers who had gathered near the windows. All of them remained on the platform until the train was out of sight.

Once inside the depot, Jacob reached for Sarah's hand. "I have a special gift for you. I'd like to give it to you this evening rather than in the morning, if that's all right."

Sarah grinned. "I've never liked to wait to open presents."

Jacob led her to the far side of the depot to the small alcove where they'd first kissed, and he reached into his pocket. "I hope you like it."

A Pinch of Love

Sarah gazed at the small box that had been tied with a thin piece of red ribbon. Instead of the gift, Jacob stared at Sarah. He wanted to gauge her reaction when she opened the gift he'd so carefully chosen for her. When she lifted the lid and withdrew the heart-shaped locket pin, her lips curved in a huge smile, and her eyes shone with delight when she momentarily looked up at him before snapping open the locket.

"I was hoping I'd discover your picture inside. It's a wonderful gift, Jacob. Now I can keep both you and Samuel close to my heart."

He nodded, somewhat embarrassed by her praise. "I didn't have time to have it engraved, but I'll make sure there's an inscription before I go back to Cairo."

"And what words have you planned?"

"*To my future wife.*" He grinned. "Would that be acceptable?"

"That would be most acceptable."

He leaned down, wrapped her in a warm embrace, and captured her lips with a kiss to seal their future.

About the Author

Judith Miller is an award-winning author whose avid research and love for history are reflected in her novels, many of which have appeared on the CBA bestseller lists. Judy makes her home in Topeka, Kansas. You an find her online atwww.judithmccoymiller.com

Endless Melody

by

Nancy Moser

"My Dear Friend. You are not my husband nor son; but you are the husband or son of some woman who undoubtedly loves you as I love mine. I have made these garments for you with a heart that aches for your sufferings. . ."

—*Note accompanying an aid society shipment to the US Sanitary Commission's Northwest Branch at Chicago*

Chapter 1

November 1862
Decatur, Illinois

Zona Evans cringed.

She wasn't the only one.

The singing voice of Gertie Collins caused heads to turn, shoulders to rise, and eyes to squint. Three children who were too young to know that one did *not* cross Mrs. Collins if you wanted to enjoy peace in your lifetime did what their elders wished they could—covered their ears and made the faces they usually saved for their mama's lima beans or brussels sprouts. Luckily for all the adults present at the Decatur Auditorium, one child led the others on an exodus out of the building, saving themselves—and all present—from the singer's wrath.

If Mrs. Collins would have noticed. Which she couldn't have because of her habit of closing her eyes when she sang. The blissful look upon her face indicated she thought her notes Divine—with a capital *D*.

As the director of the auditions for the Christmas musicale, Zona knew it was her responsibility to end the torture. But she also knew tact was needed to sustain the aforementioned peace.

She raised a hand, then realizing the singer couldn't see it, raised her voice. "Would you open your eyes when you sing please?"

The torture paused when Mrs. Collins stopped singing. She looked at Zona. "What?"

"A singer connects with their audience through their voice *and* their eyes."

"Oh. All right."

She began again from the beginning, which made Zona kick herself for delaying the end of the song.

And Mrs. Collins did keep her eyes open for the first phrase. Then they closed yet again and she sang on, immersed in her own private fantasy world.

Before she began the second verse, Zona interrupted. "Thank you, Mrs. Collins."

The older woman stopped in midaria and blinked. "I can sing more."

I'm sure you can. "I've heard enough." Zona knew she should have couched her words, but sometimes cryptic honesty had its place. "Thank you. I'll let you know if you're chosen for a part."

Mrs. Collins strode to the edge of the stage and dug her fists into her ample hips. With her smallish head and largish middle, she looked very much like a two-handled sugar bowl. "Why wouldn't I get a part? I was always assigned the lead back in Springfield."

Zona wasn't sure what to say. Perhaps the people in Springfield had a smaller talent pool than she had in Decatur? *Had* was the key word. With many of the men off to fight the Confederates, Zona's choices had slimmed. But slimmed enough to let Mrs. Collins sing a solo in the musicale?

Zona read the eyes of the other auditionees awaiting her response. Pleading. *"Don't let her have a solo. Please."*

"You can be assured I always appreciate talent, Mrs. Collins." Zona was tempted to say more but decided against it. "Thank you." She turned to the next singer on the list. "Richard? Your turn."

Mrs. Collins flounced off the stage, letting her hoop skirt assault Richard's side as she whipped past.

Zona smiled at the boy, needing the sound of his lovely voice to erase the memory of Mrs. Collins's song. "How are you today, Richard?"

He bit his lower lip. "I'm not sure."

She was taken aback because Richard was a cheery boy, eager to use his voice in whatever capacity Zona chose. She already had him pegged to sing "O Holy Night" as a solo.

"Go ahead, son," Zona said. "Whenever you're ready."

He moved to the front edge of the stage, taking the place vacated by Mrs. Collins. But instead of her huff, he appeared humble. He squatted and spoke softly for her ears alone. "My voice is acting up, Miss Evans. I'm not sure you'll want to use me this year."

"Balderdash. You have a lovely voice."

"Had."

In that moment, Zona saw him with new eyes. He'd grown six inches in the last year, which probably meant. . .

She gave him another encouraging smile. "Let me be the judge."

He stood, took a step back, cleared his throat, and began to sing "It Came upon a Midnight Clear." By the second note, with its jump of an awkward sixth, Zona's fears were confirmed. Richard's voice cracked.

Zona heard giggles behind her to the right and flashed the

three female offenders a look that silenced them. She turned back to Richard, hiding her own distress in order to ease his. "You've become a man. That's something to be celebrated. Your voice will settle down, and when it does, you know you are most welcome on this stage. This year. . .perhaps you could help with the set design?"

He looked to the far corners of the auditorium, as if searching for something. Then he said, "Actually, I'm going to join the army with my brother. I want to go fight."

Zona shuddered. "You are not eighteen yet, Richard. They won't let you fight."

"I've heard of some boys *saying* they was eighteen and getting in."

The idea of true boys fighting in a war made her cringe.

"And if that don't work, then I'll be a drummer boy. I'm going with Timothy. We want to go together."

Mrs. Collins spoke up. "I'm sure that won't please your mother, young man."

"No, ma'am, it won't. But Pa says he's proud of us."

The sound level of the auditorium rose as people shared their opinions with each other. The thought of this sweet boy putting himself in danger made Zona want to take a train to Washington and tell President Lincoln enough was enough.

As if he would listen.

"Sorry, Miss Evans," Richard said. "Will you wish me well?"

Zona met him on the stage and pulled him into an embrace. "Of course I do. And I'll pray for your safety."

"Timothy's, too, please."

"Timothy's, too."

Unfortunately, Zona's prayer list for local boys was far too long.

☙

When the auditions were complete, Zona herded everyone out of the auditorium and closed the front doors. She blew out the kerosene sconces then made her way backstage and through another door leading to her private living quarters.

Mary Lou was setting the kitchen table for dinner. "Done so soon?"

Zona set down her notes and let the savory scent of stew warm her from the inside out. She lifted the lid and gave the stew a stir, only to have her hands slapped by her former governess and lifelong friend. "To answer your question, I'm home early because the pickings were slim."

"Speaking of someone who's *not* slim. . . Did Mrs. Collins audition?"

"Unfortunately."

"If you want something to do, slice the bread." Mary Lou sprinkled some pepper in the stew, gave the spoon a swirl, and put the lid back on. "I heard her talking at the mercantile. She expects at least one solo."

"So she told me. I have too many women and not enough men. Even Richard is unavailable because he's going off to fight with his brother."

Mary Lou was taken aback. "Both of them?"

Zona nodded.

"His poor mother." She shook the thought away and changed subjects. "Instead of three kings, you'll have three queens?"

Oddly, Zona *could* imagine Mrs. Collins wearing a fake beard.

Mary Lou moved the pot to another burner and covered the hot one with a burner cover. "Jeb Gruning joined up."

It took Zona a moment to change her thoughts from the pageant to the patriotic. "He's got to be in his fifties."

"Fifty-nine. Amelia is upset."

"Rightly so." Zona brought bowls close, and Mary Lou ladled in the stew. They sat at the table, bowed their heads for grace, then tore off pieces of bread and dunked them in the rich broth. "I used to be one of the only single ladies around, but this war has given me company."

Mary Lou shook her head. "Unlike the rest, you chose to live alone."

It was an old subject that still bore sharp teeth. Mary Lou was technically right, yet not completely. Fifteen years ago, Zona's fiancé, Cardiff Kensington, chose to leave her to fight in the Mexican War. She hadn't heard from him since.

She hoped he was alive. Prayed so every night.

Mary Lou reached across the table and touched her hand. "Forgive me. I'm grouchy today. It was wrong of me to open an old wound."

Zona offered a smile of forgiveness then pressed a mental hand on the sore subject, refusing to let the bleeding continue.

⌒

Dr. Cardiff Kensington sat in the office of his medical practice in St. Louis, staring at the door. The door had done nothing to earn his scrutiny. It was a simple six-panel door, painted white, the doorknob shiny brass only because there had been little else for his hired attendant to do these past six months except keep it polished. His office had never been in better order, with every bottle dusted and labeled, every surgical instrument laid in a row, ready to meet a patient's needs.

The door was of interest because of its lack of use. Cardiff couldn't remember the last time it had opened, letting in a patient who needed to partake of his curative abilities. Not that he wished accident or disease upon anyone. But to sit in the empty office day after day, accompanied only by the tick and tock of the mantel clock was driving him near crazy.

What distressed him the most was his lack of foresight in

anticipating this dearth of business. When the war started eighteen months earlier and the young men took up the call to arms, his thoughts and prayers went with them. He remembered heeding the call fifteen years earlier, when the United States had fought with Mexico over southern borders. He knew the lure of adventure in the name of patriotism. He also knew the awful trauma as adventure turned to panic and pain.

His lack of foresight involved those left behind. At the risk of being indelicate—even in his own mind—with so many men gone off to war. . .he couldn't remember the last baby he'd helped bring into the world. With no births, and no infants and new mothers needing care, his practice had dwindled to the occasional sprained ankle or sore throat. Nothing of particular interest, and nothing that provided an income that could sustain employing an assistant at all. He'd let Bobby go last month.

Cardiff's attention was diverted to the window as he saw Mr. Cooper peer inside. The man tapped on the pane and pointed at the door. At least the door would get some business.

Cardiff remained seated as Cooper entered the office, his jowls vibrating with the effort. Although he was in his twenties, his penchant for rich food and poor drink had made him a man of extravagant girth long before the time of normal age-related corpulence.

"Kensington."

"Cooper." It was not Cardiff's habit of omitting the Mister as he addressed any man, but in this case, since Cooper had yet to deem him worthy of his doctor-title, he followed suit.

"Are you joining up?"

Cardiff felt his right eyebrow rise. "Are you?"

"I am."

Cardiff's eyebrow lowered in shock. He restrained himself from sharing his initial reaction, which involved asking the question, "They'll take you?" His second thought was in reference to the Union army ever finding a uniform with the required yardage.

After a few moments of unspoken rudeness, he said, "Good for you."

Cooper's chins rose. "I join the regiment tomorrow."

"I wish you Godspeed."

Cooper let out a huff, as if Cardiff's response did not fulfill his expectations. "I thought you'd tell me not to go."

"Why would I do that?"

"Because of my gout. Because my mother needs me at home. Because—"

"Why did you volunteer?"

Cooper unbuttoned his waistcoat and lowered himself into a chair. "I didn't plan to. I was spurred into it by some friends who are going. Actually, many have already gone." He paused to corral a new breath. "Why aren't you joining up? You're not much older than me."

"I'm thirty-six."

"As I said. Plus, you have no family to keep you from service."

Cardiff didn't appreciate the latter remark. To answer his other point, Cardiff took hold of the cane that was hooked on the side of his desk and raised it. "This. This is my reason. I doubt a regiment would want a soldier who hobbles, ambling across a field of battle, unable to aim and shoot the enemy. I'd be killed in the first volley."

Cooper considered this a moment. "You could help in other ways." He spread his arms to encompass the empty office. "It's not like you're busy."

It bothered Cardiff that this fact had been noticed by others.

Having had enough of the conversation, he stood, employing his cane for support. "I wish you well, Cooper."

The man's fleshy cheeks reddened as he rose. "*I* will serve my country well and with honor."

"I'm sure you will."

Cardiff saw him out and watched him waddle across the street. When the clock behind him struck five, he locked his thoughts away and headed home for his evening meal.

Cardiff sat alone in his dining room, awaiting his roast beef and cauliflower. He knew what had been prepared by Mrs. Miller because it was Tuesday. He wasn't keen on cauliflower but did enjoy Tuesdays for the cinnamon butter cake that crowned the meal.

As if beckoned by Cardiff placing his linen napkin in his lap, Cardiff's butler entered the room and served the dinner. "Thank you, Gregory."

"Sir." Gregory moved to his place beside the walnut sideboard, his eyes straight ahead.

Cardiff bowed his head for a moment of silent prayer then ate his meal. When he was finished, he put his knife and fork across the plate and it was removed. Cardiff drank his glass of wine down to the one-third mark just as the plate of cake was set before him. Although he would have liked to ask for another piece, he didn't consider the inclination long. One piece was the norm, so one piece he would have.

The rest of his evening was spent in carefully determined segments of time, with each portion accomplished with the satisfaction of completing another neatly ordered day in a neatly ordered life. Although Cardiff suffered an occasional thought about Cooper and their earlier conversation, he didn't allow the discussion to ruin his evening. Cooper chose his course and Cardiff chose his.

Later, with the time for sleep upon him, Cardiff sat on the edge of his bed and removed his slippers, set his spectacles on the bedside table, hooked his cane over—

His routine was disrupted by a knock on the bedroom door. "Yes?"

Gregory came in, rotating a folded letter in his hands. "I am so sorry, sir. I don't know why I didn't remember to give this to you, and if you'd like to wait until morning, I will gladly keep it until then."

With a sigh, Cardiff motioned him forward. He immediately saw it was a telegram. "When did this arrive?"

"Just before you came home for dinner, sir. Again, I apologize for not giving it to you. Mrs. Miller had issues with the stove and my time was taken helping her and. . .it will never happen again." With a nod he left.

Cardiff opened the envelope and saw that the sender was Dr. Stephen Phillips.

DEAR CARDIFF:

I WRITE TO YOU AS A COMRADE AND FRIEND. YOUR HELP IS NEEDED AT ARMY HOSPITAL IN CHICAGO. PLEASE COME.

SINCERELY SP

Once again, Cardiff sat on the edge of the bed. He and Dr. Phillips were friends from the other war. Both had been commandeered to work as orderlies, assisting with amputations and battle wounds. Both had found purpose in medicine and had gone their separate ways in pursuing that occupation.

They'd kept in touch. Cardiff had settled in St. Louis to work under their wartime mentor, Dr. Niles, eventually taking over his practice. Stephen had gone to Chicago, working in a hospital there.

Cardiff's earlier conversation with Cooper about enlisting returned with a strength that forbade him from casting it aside.

"I will serve my country well and with honor."

Memories of gaping wounds, shattered limbs, and destroyed lives rushed into his mind. He pressed his hands against his eyes, willing the images to leave.

He didn't want to tend to soldiers again. He didn't want to enter that world.

He looked around his shadowed room. He was not a wealthy man, but he'd created a fine life for himself. His home was spacious enough for all his needs, its running kept on track by Gregory Miller and his wife. They were twenty years his senior, and Mrs. Miller had a bit of rheumatism in her hands, but they were capable and loyal. They depended on him as much as he depended on them. He couldn't leave them and this carefully established life to go north to relive a life he'd left far behind.

And Stephen shouldn't ask him to.

He refolded the telegram and set it on the bedside table. Then he blew out the lamp and went to bed. The chime of the clock noted that it was fifteen minutes past his bedtime.

Zona turned over in bed, feeling like a flapjack on a hot griddle. Odd thoughts fueled her restlessness, with Mrs. Collins's dreadful voice singing a duet with the squeaking young Richard. The issue of casting the Christmas musicale churned with no resolution, spurred on by a single image of a man from her past until—

She flung off the covers and sat upright. "Stop it!"

Fortunately, the voices of Mrs. Collins and Richard were silenced, the only sound being the heavy in and out of her own breathing. Zona cleansed herself of the moment with a deep sigh and rubbed her hands roughly over her face, trying to completely rid herself of the inner chaos.

But with her hands resting over her eyes, the image of Cardiff returned. His blond hair was swept smoothly to the side, his pale blue eyes like the aquamarine brooch she inherited from her grandmother: clear, light, and pure.

She got out of bed and went to her dressing table drawer, retrieving the daguerreotype of herself and Cardiff, which showed her sitting and him standing with a hand upon her shoulder. With an intake of breath, she realized that except for the lack of color, her mental image of him exactly matched the one before her. She slid onto the bench, squeezing her eyes shut, trying to capture a different image of his face.

Many moments appeared—and disappeared—like flashes of lightning on the horizon, but she couldn't hold on to any long enough to fully *see*.

"Is this the only way I can fully remember what you look like?" *Looked like.*

For this image was taken fifteen years earlier in commemoration of their engagement.

She looked at the image of the girl. It was hard to comprehend that this was *her*. Zona looked into the moonlit mirror in front of her then down at the picture. It was difficult to reconcile that both were the same woman.

And it wasn't just because she'd grown older in appearance. She was no longer the girl in the picture in any way but that they shared the same name and body. The girl who'd just become engaged back in 1847 was spoiled and used to getting her own way. She'd been proud of procuring a proposal from Cardiff and was certain she could get him to permanently work with her father in his printing business. She knew Papa would be very willing to pass the successful company on to Cardiff. And as such, Zona knew her life would continue along its previous path, living within blocks of her parents, with a multitude of friends she'd grown up with, three children when the time came (two boys and a girl), and a life made better because she would rise in stature to that of missus instead of miss.

A bitter laugh broke the moment, and Zona shut the photograph away in the drawer. Her life had no room for childish dreams or the regrets that were born when she realized they would never become a reality.

"Leave it be," she whispered, and got back in bed.

She was too old for dreams.

Or regrets.

Chapter 2

Zona brought her breakfast plate to the sink, still chewing her last bite of bread. "I'm off to post the cast list for the musicale, and then I'll go to Lucy's sewing bee to bring them the blanket you made." She glanced at Mary Lou's legs. "Your rheumatism must be especially painful for you to miss that."

Mary Lou sat at the table and rubbed her knees. "A storm must be coming."

Zona glanced out the window. The late-November sky was swathed in a coat of solid gray. She'd learned to believe in Mary Lou's knees. She put on her cloak and tied her bonnet under her chin then took up the neatly folded quilt Mary Lou had made for the soldiers on the hospital train.

She was just reaching for the cast list when Mary Lou plucked it away and had a look. "I don't see Mrs. Collins's name."

"No, you don't."

"She's going to be upset."

Zona held out her hand for the list. "I have to be true to the ensemble as a whole. I will not be bullied into choosing anyone who does not deserve to be included."

"Her husband is a powerful man in town."

Zona was well aware. The stage curtains were purchased due to a contribution by Mr. Collins, who owned a bank. "I'll find a way to use her. Everyone can contribute in a way that best suits their talents. Her talent simply does not involve singing."

Mary Lou shook her head. "Off with you, then. And may God be with you."

Zona laughed, but as she went outside to post the list, she repeated the prayer.

◯◯

The sewing bee at the Maddox mansion was buzzing when Zona arrived. The ladies were seated around the elegant parlor, their hands busy with various stitching and knitting projects. Lucy sat at a sewing machine as another woman cut squares out of fabric on the dining table on the other side of the foyer.

"Morning, ladies," Zona said, quickly closing the door against the cold air. "I've brought a blanket from Mary Lou. She sends her regrets, but her knees are acting up."

Lucy got up from the machine and nodded at the weather outside. "I wondered as much when it looked stormy." She took the blanket. "She does such beautiful work. Give her our thanks."

"I will." None of the ladies asked her to join them, which was fine with Zona. Sewing was not her gift, and the women had long ago made it clear her help was not needed in this capacity.

Zona remembered the letters in her pocket and placed them in the basket on top of the piano. "Here are two letters for the soldiers from myself and Mary Lou."

"Very good," Lucy said. "The men so appreciate kind words." Then she added, "Zona. . .we ladies were thinking that once Advent starts, it might be nice if you and some singers met the train every evening and sang Christmas carols. Would that be possible?"

Suddenly, a woman who'd been sitting in the corner stood up. "Oooh. I'd like to be involved in that."

It was Mrs. Collins.

"But," Mrs. Collins said, "I may not have time for that in addition to the musicale rehearsals. When do they start?"

Time slowed as Zona tried to think of an answer, and in the interim, she gained the gaze of the entire room.

"I. . .I posted the cast list this morning."

"Very good. Do we start this evening?"

If only Mary Lou's knees hadn't been hurting, Zona wouldn't even be here. Although a verse passed through her mind—*"And the truth shall make you free"*—she wasn't so sure. But what choice did she have?

"I'm sorry, Mrs. Collins, but your name is not on the list." *It's the list's fault, not mine.*

All movement stopped, and slowly all eyes moved from Zona to Mrs. Collins. The woman's breathing turned heavy, and her cheeks reddened. "There must be a mistake."

"I'm sorry, but this year there were so—" Zona was about to say "so many talented singers," but everyone knew the situation with the men gone off to fight.

"Are you implying others were more talented than I am?" Mrs. Collins's eyes widened, revealing a disturbing amount of white around her irises.

Zona scanned the faces of the other ladies, who one by one took solace in the sewing work on their laps. She was in this alone.

Mrs. Collins stood and tossed her sewing on her empty seat. "This is ridiculous. Back in Springfield I played the lead in every production and was *the* soloist everyone cherished."

Zona noticed a few eyebrows rise. "I'm sorry. Perhaps next year?"

Mrs. Collins strode into the center of the sewing circle, taking her place on the oriental rug as if there were an *X* marking her spot. "Let's let the ladies decide if I deserve to be in your silly musicale."

No!

But before anyone could stop her, Mrs. Collins cupped one hand in the other at bosom level, closed her eyes, and began to sing. "'Drink to me only, with thine eyes. . .'"

The ladies' reaction was immediate as eyebrows dipped and mouths grimaced. Then Zona had an idea. Perhaps if the woman *saw* her audience's reaction. . . "Remember to open your eyes, Mrs. Collins."

The woman nodded once, opened her eyes, and continued singing.

And then a miracle. As she sang, her eyes scanned the faces of her audience, and though the ladies politely tried to remove the pain from their faces, some were less successful or not swift enough to prevent Mrs. Collins from seeing their instinctive reaction to her voice.

Her facial expression changed from pride to panic. When she stopped singing, more than one woman let out her breath as relief took over the room.

Lucy began the applause, but the smattering that followed was pitiful.

Mrs. Collins turned a full circle. "I was that bad? Truly, my singing was that dissonant?"

"Not *that*," Lucy said, being the kind hostess.

Mrs. Collins pointed at her. "It was. I saw your faces."

Zona came to their rescue. She slipped her arm through that of Mrs. Collins. "Why don't we go into the dining room to talk about it."

Endless Melody

The woman who'd been cutting out squares on the dining table willingly relinquished the room, and Zona closed the pocket doors behind them. She offered Mrs. Collins a conciliatory smile. "I'm sorry I didn't choose you, but—"

"They cringed," she said. "They looked as if they were in pain!"

So what did you learn from this?

But what Zona assumed would be a moment of revelation. . .

"What's wrong with the people in this town? I have a lovely voice."

Zona was at a loss. If the women's reactions didn't make Mrs. Collins recognize the truth, there was little hope. She pulled out two chairs. "Sit down. Let's work through this."

Although the woman sat, it was only for a moment as she popped up and resumed her pacing. "What is there to work through? I am a woman of great generosity, willing to do the work that is required to share my gift. That the citizens of Decatur are blind to it. . ."

But not deaf.

The mention of her "gift" gave Zona an idea, which was solidified as she noticed Mrs. Collins's dress that sported a jaunty trim along the sleeves and bodice. "Did you make your dress?"

Mrs. Collins looked down, as if remembering what she was wearing. She smoothed her hands along the skirt. "I did."

"There you are. Look at your fashion sense. I don't know any other woman in town who would think of using that trim in such a delightful manner."

"Thank you. I ordered it from Chicago before the war."

"It's very lovely." Zona stood. "Would you be willing to be in charge of the costuming for the musicale? It's not an easy task as we have to make do with what clothing people have and the costumes we've kept at the theater from past productions, but I know with your creative eye you could make what's old seem new and fresh.

273

Singers, I have, but a woman with an eye for fashion. . . . I could really use your help."

Zona held her breath, waiting for her reaction.

Mrs. Collins fingered the edge of the trim on her bodice. "Well, perhaps. Actually, I think I would like that."

The tightening in Zona's belly eased. "I'm so pleased. You will be our official costume mistress."

A smile spread across Mrs. Collins's face. "I like that title. I accept."

Zona offered the woman her arm. "Shall we go tell the others?"

∞

"Here you are, Mrs. Byron." Cardiff handed her the packet of headache powder. "If you don't find relief, come back and I'll do a bloodletting."

She handed him a coin and left. When he saw that it was a quarter, he sighed. Not only had the war put a damper on his quantity of patients, but also their ability to pay. He usually charged a dollar for the office visit and twenty cents for the headache powder. And most of his wealthier customers wanted him to come to their homes, which meant he could charge higher fees. As such, he made a good living. Made. As it was, he wasn't making enough to pay the Millers. And he was not alone. With many of the men off to war, everyone's business had slowed.

He tossed the quarter into a dish on his desk and stood at the window, leaning on his cane. It was a good bet Mrs. Byron's quarter would be his total income for the day.

He spotted a young man he knew reading a recruiting poster nailed to the shop across the way. Cardiff had brought Will Thompkins into the world. Actually, Will was the first baby he'd ever delivered.

Will touched his fingers to the poster, on top of the word *You.*

RECRUITS! WE NEED YOU!

The thought of Will going off to fight spurred Cardiff to grab his coat, rush out the door, and cross the street.

"Will!"

The boy turned around. "Hello, Dr. Kensington."

Cardiff nodded at the poster. "You're not thinking of joining up, are you?"

The boy's fingers strayed toward the *You* again. "My pa and my older brother have gone off, and I can't stand just sitting here, not doing anything to help."

Cardiff thought of the Thompkins family. Will had three younger siblings. With Mr. Thompkins also gone. . . Cardiff put a hand on the boy's shoulder. "You're needed here, Will. You're the man of the family while they're gone. How would your mother survive without you here?" *How would she survive if you were killed?*

Will drew in a breath that made his shoulders rise, then let it out. "I know you're right, but don't all this make you want to help? Sitting here, doing nothing, seems wrong. Dishonorable."

His innocent face pulled with sincerity, his eyes revealing the depth of his heart. Will waited for Cardiff's response, yet Cardiff didn't know what to say. The boy's argument couldn't be disputed. Yet to agree to it would require him to take personal action he didn't want to take.

"Doctor?"

Will was needed here. But Cardiff wasn't. Images of Cooper and Dr. Phillips invaded his mind. Their words doggedly resounded in his head: *"I will serve my country well and with honor. . . . Your help is needed. . . . Please come."*

Cardiff was surrounded by these men, their words, the recruitment poster, and this earnest boy. He could make excuses and return to his empty office, go home for lunch—it was carrot soup day—and let today play out as yesterday had, and tomorrow would.

Or...

Cardiff took his own deep breath and released his answer, letting it loose of its own volition, for if he thought about it too much, he would find a reason to take it captive, and find yet another reason to lock it safely away for the duration of the war.

It was now or never.

"You have inspired me, Will. I do want to help. I do want to pursue the honorable choice."

The boy's eyebrows rose, and he glanced at Cardiff's cane. "You're signing up?"

"I have been called to other service at a hospital in Chicago where I will attend our soldiers, wounded in battle."

Will nodded. "That's terrific, Dr. Kensington. I'll feel better about my pa and brother fighting if I know you're there to help them if they get hurt."

He was naive, but Cardiff accepted the compliment.

"When are you leaving?"

First things first. He pulled a pencil from his pocket and jotted on a scrap of paper. "Would you take this to the telegraph office for me, Will?"

"Of course."

Cardiff's response to Dr. Phillips was short and to the point.

I'M COMING.

"But what about us, Dr. Kensington?"

Gregory and his wife stood before him in the parlor, deep furrows between their eyes. He understood he was blowing apart their neatly ordered world, which revolved around creating *his* neatly ordered world.

"I need you to stay here and take care of the house and my office."

"Without you here?"

"Without me here." He offered them a smile. "My absence will allow you to vary the menu, will it not, Mrs. Miller?" She often complained about his need for a culinary schedule.

"I suppose, but it won't be the same."

"No, it will not," he conceded. "But in many ways it will be easier, for you will have only yourselves to care for."

"But who will draw your bath and set out your suits?"

"And mend them," Mrs. Miller added.

Who indeed? Cardiff wasn't used to fending for himself, be it for meals or his daily toilette. "I will make do without you." He thought of a reason they couldn't dispute. "As a sacrifice to our country."

Gregory nodded once. "What about your patients? What will they do without you?"

"They will have to go to Dr. Smith in St. Charles." He did worry a bit for the emergencies that would no doubt crop up. But it couldn't be helped. "Our brave soldiers need me, and I must go." He said it as much for his own convincing as theirs. "Perhaps you could use this time to visit your daughter? She lives in Columbia, does she not?"

Mrs. Miller looked at her husband. "It *would* be nice to have time to visit. We haven't seen our newest grandson."

"Very good, then," Cardiff said. "Take this as a blessing in disguise."

It was good advice.

∞

"Go ahead, Anabelle. Play the song."

As twelve-year-old Anabelle played Zona's piano, she hit far more wrong notes than right. With a sigh, she stopped and let her hands fall into her lap. "The notes blur together. I can't do it."

"Of course you can. What have I told you about the posture of your fingers?"

Anabelle looked to the ceiling. Suddenly, she held her hands like she was mimicking a bear's paw.

Zona laughed. "I knew you'd remember, though you need to relax your fingers as you curve them." She took hold of the girl's hand and helped them relax from their animal-attack mode. "In order to smoothly move from note to note, you have to strike the key with the pad of your finger, not the length of it. Try again."

This time, there were far fewer mistakes. "There you are. Can you actually hear the music in it now?" As much music as there could be in the simple version of "I Dream of Jeanie with the Light Brown Hair."

Anabelle finished the song, her cheeks pink with pleasure. "I did it!"

"Indeed you did. Now, please remember: curved fingers."

"I will. I'll try."

Anabelle looked to her lap, and it was clear she had something on her mind. "I wanted to thank you for letting me be in the Christmas musicale, Miss Evans."

"You're welcome. You're a very good singer." *A better singer than a piano player.*

"Too bad about Richard's voice."

"Next year his voice will be all settled—though lower."

She nodded once. "I know a boy who sings prettier than Richard ever did."

Zona felt her eyebrows rise. "Why don't I know about this boy?"

"Cuz he's shy. I don't think he likes to sing in front of people."

"Then how have you heard him sing?"

She bumped shoulders with Zona. "He didn't know I was listening. He was walking a horse with a game leg from the Sandersons' to his grandpa's livery and was singing."

Livery. "Johnny Folson?"

Anabelle nodded. "He sings like an angel, Miss Evans. You need to get him for the musicale."

Everyone knew Johnny. He was ten or eleven and worked at the livery with his grandfather, but also did odd jobs around town.

"I'll go have a talk with him," she said. "Thank you, Anabelle."

⌒

"Miss Evans."

"Mr. Folson."

Johnny's grandfather removed a handkerchief from his pocket and wiped his face, which was glistening with the heat of exertion and the forge. "I don't remember you having a horse."

"I don't."

Johnny hauled in a bucket of water from outside, a layer of ice skimming its top. "Hello, Miss Evans."

"Hello, Johnny." She turned to his grandfather. "Actually, I came to talk to your grandson."

"You have some odd jobs that need doing?"

She hesitated, hating to lie but sensing a partial truth was the only way to gain a moment alone with the boy. "I may have."

Mr. Folson nodded to the boy and took up his hammer and the tongs that held a horseshoe ready for shaping. "Go on, then. But bring in more wood when you come back."

Miss Evans led Johnny outside. As snow was beginning to fall she got right to the point. "I hear you're a wonderful singer, Johnny."

He looked as surprised as if she'd told him he was a wonderful ballet dancer. "Who told you that?"

"Someone who's heard you sing."

He shook his head and scuffed at the snow. "I don't let nobody hear me sing."

She lifted his chin with a hand. "God says we shouldn't put our light under a basket."

"Huh?"

His eyes were the deepest hazel. "Your light—your gift of singing—is meant to be shared, not hidden." She dropped her hand. "Sing something for me."

"Now? Here?" He scanned the street, shaking his head. "I can't."

"Then come to my house when you're free today."

"Grandpa won't let me."

She thought a moment. "I do need help taking some props out of the storeroom. I'll pay you a nickel for your time."

He hesitated then said, "All right, then. I'll come." He turned to head back inside. "But I'll only sing for you, Miss Evans. No one else."

This could be a problem.

∞

A knock rattled the door.

Zona peeked out a window and saw that it was Johnny. "Go!" she said to Mary Lou. "Go upstairs or he'll never sing."

"I'm not sure this is wise, sneaking around his grandfather."

"I'm not hurting him. Now, go!"

Although grumbling, the older woman disappeared up the stairs. Only then did Zona open the door. "Johnny. I'm so glad you came."

He entered warily, looking around the small front room. "I can't be gone long."

"And you won't be. I promise."

She started to sit on the settee then realized it might frighten him by placing her in the position of being an audience. "Let's go into the auditorium."

She led him through the connecting door to the piano. She took a seat and patted the place beside her on the bench. "I do love Christmas carols, don't you?"

"I remember Mama singing 'em when I was little."

Little-er. She remembered hearing that Mrs. Folson had passed away in childbirth a few years previous. The baby had died, too. And now Johnny's father was off to war.

"Do you know 'Joy to the World'?"

When he nodded, she played the last few measures as an introduction then began to sing, to entice him into the song. "'Joy to the world, the Lord is come. . .'"

When he joined in, it was as though she had Richard back, yet a better Richard, for Johnny's voice had a simple purity that made her forget every other voice she'd ever heard. She let her own voice fall away and let him sing a phrase by himself.

He stopped singing.

She looked at him. "You have a tremendous gift."

He reddened, looking to his lap. "I like to sing."

"You are meant to sing. Born to sing."

He looked up at her, his eyes mournful. "Pa didn't think so. Grandpa doesn't think so."

"So they've heard you?"

He shrugged. "They heard me once, but they told me to stop because I reminded them of Mama and it made them sad."

"That makes *me* sad. Your mama was a good singer?"

"She was always singing. When she was cooking dinner or mending or tucking me in at night. She couldn't walk to the pump to fetch water without singing."

Zona put an arm around his shoulders. "What wonderful memories you have."

"I miss her."

"I miss my mother, too. And my father."

He looked at her with new eyes. "You don't have neither?"

She shook her head. "My mother was musical just like yours was. That's why I play the piano and put on the musicales. In her honor. You could do the same."

He slid off the bench. "I can't. It's not allowed. I needs to go. You needed help with some props?"

"I can handle it." She led him toward the exit then remembered. . . "Here's a nickel for your trouble."

He palmed the coin and looked up at her, his eyes sad. "Sorry I can't sing with you, Miss Evans."

She closed the door behind him feeling sorry for herself, for Johnny, and for the world.

Chapter 3

Cardiff settled into his seat on the train, his heart pumping with the exertion of the trip preparations. When he'd come downstairs this morning, he'd spotted three trunks stacked neatly in the foyer and had informed Gregory that one trunk and his medical bag would have to suffice. He was taking up residence in a rooming house near the hospital—arranged by Dr. Phillips, who had telegraphed last night, expressing his joy at Cardiff's affirmative answer.

Sorting through his belongings, choosing just the basics, was taxing on both men's nerves. By the time Cardiff got to the depot, bought his ticket, checked his trunk, and chose a seat, he was exhausted and relieved he'd made it on time.

He checked his pocket watch. Three minutes to spare.

As the train filled, he watched the final soldier on the platform, his hands cupping the face of his beloved. Their gazes were locked upon each other, her chin upraised, their bodies as close as propriety would allow. Closer.

Suddenly, Cardiff was taken back to another soldier leaving his love. . .

He closed his eyes and saw Zona's face peering up at him, her eyes rimmed with tears. It was another depot in another time. Another war. And other emotions beyond love and longing.

Anger was involved. And bitterness.

For they were betrothed, and Zona had designed a life for them to suit her girlish dreams. They would marry and have three children. They would live in a house near her parents in Chicago, and Cardiff would work in her father's printing company, grooming himself to take over one day.

Because he loved her, Cardiff had let her weave the dream around the two of them. But as the weeks wore on, as Zona began making wedding plans, he found himself pulling away. He'd been on his own since he was orphaned at twelve. He wasn't used to anyone else making plans. He made his own.

He'd been thrilled by Zona's attention, for he was but an employee at her father's printing company. Who wouldn't be flattered? She was a petite and pretty girl with auburn hair and brown eyes that flashed with wit and a zest for living. And willfulness.

Unfortunately, what Zona wanted wasn't what Cardiff wanted. He'd thought it was. He'd tried to embrace her vision of their future, but he'd felt boxed in, as though his hard work and ambition were of no value.

Everything changed when the Mexican war broke out and a friend got the idea to go off and fight. *"Come on, Card. We're too young to settle down. We need an adventure."*

His memories evaporated as the train whistle sounded and a conductor warned the soldier on the platform that he must board immediately. The young man jumped onto the steps beyond

Cardiff's view. But Cardiff saw the girl take a few running steps toward him, her arm outstretched, her face pulled in grief. As the train moved away, she blew kisses until she disappeared from view.

Cardiff's throat tightened as he remembered Zona standing on the platform as his train pulled away. Her arms had been wrapped tightly around her body, her eyes glaring at him, her jaw tight against him. How dare he tell her no.

He remembered his first thought as the train took up speed, widening the space between them and cementing the finality of his decision. *What have I done?*

He took full responsibility for breaking their engagement. Yet since then, he held Zona accountable for not responding to any of his letters—letters sent from the war, in which he'd declared his love, asked for forgiveness, and begged for patience until he returned and they could talk about their shared future.

He cleared his throat, letting the old anger shove the sentiment away. He hadn't been totally surprised at her stubborn silence. In truth, he'd been guilty of his own obstinacy. That their combined vices had totally destroyed a shared future was an ache that never left him, dogging him with an unrelenting pain that surpassed the constant throbbing of his injured knee.

Cardiff saw the soldier from the platform enter his car and nodded to him as he found a seat. His black hair reminded Cardiff of his friend who'd tempted him to go fight Mexico.

Unfortunately, the friend had died in the first battle, and Cardiff had been wounded, his knee shattered. So much for adventure.

Yet the wound that still plagued him had changed his life. For as he recuperated, he found that he had a penchant for medicine, and when Dr. Niles had asked for his assistance in treating the soldiers, he'd readily agreed.

After the war, when that same Dr. Niles had asked Cardiff to apprentice under him in his St. Louis practice, Cardiff had jumped at the chance. It would be a way to start over and forget Zona.

All had turned out. Hadn't it? He was successful and had taken over the practice when Dr. Niles retired. He'd created a good life for himself—he lacked no material thing. He lived in a lovely home.

An empty home.

He shook his head against the traitorous thought that poured salt upon his wound. He applied his usual tourniquet, trying not to think about what could have been. Zona was surely married by now, with three children, just as she'd planned.

They'd each chosen their own way. Their own wrong way.

Cardiff stared out the window of the train. A flurry of snowflakes had begun to fall when he passed through Decatur, and he hoped it wouldn't worsen. The last thing he wanted was to be stranded in a strange town. He wrapped his overcoat tighter around himself and hunkered down to sleep. Perhaps when he awakened, he'd be in Chicago.

Was Zona still living in Chicago?

He was just dozing off when he felt a presence nearby and opened one eye. A little girl of six or seven stood in the aisle near his seat.

"Hello," she said.

"Hello yourself." She didn't move away, so he continued. "May I help you?"

From behind her back she presented him with a pitiful rag doll that only had one eye, a lone button.

"What happened to her other eye?" he asked.

"She lost it in the war."

He wanted to laugh, but the serious look on her face stopped him. "I'm so sorry."

Then she presented him with a far more serious problem by holding up the doll's left arm. "It's loose."

"I see that." Its odd dangling indicated it was being held by just a few threads. "Maybe your mama can sew it back on."

She shook her head no. "Mama doesn't have time."

"Why not?"

"She's morning, and even though it's afternoon, she says she's still in morning." She cocked her head, making her blond curls bend against her shoulder. "I don't understand, but she says to hush and I should be in morning, too."

Cardiff looked over his shoulder and saw a woman who was staring out the window. She was dressed in black with a heavy veil. *Mourning.*

"I'm so sorry."

"Daddy isn't coming home, so we're going to Grandpa and Grandma's house to live."

"I hope you'll be happy there."

She shrugged. "I'd be happier if Betsy's arm wasn't falling off. You're a doctor. Fix it, please."

"How do you know I am a doctor?"

She pointed to the shelf above his seat. "I saw your doctor's bag. Doc Headly had one just like it."

"You're very observant."

"So? Will you make her well?"

How could he refuse? He retrieved his bag and pulled out some suture and a needle. "First off, I should know your name."

"Dorothy. What's yours?"

"Dr. Kensington." He held out his hand and shook hers. "Nice to meet you, Miss Dorothy. Now, will you prepare the patient for me by removing her dress?"

She nimbly removed the blue calico, leaving the doll wearing only pantaloons and a chemise.

Cardiff gently took the doll and laid her on his leg. "There now, Betsy. Soon you'll be good as new."

"To comfort her, can I hold her hand—her other hand?" Dorothy asked.

Although it would make his sewing more difficult Cardiff said yes. Within minutes he'd reattached Betsy's arm. Dorothy let out a breath and pulled Betsy to her chest, giving her a hug. "There, there, you made it through."

"You can get her dressed now."

As Dorothy put the calico back on, Cardiff had an idea. He unbuttoned a portion of his shirt and clipped off one of the buttons. "May I have her back, please?"

Dorothy handed her over, and Cardiff sewed the button in the place of the missing eye. It was a little larger than the other and a whiter white, but. . .

"There," he said.

Dorothy grinned. "She can see again!"

"Good as new."

Dorothy surprised him by giving him a hug. And then a kiss on his cheek. "How can I ever thank you?"

You just did.

∞

Chaos. Happy chaos.

Zona relished the commotion and exuberance that came with the first rehearsal. It was a time of excitement and anticipation, as all those present could bask in the knowledge that they were *chosen*. Zona heard a few whispers about those less fortunate but let it go. That was part of it, too.

Victory was meant to be celebrated but came at the price of hard work. And so she took center stage and looked out over her cast, who were seated in the chairs of the audience. The auditorium was also set with tables as there had been a city meeting in the space the previous week, but there was time enough to set the tables against the wall to allow for more chairs. The Christmas musicale always played to a full house.

Zona clapped her hands. "People? Come now. Everyone take a songbook and settle in. Women in the front row and men in the back." She pointed at the two little boys who were eight and ten. "You sit with the ladies, please."

"But I'm a boy," the older one said. "I don't want to sit with the ladies again."

"I realize that, Seth. But you two will sing the melody, which is the soprano line."

Seth reluctantly sat in the front with his cohort, the ladies making room for them in the center. The boys pushed the women's offending skirts to the side, as if the touch of their feminine fabric accentuated that this was not a row for males.

Twelve singers sat before her, most veterans of the musicale.

She was a little concerned that Mr. Pearson needed help sinking into a chair, his legs obviously weakened over the past year. He had to be near eighty, his rumbling bass voice providing a dependable and strong foundation to every song, especially "Good King Wenceslas."

A slightly younger Mr. Fleming was a strong tenor, his only fault being that he was enamored of his own voice and sang too loudly.

The giggling Martin sisters continued to try her patience—would they ever grow out of it? Despite their annoying ways, Anabelle and her sisters had been a melodious addition for the past three years.

Two new women had been added: Mrs. Smith and Mrs.

Schmidt, whose children were finally old enough to fend for themselves during the time their mothers needed to be at rehearsal. And three additional women had proven themselves to be very reliable ensemble singers.

Most noted were those who were absent. Richard and three other men were missing from the cast because they'd gone off to war.

If only she had Johnny.

Her musing was interrupted when the accompanist took her place at the piano. Zona gave her a nod, and the opening strains of "God Rest Ye Merry Gentlemen" filled the space.

"Page four of the carol books, please. Women, divide into soprano and alto. Mr. Pearson and Mr. Fleming, take up the men's parts."

Zona began to direct, assessing the balance of the voices. She noticed Seth wasn't singing and stopped the song. "I will not condone pouting, Seth Green. There are plenty of other boys who would love to take your place."

"No there isn't," he said.

Mrs. Schmidt poked his leg. "Behave yourself, young man."

"But it's true. I saw how many boys tried out, and we're *it*."

Zona had to nip this rebellion in the bud. "I assure you that the musicale can and will go on without you."

Seth bit his lip. The other boy, Gabriel, looked at him imploringly. But Seth had more to say. "I don't want to sit with the ladies no more."

Mr. Fleming rose. "They are welcome back here with us, Miss Evans. We'll keep them in line."

Seth's hopeful eyes did Zona in. "Fine. Go sit with the men, but there will be no more complaints, is that understood?"

"Yes, ma'am." The boys quickly moved their chairs next to their savior, Mr. Fleming.

"Now, can we continue?"

Both boys nodded.

Zona was just about to begin again when the door to the auditorium opened a few inches. Johnny Folson slipped in.

Saints be praised! "Johnny! Come join us!"

He shook his head. "Can I talk to you, Miss Evans?"

Her hope on hold, she looked to the accompanist. "Begin again, please."

The singing that ensued was marginal, as each head turned to watch Zona take Johnny aside.

"I'm so glad to see you," she told the boy. "We're just starting rehearsal, so you haven't missed a thing."

He shook his head, his eyes on the floor. "I want to come. I want to sing, but it ain't going to work out. There's not time enough in the day."

The words sounded as though they came from an adult. "So you talked with your grandpa about it?"

A nod. "He says schooling takes enough time, and this music stuff being after school is just too much. With Pa gone to fight, he needs me at the stables."

Decatur was abuzz with similar reasoning. Now more than ever, children were expected to help their parents, especially if the business was family owned.

"So he doesn't object to the singing itself, just the time?"

Johnny cocked his head. "I told you he doesn't like to hear me sing because it reminds him of Mama, but he didn't specifically say anything about the singing this time. Just the time away from work."

Zona had an idea. "Can you read music?"

"Mama taught me."

"Wait here." Zona went back to the stage and returned with

the book of carols. "Take this with you and learn the songs on your own. Can you do that?"

He leafed through the pages. "Which part?"

"The melody." She pointed at the book. "And I'd like you to sing a song as a solo."

"I'm not sure I can do that."

"You can, Johnny. I know you can."

He eyed her a moment. "Which one?"

" 'O Holy Night.' "

"I'll take a look." He glanced out the window, as if remembering that time had passed. "I need to get back."

She opened the door for him. "Come by any time and I'll help you."

He nodded, stuck the carol book inside his jacket, and ran out into the cold.

Zona returned to the stage with renewed enthusiasm. "Well then," she said, as the singing stopped.

"Is *he* going to be singing, too?" Seth asked.

Although she hated to lie, she didn't want word to get back to Mr. Folson. "Probably not," she said.

But she certainly hoped so.

∽

"Sorry I'm late," Zona said as she came into the kitchen.

She'd expected to find Mary Lou at the stove, making sure their dinner didn't burn. Instead, she saw her sitting at the kitchen table with a small wooden box nearby. She quickly slipped something in her lap. Hiding it.

" 'Tis no problem," Mary Lou said. "I assumed the first rehearsal would run long. How did it go?"

The flush on her friend's cheeks added to Zona's need to know what she was hiding. "What's in your lap?"

Mary Lou didn't look down. "I was simply going through some of your mother's old papers."

"Show me." Zona took a seat at the table and held out her hand.

Mary Lou took two full breaths before she answered. "You don't want to see."

"As you say that, I certainly *do* want to see."

"They will make you sad."

Zona's curiosity was fully piqued. "I'll take the risk. Show me."

Mary Lou handed over a stack of letters. There were no envelopes, the address merely written on an outside portion of the folded page. Zona looked at the addressee of the top one then the others. "They're addressed to me."

"They're from Cardiff."

Her words coincided with Zona reading the return address: Corporal Cardiff Kensington, Republic of Texas. The postmarks were mostly illegible, but she didn't need confirmation as to the dates. "These are from Cardiff when he was off at war."

"That is correct."

"I never saw them."

"Unfortunately, I believe that is also correct."

Zona pulled the wooden box close. It was filled with letters. "Where did you find this?"

"In a dresser drawer that still held some of your mother's things. I haven't gone through it since we moved out of the family house. Today I was rearranging the linens in the storeroom and thought about using that dresser for storage."

Zona opened the top letter and read aloud. " 'My darling Zona. I regret the way in which we parted. How I wish we would have come to terms. I fear you think I do not love you. I do, dearest girl; I love you greatly.' "

She felt the threat of tears. "Cardiff apologized? He still loved me?"

"Apparently."

The implications tightened her throat. "I find this out after all these years?"

"I know it must be hard to read."

Zona swallowed with difficulty. "If he loved me, he shouldn't have left me."

"Perhaps not, but. . .read on."

The words were read aloud with difficulty. " 'Do not worry over my well-being, as I am doing my best to stay safe. Although I was shot—' " Zona looked up. "He was shot?"

"Read on."

" 'Although I was shot in the leg, I am recovering. Meanwhile, I have been assigned to a civilian doctor who takes care of the wounded on the battlefield. Dr. Niles is teaching me so much, and I find I have a talent for medicine that I didn't know existed before now. But enough about me. I want you to know I think of you always, and hope you understand my need to leave Chicago.' "

"I did not understand. I do not."

"Perhaps after reading all these letters you will."

Zona wasn't sure she wanted to understand. For what good would it do? She handily moved her thoughts beyond the issue of love. "Medicine? There was never any indication."

"Perhaps the war was a blessing in this regard. Do you suppose he became a doctor?"

Dr. Kensington. Zona would have liked being married to a doctor.

"Finish the letter," Mary Lou said.

Although she wasn't sure she wanted to know more, she continued. " 'I must go now, but I will write again when I can. Please know that I love you and ask your forgiveness and your patience as you wait for me to return. Yours always, Cardiff.' " She set down the letter and rose from the chair, her emotions requiring movement. "Why didn't I see these? Why did Mother keep them from me?"

Mary Lou's head shook back and forth then ended in a shrug. "Your heart was broken. You were angry and hurt that he left you. Perhaps she didn't want the hurt to continue."

Zona looked at the stack and saw that each letter was opened. "Did you open these?"

"I did not."

Which meant. . . "Mother read the letters! She knew he still loved me and wanted me to wait until he came home. I would have waited if I'd known his feelings remained. I thought he left me because he didn't love me anymore."

"Surely he never told you that."

No. Up until she'd seen him off at the train station, Cardiff had insisted his love was constant. He simply needed time away to. . .

To what? She tried to remember his words. Reluctantly, they came to her, and she heard his voice saying, *"I love you, Zona. I am fully committed to you, but find I cannot commit to the future you've planned for us. Knowing of no better future to offer you, I must go and see if I can discover a different path for the two of us."*

Us. He'd said us.

Now, as an adult woman instead of a flighty girl, she heard his words with the maturity she'd previously lacked. She pressed a hand to the space between her eyes, pushing against the new insight and its subsequent hailstorm of regrets.

"Are you all right?" Mary Lou asked.

"Not really." She sighed and let the awful truth have a voice. "I was angry that he gave up a position in Father's printing company. I was angry that he chose adventure over me. I was—"

"You said you never wanted to see him again." Mary Lou's voice was soft.

Zona's memory of those words—said more than once with the vehemence of youth—returned with fresh teeth. "I didn't mean it. I was a child. I was hurt. My pride was hurt."

"You were used to getting your own way. You were determined to get the life you wanted. Your own house. A family. Status of your own apart from your parents."

Yes, it was true she had wanted all those things, but one past desire rose above the rest, one that should have taken precedence above everything else. "I wanted him! Yes, I wanted all the rest, but. . ." Memories of her indulgent rants and demands stepped forward to demand inspection. She'd made the details of their future very clear. She had allowed no discussion.

Acknowledging her past faults made her uneasy. Yes, she'd been unreasonable, but wasn't the greater sin sitting on the table before her now? She put a hand on the letter. "I could have had him back. He would have returned to me if I'd given him encouragement." Her throat tightened. "I never wrote him. I didn't know where he was."

"Would you have written him if you'd known?"

Another sorry truth. "Probably not. Not without seeing these letters." Another point loomed. "He never knew my anger could be overcome. He never knew I still loved him."

"Love him?"

Zona shoved the letter in the box, closed the lid with a snap, and pushed it aside. "Don't be silly."

"Then why have you never married another? You had suitors."

The images of Timothy and Dwayne and Oscar passed through her thoughts, a procession of nice-enough men who had not been *enough* for her to bind her life to theirs.

The reality of her life wrapped around her too tightly and tears began to flow. "This isn't fair. We loved each other, but now I'm alone. I could have had a life with Cardiff. Not the life I concocted, but still a life." She glared at Mary Lou. "Mother stole that life from me! How could she do that?"

Mary Lou shook her head. "I don't know. It was wrong of her."

It felt good to have her feelings confirmed, yet the validation was hollow. Zona struggled to her feet, her entire being emptied. "I can't regain the past. It's gone forever." Mary Lou's nod infuriated her, yet what could she say to offer comfort?

There was no comfort.

Zona's practical nature stepped forward, once again coming to her rescue, defending her against the things she could not change.

"This entire discussion is wasted. Why talk of my love for a man who's disappeared from my life so completely? Surely Cardiff has moved on."

"As have you?"

Until now, perhaps yes. But this evening, everything had changed. The letters had fully awakened the dormant pain of what could have been. Her chest tightened as the old wound that had been patched by years of determination was torn open.

She smarted with a new rush of regret.

Cardiff's landlady stood in the doorway of his room. "Breakfast is served at seven in the morning and dinner at seven in the evening. Does that suit you, Dr. Kensington?"

He dropped his trunk beneath the single window and set his medical bag on top. "I'm not sure I'll often be here to dine. Work at the hospital creates variable hours."

"Be here or not, those are the hours I serve the meals."

"I understand." He leaned on his cane. His knee screamed with pain. He didn't want to be rude, but he needed her to leave. His body was weary, and his mind needed silence and solitude.

She pointed to the washstand. "There's a water pump in the kitchen. I don't abide by sloshing water on my carpet runners."

"I'll be careful, Mrs. Driscoll."

"I filled the pitcher this evening since you are new, but from now on, it's your job to get it and pitch it."

"I understand." *Go now. Go.*

She took a new breath, making the bodice of her dress rise. "Each boarder gets an evening to have a bath in the kitchen. Thursdays are free, if that will suit you."

"Thursdays will be fine."

She looked a bit surprised, as though she'd expected an argument. "Very well, then. I'll leave you to settle in."

Upon her exit, Cardiff's survey of the room didn't take long. It was barely ten-foot square, with a narrow bed, a dresser, a washstand, and a chair. The only benefit of the room was that it faced the alley at the back of the house, which should allow him to sleep whenever he got the chance.

Which he needed to do as soon as possible. He'd missed Mrs. Driscoll's dinner, and knowing that back home shepherd's pie and plum pudding were on the Wednesday menu made his stomach growl. Although he hadn't experienced true hunger since the last war, the issue couldn't be helped, so he set it aside.

He unpacked the trunk, using the bureau and the hooks on the wall, then got ready for bed. His shoes were dusty, and his impulse to tell Gregory to clean them was met with the reality of being totally on his own. He sacrificed a handkerchief to the task, washed, brushed his teeth, and climbed into bed.

His feet hit the footboard, and when he scooted up, his head hit the headboard. Sleeping diagonally on the narrow mattress was impossible, so he turned on his side, missing his more generous and softer bed back home. His left knee did not like to be bent to such a degree, so full comfort was impossible.

You didn't have to come. You didn't have to take this job. You chose to be here. But then he thought of Will Thompkins and his friend Cooper, and his commitment was renewed. *I will serve my country well and with honor.* In a hospital far from the battlefield. In Chicago, his hometown. It could have been worse.

A small room and a too-small bed were small sacrifices compared to the horrendous conditions the doctors and soldiers endured in the field.

He fell asleep, counting his blessings.

Chapter 4

The hospital was a sea of white, a ward of beds made with white linen that covered pallid men swaddled with white dressings. Bandages covered wounds on heads, arms, legs, and hands. Some wounds would heal and some would not. Notable were oddly shaped appendages where hands and legs and feet should have been.

The men took little notice of Cardiff, many groggy from morphine or despair. All seemed uninterested in seeing yet another person who couldn't make them whole again, turn back time, or make their futures worth living.

The soldiers ignited memories of Cardiff's other war, where he assisted in a never-ceasing parade of amputations on the battlefield, soldiers with limbs shattered, their guts oozing, their blood mixing with the dirty ground, creating a ghastly mire. The memory of it made him look to the floor, and for a moment, he was surprised to see that it was made of wooden planks instead of dirt.

"Dr. Kensington!"

He looked up to see the familiar but older face of a man who also belonged in the war memories of his past.

They shook hands. "Dr. Phillips. I'm here."

"Indeed you are." His smile still had the power to charm. "But call me Stephen. We've known each other too long to be so formal."

For a moment, Cardiff was taken aback. He was used to "formal." His life was deeply rooted in order and protocol. The hospital was a serious setting that demanded a level of formality. Not knowing what else to say, he got to the point. "Put me to work."

Dr. Phillips—Stephen—laughed. "That's the Cardiff I remember. No dilly-dallying. Straight to the task at hand."

And what is wrong with that?

Stephen clapped him on the back. "Come. Let me show you where to put your things, and then I'll tell you what's what, who's who, and how things work around here."

Stephen led him to a small office off the hospital ward, where Cardiff removed his coat and hat and took a seat in front of a small desk.

"Well then." Stephen sighed and sank into a chair. "Since you are *the* expert on amputations, I—"

Cardiff balked. "Please don't give me that distinction. During the last war, I did no more than you. We learned on the battlefield. And in my practice, I've thankfully had little need for that procedure."

"But you had a knack for it more than I."

Cardiff was repulsed by the praise—if that's what it was.

"Come now, Card. Where I cowered you had courage. You learned very quickly what to do—and what not to do."

His mind tumbled with successes and failures. Under such horrible conditions, there were more of the latter. "These are not positive memories."

"Remember how Dr. Niles always emphasized that more can be

learned from failures than successes?"

Cardiff couldn't help but smile. "A philosophy he held on to when I apprenticed under him in St. Louis."

Stephen's tone changed from welcoming to work. He nodded toward the ward. "Unfortunately, this war has created a need for new knowledge. In play is a far more deadly weapon than we've ever known before. The soldiers are supplied with a new rifled gun with a ridged barrel that can shoot with more accuracy than the smoothbore musket of past wars." He opened a drawer then handed Cardiff a small iron musket ball.

"I've seen too many of these," Cardiff said. Then Stephen handed him something else. "What's this?"

"A minié ball, the bullet used in the new rifles."

Cardiff set it next to the musket ball in his palm. "It's huge." It was a good inch tall, with a pointed end.

"It's a .58 caliber compared to the .69 caliber of the musket ball. So it's smaller in diameter, but—"

Cardiff turned it over. "It's hollow."

"And has ridges that make it spin with more power. It's also made of softer metal that spreads as soon as it is shot, which means—"

"It makes a larger hole when it hits flesh and bone."

"It shreds flesh and shatters bone instead of passing through cleanly. And the exit wound is larger than the entry wound."

Cardiff's usually strong stomach turned over. "So the boys here at the hospital are the lucky ones."

"A questionable term. But yes, they are lucky in that they were shot in their extremities. The ones shot in their head, torso, or stomach were left to die, there being no hope to repair those obliterated organs."

Cardiff let out the breath he'd been saving. "So what do you need me to do?"

"I need you to clean up the quick work of the battlefield hospitals, help me treat the gangrene, and do whatever we can to make our boys heal so they'll be able to get back to their lives once the war is over."

Cardiff thought of his sheltered world back in St. Louis where his days were filled with bellyaches, births, fevers, and the occasional sprained ankle. Yes, he had on-the-battlefield experience with amputations, but repairing the extensive damage of the current war might be beyond his abilities.

"Now that I've thoroughly horrified you, would you like to go on rounds with me?"

Before they exited the office, Cardiff felt compelled to say, "Stephen, I will do my utmost to help, but you are the expert here, and I am but the pupil."

A crease formed on Stephen's brow, but he nodded. "Together we shall learn how to best repair our boys."

∞

Both Zona and Mary Lou heard something at the kitchen door and simultaneously turned their heads in time to see a folded paper slide beneath it.

Zona retrieved it then swung open the door to see who might have left it, letting in a whoosh of November air. There was no one in sight.

"Close that door!" Mary Lou poked at the fire in the stove and added another log. "It must be an important message to venture out in this weather."

Zona unfolded the small page and read it aloud. " 'Meet me at Trinity Church at 4. J.' "

"You have a secret admirer?"

Not likely. Zona was a bit confused until she added up the childish printing and the initial. "It must be from Johnny."

"Why didn't he just come in and tell you in person?"

She glanced at the clock. "He's probably on his way to school."

"What can he want?"

"Maybe he has a question about the music I gave him."

Mary Lou's eyebrows rose. "His grandfather will not approve."

What he doesn't know won't hurt him.

Even with a knit cap beneath her bonnet and the hood of her cape raised and held shut at her neck, Zona walked to the church with her head bowed to the wind. She hugged the storefronts and took a deep breath at every intersection before braving the full force of the wailing winter wind.

She reached the church and hurried up the steps. She was just about to open the door when Johnny emerged from a crouched position nearby, hunkered down against the cold. "Miss Evans."

His cheeks were bright red, though she was glad to see he wore a hat and mittens. "You should have waited inside."

He didn't answer but held the door open for her. When the door closed behind them, Zona's body relaxed enough to shiver. "I suppose we should seek out Pastor Davidson. Have you ever met—?"

"Johnny!" The pastor entered the narthex from the nave of the church. "So good to see you again."

Zona was surprised they knew each other. She'd never seen Johnny in church.

"And Miss Evans. May I help you?"

Before she could speak, Johnny did it for her. "Would it be all right for Miss Evans and I to sit in here and talk?"

"As I've told you before, you are always welcome in God's house. Any time, any day." With a bow, he said, "I'll leave the two of you to your discussion."

Johnny removed his cap then led Zona into the sanctuary to the first row, just to the right of the center aisle. "This is my place."

Now Zona was really confused, for this spot was usually taken by the Dormish family on Sunday morning. Although there wasn't assigned seating, most of the congregation had their favorite spots. "I've never seen you here."

He set his cap and mittens on the pew. "I come other times. Pastor says he don't mind a bit. Grandpa and Pa don't abide by God since He saw fit to let Mama and my sister die."

"But you do—abide by God?"

He hesitated a moment then set a hand on the pew between them. "Mama used to sit here every Sunday, and I sat beside her." He looked to the stained-glass window above the altar that depicted Jesus with His hands extended. "She'd sing every hymn by heart, looking at Jesus' face, smiling like she was singing just for Him." He stared at the window, caught in the memory.

Zona felt it would be disrespectful to disturb the moment. She felt privileged to learn more about this boy.

Finally, Johnny turned toward her. "I been singing the music you gave me when I make deliveries and can find some time alone. I know most of the carols by memory now."

"Already?"

"They ain't that hard. And I remember some of 'em from Mama." He looked at Zona, his eyes bright. "I heard you're going to sing at the train station for the soldiers?"

"We're starting soon."

Johnny nodded once. "I want to do that. I can't do the other, the big musicale with all its rehearsals, but I want to do the caroling for the soldiers. It'll make me think of Pa."

"I'm so glad, but. . .will your grandpa let you go? The train comes through at half past five every day. Aren't you working then?"

He squirmed in the pew, pushing himself back so his feet dangled. "I wasn't going to tell him. The depot's close by the livery. And I told Miss McHenry that I would come help her set up the tables for the basket ladies, so I'll already be down there. I'll be back before Grandpa misses me too much."

Actually, that did sound like the best alternative. But Zona's conscience and the memory of Mary Lou's words that morning dogged her. She was the adult here. Shouldn't she set a good example and teach the boy the virtue of honesty? Shouldn't she insist they not go behind his grandfather's back?

But he'll forbid it.

Zona weighed what was right against her own needs. Wasn't it her responsibility to bring joy to the wounded soldiers as they passed through Decatur? Didn't that need override the illogical directives of one man? She thought of the biblical defense she'd originally used to get Johnny to sing for her: God didn't want people to hide their gifts under a basket but to share them for all the world to see.

Accompanied by a small but ignorable twinge, she made her decision. "If you think you can be there, we'd love to have you."

He agreed with a nod then said, "Would you like to hear 'O Holy Night'? I been working hard on that one—practicing in the church here."

"I'd love to hear it."

Johnny stood and moved to the center aisle, but instead of facing Zona, he faced the window depicting Jesus. As he began the song, his face rose in a rapturous communion with its subject, as if the music was the boy's offering. Zona felt a stitch in her heart and her throat tightened. She saw Pastor Davidson standing at the back of the nave, leaning against the doorway, his arms crossed, a look of pure pleasure on his face. He nodded at Zona.

She nodded back. This boy was meant to sing. He was born to sing this song.

When Johnny finished, he paused a moment, letting the last notes hang in the air. Then he blinked and lowered his gaze back to earth, to Zona. "Was that all right?"

She stood and put a hand upon his shoulder. "Your mama would be so proud."

Johnny beamed and nodded toward the window. "Him, too?"

"Him, too."

○○

After dinner, Zona retreated to her room, foregoing the usual reading aloud with Mary Lou in front of the fire. She used the excuse that she felt a headache coming on, but it was only partially true.

The memories of Johnny's gorgeous voice soaring through the sanctuary collided with their collusion at keeping their meetings secret and having Johnny sing at the depot. She knew if she spent much time with Mary Lou, the older woman would ask questions, and Zona simply wasn't in the mood—or ready—to discuss anything.

In an attempt to calm her mood, Zona shucked off her shoes and sat on the window seat, tucking her feet into the warmth of her skirt and petticoat. She pulled the curtain aside, but the darkness prevented a view. She hated the short days of winter, when darkness took the day captive far too soon.

She scraped a fingernail on the frost. Only after the fact did she realize she'd written CARDIFF.

She let the curtain cover the name. Then her thoughts returned to the box of letters her mother had hidden away. How dare her mother do such a deceitful thing?

Cardiff's words came back to tease her: *"Please know that I love you and ask your forgiveness and your patience as you wait for me to return."*

Love. Forgiveness. Patience. Three honorable qualities.

Which you *don't possess.*

She pulled her legs close and let her forehead touch her knees. *I could have been patient and loved him and forgiven him, if only I'd known.*

Suddenly, Zona needed to read *all* the letters. Every last one. Reading wouldn't change anything, but not knowing their content was no longer an option. She longed to read his words and imagine his voice. She longed to know everything she could about him.

But where were they?

Zona could ask Mary Lou, yet she didn't want her to know of her interest. She lit a candle and quietly slipped out of her bedroom to the hall. Mary Lou had found the box in the storeroom dresser. She'd been cleaning it out, so it was unlikely she'd return them to the same place, but it was a starting point. Zona tiptoed down the hall to the storeroom and went inside, the candlelight creating flickering shadows on the walls. She opened the top drawer. It contained table linen. The middle drawer contained towels and dresser scarves. The bottom drawer. . .

There it was.

Zona put the box under her arm and retraced the steps to her room. She set the candle and the box on the small desk, pulled up a chair, and only then allowed herself to take a deep breath.

She let her fingers rest upon the box, giving herself one last chance to keep it closed forever. Would it do more harm than good to find out what Cardiff had written so many years ago? Would it cause pain?

Yes, and probably yes.

But not knowing caused its own harm and pain.

She opened the box and removed the stack, noting that they were sorted chronologically. She recognized the letter she'd read the day before and set it aside. On to number two. . .and three. And four and all the rest. She read every word, yet her eyes lingered on certain lines:

> *My darling Zona. . . .*
>> *I yearn to hear from you. . . .*
>> *Are you still angry at me for leaving? I regret it, yet the distance has made me appreciate what we had. Have. . . .*
>>> *We are a stubborn pair, each used to having our own way . . . . I regret my part in our separation. Please forgive me. . . .*
>>> *Why do you not answer my letters? If I could, I would come back to Chicago and speak to you in person. . . .*
>>> *I found my calling—I wish to become a doctor. . . .*

This last line brought her back to the present. Cardiff, a doctor? He'd never shown any inclination. He'd worked in her father's printing company. She'd begged her father to groom Cardiff to take over.

Which had been one of the reasons he'd left her.

Left her to go fight a war that had nothing to do with him. Who cared about Texas or Mexico?

That he chose war over marrying her and living a normal life still infuriated her.

She remembered a passage she'd read and found it again:

> *We were like two rams, our horns locked, pushing too hard at cross-purposes. I know the life you wanted for us, but I just couldn't see myself there. I could see myself married to you, having a home and family. That was not the detail that sent me away. As I told you, I could not see myself as a printer for the rest of my life. It was your father's calling, not mine.*

Unfortunately, I had nothing better to offer you. And so like a coward I ran away, letting my friend lead me to battle.

Jeffrey died after a week. And I was wounded. Some soldiers we were.

But as I mended and saw the need around me, I met a man who was to change my life. Dr. Niles noticed my interest and took me under his wing, letting me assist him in the messy business of attending to the wounds of battle.

Because of him, I found my calling—I wish to become a doctor.

Zona let the letter rest in her lap. Medicine was a noble calling. Nobler than being a printer?

She sighed. One vocation wasn't better than the other, but for one fact: Cardiff had made the choice. Not her.

The memory of her willful insistence regarding the details of their future ignited a wave of embarrassment. She'd been nineteen years old, an only child who prided herself in her ability to get people to give her what she wanted. She'd wanted Cardiff and, as such, had set her sights on getting him.

He had succumbed to her charms, and with that victory, she'd pushed harder to gain the rest of her wish list: a home, family, status, and wealth.

She looked across her bedroom. The living quarters she shared with Mary Lou were comfortable but far more humble than her youthful dreams of a mansion with servants.

"What's done is done."

The words rang hollow, yet not wanting to argue with herself, she picked up the final letter.

It began without the usual "My darling" salutation.

Zona,

I have no choice but to take your silence as a rejection of my pleas for forgiveness, understanding, and a second chance.

The war is over, and Dr. Niles has offered me an apprenticeship in his private medical practice in St. Louis. As you have obviously moved on, so must I.

Perhaps it is for the best. I will cherish what we had, and wish you full happiness in the future.

Sincerely,
Cardiff

Zona jumped to her feet, the stack of letters falling from her lap. "He moved to St. Louis? He gave up on me?"

There was a knock on her door, and Mary Lou peeked in. With a single look, she took in the scene. "You found them."

"You didn't hide them."

"I wanted you to read them."

"Have you read them?"

"I have."

Zona shook the final letter at her. "He gave up on me. He moved to St. Louis. He became a doctor."

"I know."

Her chest heaved with a heart beating too hard and lungs seeking more air. She pointed at the letters on the floor. "My entire life would have been different if I'd seen these letters."

"I know."

"Mother had no right keeping them from me!"

"I know."

"Is that all you can say?"

Mary Lou removed the letter from Zona's hand and led her back to the window seat, resting their clasped hands upon her knee.

"I didn't agree with your parents' choices and suggested you might benefit from seeing his letters. But they wouldn't listen. Your heart was broken, and they didn't want you to be hurt again."

"He said he wanted to come back to Chicago. If he would have received some encouragement, I'd be married. We'd be married."

Mary Lou nodded. "Which is why your parents moved you here."

Zona was confused. "I always thought they approved of our match. But to move because of his letters. . . They disliked him that much?"

"Let's say they considered your match unequal."

"Because Cardiff grew up poor and worked manual labor?"

"Not just that." She hesitated. "Perhaps they believed you wanted the dream more than the reality."

In hindsight, Zona knew this was true. She'd known very little of real life.

For a moment, she didn't breathe. "You said they moved here because of the letters. We moved to Decatur because Grandmother was sick."

"Not so sick. Not that sick."

Another memory surfaced, of her grandmother getting well. "She lived until last year."

"As I said."

"So it was all a ruse to get me out of Chicago so Cardiff couldn't find me?"

Mary Lou hesitated then said, "Yes."

"Why didn't you tell me?"

"I didn't know the full truth until I read the letters the other day. I knew you had received letters, but not their content. I thought Cardiff had left for good."

"He did leave for good! He went to St. Louis. He's probably in

St. Louis now, married, with children." She flashed a look at Mary Lou. "He's probably living the life that should have been ours."

Mary Lou shrugged. "It was not to be. He moved to St. Louis and your family moved here."

Zona paced in front of the window, her thoughts skipping like pebbles on a lake. "Papa sold his business in order to move here. Were they that anxious to keep me away from him?"

"I remember hearing talk about an offer on the business, even before Cardiff left." Mary Lou retrieved the fallen letters and stacked them neatly. "Perhaps Cardiff wasn't as good a worker at the printing company as you thought he was. Perhaps your father didn't like your plan of letting him take over."

Zona had never thought of that. Cardiff's working ability and her father's wishes had never been a consideration to her plans. And then it hit her.

"I didn't think about anyone else and what they might want, did I?"

"No."

"You don't have to answer so quickly. You could ponder it a moment."

"The truth is the truth and needs no pondering."

But the truth hurt.

Zona spotted a stray letter on the floor near the bed and returned it, along with the others, to the box.

"Do you want me to put them back in the dresser?"

"I need them here. Close. For they are the evidence of my folly and its consequences."

Mary Lou pulled her into an embrace. "Don't be too hard on yourself. You were just a girl. And your parents were in the wrong, too."

"Were they?"

Mary Lou let go, looking into her eyes. "You approve of what they did?"

"I understand it." New thoughts revealed themselves with a stunning clarity. "If I'd had my way, Cardiff and I would be married."

"You loved each other."

"We did. But did I love him enough to let him be who he was destined to be? Or would he have lived a miserable life, running my father's company?"

Mary Lou moved a stray hair behind Zona's ear. "We'll never know."

It was a fact that was heavy with its own pain.

Mary Lou left her, and Zona returned to the window seat, knowing that sleep would be elusive. She pulled the curtain aside and saw the name she'd written in the frost. CARDIFF.

She drew a heart around his name then pressed her hand against the pane, melting the letters into nothingness.

∽

If Cardiff could have managed it, he would have gone to sleep on the front stoop of Mrs. Driscoll's boardinghouse. His good leg was leaden, and his bad leg pulsed and ached so badly he would have gladly cut it off to be rid of the pain.

Just a few more steps inside then upstairs to my room. One step at a time.

Once inside, Mrs. Driscoll stormed toward him from the back of the house. "You missed dinner, Dr. Kensington. It's after nine, and I specifically told you I served promptly at seven."

His legs gave out, and he faltered on the first stair, grabbing for the banister. Mrs. Driscoll rushed forward to help him stay erect.

"I'm sorry for missing it, ma'am. And I'm all right now." He stood straight, though his balance remained tenuous.

"You are not all right. You look terrible. Your face is ashen."

He turned toward the stairs and, with all his determination, gained ownership of the second step. "It's been a long day."

"Have you eaten?"

"No, ma'am. We had an emergency when one of our boys stopped breathing."

"Did he recover?"

Cardiff didn't want to talk about it. "No, he did not."

"I'm. . .I'm so sorry."

"Me too, ma'am. So if you'll excuse me, I really need to get to bed."

"Would you like some help with the stairs?"

"No, ma'am. I'll make it."

And he did. Barely. He fell into the chair in his bedroom, his torso bouncing off the back cushion, unable to keep control of itself. His head felt too heavy for his neck, and he leaned it back against the wall. The bed beckoned, but he didn't have the energy to move from here to there. He considered sleeping where he was—though the muscular consequences in the morning would be great.

But maybe if he could rest for just a few minutes, he could gain enough energy to conquer the bed.

His eyes snapped open to a tap on the door. "Dr. Kensington?"

What time was it? Surely it wasn't morning already. He pushed himself upright and groaned with the ache of the movement. "Yes?"

"I've brought you dinner. May I come in?"

He gave his consent, and the door swung inward. Mrs. Driscoll entered, carrying a tray of food. "I couldn't let you go to sleep on an empty stomach. Here is a roast beef sandwich, some squash and potatoes, a piece of spice cake, and some wine." She set the tray on the dresser, moved a small table in front of him, then transferred the tray within his reach. "There," she said. "A hard-working man like yourself needs proper nourishment." She waited for him to take up his fork, and when he did not, she handed it to him. "Eat. Leave the tray outside when you're finished."

He ate a bite of squash. It was garnished with butter and sugar. "It's delicious."

"Of course it is. Now, finish every bite." On her way out, she retrieved his wash pitcher. "I'll bring you some fresh water."

"Thank you, Mrs. Driscoll. You're very kind."

"Of course I am."

Cardiff devoured every bite.

Chapter 5

Cardiff studied the soldier's amputated leg. It was puffy and colored green and black from gangrene. If soldiers weren't killed outright by the bullets, such horrible infections gave death another chance.

But hopefully not this time.

He looked at the orderly. "When the time comes, I will need you to hold his leg steady."

It was clear the private was not meant for such work. His breathing was labored, he made fists at his side, and he gazed at the wound with an expression of disgust.

He had reason to be repelled. Rotting flesh was not a pretty sight and smelled worse than it looked. Yet his reaction was unacceptable, as it was noted by the patient—who looked petrified.

Cardiff needed to remedy his fear as quickly as possible. He offered the patient a smile and said, "We'll let you sleep. When you awaken, your leg will be better." He looked to the private. "Give him the chloroform now."

The private nodded and held a cloth doused in the drug over the patient's nose and mouth. Soon the man slept.

Cardiff worked quickly, cutting away the putrid flesh then filling the cavity with bromine-soaked lint before reapplying a bandage.

Unfortunately, before the morning was over, Cardiff had to repeat the process on a dozen soldiers. It was nearly one o'clock when he finally took solace in Dr. Phillips's office. He massaged the back of his neck.

Stephen appeared in the doorway. "You look done in."

Cardiff sat up straighter. He didn't want to show his weariness this early in the day. "The gangrene cases are attended to."

"Nasty stuff, that." He smiled. "You could have dysentery duty if you'd like."

"Nasty stuff, that."

Stephen studied him a moment then retrieved some paper and a pencil from his desk. "Here. For a change of pace, go sit with some of the boys and let them transcribe a letter home."

"I'm here to help with the medical issues."

"There are physical needs and emotional ones, Doctor. Both need attention." He handed Cardiff the supplies. "Go on, now. Corporal Meyers, third bed on the right, is due to send a letter home. It'll be good for both of you."

"I want to send a letter to my wife."

Cardiff held the paper and pencil at the ready. "Go ahead."

"To my darling Zona."

Cardiff fumbled the pencil. "Zona?"

"No, sir. I said Rhona."

Cardiff's hand transcribed the corporal's words, but his mind traveled elsewhere.

Was Zona well? Surely she had a husband and a family. She was quite a catch, fifteen years ago. Feisty, smart, and talented. She was a woman who knew her own mind and was happy to share it with whoever would listen—whether they cared to hear or not.

He'd often been a reluctant listener. When they first began courting, he'd been working at her father's printing company as a typesetter. It was boring work, and when the boss's daughter had shown interest in him, he'd found her joie de vivre a welcome diversion from the tedium of his day. He'd been surprised when he was invited to the Evanses household for dinner. He'd been so nervous, hoping he wouldn't do anything to offend the boss and his wife. Up until then, he'd only met Zona in passing, when she'd come to the plant to bring her father lunch each day. How those fleeting moments had turned into a dinner invitation was beyond his understanding.

Until Zona later explained that she'd found the intensity with which he set the type inspiring. At first, he'd thought she was teasing him—for he found his job anything but inspirational—but when her interest continued and the invitations to be with herself and her family came with more frequency, he stopped second-guessing what had sparked her interest in him.

The important thing was that she *was* interested, and *her* interest had sparked his own.

Zona was unlike any woman he'd ever met. Not that he'd met that many. He hadn't had time to court or flirt. His parents died when he was twelve, and he'd been on his own ever since. A friend of the family had let him sleep in their attic—which was where he was still living when he met Zona. He'd had a variety of odd jobs during the day, but his favorite job was cleaning the classrooms in a schoolhouse. There, after everyone had gone home, he'd grabbed himself an education. He read the lessons on the chalkboard and pored through the schoolbooks left behind. When he'd taken a book on Greco-Roman history home and had been accused of stealing, he'd made a friend of the teacher, who thereafter let him borrow as many books as he wanted.

Reading so much, learning to spell as he read the words on the page, helped gain him the typesetting job. On more than one occasion he'd been commended by Mr. Evans for catching the occasional misspelled word before it went to print.

In hindsight, he realized Zona had pursued him—and caught him. Although such feminine aggression was not often looked upon kindly by society, he welcomed it. For with his lack of experience, he was all too happy to have a wonderful girl like Zona choose him. If only he'd—

"Doctor? Did you get that last line?"

His mind returned to the present. He was surprised to see that he'd transcribed a two-page letter for Corporal Meyers. He cleared his throat and read back the last line. "'I love you and miss you more than words can say.' Is that correct?"

"That's it," the soldier said. "Sign it, 'your loving husband, Rolf.' "

The letter finished, Corporal Meyers gave Cardiff the address for Rhona.

Zona.

Where was she now?

❦

"Come now, singers. Please pay attention." Zona waited until all had quieted down. "I would like the following people to come in early tomorrow afternoon so we can work on the vocal parts for the caroling at the train station."

"Don't we all get to sing?" young Seth asked.

"You all get to sing in the musicale, but I only need a small group to sing for the soldiers."

"How many?" Mrs. Smith asked.

"Four." She thought of Johnny and covered herself. "Perhaps five." Before there was more discussion, she gave the assignment. "Mrs. Smith will sing soprano, Mrs. Greer on alto, and of course Mr. Fleming and Mr. Pearson." *And Johnny.*

"What about me?" Seth asked.

Zona was already weary of the boy, whose daily complaints over this and that hounded her. "Not this year."

"Then when?"

Luckily, Mr. Fleming shushed him. "Quit yer bellyaching, boy. It's wearing on all of us."

"But if the rest of us ain't singing there, why do we need to sing the songs now?"

"Because we will also be singing carols in the musicale on Christmas Eve."

Seth crossed his arms and began his daily pout. "It ain't fair. Not at all."

Life's not fair.

"Let's turn to 'O Come, All Ye Faithful.' "

"I'm glad we're not singing this in Latin," said one of the young ladies.

"Latin is beautiful," Mr. Pearson said. "You young people don't know what you're missing."

Zona agreed, but disagreed. "What the listeners would be missing is understanding the meaning of the lyrics. Now, come. Let's begin."

Since it was a familiar song, the parts were easily conquered. So much so that Zona dropped her arms and closed her eyes, letting the harmonies waft around her.

Then suddenly she was thrust into a memory of another group of singers offering up this very song. Two parts took precedence:

her own voice singing the melody, and to her right, their shoulders touching, was Cardiff singing the baritone line with a mellow voice that melded perfectly with her own. *We belong together, our lives melded together.*

"'Come and adore Him, born the King of angels. . .'"

As suddenly as the memory was born, it died. With a jolt, Zona realized she was singing alone.

She opened her eyes.

Everyone was looking at her.

"Sorry. I was caught up in a moment."

"A moment far from here," Mr. Fleming said.

Very far.

∞

Zona was right in the middle of directing when she noticed Mrs. Collins come on stage with two costumes folded over her arms. She ignored her and continued the song to its end. "A little less tenor, Mr. Fleming."

He gave her a familiar grimace—as he did not like to be told to sing softer. Zona was just about to begin the next song when Mrs. Collins interrupted.

"May I speak with you a moment, Miss Evans?"

"We're right in the middle of rehearsal. Can it wait?"

"If you want the singers to sing naked, I suppose it can." She stood her ground amid a flurry of giggles.

"I really would rather you waited until the end of rehearsal for your questions."

"I've tried to wait. But you're always hurrying off. Where do you go day after day with such speed and determination?"

Seth's hand shot up. "I know! She's helping—"

Zona's stomach flipped. She interrupted before he could finish. "Carry on, singers." She hurried off with Mrs. Collins. She was dismayed that her quick exits had been noted. Had Seth followed her? She'd cut him off just before he said Johnny's name. Her secret rehearsals with Johnny had been very productive. But if anyone beyond Pastor Davidson knew—especially Mrs. Collins—then word might get back to Johnny's grandfather. The caroling for the hospital train was starting tomorrow at five-thirty. Johnny was poised to sing. At that time, word would undoubtedly get out to his grandfather, but after the fact. Mr. Folson would hear praise about how good the boy sang, realize how much his singing pleased the soldiers, and relent.

It was a logical string of events. Yet life was known to break such strings.

"What do you need, Mrs. Collins?" she asked from the side of the stage.

"What was Seth going to say?"

Zona didn't dare glance back at the boy. "Who knows? Now then, you have a question?"

Mrs. Collins hesitated, as if she was reluctant to leave one conversation for another. Finally, her own concerns took over. "Look at these costumes for the three kings. They are positively pitiful, not even worthy of three peasants."

"They've served their purpose well enough."

"Served, past tense. They look old and worn. I would like to redo all three of them and add some extra trim."

"Who is going to pay for this?"

"The theater of course."

There was no *of course* to it. "I'm afraid you have a misconception regarding our funds. We subsist solely on donations." At the last moment, she remembered the curtains the Collinses had donated. "Generous donations, as you well know."

Mrs. Collins's face pulled as though she'd been ready to jump

325

on Zona's misspeak and was rather disappointed her recognition of the donation prevented it. "Surely my husband and I are not the only citizens of Decatur contributing."

Pretty much. "War times are tough, wallets slim, and contributions are rightly going to help our soldiers."

Zona remembered seeing Mrs. Collins at the sewing bee at Lucy Maddox's. "Of course, you know about sewing for our boys with the other ladies of the Basket Brigade."

Ha. Foiled you again.

"Indeed I do. I've sewn two shirts this past week and baked three dozen muffins. How many shirts have you sewn, Miss Evans? How many food items have you contributed?"

"Sewing and baking are not my talents." *As you well know.*

"Or perhaps you are too busy with your. . .other projects?"

Zona's stomach flipped. What did she know? Had she seen or heard Johnny practicing?

With a look of satisfaction at her discomfort, Mrs. Collins moved on and gave her attention to the costumes. "I do believe I have some soutache braid at home that I was going to use on a new dress. But I would be willing to sacrifice my own ensemble to dress up these sad sacks."

"That's very generous of you. Now, if you'll excuse me, I must get back to the rehearsal."

As Zona walked away, Mrs. Collins whispered after her. "The sopranos seem a bit weak."

Touché.

⚬

As Cardiff studied the stump of a newly arrived soldier who'd had his leg amputated on the battlefield, he sensed someone standing nearby. He didn't let himself be distracted and kept his focus on the badly sewn flap of skin over the stump.

When he heard the person breathing behind him, he said, "State your business, then leave me to the work."

"I'm not here to leave you to anything, Doctor. I'm here to do the work for you."

The words themselves were shocking in their audacity, but it was the gender of the speaker that caused Cardiff to turn around.

A middle-aged woman in a simple black dress and apron stood nearby. She peered around him and pointed. "You really should use finer suture for that."

Cardiff couldn't believe his ears. "Excuse me?"

She pointed again. "I could get some for you if you'd like." While she was talking with him, she tucked in the sheets of the soldier in the next bed. "When was the last time these sheets were washed?"

Cardiff was taken aback. Who was this woman?

The soldier answered. "I been here three weeks, ma'am. They's never been washed since."

"That's ridiculous." She scanned the room. "All these linens need to be washed immediately."

Cardiff was rendered speechless. How dare she act like she was in charge? He looked around for Dr. Phillips, but he wasn't in the ward. "Under whose authority do you come in here and order things done?"

The woman lifted her chin, met Cardiff's gaze, and said, "On the authority of our Lord God Almighty. Have you anyone who outranks Him?"

Some of the patients and attendants laughed.

Cardiff glared at them then put his needle down and escorted the woman to a private corner.

"I demand to know who you are and why you are here."

"My name is Mrs. Breston. And I'm here to give aid to my boys."

"Your boys?"

She gave a strong nod. "All of them. Mine to care for."

"Who hired you?"

"No one."

"What does that mean?"

"I am not an employee of the army or the hospital. Or you."

"Then you have no business being here."

"I have every business being here—without pay. Think of me as an angel of mercy." She swept an arm toward the soldiers behind her. "As long as they're here, I'm here."

Cardiff spotted Dr. Phillips coming into the ward and motioned him over.

Stephen joined them and kissed the woman on both cheeks. "Mrs. Breston. I'm glad you're here."

She gave Cardiff a smug nod. "Just arrived—and just in time from what I can see."

"You invited her here?"

Mrs. Breston answered for him. "I have no need for an invitation. I go where I'm needed." She looked at Cardiff directly. "As I told Dr. Phillips, I have worked in four hospitals near the battlefields—I was an eyewitness to the carnage at Fort Henry and Fort Donelson. And I set up hospitals in Cairo, down south."

Then why are you here?

As if she'd read his thoughts, she said, "I am here because I am a widow with two boys of my own, and though relatives are kind enough to keep their care, I returned to Chicago to be near them. And while I'm here. . ." She turned her attention to Dr. Phillips. "I need vats of boiling water to get these sheets washed. Where can that be set up?"

"There's a barn outside."

"That will do." She strode away and pointed to an attendant.

"Boy? I need you and two others to move four of these soldiers to these clean, empty beds, carry their sheets down to the vats, wash them, dry them, make up the beds, then transfer more boys to the clean beds and—"

The attendant looked aghast. "I ain't no washerwoman."

"You'll be whatever I need you to be—whatever these men need you to be. Do you understand?"

The man looked to the doctors, clearly wanting to be saved. "Best do as she says, Corporal Hines," Stephen said.

With a nod and a thank-you, Mrs. Breston left them.

"I'm not at ease with a woman in the ward," Cardiff said.

"Neither am I. But times are changing. She seems capable and willing to work hard. She brought along letters of recommendation from Generals Grant and Sherman. I can't turn her away. Can you?"

I'd like to try.

Yet as Cardiff returned to his suturing, he *did* think about getting some finer thread.

But no. He was the doctor here, and he refused to let this woman bully him into changing his ways.

∞

After rehearsal, Zona went to the kitchen, expecting to help Mary Lou with dinner. But the stove was cold, the pots empty. And Mary Lou was absent.

She looked on the table, hoping for a note to explain her absence. There was nothing.

It wasn't like Mary Lou to be late, and she was always good about leaving a note when she went out.

Just as Zona was making the decision whether to go look for her or start dinner herself, the kitchen door opened and Mary Lou came in.

"Where were you? I was worried."

Mary Lou removed her bonnet, dusting away the snowflakes.

She hung up her cape. Only then did she face Zona. "You need to sit down."

Zona's mind swam with horrible possibilities, but she gratefully took a seat. "What happened?"

"Richard Grimble was killed."

Zona felt the air go out of her. Richard, whose voice had just changed, who'd gone off to war to be with his big brother. "He wasn't a soldier. He wanted to be a drummer boy."

"Bullets don't discriminate." Mary Lou took a seat at the table. "I've been at the Grimbles'. Martha is devastated and worried about her other son."

"Have they heard from him?"

Mary shook her head. "It's very hard for letters to get through to a specific soldier." She pressed her open hands on the table and took a fresh breath. "I feel the need to do *something* to help our boys. And so I'm going to write another letter for the Basket Brigade to distribute. I'll leave it to God to deliver it where it's best needed. Would you like to join me?"

Of course.

"Well, well," Mrs. Driscoll said when Cardiff entered the foyer. "Home for dinner. Will wonders never cease."

Cardiff removed his hat and coat and brushed the flurry of snow off his boots onto the entry rug. He didn't want to endure the battle that would ensue if he got his landlady's floors wet. He'd had enough female battles for one day.

"I think I'll just have a plate in my room, if you don't mind."

"I mind very much, Dr. Kensington. Once was a favor. Twice is an imposition." She pointed toward the dining room where the two other boarders sat with their napkins tucked into their collars.

"Come, Doctor." The speaker was a man who'd previously

introduced himself as a lamplighter.

"Since we can't beat Mrs. Driscoll, we might as well join her," the hack driver added.

Mrs. Driscoll put her hands on her hips. "And who would want to beat me? Who would dare try?"

The other men laughed, and Cardiff took up his place, tucking in his napkin. "I am surrounded by strong women today."

Mrs. Driscoll ladled soup into bowls—it smelled like squash or carrot. "Of whom are you speaking?"

"A woman has come to work at the hospital."

"Is that allowed?" the lamplighter asked.

"It's certainly not proper," the hackman said. "Women shouldn't see such awful things."

When she was finished serving the soup, Mrs. Driscoll took her place at the head of the table. She bowed her head, and the men did the same. "God bless this food and the people eating it. Amen."

Short and to the point. Cardiff was glad for the brevity and noted the prayer's directness corresponded with the prayer's nature. And personally, he found more poignancy in brief prayers said from the heart over the rambling prayers of people who overvalued the sound and eloquence of their own voice.

The men waited until Mrs. Driscoll took her first taste. "Back to your comment about women in the hospital, Mr. Johnson," she said. "Do you think I haven't seen awful things? Your room was a sight."

"Sorry. I'll try to keep it in better order."

The soup warmed Cardiff from the inside out. "I don't think Mrs. Breston cares whether it's proper for a woman to work in a hospital."

"Mrs. Breston?" Mrs. Driscoll asked.

"You know her?"

"I certainly do. And a finer woman you'll never find."

That was just dandy. They were two stubborn peas in a pod. Yet perhaps their acquaintance could be put to good use. "Tell me about her," Cardiff asked. "Has she always been so zealous about caring for soldiers?"

Mrs. Driscoll considered this a moment then said, "Her eldest son joined up back in sixty-one and was wounded early on."

She only mentioned two sons at home.

"Probably didn't even know how to shoot," the hackman said.

"He died, Mr. Johnson. Show a little respect."

"I'm sorry. I apologize."

Mrs. Driscoll continued. "She was already a widow of two or three years when he died." She shook her head. "So much sorrow."

Mr. Johnson tried to make amends. "So much sorrow for too many families."

"Such is war," Cardiff said.

Mrs. Driscoll looked to the heavens with open hands. "May it be over soon."

Amen.

∞

Cardiff sat at the desk in his bedroom and readied a piece of paper.

The talk of Mrs. Breston's loss, coupled with his downtime habit of writing letters for a few of the soldiers, inspired him to write his own. What continued to surprise him was that none of the men spoke of battles or victories. Even their infirmities were quickly dealt with. What permeated their letters were memories of home, expressions of love for their family, and hope for a swift return to the life they had led before the war tore everything apart.

He took a bite of the apple Mrs. Driscoll had offered him for an evening snack and let his mind turn to his own letter.

He wrote "Dear" on the page then found himself stumped. Dear who?

He held his breath, waiting for a name to flow onto the page.

But there was no name. No family. No bosom friends who would value his letter.

"Gregory. I could write to Gregory and Mrs. Miller."

The content of the soldiers' letters was rich with memories of family and love and times shared. Although he held the Millers in high esteem—and they him—an invisible barrier existed between them, keeping master and servant in their proper places. Any letter to them would be filled with questions of logistics—and perhaps a note asking about their visit with their daughter. There was no common well of emotion to tap into, such as the emotion that filled the soldiers' letters to overflowing.

When was the last time he'd written a heartfelt letter?

"Zona."

To hear her name said aloud made him draw in a breath. He'd sent her numerous letters from Mexico and Texas.

Asking her forgiveness.

Begging for her understanding.

Declaring his love.

Defending his new ambition to become a doctor instead of a typesetter.

When he'd received no letters in return, he'd stopped writing, let the war end and his career in medicine continue.

Alone.

Without her.

His ambition had come at a cost he'd reluctantly been willing to pay.

Until now?

Depressed by the memories and emptiness, he set the pen back in its stand and returned the paper to a drawer.

Chapter 6

Cardiff was ready to slice into the soldier's vein when he felt the presence of Mrs. Breston.

Again.

"May I help you?"

"You can help Corporal Statler by halting that venesection this very minute."

Cardiff glanced at the soldier's face to see his reaction to this act of insubordination, but luckily, the patient was sleeping.

In spite of this, Cardiff angled his back to him and drew Mrs. Breston into the main aisle that bisected the rows of beds. "I cannot let you interfere with the medical care that I deem necessary for my patients."

"Cannot or will not?"

He felt his ire rise and took a deep breath to try to get himself under control. "Mrs. Breston—"

"Mother Breston. My boys call me 'mother.'"

But I am not one of your boys.

He ignored the salutation. "I cannot"—he caught himself—"will not allow you to undermine my authority. I have been practicing medicine for nearly fifteen years."

"Seems like you need more practice."

Cardiff spotted Stephen and called him over. "Dr. Phillips, I insist you do something about this situation. It is highly improper for my decisions to be contradicted."

Mrs. Breston folded a towel neatly over her arm. "Even if you're wrong? The letting of blood only weakens a patient."

"So that's why it's been practiced for hundreds of years?"

"They thought the earth was flat for longer than that, and it was proven wrong."

"I am not wrong."

She pointed at the patient. "Will it take the death of that boy to make you admit your mistake?"

Appalled, Cardiff took a step away, spreading his free hand toward his tormentor as if to say, *You see what I have to deal with?*

Stephen offered them a smile. "What stands before me are two capable people who are passionate about their professions. Surely you can find a point of conciliation between you for the good of the patient."

Cardiff was incensed. If he didn't have Stephen's support, this woman was going to run rampant throughout the hospital, weakening his authority. How could he possibly be asked to work in such conditions?

He'd had enough of them both. "Excuse me. I have a patient to attend to."

He returned to the soldier, adjusted the bowl beneath his arm, and sliced into his vein. Everyone knew that bloodletting was *the* course of treatment in regard to ridding the body of infection.

∽

"The time for your carolers' debut is here," Mary Lou said as she accompanied Zona to the depot.

Zona's stomach was knotted as she entered the train station to sing Christmas carols for the first time. She was relieved to see that all four of her designated quartet were already there, talking to the ladies of the Basket Brigade who were gathered for the evening train with their baskets of food and other comforts. She scanned the crowd, looking for Johnny.

He wasn't there.

Mr. Pearson saw her, and the singers gathered close. "Where would you like us to stand?" he asked.

She wanted the singers close to the tracks so their voices would carry into the train. The wounded soldiers needed to see them from the train windows. She moved to a spot on the platform, front and center, waving her arms to claim the space for her singers. "Excuse me. . .if you don't mind. . .we're going to sing here. . .thank you."

Mr. Pearson and Mr. Fleming used their height and male authority to further clear the space.

"There, now," Zona said, trying out the spot where she would stand to direct them, her back to the train.

"Shall we start?" Mrs. Greer asked.

"The train's not here," Mrs. Smith said.

"I wouldn't mind running through a piece," Mr. Pearson said.

Zona knew that was a good idea, but she really wanted Johnny present, for he had never rehearsed with the quartet.

And then she saw him, walking toward her with his grand-father. And Mrs. Collins. And was that Seth? The smug smiles on the faces of the latter told the story of the day. They'd tattled. Somehow they knew everything and had shared their informa-tion with Mr. Folson.

Zona pursued her first instinct. "Let's sing 'Midnight Clear.'" She stood in front of her quartet, fumbled for her pitch pipe, and unable to retrieve it in a timely manner, gave them a random note as they quickly got in place. She raised her arms and gave the downbeat. "'It came upon a midnight clear. . .'"

She dared not look beyond her singers, but goose bumps traveled up her arms knowing the army of protesters was heading her way. She wasn't even able to enjoy the appreciative faces of the Basket Brigade ladies who gathered around.

As the song neared its end, she tried to think of another, but her mind was blank.

Then Mrs. Collins strode forward and took a place at the edge of the quartet, next to Mr. Fleming.

"Miss Evans."

Her throat was dry. "Mrs. Collins." She glanced beyond the woman to see Johnny, under his grandfather's arm, his eyes downcast.

Seth pushed in between the women. "You met with Johnny in secret. I followed you! I saw you!"

Mrs. Collins moved to Zona's side, facing the audience of the crowded depot. "I'm afraid Miss Evans has abused her position as musical director by ignoring the wishes of Mr. Folson regarding the participation of his grandson." She beckoned the man closer. "Isn't that right, Mr. Folson?"

The man placed Johnny in front of him, gripping the boy's shoulders. "I forbade it, and she ignored my wishes."

Murmurs flit across the crowd like fireflies.

"Why did you do it?" Lucy Maddox asked. "We appreciate your musical talent, but to go against the family's wishes. . ."

Others nodded.

Zona glanced at Mary Lou, who looked as unnerved as she. Zona wanted to flee, yet the glee with which Mrs. Collins and Seth called her out pressed her need for escape aside and ignited the fuller truth.

She raised her arms in the air, quieting the crowd. "Yes, I went against Mr. Folson's wishes but with good reason."

Mrs. Collins raised her voice above Zona's. "So your authority supersedes that of a grandfather?"

"No, I mean. . ." She pressed a hand to her forehead, trying to find the words to make it right. Her thoughts landed on the core of her deception, the justification for her actions. She moved through the crowd and faced Johnny and his grandfather. She cleared her throat and addressed Mr. Folson. "Your grandson has a great gift. He sings with a depth of talent greater than anyone I have ever heard."

Johnny glanced up at her, smiled, then looked down again.

"That may or may not be true," Mr. Folson said. "But it is not your gift to commandeer."

"Nor is it your gift to hoard."

Oohs spread through the crowd, and she heard Mary Lou whisper, "Zona. . ."

Zona sighed, knowing her words had been too harsh. "Have you ever heard him sing?"

"That's not the point. I forbid it."

"But it is the point," she said. She spotted Pastor Davidson nearby and moved toward him. "Pastor! Please tell Mr. Folson about his grandson's great gift."

Pastor Davidson moved close, his face twitching a bit under the sudden scrutiny. "It is true, Mr. Folson. Johnny's voice is unlike any I have ever heard. I can't imagine the angels singing any better." He took a step toward Mr. Folson. "Your daughter used to sing with such conviction and joy. The boy has her gift—and more. Gifts are meant to be shared, Herman."

Zona saw the muscles in Mr. Folson's jaw contract. When he spoke, his voice was soft. "Hearing him sing reminds me of my Violet." He shook his head, looking to the ground. "God took her away from me, and little Flora, too." When he looked at Zona, his eyes glistened. "My heart breaks every time I think of 'em. And music makes me think of 'em."

Johnny looked up at his grandfather. "I remember Mama singing. I sing for her, to remember her. And I want to sing for the soldiers. It makes me think of Papa, off somewhere, fighting."

Zona's throat tightened, and she noticed more than one hand brought to a mouth, moved by the boy's words.

Everyone's attention was diverted when the sound of a train whistle announced its pending arrival.

Zona had one last chance. "Please, Mr. Folson. Let him sing to the men. For his mother. And his pa."

Mr. Folson glanced at Pastor Davidson, who offered him a nod. He drew in a deep breath and let it out with the words, "Go on, then. Sing."

The depot platform surged with commotion as the women of the Basket Brigade scurried to get in place to board the train. Zona led Johnny to the other singers and set him at the center. "When I tell you, sing 'O Holy Night.'"

"All by myself?"

She looked at the other singers. "All by yourself."

They nodded their assent, and Mr. Fleming said, "You can do it, boy. Sing for your ma and pa."

The train pulled in with a rush of air, smoke, and sound. The wheels squealed to a stop. Zona gave Johnny an encouraging smile and used the pitch pipe to give him a note. When she heard him hum it, she moved beside Mrs. Smith so the soldiers could fully see the source of the voice.

Then he began.

"'O holy night, the stars are brightly shining. . .'"

The song rang off the metal of the train and filled the platform, as if the heavens had opened up and let the songs of the cherubim descend. All eyes were on the boy, the business of delivering baskets or greeting passengers momentarily forgotten.

Zona could see the faces of the soldiers on the train, craning to see the singer. Their hurting eyes softened, and she saw many ease their heads to their pillows, wallowing in the music.

She glanced over her shoulder to see Mr. Folson's reaction. His face was lifted to the sky, as if searching for his daughter and granddaughter. Tears flowed down his cheeks, yet he was smiling.

Thank You, Lord. Thank You for making it all turn out.

The song ended, and a moment of respectful silence fell upon them. Johnny looked around, his face panicked. But then the applause and congratulations assured him that all was right with the world.

Johnny seemed to care nothing for the praise of others but ran into his grandpa's arms.

"Did you like it? Did you, Grandpa?"

Mr. Folson kissed the top of his head. "It was a gift. You are a gift."

Zona's heart was full to overflowing. As the women commenced the delivery of the baskets, her quartet began singing the carols.

The evening was complete when Johnny joined them, his face radiant with joy.

As was Zona's heart.

Cardiff was just about to leave for the day and was making the rounds of his patients. Most were doing well.

But when he came to Corporal Statler's bedside, he was appalled to see that his face was gray. He felt his forehead and listened to his heart. The man was cold and the heartbeat weak. His breathing was shallow.

I'm losing him.

He checked the slit in the man's arm where the blood had been taken. His arm was limp. Lifeless. He touched his hand. *He looks as if all the life has drained out of him.*

All blood.

For a moment, he questioned the venesection he'd performed. The practice usually worked, but—

"Seems like you need more practice."

The possibility that Mrs. Breston could be right—at least in this case—disrupted his equilibrium and shook his confidence. He made fists, trying to force the doubt away.

"I'm concerned," Mrs. Breston said as she approached the bed.

Although it was hard to admit, Cardiff agreed. "So am I."

She smoothed the sheets and ran a hand through Statler's hair. "Come on, son. Come back to us. Your wife and son need you at home."

"He's married? With a boy?"

Mrs. Breston nodded. "His wife's name is Abby, and his son, Caleb, is three."

Cardiff turned to leave then thought better of it. "I think I'll stay with him, to see him through the night."

Mrs. Breston nodded and pulled two chairs close. "Let us keep vigil together."

They settled into chairs, angled toward each other on the right side of his bed. Then Mrs. Breston surprised Cardiff by saying, "I apologize for being so brusque. My late husband used to chide me for my lack of tact."

"I could use a bit of that myself."

She adjusted the cuffs of her black dress. "I also know that my ways may seem revolutionary and sit against the grain."

"They do. And whether you wish to believe it or not, I do have

342

experience with soldiers. I worked in an army hospital during our war with Mexico."

"My issue lies in the observation that not much has changed for this war. There are still too many unsuccessful amputations. And still the disturbing, unsanitary conditions."

"I assure you we always try our best to save a limb."

She nodded. "I'm sure you do. It's not you in particular, Dr. Kensington. It's the medical field in general that I battle. Common sense is often absent. Beyond the tending of their wounds, what the boys need are clean bodies, unsoiled sheets, fresh air, and healthy food."

Her thinking was far too simplistic. "They need more than that."

"Indeed they do," she said. "They need doctors to wash their hands and surgical instruments. They need time for the body to heal itself through rest and common care."

"In the field, there was often no time to wash."

"There must always be time to wash! We've both seen how even the simplest of cuts heals faster when it is kept clean. Doesn't it make sense that larger wounds would react the same?"

"Yes, but—"

"No *buts*, Doctor. There is too much we don't know about the body and how it works. Until that knowledge is obtained, we must use logic and common sense to do our work."

He knew there was no arguing with her.

She plucked at the fabric of her apron. "My George would still be alive if he'd been taken to a hospital that possessed sanitary conditions."

Cardiff remembered Mrs. Driscoll's mention of Mrs. Breston's loss. "I am so sorry."

"As am I." She took a fresh breath. "His death was the impetus to my fervor regarding the boys' care. If someone had been there for my son George, I am convinced he would not have died."

They lacked proof one way or the other, and battlefield conditions often negated any consideration for care beyond what was quick and nominal. But Cardiff knew this moment was not a time for proofs but a time for compassion. "Again, I am sorry for your loss." He tried to find a happier subject. "You mentioned two other sons?"

She smiled. "Timothy and Carl. I am very blessed." Thinking of her boys seemed to clear the sorrow from her face. "Do you have anyone back home, waiting for you?"

"No. There's just me."

"*Was* there anyone?"

He balked.

She reached across the space between them. "There was someone, wasn't there?"

Cardiff looked around the ward. Most of the soldiers were sleeping. What would it hurt to tell this woman the truth? "Her name was Zona."

"That's a distinctive name."

"She was a distinctive woman."

"Was?"

"Probably still is. We were engaged but lost track of each other."

"On purpose?"

He thought of his unanswered letters. "On her part. I wrote letters while I was off in the other war. She did not answer me."

"Perhaps she didn't get them."

He'd never thought of that. "I assumed she did."

She slapped his knee. "You let an assumption dictate your life?"

It sounded as lame as it was. "She went her way and I went mine."

Mrs. Breston's hands fluttered around her head. "I cannot

believe what I'm hearing. You let a woman you love get away without going after her? Talking to her in person? Making sure it's what you both wanted?"

He tried to think of his reasoning back then, but logic eluded him. Finally he came up with, "I went to St. Louis and apprenticed under a doctor I'd worked with during the war. I took over his practice."

"And what of Zona?"

"I—I don't know." He tried to think of some excuse for his actions. "She was angry at me for going to war. She wanted to marry me and wanted me to work in her father's printing business."

"Sounds totally appalling."

He caught her sarcasm. "I didn't want to work there."

"Then stay and say no."

He shook his head. "It wasn't easy saying no to Zona."

She looked toward the ceiling, "Lord, what can we do with this man?"

Cardiff resented her words. "I don't need you to implore the Almighty on my behalf."

"Someone needs to do it. You need to, for He's the only one who knows where your Zona is. *If* you want to find her."

Her words smacked him like a slap. "I—I do want to find her."

"Of course you do. You need to find Zona and give yourself some closure."

"I assume she's married, with a family."

"There's that nasty habit of assuming again. So what if she is? Say hello, see how she's faring, wish her the best, and go back to St. Louis with the door to what could-have-been firmly shut."

It would be nice to know for sure.

She lowered her voice. "But if she's never married, just as you have never married. . .perhaps God has been keeping you for each other all these years, for such a time as this."

The notion made his stomach dance.

"That is, if you still love her. Do you?" Her gaze was unwavering.

A soft laugh escaped. "You are indomitable, aren't you?"

"I believe there is a bit of stubborn in you, too, Dr. Kensington. Use it to seek her out. Use it to not stop until you find her and put this past to rest, so you can begin a new future."

His mind swam with the logistics of it. Yet they quickly calmed. He knew where her family lived.

He knew where her father worked.

"She lived in Chicago. She lived here."

"Oh. My. Goodness! You're in the same city? You have no excuse. Go to her."

She was right. "I will. I'll go tomorrow."

"Perfect." She touched his arm. "It's the right thing to do."

"I know it is. Thank you for. . . ?" He couldn't think of the proper word for what she'd done for him.

"Prodding you into it? Prodding is my job. Now then. Let's say a prayer for Corporal Statler and for you to have a successful quest in finding Zona."

He couldn't—and didn't—refuse.

A few hours later, Cardiff was back at the boardinghouse. Corporal Statler's breathing and heartbeat had stabilized. Had God heard their prayers?

He had no other explanation. And since they'd prayed about their patient and about finding Zona, Cardiff was compelled to take the next step.

As he reached the upstairs landing, he stopped at Mr. Johnson's door and knocked.

The door opened. "Doctor. What can I do for you?"

"I need the use of a horse for a day. Can you get me one?"

"I'm sure that could be arranged." He gave Cardiff a sideways glance. "Care to tell me why you need it? I could take you wherever you want to go in my hack."

"Thank you, but I'd prefer to go on my own."

"Go where?"

He thought a moment. "To visit my past."

Mary Lou set a bowl of stew in front of Zona. She took her seat at the table and placed a napkin in her lap. Without looking up, she extended her hand to Zona and began grace.

"Heavenly Father, thank You for this food and for handling the confrontation at the depot today with such grace and mercy. Help Zona know what she needs to do next."

Zona pulled her hand away. "That was subtle."

"Wasn't meant to be."

"Everything worked out. Johnny sang, and his grandfather saw his talent."

"You got what you wanted."

"Johnny got what he deserved."

"And you got to use his talent for your own purposes."

She was turning everything around. "The soldiers loved it. So did everyone who heard."

Mary Lou sighed dramatically. "So the end justifies the means?"

Zona pushed her bowl aside. "You're siding with Mr. Folson?"

"You hurt him."

"I helped him see his grandson's talent."

"Was that your place?"

Zona couldn't believe what she was hearing. "It was for his own good."

"And who are you to determine that?"

She pushed away from the table and stood. "He gave me no choice. I put the boy above all else."

"Hmm."

"You heard Johnny sing. It would be a sin to let a voice like that be silenced."

"I agree."

"You agree?"

"I am happy for the result but question the method. Slinking around, forcing the boy to slink around—"

"It was his idea!"

Mary Lou gave her the look she deserved.

"I know. I'm the adult. I should set a good example."

With a nod, Mary Lou moved to another point. "Your willfulness and need to get your own way has hurt you before and cost you everything."

Zona couldn't believe she was bringing it up. "Cardiff."

Mary Lou shrugged. "I thought this time you'd think of others first."

"But today everything turned out all right. Doesn't that count for something?"

"You have Pastor Davidson to thank for that. He diffused what could have been a very humiliating situation."

Didn't she see Zona's point at all? "It *was* humiliating. Thanks to Mrs. Collins and Seth tattling to Mr. Folson. Did you see the smug look on their faces when they came storming onto the platform?"

"You pushed them into it."

"So their behavior is also my fault?"

"Without your lies to them and to Mr. Folson. . ."

"I didn't lie outright, it was more a sin of omission."

"Zona."

The glory of the day's success dimmed. "What do you want me to do?"

"What *should* you do?"

One word sped front and center into her thoughts: *apologize.*

She wanted to ignore it.

So she left the room.

"You hate when I'm right," Mary Lou called after her.

Not as much as I hate when I'm wrong.

Zona lay on the bed, fully dressed. The room was dark but for the moonlight. She was disappointed Mary Lou hadn't come to check on her. Didn't *she* deserve an apology?

Do you?

Zona wrapped a pillow around her ears, trying to drown out the inner voice.

Suddenly she remembered another time she'd used a pillow in such a way, in another darkened room, in another town. Cardiff had left her behind. He hadn't married her, hadn't accepted her father's offer to rise up in the printing company, hadn't—

Given in to your wishes?

The fifteen years between the first childish reaction to disappointment and today's forced her to sit up and toss the pillow across the room. "What's wrong with me? Why do I always push to get my own way?"

Why do you always think your way is the best and only way?

Thoughts of Cardiff superseded the events of the day. She retrieved their old daguerreotype from the dressing table and took it to the window seat. The moon provided a gentle light, allowing her to study him—study them. What would have happened if she hadn't been so willful and demanding? Would Cardiff still be with her? Would they be happily married in Chicago, with umpteen children underfoot?

A drastic thought burst forward and demanded a voice. "Did I upset God's plan for us by insisting on my will over His?"

The notion that she'd upset some divine balance overwhelmed her, and tears fell. "I'm sorry for being so stubborn and spoiled. It's my fault he left. If I'd been reasonable and allowed him to have a say in our future, we could have compromised. Losing Cardiff is the consequence I deserve." She looked at the picture again. "I accept the life *I* have. It's a good enough life. But Cardiff deserves the best. Please make sure he's happy and well."

Her thoughts turned to Johnny, Mr. Folson, Mrs. Collins, Seth, and all the other singers. "Thank You for Your mercy today. My humiliation could have been much worse if not for Pastor Davidson. Thank You for letting Johnny's talent outshine the drama of my methods. Help me make amends." She asked God the same question she'd asked Mary Lou. "What do You want me to do?"

The same answer entered her mind. *Apologize.*

But this time, instead of running away from the directive, Zona embraced it. It was the least she could do.

Chapter 7

Cardiff was up with the dawn. After checking on Corporal Statler and renting a horse for the day, he began his journey into the past. His stomach was unsettled, though he wasn't certain if the cause was excitement or trepidation. Today *could* change his life. To have such a possibility within his grasp was almost too heady to handle.

And so he decided to ease himself into the journey by riding past the house where he'd grown up. It wasn't his family's house but the house belonging to the family friends who'd taken him in when his parents died. It had looked old and tired then, but now seemed on its deathbed. The trees around it were overgrown and forlorn, yet people lived there, for a pair of boots sat on the front porch. It must have been freezing inside, as a large chunk was missing out of the small attic window.

The attic that used to be his.

He paused and let his memories rush back to that life that had been thrust upon him. The boy he was then and the man he was now seemed unrelated, like mere acquaintances. Yet if he let his thoughts return to the days before he was twelve, when his parents were alive, he found few memories at all—only fleeting images of being tucked in by his ma or poking the fire with his pa. The most vivid memories were of the fever that had killed them both, when he hid behind a dresser and listened to them fight for each breath.

He shucked that remembrance away and looked back at the attic. More substantial images came to mind. The Thompsons had five other children and made it known that keeping him was an imposition. That's why he'd taken odd jobs during the day and cleaned the school after classes ended. He'd read the borrowed books by candlelight before falling into an exhausted sleep.

Alone as a child, alone as a man.

One situation was thrust upon him, the other created by choice. He chose to run away from Zona and marriage. That he soon had second thoughts and attempted to reconnect with her was pitiful and obviously too late. He should not have been surprised that her broken heart could not be mended by a few letters.

Then why are you trying to find her now? The wounds of the past had scabbed over. If Cardiff persisted, the wounds could reopen and the pain could be awakened.

Unable to dissect the right course on his own, he bowed his head, aching for God's direction. *Help me. Lead me.*

Suddenly, his horse began to walk, past the house, down the street. Was this God's answer?

He chose to believe it was, and as he made the acknowledgment, the burden in his heart lightened.

"To Zona's?" he asked the air. "Stop me if it's not what You want."

But as Cardiff came to each intersection that led him closer and closer to Zona's family home, he felt no pull to turn back or go another way. As the distance shortened, his confidence grew, and he actually found himself smiling. To see Zona again, whether she was married or not, filled him with a long-dormant anticipation. And hope.

When was the last time he'd felt either?

Turning into her neighborhood, he was glad to see the houses had been kept in good condition. Other than the trees being taller and grander, the essence of the stately neighborhood was intact.

And there it was. The house where Zona lived.

Lived now, or once lived?

That was the question whose answer would change everything. As Cardiff rode close, doubt returned, and he found himself gripping the reins as if the horse was at a full gallop rather than a slow walk. He wasn't even certain how he wanted this day to play out. What if Zona came to the door with three children bouncing around her skirt? That's what he expected.

But what if she came to the door with her elderly mother or father calling to her from the parlor, "Who is it, Zona?" What if she'd continued her life in this house where he'd left her, living year after year as a daughter and never a wife or mother? The thought of it stirred his innards while it also made him sad. For if she had never married, was he to blame? He remembered how important marriage and family were to her.

He stopped his horse in front of the house, trying to find the courage to dismount and knock on the door. Another prayer burst forward. *Please help me. Make this turn out as it should, as You have planned.*

His heart skipped a beat when he saw the front curtain pulled to the side. A woman peered out then let it drop.

Zona?

If it was Zona, would she come out to greet him? Images of a romantic reunion slid through his thoughts, with Zona running into his arms, her words of timeless love muffled against the wool of his coat. He would hold her close, kiss her hair, call her darling, and all the years would fall away.

But no one came outside. The house remained as it was when he first saw it. Was she inside, panicked at his sudden appearance? Was she arguing with her husband either for or against speaking with Cardiff? Or had she gone on with her day, letting the wall that separated them grow thicker and taller, an impenetrable fortress keeping them apart?

Suddenly the door opened and a middle-aged man came out of the house. Cardiff's horse shied at his approach, but Cardiff held his ground.

"What business have you here, sir? My wife noticed you peering at the house."

"I apologize for causing you concern. My name is Dr. Kensington. I used to know the lady of the house."

The man's brows leaned toward the middle. "You know my wife?"

Cardiff knew he had to tread lightly. He didn't want to cause Zona any domestic trouble. "I knew Zona fifteen years ago. I worked at her father's printing company."

The man expelled a breath, and his brows regained their usual position. "You speak of Zona Evans."

"I do. I assure you my intentions are honorable. I am in the city working at the military hospital and wanted to pay my respects to an old friend. If you will express my greetings to your wife, then I'll be on my way."

"You are mistaken if you think my wife is Miss Evans. Her family moved away years ago. We've lived here over fourteen years."

Relief collided with more questions. "Do you know where they went?"

"South, I believe. There was some relative who was ill?"

Cardiff remembered some grandparents in central Illinois but could not remember the name of the town. "What of the printing company?"

"It was sold, too, but I don't know the details. Sorry I couldn't be of more help."

The man turned toward the door as the wife came outside, a shawl around her shoulders. She stood on the front step.

"Morning, ma'am. Sorry if I spooked you."

She nodded, and Cardiff knew it was time to go. But then he thought of one more question. "Do you remember if Zona was married when they sold and moved away?"

"I'm afraid I don't," the man said.

"I remember," said the wife. "I spoke to Mrs. Evans and the daughter while the men were negotiating the sale of the house. Zona was unmarried, and was in fact rather upset about some beau who'd left her." She blinked once then stepped off the stoop. "Are you the man who broke her heart?"

"Maddie!" the husband said. " 'Tis none of our business."

"But he asked. . ." She gazed at Cardiff, awaiting his answer.

"I am that man." He didn't expand. "I never meant to hurt her."

"Men never do."

The husband took his wife's arm and moved toward the door. She called out over her shoulder as he led her inside. "I hope you find her. It's never too late for love."

Her last word was spoken as the front door swung shut, leaving *love* hovering in the air between them.

But then confusion wrapped around the word. What about all the letters he'd sent to Zona, admitting how wrong he'd been, telling her he loved her? If she had a broken heart, it meant that *she* had still loved *him*.

Could it be that the family moved before she received those letters? Could it be that fifteen years had come between them through a fluke of miscommunication?

Cardiff shivered at the thought and only then realized he was cold. A soft snow began to fall, and he could feel the muscles of his horse shift and tremble in an attempt to stay warm. "Come on, boy. Let's get you home."

Wherever that was.

∽

Zona paused at her bedroom door and took a deep breath before exiting. "Help me get through this day. Give me the words to make things right."

She startled when there was a tap on the door from the outside. "Zona? Who are you talking to?"

Zona held back a laugh and opened the door. "God."

Mary Lou's eyebrows rose. "Really?"

"Yes, really. Is it that hard to believe that I pray?"

"Of course not." She moved toward the stairs then turned back. "Did He answer?"

Zona only hesitated a moment. "I believe He did."

Now Zona had her full attention. "And?"

"The first order of the day is to eat some crow. And apologize."

Mary Lou grinned. "Want some salt with that?"

"Salt, pepper, and lots of gravy."

Mary Lou kissed her cheek. "Good girl."

∽

With each step closer to the Folsons', Zona's stomach took another stir. The mantra *Help me, help me, help me* spun an inner rhythm.

It wasn't that apologizing was difficult, for her regret was sincere. The issue that made her nervous was how the offended parties would react. Would they accept her apology gracefully, or would they use the moment to make her writhe? It didn't really matter. What must be done must be done.

Fortunately, the streets of Decatur were fairly quiet, as the combination of the winter wind coupled with the early hour had most people comfortably warm in their houses.

Today was not a day of comfort for Zona. Not until her task was complete, her penance accomplished.

She reached the Folson house, a clapboard in need of paint. The front steps were icy, causing her to fully grip the railing for support. She saw a curtain at the front window pull back then drop. Then the front door opened before she had a chance to knock.

"Good morning, Johnny. Is your grandpa home?"

"He's making porridge."

"May I speak with him?"

He studied her a quick moment then let her inside.

Mr. Folson called out from the back of the house. "Johnny, get in here and eat. I gotta get to work."

Johnny motioned for her to follow him then ran ahead. "Miss Evans is here."

"What?" Mr. Folson appeared in the doorway to the kitchen, a spoon in his hand. "Miss Evans."

It was now or never. "I'm sorry to disturb you so early in the morning, but I wanted to make sure I caught both of you at home."

"Is something wrong?"

"Didn't you like my singing?" Johnny asked.

She put a hand on his hair, which needed a good combing. "You sang beautifully."

Johnny offered her a quick smile then looked to his grandpa, who said, "Yes, you did."

His acknowledgment led Zona to rush forward with her

apology. "I am here to apologize for deceiving you, Mr. Folson, for going against your wishes that Johnny not sing and for practicing in secret. I went too far. It was not my place nor my choice to make. I should have abided by your wishes."

"Indeed you should have."

Zona swallowed.

Mr. Folson pointed the spoon at her. "I have enough to worry about, having to care for Johnny on my own without the benefit of my daughter or her husband. And he's been a good boy—until this. Like Satan himself, you tempted him to do wrong. To lie. To sneak."

Johnny's face was stricken. "Grandpa, I said I was sorry."

The older man's face softened a moment—until he looked at Zona. "I blame him some but blame you more. It doesn't matter if you thought my reasons were wrong. They were my reasons." He paused and looked toward the doorway. Zona looked over her shoulder and spotted a blue bonnet hung by its ribbons on coat hooks.

No women lived in this household. Not anymore.

To see the bonnet still hanging there, years after the daughter's death. . .it made Zona think of the daguerreotype she kept of Cardiff.

With a cleansing breath, Mr. Folson said, "By letting Johnny sing, you forced me to revisit the pain of my daughter's absence, Miss Evans. You had no right."

She hung her head, not wanting him to see her shame. "I had no right."

He accepted her words with a nod but went to the bonnet, touching the flowers along its brim. "Why would God take her from me? She was the light of my life. And not just take her but my granddaughter, too." He looked at Zona with eyes drowning in grief. "Can you tell me why, Miss Evans?"

She had no words. And suddenly the meeting moved beyond an apology to a communion of two broken souls. Mr. Folson's was broken through no fault of his own, and Zona's was broken because of her own willfulness. Together, they shared a poison pill of bitterness that owned no antidote.

Except perhaps. . .

Zona closed her eyes, prayed for strength, then opened them. "We are two of a kind, Mr. Folson."

He let his hands leave the bonnet. "What?"

"You are bitter regarding the loss of your daughter and grand-daughter, and I am bitter regarding the loss of the love of my life."

"I didn't know you had a suitor."

She shook her head. "It was a long time ago, when I was but a girl."

With a nod, Mr. Folson gestured to the table in the kitchen. "Will you tell me about him?"

"If you will tell me about your daughter."

Coffee was poured out—as were their hearts. Zona heard all about Violet and little Flora, and felt a purging of her own soul by being able to share her memories of Cardiff. Regrets and laughter wove together with wistfulness and gratitude.

Through it all, Johnny was silent, looking back and forth between them, taking it all in.

When the clock on the wall struck ten, Mr. Folson sprang to his feet. "Here I've talked away the morning and now I'm late for work."

Zona rose, completely shocked by the passage of so much time. She headed for the door. "I'm so sorry for making you late."

Mr. Folson put a hand upon her arm. "I'm not. 'Twas a good conversation that's made me feel better about everything. I hope it's done the same for you."

She smiled. "It has."

"One thing before you go. One thing for both of you." Mr. Folson looked at Zona and then to Johnny. "I offer both of you my own apology. I was wrong to keep Johnny from singing when I knew he had a gift. I was smothering the fire out of him by trying to control him. It was my problem to overcome, not his." Johnny beamed.

But to Zona, Mr. Folson's words elicited a meaning beyond his original intent. "*I was smothering the fire out of him by trying to control him. It was my problem to overcome, not his.*"

"Is something wrong, Miss Evans?"

She repeated her thought out loud then added, "I forced him away. I was in the wrong. It was my problem to overcome, not his."

Mr. Folson nodded. "Life lessons learned are earned."

Indeed.

Then he added, "If it's all right with you, Miss Evans, I wonder if you could find a spot for Johnny in your Christmas musicale."

Zona walked home with a spring in her step. She'd apologized, been forgiven, and had achieved her original purpose in getting Johnny for the musicale. And more than that, she felt good about sharing some of her memories and culpability regarding her relationship with Cardiff.

Yet as she walked, her pace slowed, as if this last issue wasn't completely resolved.

"Good morning, Miss Evans."

Zona looked up and saw that she was in front of the church. Pastor Davidson had just come out and stood on the steps. "Good morning, Pastor."

He walked down to her side. "You seem consumed with thought. Are you upset about what happened at the depot?"

The memory of that humiliation seemed further away than the memory of her sins from the distant past.

"Would you like to talk about it?"

Although it might have been advantageous to talk to a godly man like the pastor, she felt compelled to talk to his Boss, alone. "May I go in the church and sit for a while?"

He waved a hand toward the door. "The Almighty is waiting for you."

Zona entered the empty church and began to take her usual place in the front pew where she always sat while working with Johnny. But then, she decided against it. That place belonged to *before*. It was time to begin a new *after*.

She walked down the aisle to a random pew then let the sacred silence tuck her in. She looked up at the vibrant colors of the Jesus window above the altar. His face was forever kind and full of peace, and His arms reached out to her, drawing her to Himself. *"Come unto me, all ye that labour and are heavy laden, and I will give you rest."*

Zona drew in a deep breath and expelled it raggedly. Then she put a hand to her mouth and let the tears come. The tears turned to sobs that echoed in the rafters, returning to her many fold. She wasn't even sure why she was crying. Was it the humiliation of the depot, her own wrongdoing in deceiving Mr. Folson, her less-than-kind treatment of Mrs. Collins, Seth, and the other singers?

Yes.

But she sensed the sobs came from a deeper, hidden place, where old fears, doubts, and shame squatted without her consent. All previous rationalizations for her actions stepped out of the shadows, demanding attention. *You can't hide from us forever. We are the ugly part of you. We hover close, awaiting our next chance. You pretend you are a good person with pure motives, but we know better.*

We are patient and take our chances when you let us loose.

Zona covered her face, shaking her head, trying to make the ghosts of her sins disperse. Yet they stood firm, waiting for her to fully notice them. Name them.

She saw Pride and Selfishness in the front row, with Stubbornness and Obstinacy right behind, until Impatience and Manipulation shouldered their way into view.

No, no, no. Go away! I don't want you to be a part of me anymore!

Zona hugged herself, longing to disappear, leaning forward, her head bowed, ashamed. "I'm so sorry for putting my plans and schemes above all else, above everyone else. Above You. Please forgive me. And if there is any good in me, bring it forward and make positive attributes take over my life."

The prayer lingered in her mind, and slowly Zona sat upright. She opened her eyes and risked a look at Jesus. He had not turned away from her, and His face was not full of disgust and anger. He looked upon her with compassion, and His arms were still outstretched, drawing her in.

His love allowed hope to enter her soul. She closed her eyes and let the peace of His forgiving presence fill her entire being. Her shadowed places were overcome as they filled with His light, leaving no corner unlit.

Finally, she drew in a new breath, and a new Zona was freshly born.

∞

"She's here."

As soon as Zona saw Mrs. Collins walk by the kitchen window, heading for the musicale rehearsal, she hurried into the auditorium to greet her.

"Hello!" Zona said as Mrs. Collins entered.

Mrs. Collins put a hand to her chest. "Gracious sake, you scared me half to death."

"Sorry, I didn't mean to."

Mrs. Collins removed her cape, bonnet, and gloves. Then she faced Zona, her face skeptical. "If you're going to get after me for telling Mr. Folson about your secret—"

"I want to apologize to you, for the deception." She took a cleansing breath. "I was wrong."

"Well now." Mrs. Collins draped her cape over a chair, setting her bonnet and gloves on top. "It *was* wrong of you."

Zona laughed inwardly. If anyone was going to make her apology difficult, it would be Gertie Collins. "I offer no excuses."

Mrs. Collins smoothed her skirt, as if unsure how to respond.

Her silence nudged Zona to say more. "I also apologize for not letting you sing in the musicale. Who am I to keep you from using your talent?"

Mrs. Collins's eyes batted in a flutter, as if Zona's words were a swarm of pesky gnats.

"Would you like to join us?" Zona asked.

"I. . ." She rearranged her bonnet on the chair. "Actually, I had a talk with my husband and asked him to be honest with me about my singing." She cleared her throat as she fingered a feather in her hat. "He suggested I focus on costume design."

Although she tried, Zona could not hold in a laugh.

At first, Mrs. Collins looked appalled, but then she smiled. "The truth is, I wish someone had been honest with me sooner. When I think back to all the solos I probably desecrated. . ."

"That's far too harsh a word." Although it wasn't.

She waved Zona's appeasement away. "Actually, I need to apologize to you for the trouble I caused at the depot."

"I deserved it."

"Yes, you did, but it wasn't up to me to dole out your

punishment—especially in public." She sighed deeply. "Sometimes I can be quite wicked."

Zona remembered the shadowed vices she'd confronted at the church. "So can we all."

∞

"And so, I want to ask your forgiveness for not being totally honest with you by working with Johnny in secret. I have come to realize that secrets breed tension, and truth breeds peace."

At just that minute, Johnny slipped in the door of the auditorium.

"Come in, Johnny. I was just telling the others you were going to join us."

Mr. Fleming moved a chair between him and Mr. Pearson. "Come sit here, boy."

"No," Seth said. "Let him sit with me and Gabriel."

The eldest of the Martin sisters giggled. "He can sit by us."

Johnny blushed.

"Next to Seth and Gabriel would be fine," Zona said. "Now then, let's run through the staging for 'Joy to the World.' "

An appropriate song, all in all.

∞

Cardiff didn't remember much about the ride back to the stable, nor his subsequent walk to the boardinghouse. Hours had passed as he wandered the streets of Chicago, thinking about the past and what could have been, what should have been. So many errors of timing and intent.

By the time he reached the boardinghouse, he was covered with snow and couldn't feel his hands or feet. Somehow he stumbled up the steps and inside, where his cane clattered to the floor.

Everyone was eating dinner, but upon seeing him, they erupted into motion, drew him to the fireside, and removed his outer garments. The two tenants rushed to fulfill Mrs. Driscoll's orders of blankets and hot coffee. Cardiff let them fuss around him, too stiff and miserable to protest.

Mr. Johnson put another log on the fire and poked it to higher flames. "You're just getting back?" he asked. "You've been gone since morning."

"I got the horse back safely. No worries."

"I'm not worried about the horse, but it's far too long to be outside, especially in this weather."

Cardiff had no defense. "I lost track of time."

"Pooh to that," Mrs. Driscoll said. "Lose time and lose your life. What were you thinking?"

I wasn't thinking. Or perhaps I was thinking too much.

The other tenant brought him coffee, but Cardiff's hands were too stiff to hold the cup. Mrs. Driscoll pulled another chair close then took his hands in hers and rubbed them vigorously. "Where did you go all day? I insist you tell us the reason for risking your life like this."

Cardiff hunkered his shoulders into the blanket. The tops of his ears stung with the cold. He didn't want to tell them. For one thing, it was none of their business; for another, it was old business, done business, business that made his heart ache.

"We're waiting."

"Maybe he doesn't want to say," Mr. Johnson said.

"He has no choice in the matter. He comes home near death? We deserve an answer."

Cardiff closed his eyes a moment and realized sleep was imminent. Best to answer her quickly so he could be left alone. "I sought an old friend but found she had moved away."

"She? Was she your sweetheart?"

He was too weary to deny it. "Yes."

"Do you still love her?"

Such a question. And yet, "I believe I do, though it doesn't do me much good after all these years."

"How many years?"

"Fifteen."

"Gracious."

Mr. Johnson poked the fire again. "You have no idea where she is?"

"Her family moved to help an elderly parent in central Illinois."

"No city known?"

"No city known."

Mrs. Driscoll put a hand on his arm. "Surely there's some way you can find out where she went."

Mr. Johnson leaned against the mantel. "He can't very well send dozens of letters to every town."

Mrs. Driscoll's eyes brightened. "Why not? Surely one would stick."

"I don't even know if she's still unmarried."

Mr. Johnson frowned. "Fifteen years *is* a long time."

"Too long," Cardiff said.

Mrs. Driscoll shook away the negative thoughts. "It is never too late for love."

Cardiff looked at her. "That's what the woman who lives in Zona's old house said."

"See?" She spread her hands as if they held the truth. "It is never too late, *and* I know what we *can* do. We can pray."

"For what?" Mr. Johnson asked.

"Pray that if this woman—what is her name?"

"Zona Evans."

"Pray that if Zona Evans is unmarried and willing to meet up with our doctor, God arranges it."

"That's absurd," the other tenant said.

"Prayers are never absurd." She pointed at each one of them. "Take hands and bow your heads. I'll do the praying for us."

The men did as they were told, and Cardiff let his landlady's prayer spin a cocoon of hope around him.

Chapter 8

Cardiff stood by Corporal Statler's bed. "Your color is better. How are you feeling?"

"Fair to partly cloudy."

His wit was a good sign. Cardiff had dodged his own bullet with this patient and thanked God for it. And Mother Breston.

"Can I get you anything?"

The corporal nodded at the bedside table. "I got a letter there, from one of those nice ladies who bring them onto the hospital train. Never got a chance to read it."

"What ladies?"

"In Decatur. When the hospital train stopped there, all sorts of ladies came on board and gave us food, letters, socks, and blankets."

Cardiff vaguely remembered passing through Decatur on his way north. No ladies had tended to his train.

But it wasn't a hospital train.

He retrieved the letter and read it aloud: " 'My Dear Friend. You are not my husband nor son; but you are the husband or son of some woman who undoubtedly loves you. I send you my prayers and support with a heart that aches for your sufferings. Signed—' "

Cardiff's breath left him. He stared at the name. *No. It couldn't be.* "Signed *who*?"

Cardiff's throat was dry, and he suffered a ragged swallow before answering. "Signed Zona Evans."

"Zona. What an interesting name."

Cardiff, who could endure the sight of wounds that would make most people faint, felt his legs lose their strength. He fell onto a chair just in time.

"Is something wrong?"

He stared at the letter, uncomprehending. *She's in Decatur. She's unmarried.*

"Dr. Kensington? Are you ill?"

It was Mother Breston. Cardiff couldn't answer her with words. Instead, he thrust the letter toward her.

She read it silently then exclaimed, "Zona! Is this your Zona?"

He could only nod and was appalled to feel tears threaten.

She put a hand on his shoulder. "Is Evans her maiden name?"

He nodded again.

"So she's unmarried and lives in Decatur."

Cardiff finally summoned the words that sped through his mind. "God did it. He brought us together."

"Not yet He hasn't. You need to go to her. Immediately."

When Cardiff stood, he nearly toppled the chair. "I need to go to her."

Mother Breston took his arm. "Yes, you do."

He looked around at the other soldiers and Dr. Phillips. They were all looking at him. Had they overheard?

By their grins, he knew they had. "Go on, Doc. Go see your girl."

A chorus of support filled the ward.

Dr. Phillips waved him off. "We'll handle things while you're away."

Mother Breston put her hands on her hips. "What more prodding do you need?"

None. He kissed her cheek and left to the accompaniment of applause.

∞

After a quick stop at the boardinghouse, Cardiff was on a train heading south. Although the train was full, he gladly sat next to a man who dozed, allowing him time to process his thoughts.

He was on his way to see Zona!

The concept was almost too much to grasp. He looked at the snowy landscape rushing by and suddenly his thoughts grabbed on to the memory of another southbound train, heading to war, leaving Zona behind.

When the war with Mexico had proved to be less of an adventure than a horror, and after receiving no replies to the letters he sent to Zona, Cardiff had forced himself to set her on a mental shelf, a charming thing of beauty to gaze at fondly as a reminder of a long-lost time. Year after year, he'd moved her to a higher shelf, until she was finally out of reach and rarely noticed.

Until recently, when her name and image vied for his attention. He'd fought moving her to a lower shelf again, making excuses, wary about letting their shared past invade his present.

Yet he hadn't simply heard Zona's name once but had thought of her many times: the couple saying their good-byes on the train platform back in St. Louis; the soldier writing to his wife, Rhona; Cardiff writing his own letters and thinking about the ones he'd sent to Zona; finding her family home and hearing her history; two women telling him it was never too late for love. Then finally discovering that she lived in Decatur—and was unmarried. He sighed deeply at these stepping-stones, leading him toward this train headed south.

The man next to him awakened. "Forgive me. Was I snoring?"

"Not to worry. My mind has been elsewhere."

The man sat up straighter, shuffled his shoulders, then studied Cardiff, making him feel uncomfortable for the scrutiny.

"Excuse me?" Cardiff said.

"Who is she?"

"Pardon?"

"The woman who's fully captured your attention." He made a curlicue near Cardiff's eyes. "You're looking at me but not looking. And you're smiling."

The man's observations were disconcerting. "You are very perceptive."

"So I've been told. Now, out with it. Tell me all about her."

Although Cardiff was not one to confide easily, he told the man everything.

"Sounds like the Almighty has you where He wants you."

"Why do you say that?"

"God did the same for me and my dearly departed wife. He led us step-by-step, closer together, and thankfully neither one of us were stubborn enough to tell Him no." He took out his pocket watch then placed it back in his vest pocket. "When everything seems to be pointing you in a certain direction, it is not a coincidence. It's God. 'For God speaketh once, yea twice, yet man perceiveth it not.' "

"You're implying God has been speaking to me?"

The man shrugged. "You have a better explanation?"

Cardiff glanced out the window then back at his seatmate. "Actually, no, I don't."

"There you are. On a journey that He has set in place, bringing you and your Zona back together."

The notion that God was behind all that had happened was inspiring, and humbling. He thought of the prayer said in Mrs. Driscoll's parlor. "But what if Zona rejects me? Tit for tat."

"That's where faith comes in, my friend. Since you've come this far—and you could have ignored each and every nudge—I have to believe God has been working on Zona's heart, too."

Cardiff felt his demeanor soften as his muscles let go of the tension that had followed him onto the train. "I pray you're right."

"I will also pray. It's never too late for love."

Cardiff couldn't deny that hearing the same phrase for the third time was not a coincidence. And so he followed the man's lead, bowed his head, and surrendered the upcoming meeting to God.

∞

"De-ca-tur!" yelled the train's conductor.

Although Cardiff was confident everything would work out, he suffered a tinge of disappointment that God hadn't arranged for Zona to be on the platform, waiting for him. *That's how I would have handled things if I were God.*

Just to make sure, he scrutinized each and every person who milled around the depot. But then he realized that the Zona he was seeking would not be a nineteen-year-old girl but a mature woman. Upon making that realization, he had to acknowledge that he was no longer a twentysomething boy, either, but a well-worn man of thirty-six. Although the hair on his head wasn't gray, his beard had recently betrayed him by adding some salt to its pepper.

They had both endured the effects of fifteen years apart. He was still slim, but he knew his shoulders had slumped forward, and his gait had slowed, adjusting itself to life with a bum leg and a cane. Would Zona look similar to the girl he'd left behind? Or had she grown plump with age? Did her red hair reveal a stray strand of gray?

It is what it is, and we are what we are.

Cardiff saw a sign for the Depot Hotel and Restaurant. Perhaps someone inside would know where Zona lived. And food would be good. He hadn't realized that he'd missed breakfast until he'd boarded the train, and even then, with the dance of his stomach mimicking the rocking of the railcars, he knew an empty stomach was better than a full one.

Upon entering the restaurant area off the main lobby, he was greeted by a woman who smoothed a tablecloth. "Good afternoon, sir. Would you care to dine? We're smack dab in between the midday and evening meal, but I'm sure we could accommodate you."

"That would be nice."

The woman handed him the menu then said, "My name is Mrs. Slade, the proprietor of this restaurant. My son Matthew runs the hotel. Will you be needing a room?"

"I believe I will."

"And you are?"

"Dr. Kensington. I work at the army hospital in Chicago."

The woman smoothed the cloth again. "Do you receive the wounded that come through here on the hospital train?"

"I believe so."

"It comes through everyday. I'm sure they would appreciate any care you could give them while you're here."

The next moment was awkward. "Actually, I'm here on personal business."

Mrs. Slade's left eyebrow rose.

"I could use your help. My friend's name is Zona Evans, and—"

"The musical director for productions at the Decatur Auditorium?"

"I'm not sure." Though Zona *had* been musical. "Certainly there aren't two women bearing her name. Could you give me her address?"

Mrs. Slade released the tablecloth to itself. "I'm not sure I'm comfortable doing such a thing," she said. "Here in Decatur we are protective of our womenfolk—especially those who are unmarried."

Cardiff's stomach danced at the final affirmation that Zona was single. "I assure you, I mean no harm."

"That's all well and good," Mrs. Slade said. "But I must stand firm on this."

Cardiff felt the life drain out of him. God or no God. Plan or no plan. If Cardiff couldn't find out where Zona lived, then it was all for nothing.

"Actually," she said, her voice softening, "I do believe there is another way you can see her."

"How's that?"

"She's due to come to the depot for the hospital train at half past five. She directs a small group of carolers who entertain the soldiers."

Cardiff looked at the large clock on the wall of the restaurant. It was already half past three. "I will wait, then."

"As soon as you eat, come to the front desk and check into a room. Until then. . ." She motioned to a waitress. "Miss Wallace will be happy to take your food order."

Cardiff was glad for the bowl of soup and some bread, though he was unable to imagine eating more substantial fare. Then he checked into his room and found that its window overlooked the platform. It was perfect. He pulled a chair close and settled in to wait.

Zona was coming!

∞

Cardiff's chin fell off his hand, and he was jerked awake. It took him a moment to realize he was seated at the hotel window in Decatur, his elbow on the sill, waiting for Zona.

The depot was abuzz with dozens of ladies carrying baskets, waiting for the train. And then he saw Zona, marching a small contingent to the edge of the platform.

He couldn't take his eyes off her—he didn't dare. He pressed a hand to his mouth, covering a gasp and a smile. The image in his mind melded with the image before him. Although he was too far away to see strong details, and though the evening was upon them because of the shortened December days, the gas lights of the depot allowed him to see the essence of her, which hadn't changed. He recognized her strong gait. Zona had never been one to glide from place to place with her skirts gently offering a charming ding-dong to her sashay. Zona captured the ground beneath her as if it was hers to claim.

The way she directed the singers to their places, moving each an inch here or there, made him laugh. Her ability to dictate and achieve her own well-imagined plan was very familiar.

Even the way she shuffled her shoulders to adjust the flow of her cape brought back memories, with the voice of Zona's mother admonishing her to "Be still, girl."

As a whistle announced the arrival of the train, the singers began their first song.

" 'Joy to the world, the Lord is come. . .' "

Cardiff absorbed the moment, mesmerized by the music and the familiar combination of his Zona and song.

Then, with thanks to the Almighty on his lips, he retrieved his coat and hat.

It was time.

%

" 'O come, all ye faithful, joyful and triumphant. . .' "

There was too much soprano, and Zona glanced at Mrs. Miller, giving her a small signal to sing softer.

As they started the second verse Zona heard another voice join them. A man's rich baritone. " 'Sing choirs of angels, sing in exaltation. . .' "

She drew in a breath and held it. No. It couldn't be.

She scanned the crowd, looking for the singer.

And there he was, walking toward her. Time stopped, then began again in slow motion.

Cardiff stepped into place beside Mr. Pearson and continued singing the song. His smile made her skin tingle and her legs weaken. Her heart beat double time, making it impossible for her arms to conduct another note.

The rest of the quintet leaned forward to check out the newcomer in their ranks then looked back at Zona. She felt their gaze. She felt their questions. She had plenty of her own. How had this happened? How had Cardiff found her? Why was God giving her this blessing after she'd behaved so badly?

Although she assumed the carol was sung to the end, she didn't hear it.

But with the music stilled, she stepped toward Cardiff and looked up at his face for the first time in fifteen years. His soft eyes, his strong jaw, his glorious smile. "Is it really you?" she whispered.

He put a hand upon her cheek. "It's really me, my love. I've come to finally claim you as my own, for now and for always."

With an expulsion of breath, she wrapped her arms around his waist and pressed her face into the wool of his coat. Its roughness and the solidity of his body against hers confirmed the truth. "You're here. You're actually here." *And I'm never going to let you go.*

He held her close, and they found a rhythm from their past, two hearts beating as one.

A multitude of eyes watched the happy couple, yet Zona was only partially aware of their murmurs and stares. Her world had grown very small, the miracle keeping the rest of the world at bay.

"Thank You, God," she whispered into Cardiff's chest. The simple words did little to convey the extent of her awe and gratitude.

Cardiff lifted her chin and gazed into her eyes. "I thank Him, too, my dear. Merry Christmas, darling."

As they kissed, the years of separation melted away and were replaced by the endless melody of their love.

About the Author

Nancy Moser is an award-winning author of over twenty novels that share a common message: we each have a unique purpose—the trick is to find out what it is. Her genres include contemporary and historical novels including *Love of the Summerfields, Mozart's Sister,* and the Christy Award–winning *Time Lottery*. She is a fan of anything antique—humans included. www.nancymoser.com.

A Basket Brigade Christmas

Recipe Collection

From Stephanie Grace Whitson, *A Stitch in Time*:

This novella collection was inspired by a visit to an exhibit at the Illinois State Museum, where I learned about the Basket Brigade and in subsequent research "met" Jane Martin Johns, author of a fascinating memoir about daily life in Decatur, Illinois, before and during the Civil War. The memoir mentions a "tall gentleman" who threw off "a big gray Scotch shawl" and helped move Mrs. Johns's new piano out of a delivery wagon and into the parlor. "That," Mrs. Johns writes, "was my first meeting with Abraham Lincoln." As a historian, I loved reading the memoir, and when it was time to share history-related recipes, I went looking for something not only fitting for the Basket Brigade but also connected to Mary Todd Lincoln. One biographer provided the name of a cookbook known to have been used by Mrs. Lincoln. The two recipes below are reprinted from the 1851 edition of that cookbook titled *Miss Leslie's Cookery*.

Scotch Cake

Fictional Martha Jefferson's specialty in *A Stitch in Time*

INGREDIENTS:
¾ pound butter
1 pound sifted flour
1 pound powdered sugar
1 tablespoon cinnamon
3 eggs

DIRECTIONS: (from the historical cookbook)

Rub three quarters of a pound of butter into a pound of sifted flour; mix in a pound of powdered sugar and a large table-spoonful of powdered cinnamon. Mix it into a dough with three well beaten eggs. Roll it out into a sheet; cut it into round cakes, and bake them in a quick oven; they will require but a few minutes.

Beef Tea

This recipe is offered in Miss Leslie's chapter, "Preparations for the Sick." It's appropriate for our Basket Brigade angels as they minister to the wounded warriors on the daily train.

INGREDIENTS:
1 pound lean beef
Salt

DIRECTIONS: (from the historical cookbook)

Cut a pound of the lean of fresh juicy beef into small thin slices, and sprinkle them with a very little salt. Put the meat into a wide-mouthed glass or stone jar closely corked, and set it in a kettle or pan of water, which must be made to boil, and kept boiling hard around the jar for an hour or more. Then take out the jar and strain the essence of the beef into a bowl. Chicken tea may be made in the same manner.

From Judith Miller, *A Pinch of Love*:

While researching materials for *A Pinch of Love*, I was particularly interested in some of the foods that were served to the wounded soldiers arriving on the trains. One of the documents contained the following comment and inspired me to share a recipe for pickled peaches and old-fashioned doughnuts. A quotation from the time:

Every woman insisted on passing her own basket. Mrs. Peddecord had baked a hundred of her famous sour-cream biscuits, Mrs. Race had made fifty sandwiches, Mrs. Ryan had a bucket of pickles, Mrs. Oglesby, a big basket of doughnuts, which Mrs. White had fried. Some one, I wish I could remember who, brought a jar of pickled peaches, "enough to go around twice." Laura Allen's basket of red winter apples was "the last we had and just fifty of them." In other baskets there was food enough for every man to eat his fill, and the fragments were given to the commissary, for another time.

Pickled Peaches

INGREDIENTS:

4 cups sugar

1 cup white vinegar

1 cup water

2 tablespoons whole cloves

4 pounds fresh clingstone peaches blanched and peeled

5 (3 inch) cinnamon sticks

DIRECTIONS:

Combine sugar, vinegar, and water in large pot, and bring to boil. Boil for 5 minutes. Press one or two cloves into each peach, and place into boiling syrup. Boil for 20 minutes, or until peaches are tender.

Spoon peaches into sterile jars and top with liquid to ½ inch from rim. Put one cinnamon stick into each jar. Wipe rims with clean dry cloth, and seal with lids and rings. Process in hot water bath for 10 minutes to seal.

Clara's Doughnuts

INGREDIENTS:

2 tablespoons unsalted butter, softened

1½ cups sugar, divided

3 eggs

4 cups flour

1 tablespoon baking powder

3 teaspoons cinnamon, divided

½ teaspoon salt

⅛ teaspoon nutmeg

¾ cup milk

Oil for deep-fat frying

DIRECTIONS:

In large bowl, beat butter and 1 cup sugar until crumbly, about 2 minutes. Add eggs, one at a time, beating well after each addition. Combine flour, baking powder, 1 teaspoon cinnamon, salt, and nutmeg; add to butter mixture alternately with milk, beating well after each addition. Cover and refrigerate for 2 hours.

Turn dough onto heavily floured surface; pat dough to ¼-inch thickness. Cut with a floured 2½-inch doughnut cutter. Heat oil to 375 degrees. (You can use a deep fryer or electric skillet, but Clara didn't have either of those conveniences.)

Fry doughnuts, a few at a time, until golden brown on both sides. Drain on paper towels. (Unfortunately, Clara didn't have paper towels, either. She would have covered old newspapers with cloth napkins or tea towels to absorb the grease.)

Combine remaining sugar and cinnamon; roll warm doughnuts in mixture. Yield: about 2 dozen.

From Nancy Moser, *Endless Melody:*

I would like to share some family recipes that have been passed down generation to generation. My mother's side of the family immigrated from Sweden in the 1800s, and my father's side immigrated from England in the 1600s. On a side note, my mother has traced our family history and found two soldiers who fought in the Civil War: Solomon Young and William Chrystal. Solomon lost an arm, and William (who was in an Illinois regiment) was made lame.

Watermelon Rind Pickles

INGREDIENTS:
1 large watermelon
Brine:
7 cups sugar
2 cups vinegar
½ teaspoon oil of cloves
½ teaspoon oil of cinnamon
1 teaspoon salt
1 lemon, thinly sliced

DIRECTIONS:

Pare and discard hard dark green rind of watermelon and trim off soft pale pink of rind. Cut pieces of white rind about 1 inch square and ¼-to-⅓ inch thick—or whatever size pickles you prefer. Cover rind with hot water and boil until rind is tender and translucent. Drain well, discard water, and place rind in heat-resistant dish.

Bring brine ingredients to boil and pour over rind. Cover and let stand overnight. Repeat process for three successive days: drain off brine, bring to boil again, and pour over drained rind. On third day, pour into mason jars and seal while hot.

Swedish Lefse

These are like Swedish tortillas and were always served at Christmas during family celebrations. They are spread with butter and sugar, or jam, and rolled up. A modern take on serving them is to spread them with peanut butter.

Lefse would have been very easily shared with the soldiers on the train.

INGREDIENTS:
10 pounds potatoes
Salt
½ cup butter
¼ cup cream
4 cups flour
Butter and/or jam for spreading
Sugar for sprinkling

DIRECTIONS:

Boil potatoes. Mash and add salt to taste. Add butter and cream. Cool potatoes (an important step). Divide mashed potatoes into fourths, which makes about 4 cups mashed potatoes in each part. Add 1 cup flour and salt to taste for each part.

Roll out on heavily floured surface to ⅛-inch thick circles of 8-inch diameter. Put between two damp towels until cooked. Grill on stove until just browned. Keep them moist between towels until served. They should not be crispy, but even if they get a little bit crispy on grill, they will soften between towels. Spread with butter and sugar, or jam. Roll up. Serve cool. They freeze well.

Also Available from Barbour Publishing

Beautiful Star of Bethlehem

978-1-63409-036-0

From bestselling author Lori Copleand comes a poignant Christmas story about tragic loss, humorous coping, and enduring love.